Praise for Wild Conviction

"Mary Dezember has created a tour de force
featuring a strong young woman
who displays integrity, independence,
empathy, and a commitment to equality—
a necessary role model for today's world and any other."

—T. A. Niles, from *T. A.'s Poetic Expressions-Plus*

Wild Conviction

Sixteen Is Power

Mary Dezember

BRILLIANT MOON PRESS ~ ALBUQUERQUE, NM USA

WILD CONVICTION. Copyright © 2023 by Mary Dezember

All rights reserved. No part of this book may be used or reproduced in any manner without written permission from the author except in the case of brief quotations embodied in critical articles and reviews. For additional information and for permission requests, contact the author at marydezember.com.

This is a work of fiction. Characters, names, titles, places, organizations, and events are fictitious or are used fictitiously. References to historical figures, persons, names, titles, places, organizations, or events are used fictitiously and are intended only to provide a sense of authenticity. All other characters, names, titles, places, organizations, and events are products of the author's imagination, and any resemblance to actual persons, living or dead, names, titles, places, organizations, or events is entirely coincidental and is not to be construed as real.

Published by Brilliant Moon Press, Albuquerque, New Mexico USA
brilliantmoonpress.com
Interior book design is by Brilliant Moon Press, using Atticus formatting program.
Logo featured (the seal of the fictional Sisterhood of Gifts) is the author's logo—the logo for Mary Dezember—is the property of the author, is provided by the author, and cannot be reproduced or used without permission of the author.
Cover art and design by nirbheek on Fiverr.

Permission was obtained for the following: Quotes from Lucretia Mott are from *Lucretia Mott: Complete Speeches and Sermons*, edited by Dana Greene, New York: Edwin Mellen Press, 1980, and are reprinted with permission from The Edwin Mellen Press.

Library of Congress Control Number: 2023903593
First Edition
Printed in the United States of America
ISBN 979-8-9872935-1-5 (hardcover)
ISBN 979-8-9872935-0-8 (paperback)
ISBN 979-8-9872935-2-2 (ebook)

Richly historical, low fantasy, high tension—*Wild Conviction* is a coming-of-age, socially conscious, epic adventure with touches of magic and love.

Summary: 1858. Memphis, Tennessee. Sixteen-year-old Twilight Adams knows slavery is wrong. But almost everyone around her disagrees and wants her to keep her beliefs to herself. After receiving a letter with secrets both wondrous and dangerous from her beloved GrandMama, abolitionist and champion of a mysterious mystical sisterhood, Twilight sets out with wild conviction to stop the enslavement of children at a wicked plantation, only to discover what the captive children know too well—survival isn't freedom.

Copyright page continued

Please note: This is a socially conscious novel, a fictional coming-of-age adventure in which the protagonist confronts social issues. Historical and contemporary derogatory words are avoided. However, please be aware that difficult situations do occur. Comments, conversations, and actions by certain characters that show prejudice, abuse, racism, and misogyny are part of those characters' personalities and are not the author's beliefs.

For this novel, the author created a scenario within a historical setting in which the terms Rich-tone and Pale are used for skin tone.

The author's intent is to create and tell a story using skin tone terms that might provide insight differing from the historical and contemporary words and connotations and to tell a story without historical and contemporary derogatory terms.

The author states, "Language, even individual words, can be effective in creating awareness."

Contents

Epigraph		X
Prologue		XI
1.	New Realm ~ and An Exchange	1
2.	The Canon Effect	11
3.	GrandMama's Letter	17
4.	The Plea	23
5.	Hypocrisy's Hints	31
6.	Tarnished Mirror	39
7.	Gala Event	47
8.	Those Words	51
9.	Target Practice	55
10.	Atrocity Square Again	61
11.	Can't We Do Better?	65
12.	Family and Kin	69
13.	Games and Love Potion	73
14.	Trying to Forget	79
15.	More Surprises	95
16.	Visitor	107

17.	That's Final	115
18.	Magnolia Bay	125
19.	The Canons	129
20.	Another Vow	135
21.	Makeshift Honeymoon ~ Two Months in One Room	141
22.	Let God's Children Live Free	149
23.	Gifts and Names	157
24.	Canon Fire	167
25.	Bedtime Conversation	181
26.	Warning Signs and Threat	187
27.	The Rider	193
28.	Meeting	201
29.	The Fire Gathering of Girls	207
30.	The Voice	213
31.	Let Me Speak So I Can Fly	221
32.	Secrets, Sacred	225
33.	Secrets, Sacred and Profane	231
34.	Independence Day Plans	237
35.	Freedom Games	241
36.	Dance with Stale Mate	251
37.	Invasion Averted	257
38.	The Importance of Stories and Names	261
39.	The Large Mystical ~ Tensions and Mysteries	267

40.	Twin Tensions	277
41.	Flight	287
42.	Escape	301
43.	Home	305
44.	Poetry and Surprise	311
45.	Northbound	317
46.	Bad Catch	323
47.	Willow Land	329
48.	Rescue	337
49.	Friendship	345
50.	Freedom Champions	361
51.	Nation Ablaze	369
52.	Division	373
53.	Learning	381
54.	Decision	385
55.	Call to Arms	391
56.	The Divided States	397
57.	War	407
58.	Wise Willow Grove and Ember's Moment	415
59.	Twilight's Time	423
60.	Finally	435

Epigraph

*Slip into these pages
To a place present and past.
~ As for tomorrow, what will last? ~
Remember as you journey within
The realm of
Twilight:
The future is ours to write.*

Prologue

Monday, June 14, 1858
3:30 a.m.
Memphis, Tennessee

This is one of those tragedies.

Those were her thoughts as she, her father, and several other townspeople were doing what they could for the injured. The day before, in the waking morning on the Mississippi River, the *Pennsylvania* exploded.

The high waters swept away the dead—and many of the living. The remaining—scalded, bruised and broken—clung in the stifling, muggy Southern summer heat to trees or to wreckage, to hope and to life. For hours, they clung to their imaginings of benevolent hands pulling them from their doom to take them to the nearest port, Memphis.

The *Diana* had arrived at 11 p.m. to the Memphis port with about twenty of the injured. The town was alerted. At 3 a.m., the *Kate Frisbee* arrived with thirty or forty wounded, who'd weakened in the water for nearly a day. The wharf, the streets, and the improvised hospital in the large courtroom at Exchange Hall created a heart-wrenching blur of aching, crying, and moaning children, women and men.

She braced the elbow of a limping girl and guided her to an awaiting mattress, trying to support her without inflicting more pain. Amid the sight of mangled and scalded people, what she noticed most were eyes of suffering. "By the full moon and its mysterious shadows," she whispered as she gazed into the eyes of a very young man being carried past her—dark eyes deep, imploring, intense, and yet, within their expression of agony, they held a soft, twinkling brightness.

She would work through the night and into the soon-dawning day to dress burns and wounds, to provide water and food, to talk if the injured wanted her to talk, to listen if the injured wanted her to listen, and to, without ceasing, whisper prayers. With the rhythm of her breath, she sent blessings for healing to each person and their families—and blessings for safety to every person aboard *Pharaoh's Run*, wherever on the Mississippi it might be.

Chapter I
New Realm ~ and An Exchange

Wednesday, June 16, 1858
Late Afternoon
Memphis

From her shrine honoring beloved GrandMama, Twilight Adams lifted a book of poetry by Phillis Wheatley, pressed it to her chest, and whispered, "It's time."

Gingerly, she opened the book and removed her patient gift: a letter that GrandMama, four years ago and near death, had tucked inside.

This was Twilight's birthday—another one her mother and sisters celebrated by ignoring it.

"By the full moon, I wish they cared." She sighed, then kissed the letter. "Doesn't matter. All that matters is this gift, full of love, waiting for me."

As she'd done countless times, she traced her forefinger along the swooping blue inscription on the back of the folded paper:

Open On Your Sixteenth, Not Before, My Darling Twilight

She took a breath, turned over the tidy dense package of overlapping pages, then slid a letter opener under the rose wax seal embossed with the image of a doe beneath the sweeping branches of a tree. Carefully unfolding the letter, she was surprised to find small gifts: three tiny gems—rose quartz, black obsidian, lapis lazuli—and a thin ring. The gems she recognized as GrandMama's. The ring was unfamiliar. Positioning the gems and the ring next to GrandMama's Bible on the small bedside table she had made into a shrine, she, excited, began reading the long-awaited words.

As she read, she could feel GrandMama's maternal caress. She could hear her soothing voice. But the words jarred her to her very core. After reading twice to be sure, she pressed the letter to her heart, then sank to the floor.

If another Earth realm exists, I'm certain I've left the place I know and entered that new world.

She read aloud GrandMama's final words to her:

Burn this letter.

Instead, she buried it in her left pocket, patted another secret in her right pocket, and strode from the bedroom to the yard. Her electrified mind worked to untangle the letter's words and how they stitched together her identity.

Who am I?

GrandMama, you told me a lot in my birthday letter, but not nearly enough. It's time I see what I've purposely avoided.

In one swift move, she leaped onto her palomino mare, Spirit. With gliding strides, Spirit nearly flew along the streets—expertly weaving through the relentless march of wagons, gigs, pedestrians, and riders—to the despicable marketplace Twilight called Atrocity Square.

On the auction block, muscles taut, a young man stood. Though Twilight was seated atop Spirit on the far edge of the crowd, she sensed the youth's quiet defiance, the restraint of his fever to break free, to know for once *his* life, unowned. Witnessing a person being auctioned caused her to shudder with fury. Raised until age twelve by her abolitionist

GrandMama, Twilight wondered how it could be that in America people were sold, bought, owned. She'd always hated slavery. Now, ignited by her birthday secrets, she hated it to the gates of hell.

Two stinky men stood near her. She'd been ignoring the one who first yelled abuse at the enslaved youth on the block then turned to yap lewdly at her. Relentlessly he spewed his wretched breath and words through his missing front teeth. She reached inside her right pocket where, waiting and loaded, a pistol hid. She'd never shot any living thing, not even a heckler. And she didn't plan to. But if her life, or her virginity, depended on it, she could. Gallatin had taught her well. A sharpshooter, she'd aim to wound. Regardless, being female, she'd probably be noosed for shooting any man, even a predatory breathing manure heap like this one.

"I said, missy, slide on down from that glittery horse into my manly arms; I know how to make you glitter," he repeated. Then to his buddy, he said, "Isn't that right, Cyrus?"

"Do as Rufus says," said Cyrus, whose putrid odor wafted up to her. Spirit shifted her twelve hundred pounds toward him and nipped close to his face. He chuckled nervously, then said, "We're just funnin' with you, missy."

"Let's leave, Spirit," she said, circling away from the harassing fetid predators and around the malignant crowd of bidders.

"As you can see, gentlemen and ladies, he's young and strong! For the field, he's a solid workhorse!" the auctioneer called, pointing a cane at the silently courageous boy. In the surrounding crowd, all the Pale men were eagerly bidding. In their midst, but closer to the crowd's edge, was a young man not bidding. Yet, he watched it all intently.

Seeing those in line next to be sold, Twilight clenched her teeth, seething, feeling hot and dirty upon realizing she didn't know what to do about scared children clutching their mama's legs. What could she do about the violation of women, men, and youths who couldn't save their families, or even themselves?

Coming forward, the youth's new owner was wearing a ditto suit in deep gray, just like the other well-dressed bidders, all exploiting the strength of nearly-naked silent men, women, and children to create their prosperity.

She hated the ditto man.

Do the enslaved feel what I feel, that I live in a hostile land I do not understand, that I belong in a world that certainly is not this one?

Sunlight pierced her view of the injustice.

Free as I am, I can't even imagine what they must feel.

She cupped her hand above her eyes, which framed, in the distance, the young man who wasn't bidding. Twilight studied him. With his top hat in hand, his wavy hair shone black in the June sun. She approved of his tanned face that looked clean and fresh without the fashionable sideburns that clung like huge hairy triangles on the faces, necks, and chins of most men, even many of the younger ones. Maneuvering through the crowd in his well-tailored bright blue ditto suit, he stopped and gazed at the block, curious but unengaged.

Maybe he was different from the Southern boys she'd met before, for his manner certainly set him apart. He turned and moved away from the block, which lessened the distance between them and put him in her line of sight. Realizing how forward she appeared by watching him, she lowered her head. Then, dismissing her training that a lady must never initiate conversation, she looked directly at him, then smiled. He smiled. He approached her. Bowing deeply, straightening, placing his hat on his head, and looking up at her, he said, "Good day, Miss—or Mrs.?"

"Miss Adams. Twilight Wild Adams."

His eyebrows lifted slightly, revealing eyes with a hue of earthy blue, rather like the Mississippi River at sunset.

"Jackson Petigru Canon at your service, Miss Adams," he said. "Twilight. The name becomes you, with your eyes blue as day and your hair black as night."

The caller's voice rose and fell.

"My GrandMama Felicia Wild told me that is one reason she chose my name."

He nodded slowly, smiling. "And you are looking for a fine enslaved laborer today, Miss Adams?"

"I most certainly am not! I hate it here, at this Atrocity Square."

"Atrocity Square. Clever," Canon said.

"I avoid this place," Twilight said.

"And yet today, here you are."

She wouldn't tell him the real reason she rode to Atrocity Square, as GrandMama's letter directed her to keep the contents secret. So, she gave a related truth. "Today is different. I was preoccupied after volunteering for two days at the makeshift hospital at Exchange Hall. I'm doing what I can for the *Pennsylvania* victims. All I've had are snippets of rest by leaning against any wall with an open space."

Her mind glanced back to the dark pre-dawn hours of Monday. With dozens of others, she had worked into the breaking day, then into Tuesday, then into Wednesday—this day, her birthday. And then she'd read her letter. And now, she was here, seeing with her own eyes the unbelievable sights at Atrocity Square, thought to be "normal" by Pale Southerners.

Canon spoke, bringing her thoughts back to him. "Yes, the downriver Sunday morning explosion of the *Pennsylvania*." Shaking his head, he said, "A terrible tragedy."

"I hear hundreds died in the explosion," she said. "And many of the survivors brought to us, despite our best efforts, are dying. The other volunteers and I are doing what we can. Three years ago, after the harbor fire that burned four steamships, my parents wouldn't let me help. But today, I am sixteen, and *no one* will stop me from helping ever again."

Canon smiled, then said, "Thank you for caring for the poor victims. Onto happier subjects, specifically, happy birthday, Miss Adams. Also, I am wondering, why were you staring at me with your blue-as-day eyes?"

"You are mistaken."

"Oh?" Canon said, again raising his dark eyebrows.

"I was merely observing the crowd," Twilight said, "of which you were a member."

"You may have been observing the crowd, but you were, without a doubt, staring at me."

Turning her face away from him, she said, "You are bold."

Spirit shifted. A quiet moment passed. She turned her face back to him. He took a step closer.

Softly, he said, "Miss, you are bold."

Twilight said, "Let's go, Spirit."

With an uncanny reflex, Canon grabbed the reins in front of Twilight's hands. Spirit halted, then reached her nose out, pushing Canon's hat off his head. Canon laughed as his hat hit the ground. Twilight leaned on Spirit's neck and whispered in her golden ear. It flicked. Straightening, Twilight sternly said, "Mr. Canon, you've made a scene."

Canon nodded toward the block. The crowd was intently vying for a maturing girl. "They are busy," he said. "No one cares about us."

"No one cares about *her*," she said, nodding toward the girl on the block. "Let go of my reins. I need to leave this maddening, wretched place."

Spirit exhaled with a huff.

"I don't want you to leave," Canon said, handing the reins back to Twilight. He bent to retrieve his hat, stood, and added, "And I don't want you to tease."

Twilight observed the young man. "What is it you *do* want, Mr. Canon?"

Canon smiled boyishly, disarming her with his charm.

"I wasn't staring, Mr. Canon," she continued, "though—I did notice you. However, if you must know, it was not your appearance that drew my attention. It was the fact that you are the only gentleman here who wasn't bidding. I have a distinct feeling that you are not here to bid at all. I was wondering, why?"

"What would you like the answer to be?"

"The truth."

"Ah. The truth. I doubt you would like the truth, and our relationship will end before it can begin. Couldn't you retain your fantasy answer until we become better acquainted?"

"No," she said. "My time is too precious to waste on giddy flirtations. I find such games insulting. For that, you should banter with my sister Rachel. As to why you did not bid, tell me or do not tell me, as I must return to Exchange Hall."

"The truth is, Miss Adams, I never bid."

"Oh?" she said, thinking his answer meant he didn't own people.

"I come to learn how much the competition is getting for their Rich-tones."

"The competition?"

"Yes. I do, shall we say, reconnaissance for Bedford Forrest."

"You work for a leech."

"As I am sure you know, Bedford Forrest is likely the city's largest dealer of Rich-tones. From humble beginnings and in a mere few years since his arrival in Memphis, he has elevated himself to be one of the most respected and wealthiest gentlemen in the area, maybe in the entire South. His devotion to Memphis, the South, and law and order is exemplary. I think he will rise even further in status to help govern our fine city." He lowered his voice, "I hear he is slated to be a city alderman starting next month. You should take care in what you say about him."

"He lives off tears and not his own. This is the last thing I wish to say to you, Mr. Canon. Memphis brims with kind, generous, and caring people. However, that does not change the fact that, overall, our society is ill, and it is people such as you, Forrest, and all here bidding who are the disease. I suggest that tonight you and Mr. Forrest dine on nothing but a thin pork rind. Now, release my reins. You are taking advantage of an unescorted lady."

"Unescorted *lady*? There is no such person."

"Maybe not in the South," Twilight answered. "But I have news for you, Mr. Canon—the South is not the world."

"Memphis lies in the South," Canon said.

"What an awful shame for Memphis," Twilight said. "Mr. Canon, we've met, spoken, argued. Our meeting has run its course."

"May I call on you tonight?"

Stunned, Twilight was curious, silent.

"Yes?" Canon persisted.

"I dislike you. In fact, I disdain you and your life," Twilight said.

"I wish to call on you."

The sun shifted. The bidding ceased.

"Why would you wish to call on someone you do not consider a lady?"

"Somehow, Miss Adams, you are successful in avoiding many of our fine Southern customs—such as your manner of sitting your horse," his voice trailed away before adding, "and of how you refuse to tie back your hair." He gazed at her as if in a daze.

"Yes?" she prompted.

He blinked. "Despite those distinct manners, you retain your social standing. Your father is Harley Adams, am I correct? Your family is one of the finest in Memphis. That, my dear young woman, might be your redemption."

Twilight's mind stopped when he said the word "woman." It wasn't just the word but the way he said it.

"Also, there is a quality about you. I suspect you will never play by the rules, yet you'll not be labeled a cheater. Regardless of your actions, you are lovely and feminine. And, yes—you are bold. While the rest of the South might dictate that a lady can never be bold, I, in fact, find compelling the combination of your loveliness and boldness."

In spite of herself, Twilight felt drawn to his words.

Canon said, "I wish to call on you. Tonight. May I see you?"

The moment lingered. She knew she shouldn't answer. She knew she should leave. But she didn't want to leave. She hated herself.

"I offer an exchange," Canon said.

Squinting her eyes, Twilight said, "An exchange?"

"One hour of your time with me, in your parlor, for my career."

Is this another man's lying game?

"I speak the truth, Miss Adams. I will end my business with Forrest if you will, in return, spend one hour with me tonight."

"Absurd."

"Say yes."

"Mr. Canon, I would gladly give one hour of my life to end your barbaric business. But I am no fool. What is your proof?"

"If you allow me to escort you home, you can accompany me as I resign my services. I imagine you live on Adams Avenue, near Bedford Forrest?"

Twilight considered his proposition as Canon's eyes journeyed into her own. Intent on the discovery, neither soul smiled; momentarily, the air between them vanished.

"You will accept my proposal then," Canon said.

She felt as if his eyes had probed all the way into her heart. She wasn't ready for this, not with this young man. Still, the intrigue of his offer and manner shifted the static places of her life. Standing in front of her was adventure. And something more.

"I will accept—except," she said, "you will not escort me. I will meet you at Forrest's." Barely had these words entered the air breaking the trance between them, when Twilight was gone, Spirit moving her away from him.

Canon smiled as he walked to Forrest's place of business—Forrest's slave mart.

Chapter 2
The Canon Effect

Wednesday, June 16, 1858
Late Afternoon and Evening
Memphis

Enslaved people of all ages—tiny children to aged men and women—trod dishearteningly in a circle, on display, in the yard of Forrest's mart.

When buyers arrived at Forrest's, they selected captives from the harsh parade. Twilight knew of this routine and, when walking or riding by—as she had with the auctioning of people before this day—avoided looking. Now, she faced it. The sight sent outrage into her chest. She hated Canon, for he was part of it all. When he arrived minutes later, she, in a heightened voice, said, "What is the matter with you? What is the matter with Forrest? What is the matter with the South and with the U.S. Congress? They are people! Each is a human being!"

"Well, what sparked this outburst?" he said. "You know the laws. In America, they are property. You have the passion of a Southerner, Miss Adams, but not the ideals. There is nothing wrong with the South. Slavery has flourished in this country for over two hundred years. I'd say that proves it is a good system for this nation. The South, as we know, produces almost all of America's exports, with most of that being cotton. In fact, the South produces about eighty percent of the cotton used by the entire world. The world wants cotton, my dear, so the world wants slavery. We could never produce that amount of cotton without the labor of the Rich-tones."

"I have no objection to the labor of Rich-tone people if the laborers are hired and free."

Nodding, Canon said, "I'm leaving Bedford's business this very hour, Miss Adams. Please do me the honor of witnessing my resignation."

Twilight moved her skirted right leg above and across Spirit's back and gracefully landed at Spirit's left side. "Stay here, Spirit," she said to her companion, who turned her head to Twilight and nickered.

Smiling, Canon motioned for her to step through the door before him. Inside, Forrest was talking with two Pale men, one who clasped then pulled down the jaw of a Rich-tone man, examining his teeth.

"You'll have no trouble with Elija," Forrest was saying. "He works hard from sunrise to sunset and through the night during harvest season, all the while singing a sweet melody. On the block, I could get a thousand for him. Here, today, he is yours, new clothes and all, for a mere eight hundred."

As one Pale man wiped his hands on an embroidered handkerchief, the other placed New Orleans dixies on Forrest's desk, saying, "He's getting along in age. Seven hundred, Bedford, in the best bills, and you have a deal. But first, I must know, is he obedient? I don't like having to whip my laborers. And I rarely spend good money for a breaker."

Breaker? Whipping? Twilight winced and feared for Elija.

"Elija obeys," Forrest said.

The man looked at Elija. "Let's see about that. Elija, jump up and down on one foot."

Elija hopped once.

"Keep jumping till I tell you to stop, you fool," the man snapped.

Elija hopped, eyes steady toward the floor.

"Now, clap your hands while jumping," the man said.

Elija clapped and hopped and stared at the floor, his eyes deepening with sadness.

"Now sing Stephen Foster's 'Camptown Races' while you jump and clap," the man said.

"No."

All the men in the room looked at the young woman who had spoken. Deftly, Elija glanced at her, the tension of either fear or surprise tugging quickly at one side of his mouth, then focused at the floor.

"What did you say?" demanded the man giving orders.

Ignoring him, Twilight faced Forrest and said, "Mr. Forrest, you told this man that Elija was obedient. The man ordered Elija. Elija obeyed. It is obvious your—," Twilight hesitated, not wanting to say "customers," then continued, "It is obvious your associates do not trust you, or they would not have to put people you enslave to such tests."

Forrest looked at her, then at Canon, then at Elija. "Stop, Elija," he said. Elija stood still, silent, face directed to the floor but eyes sneaking upward. Forrest, nonchalantly taking a knife from his vest pocket and studying it in his hand, said, "You see, Elija is obedient. Eight hundred in dixies."

"I could've spent my money at the auction today. But I came here instead because I know you get the best, Forrest. Seven hundred fifty," he said.

"Fifty more for a deal," Forrest said, directing his eyes straight into the man's eyes.

The man looked at Forrest, then at Elija, placed more dixies atop the stack on the desk, signed papers, and left with his friend and with Elija in chains. Twilight, grief defining her face, watched Elija being taken away, his precious life and body continually confiscated.

With his right hand, Forrest stood the knife on its tip in his left palm. Balancing it there, then placing his right hand in his trouser pocket, he gazed at Twilight and said, "What are you doing here, Jackson, with my rebellious albeit beautiful neighbor?"

Before Canon could answer, Twilight, deciding to discover what the horrid Forrest knew about her, flipped open her fan with flourish and said with exaggerated drawl, "Why, Mr. Forrest. I had no idea you would recognize me, just a girl from down the street."

Right hand still pocketed and with a quick twist of his left wrist, Forrest flipped the still-balanced knife and caught it by its handle. "Some girl," he said, then chuckled. "I think you, Miss Adams, should be banned from the South. In these times, we need nationalism, not criticism. Do you know why I have a proud reputation? I'll tell you why. Because I uphold Southern ethics."

No longer mocking the Southern lady's coquettish conduct and without drawl, Twilight said, "Ethics? Ha! You mean 'economy,' don't you, Mr. Forrest?"

"You do realize, do you not, Miss Adams, that your unladylike behavior is the disgrace of the fine Adams name. Your outspokenness and how you sit that horse are most shameful. I do respect the weaker sex, but you do not know your place, and I want to know why you are here, in my business, with my comrade."

"Correction, Mr. Forrest: you might show respect to *some* girls and women, but you do not respect girls and women, and certainly not Rich-tone girls and women," Twilight said.

Quickly, Canon intervened. "Bedford, she's here at my invitation. I came to tell you, I resign my services with your reputable company."

Forrest frowned and squinted his eyes. "So, you're leaving me, Jackson. A shame." With his right hand, he moved several bills from the transaction for Elija to the side of his desk then, with his left, plunged the knife through the bills into the wood beneath. "I was planning to offer you," he paused, "a better situation." Tapping his knuckles on the dixies held by the knife blade, Forrest added, "I have a great opportunity for an adventurer if you decide to return." Then, with a firm stare at Twilight, he said, "I suppose Miss Adams here has a great deal to do with your decision, Jackson?"

"That is none of your business," Twilight said.

"Being here within my mart is none of your business, Miss Adams, unless you wish to purchase a fine enslaved laborer."

"Mr. Forrest," Twilight said, "the atrocity of human captivity and ownership in our land of the free is everyone's business." Turning on her heel, Twilight marched to the door. Canon jumped to grab the handle, opening the door for her.

"Keep your money, Bedford," Canon said, smiling. "You'll need it—for our game tomorrow at the tavern."

"You know, Jackson, I never lose," Forrest said. "And Miss Adams, boldness is to be admired in a gentleman, but not in a lady."

Turning to face him from outside his threshold, Twilight glared at Forrest and said, "You have no conscience, Mr. Forrest. So, despite appearances, your money, and whatever you and others think you have accomplished," she took a breath for emphasis, "you have nothing."

A wicked fire ignited his eyes, that, under other circumstances, might send her trembling. But she felt steady, even in his nearly-crazed gaze. She added, "You will be remembered for your inhuman, brutish cruelty." With that, she walked away.

Nodding to Forrest, Canon followed Twilight out the door, saying to her, "I've kept my part of the bargain. As for your part, at what hour should I arrive this evening? Seven?"

With a one-step leap, Twilight mounted the unsaddled Spirit and said, "Half past. But not tonight, tomorrow night," then bolted cleanly away from the next evening's suitor.

Irritated at her attraction to Canon, Twilight tried to analyze what it was about him that was so magnetic. Maybe it was just that she hadn't had a caller in so long. Her sister Rachel had beaux frequently calling; her other sister Sarah, though rarely, also had suitors. But Twilight, who once had her share of beaux, had had none in the last year. Being outspoken, nearly flying bareback on her horse, and not tying her hair caused her status to teeter toward spinsterhood.

But it wasn't just beaux deprivation that made Canon entrancing. There was something more—the feeling that rushed inside her when he was near: a sensation she'd felt for only one other young man, the only man she had ever loved. The young riverboat pilot. The pilot of her heart.

She wouldn't think about her pilot now. For now, she would volunteer more hours at Exchange Hall. For now, she would ponder the amazing messages of GrandMama's letter. For now, she must try to shake the Canon effect.

⁂

As dusk etched shadows on her bedroom window, Twilight placed the pistol in the drawer of the shrine. She gazed at the weapon for a moment, remembering. At first, she'd been frightened when, exactly a year before, her fifteenth birthday, Gallatin had handed her two authentic Henry Deringer pistols—sold as a set for two shots and known as original Philadelphia Deringer pistols—which she refused. Finally, upon his insistence, she accepted one, saying, "If I miss with one shot, I shouldn't be shooting. Besides, I like knowing you have the mate to mine."

She shut the drawer, curled up on her bed, and again read her birthday letter.

Chapter 3
GrandMama's Letter

August 1, 1854, sealed by GrandMama
June 16, 1858, opened by Twilight

My Darling Granddaughter Twilight,

Happy Sixteenth Birthday, Dearest.
I love you. I wish I could be there with you celebrating this milestone in your young life. But Destiny has other plans for me, which I now accept. And Destiny has plans for you—which you can accept and shape, or deny.

Now that you are Sixteen, there are Two Secrets you need to know, and both must be kept hidden. Always. Only to your daughter, should you have one, can you entrust these secrets ~ when she celebrates Sixteen. These secrets are blessings that, in our current cruel world, carry risks. If anyone learns of what I am about to share with you ~ your life is in danger.

You recall the many stories I told you about my own dear GrandMama Rose, your Great-Great-GrandMama. I loved her dearly. Dearly. As you know, Phillis Wheatley gave a copy of her book of poetry to Rose. Rose passed it on to my mother, who passed it on to me, and I to you. Such as the gifting of the beautiful book of poetry, we gift this information to our daughters about the women in our family, a Sixteenth-birthday soul tradition. Sadly, I could not gift this information to your mother, my only daughter, as by her Sixteenth she did not have the strength of mind to carry these Two

Secrets. Because I couldn't share it with your mother, your sisters ~ with whom I've had little association ~ also do not know. As they all live in the South, I suppose it is best they don't know. Since you are probably still living in Indiana with your Grandfather, you are somewhat safer. Hopefully.

Secret One: Your loving, lovely Great-Great-GrandMama Rose was African.

I know little about her meeting, romance, and marriage with your British Pale Great-Great-Grandfather Henry Wilde, but I know she loved him and was not forced to marry him. However, marrying him meant she had to leave her home in Africa, which saddened her deeply. I'm not sure of her birth country, but my mother said she had a connection with Empress Mentewab and the Kingdom of Abyssinia. However, Mama also mentioned a vague recollection concerning Senegal, across the continent, the country from which Phillis Wheatley was stolen.

Young Rose accepted an Anglicized name. One of her daughters died as an infant; her son never had children. Her remaining daughter, my mother, carried the combined tones of her Pale father and Rich-tone mother, with more of her father's tone. The Wilde family was British Pale. End of story.

Except, it is not the end of our story.

As you know, I married your Grandfather, Johannes Wild, German Pale. I have to add here the coincidence of names, as we never really spoke of this. My mother's maiden surname was Wilde, so Wilde is my middle name. Then I married a Wild. My name, as you know, is Felicia Wilde Wild. Your mother's maiden surname was Wild, and, as you know, that is your middle name ~ Twilight Wild Adams ~ as well as the middle name of your sisters and brothers. I think this name is fitting for you and for me, my dear. On with our story:

Johannes knows me only as British Pale, though he does comment on my "lovely tone." Foolishly, I didn't consider my heritage when we sailed to America. Our Land of Equality is, ironically, a place like no other in Tone Demarcation for perpetuating Pale Supremacy. And here, though some with a faded tone like mine are considered Pale, the truth is, in America, having any heritage with African lineage can threaten a person's freedom ~ and life ~ especially if one's lineage is matriarchal. Only our country devised a "one-drop rule," referring to one drop of Rich-tone blood. I know you're aware of this "rule," as we've spoken of it in our many conversations about slavery and the atrocious treatment of anyone, whether enslaved or free, with Rich tones from any heritage.

I've felt somewhat safe living in the North, though Indiana, as you know, is just over the Southern border. The constitution of Indiana ensures slavery is illegal; however, Rich-tone people in the state have essentially no rights. Ultimately, whether written into law or not, even the Northern states are formulating a "one-drop rule." In the South, this is an accepted notion. It is a threat to you, to your sisters, and to your mother. And possibly even to your brothers. However, your brothers are raised Pale, their tone is faded, your father is highly-regarded, and society favors men; thus, Jed and Jesse are probably exempt from the threat of enslavement that you, your sisters, and your mother could face. However, we can never be sure, so know that the twins, too, might be in danger.

As you will tell no one, no one will ever know this Secret. You must protect yourself and your family. In America, "one drop" can be a death sentence.

Here is another truth: being raised Pale, we don't have, know or understand any of our African cultural heritage. For us, our heritage is "only blood." This is an irony in America, as it is also "only blood" that decides our fate: freedom or captivity; rights or oppression.

Isn't it fascinating to learn on your Sixteenth, which is also the sixteenth of the month, that you are one-sixteenth African? Beautiful, isn't it?

Know this ~ Sixteen is power.

Secret Two: This is another inheritance, though not by tone heritage but by female heritage. Dear Twilight ~ You are the heir of female-lineage mystical gifts. These gifts are subtle. You probably haven't noticed your gifts, as they are just "you" and "what you do." As of this special day, and as you age, you should receive more gifts. All women everywhere have gifts, but a woman must be aware in order to gain this knowledge and to perceive her special talents.

Sadly, many women have forgotten, or choose to deny, their abilities and intuition. They are the Deniers. Deniers choose to believe deceptions maintained by the Society for Supremacy. The Deniers erroneously claim men as naturally superior and biologically unable to keep themselves from mean-anger, violence, destruction, coercion, philandering. The Deniers are growing in number.

We who remember and embrace our special talents are the Sisterhood of Gifts. We are Champions. Sometimes we recognize each other. Often, we journey life alone in this Secret, wondering if we are the sole sister of the Sisterhood of Gifts.

The Seal of the Sisterhood of Gifts is the Doe and the Tree. Keep in your heart our time spent together in forests, woods, and groves. Remember how I told you that all of Nature is sacred, the doe is mystical, and the rare antlered doe carries magic. Nature and the Wise Ones will teach you what you need to know. Nature will give you other signs.

The signs repeat ~ Recognize Repetition. See Symbols. Discern Signs. Read the Messages.

A man can be a Champion. The man of goodwill can find a gateway to receiving mystical talents ~ he must reject Male Dominance, thereby rejecting the Society for Supremacy and joining the Band of Champions. A Champion Man gains talents, serves justice, and supports the Sisterhood of Gifts. Frederick Douglass is a Champion.

Beware ~ The Society for Supremacy upholds homogeneity. Suspecting that women have mystical flair, the Society acts to suppress us and, thus, our abilities to use our gifts. The man who supports or practices the Society for Supremacy's intimidation and domination techniques is known as an Egoman. The best are unaware; the worst are Egomaniacs.

The Pale Males wield societal control; they exert dominance over all females and over all other males. But if all males were equal, females of all tones, Palest to Richest, still would be treated as "Less Than Man." This injustice will end when the prominent practiced belief in the Dominion of Men through Male Supremacy ceases.

Further, unseen negative forces called the Beleaguers do whatever they can to make us doubt our talents. You will find yourself under attack by the Beleaguers now that you know you have female-heritage gifts. Beleaguers try to invade your mind so that you do not use your gifts. Listening is essential to learning, but never believe the Beleaguers. Never.

Dear, I hope you remember what I've often said ~

Look, Listen, Discern, Learn
The Key to Mystical Growth is Truth
Awareness Opens the Heart's Passage to Epiphany, Change, Freedom
Every Breath of Life is a Prayer
When all you have is Faith, you have All

This is what I can share, as this experience is unique for each woman, as each woman is unique. Living the experience is essential for the learning. It will include dangers. What you gain will be wondrous.

And please, Dear ~ Survive. As I have. My illness is of my failing body, not of a failing will to survive, to grow, to act. As you know, I have tirelessly fought this illness for over a year, believing I'd regain health to live many more years. Though I want to stay here, with you, I now understand that my illness is a signal that I'm needed Elsewhere, and my corporeal death is the portal.

Forever, I am a Champion and Person of Character devoted to the Mission of the Sisterhood of Gifts:

To keep love in all places, worlds, realms;
To bring justice to all women and children, to all who are oppressed;
To care for creatures, plants, water, sky, minerals ~ our mother planet, Earth;
To nurture the beauty, healing, lovingkindness, and joy of positive unseen forces.
To maintain individual Integrity.

This is incredible information, I know.

I wish I could be there to answer your questions. To hold your hand. But you are only twelve as I write this, and soon I must leave this place to venture to my life Elsewhere. Good work is waiting for me there.

My Love is with you for Eternity. I am with you for Eternity.
Wear this ring to hear the language of the Sisterhood.

Your Ever-Loving GrandMama

<u>*Burn this letter.*</u>

Chapter 4
The Plea

Wednesday, June 16, 1858
Early Night
Memphis

The third reading of GrandMama's letter jolted Twilight as forcefully as the first and second readings had.

Refolding the pages, she placed them in her pocket.

Over the previous four years, Twilight had held the sealed letter, closing her eyes and envisioning the precious words, which she imagined as loving womanly advice for her sixteenth birthday. Even though curious about its contents, she'd never been tempted to open it early. First of all, she'd promised GrandMama. If waiting until she was sixteen to read these words was important to GrandMama, then it was important to her. Anyway, the anticipation made her sealed gift even more mysterious. But, upon opening it, what she received wasn't just mysterious; it was fantastic.

In the final rays of persistent sunlight reaching through her window, Twilight held the familiar small stones of GrandMama's: blue, black, and rose. Lapis lazuli—for receiving and speaking one's truth. Black obsidian—for clarity and for protection. Rose quartz—for love and compassion. These gem powers are what GrandMama had told her long ago. But now she saw the rose quartz as even more symbolic of a quest of love honoring her Great-Great-GrandMama Rose Wilde.

She placed the tiny gems in a small silk organza bag, pulled tight the satin strings, and slipped them next to the letter in her pocket. She didn't remember ever seeing GrandMama wear the ring. *Where did this come from?* She slid it onto her right ring finger. It flashed. Was it caused by the final shining sunray through the window? Or was it only in her mind's eye?

Believing it had flashed on its own—and admiring how it fit her finger perfectly—she said, "I will call you Wondrous Ring." She inhaled deeply, waiting to hear the language of the Sisterhood. She closed her eyes and listened. She waited. And waited.

She heard nothing.

"Help me, GrandMama," she pleaded.

Touching the letter in her pocket, she slipped off her bed and went downstairs to the parlor.

Her parents, Harley and Elizabeth, peered at her over their perfectly-poised teacups. With barely a glance at her mother, Twilight curtsied and said, "Good evening, Mother." Brightly to her father, she said, "Hello, Father. Was your trip successful?"

"Yes. I've signed papers for the shipping agreement. Meeting in person to seal a deal, rather than just through letters or telegrams, always helps," Harley said with a triumphant smile.

"That's wonderful news!"

Cara, an Irish immigrant who worked as their servant, breezed through the home like an angel of light, illuminating each candle and oil lamp. Helping Cara with this twilight ritual, Twilight lit a taper, then the candles and lamps in the parlor.

"Father," Twilight said as she glided to light the home, "I've just come from Exchange Hall. I must tell you about one of the patients and about his brother who arrived yesterday."

Quickly, Harley glanced at his wife, who began fidgeting when Twilight spoke of working at the makeshift hospital. Dabbing her forehead with the embroidered handkerchief she always held, Elizabeth said with staccato intensity, "Harley. As I have said before. I cannot understand how you can. In all good conscience. Let our daughter work. We will always have problems. With this child. If you do not support me on this. Forbid her. She is to be a lady. Like Rachel and Sarah. And all good Southern ladies. Twilight should be taking art classes. She should sew samplers. She should twist her hair into jewelry. Instead, she works at your packet office. And today she worked at that makeshift hospital. Like a common laborer. And the way she sits that horse. And flying on that horse. Letting her hair fly. So outrageous. The disgrace. And, it worries me. Constantly. That she might go near that awful Pinch."

Cara, who'd returned with a teapot, tensed. She finished pouring more tea, then bustled from the room.

"Mother, Pinch is the home of immigrants. It is a neighborhood. Besides, Exchange Hall is not near Pinch; you know that. And many caring ladies of Memphis are at Exchange Hall, doing what they can for the poor *Pennsylvania* victims and their suffering families. And you also know that Spirit and I fly only about twenty feet, kind of a very long jump. And just slightly above the ground, not up into the sky."

Vigorously, her mother fanned her face with her handkerchief and ignored Twilight's comments. "It is a wonder that something horrible. Has not already happened to her," Elizabeth said, eyeing Twilight. Moving her gaze to Harley, she continued, "And if. Something does happen to her. Our family will *never* overcome. The disgrace."

"Mother, please," Twilight interrupted. "Must you forever react this way? Don't think of me as your daughter if that will help. Tell your friends it's not your fault I'm so strange. Tell them it is GrandMama's fault. They know the truth, that GrandMama raised me from nearly the day I was born until I was twelve, only leaving me because she died." *Then, Grandfather sent me here. Why, oh why, Grandfather, did you do that? Why did you send me away from you, away from Willow Land?* Twilight continued, "GrandMama was my real mother. If something bad were ever to happen to me, certainly GrandMama would care more about *me* than the disgrace it would bring to the family. And she would certainly recognize my birthday." *Which she certainly had, even from the beyond.* "Unlike you."

Choking, Elizabeth sputtered, "I feel faint. Harley, forbid that child to speak. To her mother in such a tone."

"Twilight," Harley admonished, though his eyes held their constant gentleness for his daughter. "I will not have you speak to Mother in such a disrespectful fashion. She is your mother. She is the one who nearly lost her life giving you yours. And she's been in poor health since, the sweet dear." He patted his wife's hand. Resting her head against the back of the settee, Elizabeth dabbed furiously at her face and neck with the dainty lace cloth.

Continuing to speak to Twilight as if his wife were not in the room, Harley said, "I take the blame that your dear mother"—he glanced toward the floor—"conceived you so soon, too soon, after the birth of those twin brothers of yours. She was so weak. It was unreasonable to expect her, in her condition, to bring into the world a fifth child." Focusing back on Twilight, he continued, "Thank goodness your grandmother Felicia did take you in; it was the only choice at the time."

There is never an only choice.

"I expect you to be kind to your mother, Twilight. Now call Sarah; Mother adores her company. And have Cara bring fresh tea to Mother."

Fresh tea? Cara just poured tea. Why does Father dote on her? Does he only love me when Mother's not in the room?

After delivering her father's message to Cara and Sarah, Twilight went to the library. Soon, Harley entered and said, "Happy birthday, Daughter. I should've said that as soon as I saw you. Dear, though I made the deal and got the signatures today, your diligence is creating an organized transportation system of steamers that connect to Memphis through our line. You help the Adams' enterprises thrive."

Her father's pride in her business skills always lessened Twilight's tension about her family, as did spending time in the library. The deep scent of leather from books and chairs and the cozy fragrance of her father's tobacco eased her torment of feeling unacceptable. But even finding relief in this room was an irony, for social mores dictated it was improper for a lady to enjoy a library, much less lounge in it as she did, draping herself across a leather wing chair, her house-slippered feet elevated on a huge ottoman. Her father never seemed to mind; in fact, he enjoyed her company in that female-forbidden room. Due to this, she adored her father, despite his devotion to her mother. But on this day, for several reasons, not even the spell of the library could calm her.

"Father, I have something important to tell you."

"First, dear," Harley said, "I must remind you *again*—do not upset your mother. I know you are spirited, but I'll not tolerate such behavior toward the woman who gave you life."

Twilight sighed deeply. "Father, why can't Mother be content? Our family is so blessed. We've not suffered deaths or terrible injuries. No one in our family succumbed to yellow fever three years ago, and not one of us has been in a terrible accident." The horrors of the *Pennsylvania* explosion loomed, moving as phantoms in her mind.

Harley said, "Yes, we haven't experienced illness or injury."

Twilight added, "We are not enslaved like many people in the South. And yet, for all of our good fortune, she can't be thankful."

Harley's forehead rose. "True, we are not enslaved. We are Pale."

I've been raised Pale; I have all the privileges of being Pale. It is the life I live. But Father has no idea of my truth. Nor did I, until today.

She studied the novel she was holding, *Wuthering Heights*, and said, "One of my favorite novels, and written by a woman who published under a male pseudonym. To be recognized, must one be male and Pale?"

"It would seem so," Harley said.

Changing the topic to a family suffering bad fortune, she said, "Father, I want to tell you about a young man at Exchange Hall, Henry Clemens. He has searching yet kind eyes. I first saw him that early morning of the explosion; he was being transported from the *Kate Frisbee* to the Exchange. His brother, who arrived yesterday, was a cub on the *Pennsylvania*! He had disembarked in New Orleans just days ago; if he hadn't, he also would have been on the *Pennsylvania* when it exploded. His eyes are gentle, dark, and intense, like Henry's. But the sorrow that fills them is overwhelming. More than pained, his eyes are haunted. I think you should meet him. It might ease him, talking with you, another man of the river. He mentioned that he first learned to pilot under Horace Bixby, on a different steamer, of course.

"Bixby's apprentice, you say. What a turn of events to his life since he stayed in New Orleans rather than continuing on the *Pennsylvania*. I'll have Cara wrap a dinner, and I'll take it to him. His name?"

"His name is Sam."

"Sam. Bixby's cub, Sam Clemens. Is he dark-haired and young of age, early twenties?"

"That fits Sam's description," Twilight said.

"Yes, I have spoken with him, when he was a cub of Bixby's. Once or twice, very briefly. At Duval and Algeo's wharfboat on the lower levee. Bixby told me he commanded young Clemens to write notes of the river, and since, Clemens has become a strong cub with solid piloting skills."

A bell rang, announcing supper. Giving her father a light, quick hug, Twilight turned to leave.

"Are you dining with the family tonight, dear?"

"Not tonight, Father."

"But you haven't dined with us for at least a month. And today is your birthday."

"Mother and Sisters don't care about my birthday. And worse, I can't bear their favorite dining entertainment—finding fault with me, trying to fashion me into a domestic motto, as if that were their hobby, their words like needles with me being one of their samplers. When the twins return from Nashville, I'll dine with the family. Jesse and Jed are so dear and funny that no one pays attention to me. And that's the way I like it."

He kissed her on the cheek. "Your sisters could be kinder to you. I'll tell Cara to take your meal to your room. And to add a slice of pie."

"Thank you, but not tonight, Father. I must return to Exchange Hall to replace dressings. With so many wounds on so many wounded, it takes several volunteers. Also, not tomorrow night. A gentleman will be calling at half past seven."

"You do say? A beau? That's fine. That's fine. But I'll never understand why young ladies dislike eating before beaux call on them."

"He's not a beau. Just a gentleman caller."

Chapter 5
Hypocrisy's Hints

Thursday, June 17, 1858
Evening
Memphis

When Jackson Petigru Canon entered Twilight's home the following evening, he carried flowers and the same desirable impact of the previous day.

Waiting in the parlor, Twilight tapped her fingers lightly on another of her favorite books, *A Christmas Carol in Prose, being a Ghost Story of Christmas*, by Charles Dickens. Sarah and Rachel sat nearby, doing needlework with painstaking devotion.

Upon seeing Canon, Twilight stood, leaving Charles on the settee. She was wearing her favorite dress, one that she knew looked wonderful on her—yellow chintz with ivory buttons from her neck to the floor. White panels detailed with broad yellow ribbons layered the six-foot wide frock. White sleeves, buttoned tight at the cuffs, billowed. "Roses, Mr. Canon?" she said, as he handed her the bouquet.

"Sixteen of the loveliest in Memphis. To celebrate your sixteenth." He smiled. "I couldn't decide which was appropriate for you, Miss Adams, pink or white. So I bought eight of each. Now I see sixteen yellow roses would have suited you this evening."

She lifted them to her nose. With her eyes peering over the bouquet, she said, "They are lovely. But we barely know one another. I don't believe it is proper that I accept a gift from a gentleman who isn't my beau."

"Yet," Canon said.

She studied him from under her dark lashes. "You have plans?"

Canon stared at her, grinning, looking confident and more appealing than she wanted him to be.

"Really, Twilight, have you no manners?" Rachel said. "Introduce us. Sarah and I are not mere room adornments."

Twilight said nothing.

After staring at Twilight a moment longer, Canon turned his attention to the two sisters near the window as Twilight left the room carrying the roses. "Jackson Petigru Canon, at your service, ladies," he said, bowing. Sarah and Rachel held out their hands. Taking Sarah's hand, he asked, "And you are?"

"Sarah Adams, Mr. Canon, sir," she said, nearly freezing from shyness.

Shifting toward Rachel, he took her hand and cocked his head. "I am Rachel, kind sir," she said.

"Mr. and Mrs. Adams are blessed with lovely daughters," Canon said, bowing again. "Now, if you will excuse me, I wish to speak with your sister."

Fanning and pouting, Rachel said, "I simply cannot imagine why. She's the black sheep of the family." Then she smiled and batted her long eyelashes at Canon. He assessed Rachel, who unabashedly returned his stare until Twilight entered, carrying the large bouquet in a huge vase, which she placed atop the marble fireplace mantle. Pulling his gaze from Rachel's hold, Canon took Twilight's elbow and guided her to the settee on the far side of the parlor.

"You are breathtaking in yellow and white, Twilight," he said.

"Thank you, sir. Now, I am curious, how does it feel to be unemployed?"

"Ah. You wish to avoid flirtations? Fine. I'll try not to compliment you this evening, though I've never had a more difficult task."

"Oh? Then I daresay you lead an easy life, sir. Wasn't leaving your employer 'a more difficult task'?"

"Actually, no. You were right. I wasn't particularly proud of my position with Forrest. I'm glad you insisted I leave his employ."

"I didn't insist, Mr. Canon. It was your suggestion."

"Regardless, it's because of you that I, personally, will no longer directly profit from the selling of Rich-tones."

"Ah, risking it all to do the right thing. How does that feel?"

Canon didn't answer.

"So what will you do now?"

"After nearly a year in Europe on my Grand Tour, I returned to Tennessee three months ago and began my work with Forrest for business experience. Of course, the plan has always been for me to return to my father's employ."

"Which is?"

"Managing his plantation."

"Plantation? Your father owns a plantation?"

"Yes, a fine one. He's up in years, and I am an only son. It's my place to carry on his life's work. I want him to know that his hard work will continue after he passes."

"By the stark moon! How many people does he enslave on his plantation?"

"He is an enslaver of two hundred."

Rachel's eyes raised as she smiled.

"Two hundred people!" Twilight shouted. Bolting to a stand, Twilight stomped her foot. "Two hundred! Enslaving one person is wrong. Your father enslaves *two hundred people*? And you feel righteous about leaving Forrest yesterday and not 'directly profiting' from the trafficking of people? You and your father are no better than Forrest." She pointed to the door. "Leave, Mr. Canon. Now."

"Twilight!" Rachel said from across the room. "Mind your manners. Mr. Canon should be admired. You are embarrassing Sarah and me."

"Again. Like always," Sarah whispered.

Rachel added, "I shall call Father if you continue this unladylike behavior. You disgrace us over and over again."

With tears welling, Sarah clasped her sampler against her mouth, squeaking through the cloth between sniffs, "She's horrid. Simply horrid."

With hands clenched at her sides, Twilight pointed a glare at each in the room as she said, "It is you who disgrace the entire human race. You, Rachel. And you, Sarah. And you, Mr. Canon."

Canon remained seated, looking amused. "Ladies. Now, ladies," he said. "Do try to be ladies, or I might let slip my knowledge of your behavior at one of our many fine ice cream saloons or coffee houses—or at Murray's Tavern."

Instantly, the blood drained from Rachel's face, her eyelashes fluttering like two soot-covered moths trapped on snow. "You wouldn't, would you, Mr. Canon?" she whispered. Sarah clutched the arms of the settee as if she were adrift. The implication of Canon's threat was clear: all the beaux in Memphis would avoid the Adams home, where the females did not behave as ladies.

Twilight said, "You disgusting leech. Now you're blackmailing us."

"Twilight, your language. Please. Mr. Canon is our guest," Rachel said.

Twilight sat, then said, "Don't you see? A gentleman would never threaten ladies. Don't listen to him, Rachel. I'm sure no one else does, not even at Murray's Tavern."

Crossing his legs and tapping the bottom of his boot with a cigar he'd pulled from his breast pocket, Canon said, "But I am of the finest families, the Petigrus and the Canons."

Twilight considered a moment. "Yes, with that, I suppose you win: people listen to you because of your family and their wealth. Since your father owns a plantation and two hundred people, I'll warrant that he, along with Forrest, ranks among the wealthiest men in several counties, maybe in all of the state of Tennessee. Or even in the South. Certainly, your plantation is among the largest. Not even our *honorable* Mr. Jefferson enslaved two hundred people."

"But Mr. Washington did, I'm told; actually, more than two hundred," Canon added.

"Yes, Jefferson and Washington—those scoundrels," Twilight said. Canon laughed. Twilight faintly smiled.

Rachel whispered loudly to Sarah, "I simply cannot comprehend the shared disrespect of our wretched sister and such a charming young gentleman concerning two of our country's foremost founders, fathers of our nation."

Ignoring Rachel, Canon said, "It seems, as the stories go, that Mr. Washington lamented ownership of his captives but did not provide manumission. However, his wish was that, after his death, his wife would manumit them. Apparently, she did free some of their enslaved laborers. But not all." He slipped the cigar back into his breast pocket. "Concerning Mr. Jefferson, he did *not* free his enslaved. The story is that they were sold after he died to help pay off his debt."

"Hypocrisy," Twilight said.

Rachel said, "Mr. Washington was our country's premier President and a hero of our war for freedom from tyranny. Mr. Jefferson was our country's tertiary President and penned our Declaration of Independence. Is nothing sacred to you?"

Premier? Tertiary? Twilight rolled her eyes and answered, "Yes, Rachel, human life and freedom are sacred to me. Upholding the preamble of our United States Constitution is sacred to me. Do you really know what is sacred to you?"

Rachel didn't answer. Twilight added, "Why don't you and Sarah continue your sewing? I promise that Mr. Canon and I will behave. And don't worry, he won't breathe a word about what has happened in this parlor, will you, Mr. Canon?"

"Of course not, my dear."

From their repartee, Twilight felt less hostility and even, strangely, a touch of camaraderie toward this son of an enslaver. Lowering her voice for privacy, she said, "So you will return to your father's plantation soon?"

"That depends on you."

"Oh?"

"If I may, I would like to call on you every day for a month. If we've enjoyed our visits, I might stay in Memphis longer. If we have not, I'll move to Magnolia Bay, my father's plantation. In that event, I quite possibly will never see you again."

She had only just met Canon. She wasn't sure she even liked him. That his father owned people sickened her. And yet, the thought of never again seeing this young man bothered her.

Noticing the change in her expression, Canon touched her hand lightly. "Magnolia Bay is a wonderful place," he said.

Twilight jerked her hand away from his fingers, responding, "No, it's not."

Canon blinked slowly, then said, "I think it strange that you've appointed yourself guardian of the Rich-tones. You are so quick to judge others, to call us leeches. But what about you?"

"What about me?" Twilight said. "We don't own people. So what are you implying?"

"Your elegant gown billows so beautifully over that settee. Yards and yards of material to fashionably highlight you." Canon looked into her eyes. "Yards and yards of cotton."

She felt a twinge on her finger where Wondrous Ring encircled. In a quiet voice, she asked—even though she knew the answer—"What is your point, sir?"

Jackson said, "In the words of Mrs. Lucretia Mott, renowned Quaker from Pennsylvania, those who oppose slavery must, and I quote, '…deny themselves the blood-bought sweets and the blood-stained cotton that has come through this corrupt channel.'" Then, from his inside coat pocket, he pulled a yellowing newspaper clipping and gently unfolded it.

"In the famous *Liberator* of Boston, in 1841, Mrs. Mott stated, 'Let us examine our own clothing—the furniture of our houses—the conducting of trade,—the affairs of commerce,—and then ask ourselves, whether we have not each, as individuals, a duty which, in some way or other, we are bound to perform.'"

Carefully folding the clipping and placing it back into his coat pocket, Canon said, "Mrs. Mott is a woman of her word. I hear she ceased using enslaved-laborer products in her home over thirty years ago—no sugar, molasses, tobacco, rice, indigo, or cotton—and buys only goods produced by hired, not enslaved, laborers. I've heard she even sacrifices writing paper made with cotton fiber." Stretching his long legs into the room, he added, "She insisted her husband, a merchant whose business dealt largely in cotton, abandon all enslaved-laborer products. It took him a few years to do this, as he had five children to feed, and he thought it might ruin his income. But, he switched to trading in wool rather than cotton, and apparently, it never hurt his business."

Twilight gazed from Canon to her dress. GrandMama had often spoken of Mrs. Mott, another fierce advocate for the rights of all women and of all oppressed, and considered her a friend. Hearing someone speak of Mrs. Mott again nudged a forgotten memory to suddenly emerge: when she lived with her grandparents, her clothes had been linen and silk. Never cotton. That changed when, at twelve, she was sent to her parents' home. *What happened to me when GrandMama died, and I was sent away? Have I become a hypocrite?*

Tracing with her eyes the yellow ribbon looping heavily through a white panel of her dress, she said, "Yes. Yes, you are right, Mr. Canon. I am opposed to slavery in word, not wholeheartedly in deed. As long as I am buying dresses of cotton, I am endorsing the labor of the enslaved."

She sat quietly.

Canon watched her, then said, "Of course, your use of cotton is nothing in comparison to the overall demand. If you stop buying it, no one will know the difference."

"I'll know."

After a moment of silence, she added, "Every small use adds up to millions of enslaved people. If you will excuse me, I need to find a more suitable dress."

"Nothing could be more suitable. This dress flatters you," Canon said.

Gazing at her billowing skirt, Twilight said, "Yes, it was my favorite."

"Twilight?"

She didn't answer.

"Twilight. Are you well?" Canon asked.

She laughed tightly. "Better now than I was."

"Good. For a moment, you were too sad. Your spark was gone. I can't imagine you without your lively, uncanny spirit."

"Don't fret, sir. I won't give up my spirit. Just my cotton dresses."

"May I call on you tomorrow?"

"Yes. I would like that, Mr. Canon."

"Please, call me Jackson."

"I would like that, Jackson."

Chapter 6
Tarnished Mirror

*Thursday, June 17, 1858, Evening
and Friday, June 18, 1858, Early Afternoon
Memphis*

After Jackson left, Twilight quickly climbed the stairs to her room, placed her birthday letter on the shrine, shed her gown, and in her petticoat and chemise, examined her summer wardrobe.

Only three gowns weren't of cotton weave—one of soft linen and two of silk. She had two linen frocks for chores. Without delay, she decided, she must have non-cotton dresses made. But it wasn't just the dresses; all her chemises were made of absorbent, cool cotton. She'd have to figure out how to replace those, which might take a little time.

She placed her hands on her washstand, leaned forward toward the mirror, and searched the eyes of a hypocrite. *Why had I needed the son of an enslaver to remind me of Mrs. Mott's writings and sermons? Or to hint at my hypocrisy? I am ashamed of myself. Would GrandMama be ashamed of me?* The answer came instantly: *No. Never. GrandMama did admonish at times, but always gently. But she was never ashamed of me. She thought shame was a waste of good time.*

Her dear GrandMama—adamant against slavery; adamant against all disrespectful attitudes toward and treatment of Rich-tone people and all women and children—had met Mrs. Mott and also Frederick Douglass at the first Women's Rights Convention, Seneca Falls, New York, in 1848. Twilight concentrated, pulling from her memory Mrs. Mott's words advocating freedom for all. Now that she was thinking of it, her grandparents used little sugar or molasses, no tobacco, no rice, no indigo, and few cotton products, including the rare use of cotton rag paper for letter writing.

GrandMama had also often referred to Sojourner Truth, whom she'd heard speak at the first National Women's Rights Convention, Worcester, Massachusetts, in 1850 and at the Women's Rights Convention, Akron, Ohio, in 1851. Twilight had read the autobiography of Truth, who, with her baby, had escaped slavery. She'd read the autobiography of Frederick Douglass, who, at age twenty, had escaped slavery. She'd read the autobiography of Solomon Northrup, a free man and a musician living in New York. Pale men lied to him, offering him work in performing his music in Washington D.C., where they drugged him, abducted him, and sold him into slavery. After twelve years, he made connections that aided him in regaining his freedom.

Around the time GrandMama took ill, she and Twilight read then discussed a letter printed in the *New York Semi-Weekly Tribune,* the author signing as "A Fugitive Slave" rather than with her name. A woman and mother, "A Fugitive Slave" wrote forthrightly, hoping to educate those like former first lady Mrs. Tyler, who, in an act of inflexible refusal to accept that owning people was wrong, had published a pro-slavery letter in newspapers. "A Fugitive Slave" even boldly stated what those in the South, and many in the North, knew about but denied—sexual abuse by the master enslaver.

The truths revealed by the formerly-enslaved stung Twilight's heart. It was as if the United States was a swarm of venomous Southern, Northern—and moving Westward—wasps.

Why had I pushed all this about Mrs. Mott into the hidden corridors of my mind? At only twelve, in deep grief from GrandMama's death and sent suddenly to live with a mother and sisters who abhor me, I must have been in a kind of shock. Not until this evening have I given thought to the importance of boycotts. Not until young, handsome Jackson Canon enlightened me.

Now, her head throbbed with the words of Mrs. Mott.

She touched lightly all of her physical memories of GrandMama placed respectfully on the shrine: GrandMama's wedding band, handkerchief, hair barrette and comb, a lock of her hair in a pink silk ribbon, the bottle of her favorite perfume—all arranged in a circle on an embroidered linen napkin. In the center of the circle were GrandMama's Bible, the poetry book by Phillis Wheatley, the organza bag with the three stones, and the letter. Also, the doe and tree letter stamp GrandMama, upon her death, had bequeathed to Twilight—a gift that, at the time, Twilight thought striking and beautiful but had no idea of its significance. One item that was not her GrandMama's graced the edge of the shrine: a hummingbird feather—held down by a small stone so that it would not blow away.

After lighting a candle then setting it next to the Bible, Twilight lifted GrandMama's letter to her heart, closed her eyes, tilted her face upward, and said:

"GrandMama, I am your granddaughter. And I am my Great-Great-GrandMama Rose's granddaughter. Even before I knew of my heritage, I, like you, wanted slavery to end. Now, I desperately want slavery to end. Raised in every way as a Pale young woman with advantages and freedom, I pray that my eyes be opened. Now I know that by Pale judgment and possibly even Pale law, I am a Rich-tone young woman. But the truth is, I'm not really Rich-tone, am I? I know nothing of the Rich-tone community or what it means to be Rich-tone. Who am I? Show me, GrandMama, show me who I am."

She kneeled. "I vow on my love for you, on your love for your GrandMama, on my female heritage, on these secrets I will keep, and on all that is right and humane, that I will do whatever I can to see—then end—my hypocrisy and the atrocity of slavery."

After a few moments of silence, she opened her eyes, stood, kissed the seal, then, one last time, traced her finger on GrandMama's inscription.

It was time. Time to act. Time to burn the letter, as GrandMama had directed. Cautiously, she hovered GrandMama's words near the flame. She touched an edge to the fire but instantly pulled the letter away and stopped the burn with her finger.

Clutching the letter to her chest, she knew she couldn't destroy her last communication from GrandMama. It was a vital link to the person she loved most.

Opening it was magical. It holds so much important information. I must read and re-read it to feel close to GrandMama and for clues to understanding these "gifts" she claims I have. Later I will burn it. But until then, I'll keep it safe. I have the secret pockets I've sewn inside the seams of my dresses to hide my pistol. The letter will be safe on my person. At night, I'll keep the letter in the poetry book. No one enters my room; no one snoops. I know because no one has ever found my Deringer; it would have been huge news if they had. All is safe in a book of poetry. No one in this house, except me, reads poems.

Tucking the letter back into the poetry book, then shedding her petticoat and slipping on her dressing gown, she went to the library to discuss with her father steps to end the Memphis Star Packet trafficking of cotton and people.

Folding the newspaper and laying it on his knees, Harley responded, "Profits grow as the sales of enslaved people grow. I fear our nation is being built on the selling and the buying of people as well as their unpaid labor."

Twilight looked at the design on the rug and noticed, for the first time, an obnoxious pattern. "I keep our ledgers. I know what, and whom, we transport. Did I choose to see only what I wanted to see?" Twilight shook her head. "I have been so quick to judge others but have not looked at my own use of cotton nor at our shipments of cotton nor at the shipping of people as goods." Wrapping her arms around her middle, she said, "I feel ill."

"We could decide never to ship enslaved-laborer goods or enslaved people," Harley said. "Without shipping cotton, profits will fall. And that's fine. We'll be fine. We'll still have passengers, and we have other freight to ship." He paused, then added, "However, we just signed our agreement with one more Southern packet, the one based in Louisville. They're going to want to traffic enslaved people."

Squeezing shut her eyes, Twilight rubbed her temples. "Yes, an agreement I negotiated. For more business," she whispered. She opened her eyes to see her father smile weakly at her; his eyes held a deep look of concern.

"If we end our business of transporting the enslaved now, I see legal pains ahead," Harley said. "It also means that the people we would have transported will have to walk, chained, to their next owner, or mart, or auction. Or, they will be shipped on someone else's steamer or on the rails. It does not mean we are reducing the domestic trade of the enslaved."

"Well, I don't like that they would have to walk. But *we* wouldn't be part of human trafficking, so isn't that the right thing to do?" she said. "And, Father, can we change the name of *Pharaoh's Run* to *North Star*?"

Harley's eyebrows rose. "Rechristen? I suppose so. Why?"

"Isn't it Exodus that tells the story of a pharaoh that kept the children of Israel in bondage?"

"Ah, yes."

"I know, Father, that you like the name *Pharaoh's Run* as it relates to Memphis being named for the city in Egypt on the Nile and to the Mississippi River being referred to as the Nile of North America. But—"

"But I see your point. *North Star* is a good name. Fits well for the number one steamer of the Memphis Star Packet Line. Let's discuss this more tomorrow and devise a plan. These changes might take some time," Harley said, stamping out his cigar. "Have you read yesterday's *Eagle and Enquirer*? It reported Sam Clemens' arrival."

"Oh? Every day at the Exchange, I see reporters. But no, I haven't had time to read much lately." *Except for GrandMama's mysterious letter.*

Harley opened the newspaper to page 3 and read aloud the account of Sam's overwhelmed reaction upon seeing his brother. Then he said,

"The brothers, Sam and Henry, fast friends that they are, had found work on the same steamer. Henry was the clerk. Sam, as we know, was the cub. Sam said he was put ashore in New Orleans after an altercation with William Brown, the pilot—gone now, down with the steamer, God rest his difficult soul—to stop Brown from attacking Henry. Brown had no good reason to attack Henry, of course."

Twilight's eyes were wide upon hearing of the fight. "Brown attacked his clerk? Certainly not! Then the cub attacked the pilot? Was this happening in the pilot house? While they were on duty?"

"Yes. Sam said he knew this was wrong. It seems the captain, Klinefelter, understood Sam's position on the matter—protecting his younger brother from Brown's attack. He decided to separate Sam and Brown, having Sam disembark the *Pennsylvania* in New Orleans to continue on another steamer. Sam told me, 'To correct Brown's behavior and his speech, I pummeled him and his parlance.' He told me all this in a monotone, without ever taking his eyes off his brother. It would be humorous, except for the tragic situation."

"Corrected his behavior *and* speech?" Twilight said, smiling. *Sam is witty. Even in the midst of great tragedy.*

Harley chuckled. Then he added gravely, "Sam would've been on the *Pennsylvania* when it exploded if not for his altercation with Brown to defend his brother Henry, who now might die."

"By the full moon and its mysterious shadows. Life has its twists and turns," Twilight said. After absorbing all her father had told her, she added, "More steps for steamer and river safety can be done; more should be done."

"Yes, even though inspectors are doing what they can, river travel should be safer," Harley said.

"I wish more could be done to make life travel safer," Twilight said. "Where are the inspectors for that?"

She went to her room, held the letter again, and said, "What does one do with secrets like yours?" Placing it back into the book of poems, she added, "I'm going to find out."

The following day, she took linen and silk to a seamstress, who, fortunately, didn't ask why she needed so many dresses of non-cotton, as Twilight was reluctant to discuss her anti-slavery stance to a born-and-bred Southern woman on whom she depended for her clothing. Twilight did not want to be forced to use the newest dress-making invention, the sewing machine. As it always made her think of the fairy tale about Briar Rose, who fell asleep for one hundred years after touching a spinning wheel, Twilight vowed never to go near the gadget. The sewing machine, however, thrilled Sarah and Rachel almost as much as a new beau-come-a-calling.

Next, she went to the packet office to work on the balance sheet. And to figure changing what, and who, they transported. There, leaning against her door, arms crossed against his chest, legs crossed at the ankles, stood the tall, handsome Jackson Canon, his black hair curling down his forehead toward his arched eyebrows, thick black lashes, and earthy blue eyes. He was smiling. "Good day," he said with a bow, swooshing his top hat in front of him.

"And to you," Twilight replied with a curtsy.

"You look even lovelier in linen."

"Thank you."

"Would you meet me at the dance this evening?"

Without hesitating, Twilight answered, "Yes."

He placed his hands lightly on her shoulders. She could feel the heat of his hands through the fabric. "I think of you every minute," he said. "Twilight, I long to dance with you. I'll see you tonight." He strode to his horse, then turned to look at her again, smiling.

Twilight watched him mount his horse and ride away. Her gaze drifted to the busy wharf. Chanting enslaved men, while their Pale overseers shouted at them, loaded and unloaded rows of side-wheelers and stern-wheelers. The active wharf, even with its injustices, was home to her. *What would it be like to live at the grand Magnolia Bay?*

She shook her head. *What am I thinking?*

Chapter 7
Gala Event

*Friday, June 18, 1858, Evening
and Memory
Memphis*

The Adams sisters, chaperoned by their father, arrived punctually at the city ball.

Twilight couldn't wait to dance with Jackson, to feel his body near hers, as near as a waltz would allow. Rachel and Sarah giggled, for eligible husbands filled the room.

Will the night be magic, Twilight wondered while watching her sisters, *and provide my sisters with husbands so they will soon leave the house?*

Then to Twilight's delight, two brothers, coppersmiths in their early forties, whisked Rachel and Sarah out onto the dance floor. Twilight was left standing. *I don't want to dance with an old forty-year-old anyway. Jackson will be here soon.* Anxiously, she looked toward the door. *When he arrives, we'll dance, and all of stuffy Memphis will see that someone—one of the most educated and handsome young men in the area, in fact—chooses me.*

Ten minutes passed. Twilight nervously tapped her foot to the music, fearing Jackson might not show. She tried not to stare at the door, but the swirling kaleidoscope of colorful figures couldn't keep her attention. And then, through the door walked the young man she loved.

"Gallatin!"

Gallatin—always attracted, never repelled, by Twilight's independent ways. Gallatin—who encouraged her outrageous spirit. Gallatin—the pilot of *Pharaoh's Run*. Gallatin—*her* pilot, the pilot of her heart.

※

Her moments with Gallatin forever played in her memory, devout and repetitious, like the hymns she heard each Sunday at Calvary Episcopal Church. Her favorite memory was of their meeting. Fourteen years and two weeks old, she was feeling womanly. Since that birthday, her father allowed her to work at the packet line office, a room in his general and hardware store near the public landing. *Pharaoh's Run* had docked. The new—very handsome—pilot walked through the office door and into her life. He looked too young to be a pilot, yet, he carried a mesmeric composure.

"May I help you?" Twilight said. "Mr. Adams is supervising the unloading of *Pharaoh's Run*."

"I pilot *Pharaoh's Run*, miss. Gallatin. I've come for my pay," he said. Then he smiled at her in a way that she could only describe as electric, with something more for which she had no words.

Warmth was rushing over her with so much force it shook her. Keeping her composure, however, she said, "Mr. Gallatin? One moment, please." Digging into the file drawer with a shaking hand, she pulled out an envelope and said, "Here it is, but Mr. Adams didn't write your given name." Trying to maintain a professional appearance, she looked back into the file drawer and said, "It's not written on the folder, either." She pulled out the folder, placed it in front of her, and dipped a pen into the inkwell. "I'll write your given name on here, Mr. Gallatin, just in case we should employ another man with your surname." Bent over the desk, poised with the pen, looking up at him, she waited for his name and hoped he hadn't noticed her shaking hand and flushed face. "Will you tell me your name, Mr. Gallatin?" she asked, wondering if he planned to ever answer her.

He smiled; the heat rushed more deeply over and through her. "I have only one name," he said.

How intriguing.

"Not so intriguing, actually."

Though shocked, wondering if he'd just read her mind, Twilight held her composure, trying to keep her reaction in check.

"It's that my mother died shortly after my birth. She hadn't named me, and my father didn't want to."

"I see," Twilight said. "My mother didn't name me, either."

Gallatin said nothing but considered her with interest.

Twilight continued. "She sent me away shortly after my birth. Grand-Mama named me."

"And what name did GrandMama choose for you?" he asked.

"Twilight."

A hummingbird flew through the open door and hovered. Then, another hummingbird entered. For a moment, they hovered together, then flew quickly out the door, back into the world. A tiny feather drifted as Gallatin opened his hand, where it landed.

"Maybe they lost their way," Twilight said.

Gallatin smiled, then said, "Or maybe they found their way."

Twilight opened her hand. Gallatin placed the feather onto her palm, then whispered two words so softly that Twilight couldn't hear them clearly. Then he said, "Twilight. On the river, twilight is the magic that transforms the day. I like to think of twilight as the embrace of day and night, creating a new time. Not day. Not night. Both, and also neither. Twilight is her own time."

Strange. Even though they'd only just met, she felt she knew him, somehow. Rather, they knew each other, somehow.

Deeply gazing into her eyes, Gallatin said, "Some things are eternal."

She would never have chosen to love a blonde, rugged, vagabond river prince, but at that moment, a decision from beyond her had been made.

Chapter 8
Those Words

Friday, June 18, 1858
Evening and Night
Memphis

"Gallatin!" she called again, nearly running to him.

He rested his hands gently on her cheeks for a moment, then placed them on her shoulders. Slowly, his hands slid down her arms until he was holding both her hands.

Her breath caught in her chest. As always when she was near him, waves of warmth rushed over her and through her. Her heart nearly expanded through her chest. Her soul eased with satisfaction.

"Twilight, you look beautiful in emerald silk." Gazing lovingly at her bare neck and shoulders, he added, "You are more lovely than any sight I've seen. Ever. Anywhere. Dearest, happy birthday. I am sorry I wasn't here to celebrate it with you." Then, staring deeply into her eyes, he added, "But I'm here now." He inhaled slowly, then said, "I've been running the Mississippi too long. I've missed you."

"I've missed you," she said as her breath returned and the pounding of her heart softened. But the warmth continued to envelop her, turning her inside and out. "Treacherous obstacles to navigation have kept you away?"

He nodded and inhaled deeply. "As you know, June brings flooding; Cairo was nearly immersed in places. Now the water is starting to recede, leaving much in its wake. Navigation has been difficult."

"Snags, sawyers, sand bars, new islands, the Graveyard, and more than that, I'm sure. I hope the passengers were patient."

"Ah, the Graveyard. Navigating that stretch is navigating through a growing number of sunken boats, maybe as many as one hundred."

"By the full moon," Twilight said.

"The trip has been long and tedious, but most passengers are grateful that they arrived to their destinations safely."

"Oh, Gallatin, the *Pennsylvania*. It was terrible. I'm volunteering at the makeshift hospital at the Exchange Hall."

"You're a gem for doing what you can," he said, his eyes soft.

A distasteful man whose name Twilight could never remember said loudly to Captain Merton of *Pharaoh's Run*, "Still slow even after those snag boats did all your work, Merton? Not as much skill needed now." Not looking at Gallatin even once nor waiting for a reply from Captain Merton, the man walked quickly on.

Twilight said, "What an awful man. I can't believe there are those against cleaning snags from the river, claiming that the cleared waterway takes away from the skill required to pilot. And, he's a coward. He spoke loudly enough for you to hear but wouldn't speak to you directly. Then he hurried away."

Unfazed, Gallatin said, "Those who make such claims believe more dangers equal better pilots. He and those in his camp have never piloted the river, nor do they care for human life, or so it seems. There are way too many snags and the corpses of boats they leave. The river has more than enough mysteries and dangers and takes far too many lives."

She tilted her head and said, "As we know, when he was President, Andrew Jackson affected some river improvements, but probably not for admirable reasons alone."

Gallatin said, "The clearing of snags is good; the clearing of people is not. Jackson, the scoundrel. Forcing the Choctaw, Creek, Chickasaw,

Cherokee, and most of the Seminole from their lands east of the Mississippi River." Nodding toward the disagreeable man who was arguing with someone near the entrance, Gallatin added, "Ignorance and ego. A dangerous combination that drives too many."

"And terrorizes thousands," she said. "On a different matter, Gallatin, how would you like to pilot the *North Star?*"

"Pilot the star that guides us? Sounds like quite an honor," he chuckled.

"No," she laughed. "We're renaming *Pharaoh's Run* to the *North Star*."

"I like it," he said. "It might be a scheduling nightmare for you for a while."

"Father agrees to this as long as all of the paperwork and renaming on the schedules is mine to handle," she laughed again. "Shouldn't be much different than if we were putting a new steamer into the schedule of a retired one."

"Hopefully, that's true. When do we rechristen?"

"Tomorrow. If Father agrees."

Gallatin nodded, then said, "Dearest, you are carrying your Deringer, I trust?"

"Of course, though I'm not sure why. I am at a public dance. Even though the gun is light, the habit and responsibility of carrying it feels very heavy."

"A necessary habit for a young woman as striking, outspoken, and with such pure spirit as you."

Raising her head, Twilight said, "Pure, Gallatin? I think I resent that. After all, it is the publication I detest, *Godey's Lady Book*, that preaches the epitome of true womanhood is purity. And also domesticity, piety, and my least favorite, submissiveness."

"Ah, you haven't changed. Good. Not just *Godey's*, but most publications aimed at women extol those as four essential female virtues."

"True." Twilight took a deep breath. "Gallatin, I will never become a *Godey's* fashion plate. So what did you mean about me being 'pure'?"

"Not you, darling. Your spirit. Your spirit is bright, alive, uncomplicated. When the rest of the world can't resolve even the simplest of matters, something inside of you leaps out in the knowledge of right and wrong that is beyond the understanding of most. I don't think that you're conscious of such uncanny insight. I believe you were born with it." He smiled. "It's a gift, my mystic princess."

Mystic princess. Were those the two words he had said when we met? She said, "Or a curse. I have few friends. My mother hates me. Sometimes I want to conform more to please Mother and to not be such an outcast. It's lonely, being me. But conforming always makes me feel like a liar."

Unmoving, Gallatin stared at her as if he could do so forever. And then he said, "I love you."

Those words. Words I have dreamed of hearing from him. Wanting more than anything to believe that he meant romantic love but fearful that he meant only friend-love or family-type love, she squeezed her eyes shut, then opened them and asked, "How?"

"How?"

"Yes, how do you love me? Like you love your father or like you love the Mississippi?"

He laughed. "Not like I love my father. But as you know, Twilight, I can't love anyone or anything as much as I love the Mississippi."

"Oh," she said, and the warm rush chilled.

She started to pull her hands from his, but he held them firmly and said, "May I have this dance?"

They danced. All evening. Though she was having fun, she knew she could have a truly wonderful time if only Gallatin would love her like he loved the Mississippi. But obviously, they'd be only friends forever. After the last dance, Gallatin walked with her to her father's carriage, gave her his hand to help her inside, then sat in front with Harley.

It wasn't until then that she realized she'd forgotten all about Jackson Petigru Canon.

Chapter 9
Target Practice

*Friday, June 18, 1858, Night
and Saturday, June 19, 1858, Morning
Memphis*

Stuffed in the carriage with two twittering sisters and three large hoop skirts, Twilight quietly sat, twisting Wondrous Ring and wondering why Jackson hadn't arrived.

Did he lie about wanting to dance with me? Is he ill? Or has he been in an accident? Is he dead? Her biggest question was: *Why didn't I think about him while dancing with Gallatin?*

As soon as they were home, she hurried up the steps to her room.

After a sleepless night, she found the morning held no promise of ending her confusion. She needed tea. At the kitchen doorway, she stopped abruptly upon seeing Gallatin seated at the small table.

"I've been waiting for you."

"Oh? Why aren't you on the river?"

"You want me to go?"

"Of course not," she said, putting a kettle of water on the cookstove and lighting the fire. "I just wondered how long you'd be with us. You know I always miss you when you go. When you're here, Gallatin, I don't feel so lonely."

"Or misunderstood."

Twilight nodded. She joined him at the table. They sat in silence. As the water heated, she placed her hand on top of his.

He said, "I'll be here today and tomorrow. The *North Star* needs some minor repairs. And as you know, we repair before—not after." He winked at her. "And today is the christening."

Normally, Twilight added to any conversation about packets, river travel, and especially steamer safety. But she was quiet.

"Twilight," Gallatin said, "you seem distracted. You always know the schedule—when I am expected to arrive and leave—even when that schedule has to change. And you know about the needed repairs often before you see me. And you know the christening is scheduled for today."

It was true. For the first time, Twilight wasn't framing everything in terms of her father's riverboats and, in particular, Gallatin's visits.

Gallatin breathed deeply, then said, "Twilight, I have something to say."

Looking at him with a slight grimace and pulling her hand back from his, she said, "I'm not sure I want to hear."

"I must be clear, dear one. What I said last night, I mean. I do love you. I couldn't stop myself; the feeling was, and is, too strong. But I shouldn't have said those words. It seems to me that a young lady will wait forever for a man who confesses his love for her. We both have much to accomplish in our separate lives. So the fact that I love you is futile. Don't wait for me."

The water boiled. She went to the counter, measured gunpowder tea, dropped it into the teapot, then poured the boiling water over it.

Setting Gallatin's teacup in front of him and the steaming teapot between them, she said, "Futile? That's a horrible way to think of love—as futile." She walked back to the cupboard and reached for her cup. Returning to the table, she placed her cup next to his. She folded her arms.

"Gallatin, I've always loved you, but I tell myself that my feelings are nothing more than a fondness for a special, caring friend. I wish you hadn't told me; now I'll wonder for the rest of my days what it could be like for us if only I were as important as the Mississippi."

With a lift of her head, she added, "You're not quite twenty, and you think you know what's best for us both. Well, let me tell you something, Mr. Gallatin. The Mississippi is water. I am a person." Tapping her chest with her fist, she said, "I think, breathe, and love. Really love." With a turn, she stalked from the room and up the stairs.

Gallatin followed, taking her hand and pulling her close to him. She lifted her face. Gallatin bent so that his lips were as close to hers as possible without touching. For a moment, there was only silence and breath. They lightly touched lips. Then, they kissed.

Her first kiss. And with Gallatin. Twilight thought it was the most sensational feeling she had ever known.

He pulled her closer. Pressing their bodies together, they kissed again. Moving his lips to her ear, he whispered, "I love everything about you; I love your defiance." Crunching her hair gently in his fist, he said, "Never lose your fight, Twilight."

She turned from him, hurried to her room, shut the door, sat on her bed, clasped her hands together until her knuckles turned white, and whispered, "By the full moon and its shadows, Gallatin. I'll be forever hopelessly in love with you, a man who'll never marry me."

"Twilight." Gallatin's voice was faint through the closed door. "Let's ride."

Shaking her head at her foolishness, she said, "I'll be down in ten minutes."

⊱✦⊰

Riding astride the back of Spirit as a man would ride—and, even more daring, bareback—was Twilight's greatest joy and, to date, her greatest sin. Of course, she knew how terrible it was to ride in such a manner.

No lady of high repute would ride as she did. But as a little girl, she, with a unique talent, leaped onto the bare back of her grandparents' mare, Mystica, the horse who later became Spirit's mother. Immediately, Twilight felt as if she were one with Mystica. Girl and horse moved brilliantly, first walking, then cantering, then nearly flying. This talent also happened immediately with Spirit.

As she grew, even her open-minded GrandMama mentioned half-heartedly, and just once, that Twilight might consider changing her bareback riding to sidesaddle riding, as the sight of a woman with her legs apart and against the animal was considered by society as simply too profane. Twilight refused then and refused now. Wearing trousers under her skirt, she continued to ride astride and bareback.

Across the open lands, Twilight raced for the joy of near flight on Spirit. Gallatin raced for the wild rush of speed on Charger, Harley's horse. After a bit, they stopped and dismounted. Picking up a stick, Gallatin pitched it, yelling to Twilight, "It's yours!"

Instantly, she pulled the loaded pistol from her pocket, cocked the hammer, and shot the stick just as it hit the ground. "Excellent!" Gallatin called, punctuating his praise with a muffled exclamation by clapping together his leather-gloved hands once. He tipped his hat to her, then pulled off his gloves and, holding them with his left hand, smacked them against his right hand.

Twilight sat on a large rock. Taking her powder flask, loading rod, percussion caps, and a ball from her drawstring bag, she began to reload. Gallatin reached into his right pocket and drew the twin to Twilight's Deringer. Sitting beside her, he said, "I wish you would take this one also. When I acquired the two, I was thinking of you. You accepted just one last year. But how about this? One for last year's birthday, and this one for this year's birthday."

She studied her hands reloading her Deringer as she thought of how he said the word "acquired" as if it were only two syllables rather than three, with an emphasis on the long "i" sound and an almost-missing "r" sound, soft and nearly a "w." She, having been raised just across the Kentucky border, had the slight accent of the residents of southern Indiana. However, Gallatin, who'd been born and raised in New Orleans, had the true Southern drawl, which Twilight deemed lovely and quite perfectly suited for a gentleman.

She shook her head. "No. One is more than enough for me," she said. "But I suppose one is not enough for a riverboat pilot."

"Look at this," he said. From his waistband, he pulled a larger gun and laid it on top of his palm. "It's a revolver that uses cartridges that contain the powder. And, it has a cylinder that's made so you can load from the back, a breech-loading cylinder; no powder, no ball, no ramming with a loading rod. Fires seven shots. Smith and Wesson; their first firearm. And the only one with this patent."

"By the eclipsing moon," Twilight said. "Seven shots? What next?" She shook her head again, imagining seven shots without having to reload using powder, ball, and loading rod. "Such a gun in misguided hands could easily inflict mass murder," she said, wrinkling her nose.

"I could give you my Colt. It would give you repeating shots, up to six. It's smaller than most guns. But too large for you to pocket, I suppose."

"It would be too large for me in many ways. One shot is more than enough." She finished loading. "This modest Deringer pistol is deceptively substantial. I like how its finely-curved handle fits my hand just right. It stays concealed in the hidden pockets I sew in the seams of my dresses. It constantly worries me, carrying it around. As I've said, even a light gun is a heavy responsibility. But you insist."

She wished she could tell Gallatin of her other secrets, which also were feeling heavy. Serenely walking from a cluster of trees, a young deer appeared, looked directly at Twilight, then at Gallatin, then turned and leaped, her white tail flicking once. "A doe and trees," Twilight whispered.

"Beautiful," Gallatin said.

Twilight nodded, thoughtful. *A warning to not say a word to anyone? Or just a coincidence?*

As they headed home, Twilight said, "Gallatin, I'd like to ride out to Germantown when we have a day to get there and back."

"Germantown? Do you want to see how the Memphis and Charleston Railroad is built through the community? Progress that threatens our valuable waterways."

"What's more interesting to me is to see where Nashoba was."

"Fanny Wright had a seemingly possible plan," he said. "A plantation community for the enslaved to gain education and freedom. Though she did become an American citizen the same year she started Nashoba, she was an unmarried woman originally from Europe trying to reform a U.S.-sanctioned Southern system. That's courageous. And brazen. If she hadn't gotten ill and gone back to Europe to regain her health, maybe she could've maintained Nashoba's reputation."

"We must do what we can to stop this disease of people thinking it is acceptable to own others. And to change the thinking that Rich-tone people and Pale people must not socialize. It seems that maybe there was less narrow thinking for a time. You do know that our first mayor was married to a Rich-tone woman?"

"I know a bit about my river ports, especially Memphis." He smiled. "Yes, Marcus and Marie Winchester. Since their time, there has been a terrible swing toward stricter laws against Rich-tone people, whether free or enslaved. Of course I'll ride with you to the site of what used to be Nashoba, when we have a day to do so. But what can you gain by looking at the site of a place that ended nearly thirty years ago?"

"I'm not sure. Just curious," Twilight replied as they approached downtown Memphis.

Chapter 10
Atrocity Square Again

Saturday, June 19, 1858
Noon
Memphis

When they reached Main Street, Twilight said, "The city has added gas lamps on some streets. Seems the entire country is adopting gas lighting."

"Or, for some citizens, adapting to it. And to other presumed improvements," Gallatin said. "Like railroads. Now we have the Memphis and Charleston Railroad, connecting the Atlantic Ocean to the Mississippi River. As far as I'm concerned, the best way to travel is—"

"—on water," Twilight said with Gallatin in unison. Twilight smiled and added, "So you've said. But it would be wise if you didn't say those things when you're seated upon Charger. He's twelve hundred pounds of pure muscle, and he can be sensitive." To Charger, Twilight said, "Right, fella?"

Patting Charger's neck, Gallatin said, "I didn't mean it, Charger. You're almost as fun as running the Mississippi." Charger snorted.

Twilight laughed. "Do you compare everything in your life with the Mississippi?" she asked.

"All the good things," he said.

As they approached Atrocity Square, Gallatin said, "Let's ride quickly. Neither of us wants to see—"

Instead of moving past the sight, Twilight stopped to watch. Puzzled, Gallatin stopped next to her. Twilight grabbed Gallatin's arm. Atop the block, the auctioneer pulled a toddler who was crying and trying to clench desperately onto her mother. The mother clutched her child, but another man whipped the woman with one determined lash; she dropped to the ground. The auctioneer threw an ugly glance at the man with the whip and said, "Careful with the merchandise." The man tucked the whip into his pocket, then held onto the mother, who sat on the ground.

The auctioneer lifted the screaming child.

"Who'll start the bidding at one hundred dollars for this little darlin'? She's two years old, so spend a little money here today, and you'll have a Riches worth many times more in just a few years."

Twilight flinched upon hearing the insulting and disrespectful term Riches that some used when referring or speaking to a Rich-tone person or persons. The little girl's hair swung in long ringlets about her face as she jerked her head from side to side, searching for her mama. Then, she saw her mama, who was looking in desperation at her. Mother and child locked eyes, seeing nothing but each other. Twilight watched in horror as time ticked away, each second pulling mama and baby apart to the moment when they'd never see each other again.

The bidding rose to one hundred twenty from a husky-voiced couple who called together, and Twilight thought the dreadful moment had happened, for no one spent much over one hundred dollars for a child.

"Do I hear one hundred thirty?"

Frantically looking at the crying child then at the crying mother then back at the crying child, Twilight gripped Gallatin's arm.

Seated atop shiny Charger, Gallatin moved a forefinger and nodded slightly to bid. He appeared professional and experienced, though bidding for humans was something he never thought he'd do.

"Thank you," Twilight said gently, as if in prayer.

"I hear one hundred thirty. Do I hear one hundred forty?"

The couple bid one hundred forty dollars.

Gallatin nodded again, saying, "One hundred fifty."

"We have one hundred fifty. Do I hear one hundred sixty? The man on the dark horse has a Rich-tone child unless I hear one hundred sixty dollars," the auctioneer called, searching the crowd. The husky-voiced couple glared at Gallatin and Twilight.

"Sold to the gentleman on the dark horse for one hundred fifty dollars."

Twilight released Gallatin's arm and said, "Thank you, dearest man. Now, the mother." *I wish we could free them all.*

The auctioneer dragged the young mother onto the block. He pointed to her face, then yanked off her head wrap, holding out her long hair and tightening her shift around her to display her figure, all the while verbally advertising her features. Wanting to hide, she turned her face to her child, who was being held below the block. She imagined running far away—far, far away—with her babies. The auctioneer grabbed her chin and pulled it up, twisting her face left and right for all to see.

"She bears good little enslaved babies. She's had two already; she's young and can bear many more. With these," he said, pulling her shift even more tightly, "you couldn't find a better wet nurse. And she's an experienced house servant. I'll start the bidding at seven hundred fifty dollars."

Gallatin bid with the dozens of men who wanted the woman. Finally, Gallatin ended the bidding at fifteen hundred dollars, an unheard-of price for a young woman advertised to be a wet nurse and house servant. Twilight doubted that most of the bidding men had been thinking of the woman only in those ways. Together, Gallatin and Twilight rode their horses to the mother and child and the man who held them. They dismounted. Taking the wriggly girl from the man, Gallatin placed her in her mama's outstretched arms; mother and daughter hugged then clung to each other. Twilight whispered to Gallatin, "I'm going to the bank for the money."

Gallatin tilted his head. "You have the money?"

"Yes. Father gave us each a dowry account, of course, but he made it clear that we can do what we want with it. Rachel and Sarah would never touch theirs. They intend to have large, enticing dowries," Twilight said, laughing.

Laughing with her, Gallatin said, "They'll need them." Then, serious, he added, "I want to buy freedom for the mother and her child."

"Thank you, Gallatin. But this is my doing," Twilight said.

Gallatin pulled his wallet—tethered by a strand of thin leather to his belt, as was the custom so that no one could steal a man's wallet—from its place tucked between his torso and belt. In Gallatin's hand, the wallet unfolded as if it were coming alive, opening like a breathing book that offered a story of compassion. "Money for freedom with equal rights. Capitalism be damned if it doesn't include that," he stated. To the man, he said, "This is half. Miss Adams will be back soon with the other half." The man grunted.

Twilight smiled at Gallatin and wished she could kiss him long and hard right there in the square. Instead, she glided effortlessly onto Spirit's back and trotted to the bank, Spirit's hooves barely touching the ground.

Chapter II
Can't We Do Better?

Saturday, June 19, 1858
Early Afternoon
Memphis

Ember and Makeda-Angel were their names.

The thought of legally owning two people made Twilight feel sick. However, she was making good on her beliefs and vow because, by owning them, she could also grant them freedom, which she would do immediately.

"Ember, where's your other child?" Twilight asked as waves of illness washed against the shore of her soul. "The auctioneer said you had two children. Is there another here we should—?"

Wincing from her whipping wound as she pulled her toddler closer to her, Ember said, "I see him when I see the moon, mistress."

"Oh. How painful for you, Ember," Twilight said.

Ember hugged Makeda-Angel tighter.

"And, please, call me by my name: Twilight. This is Gallatin. Ember, I want you to understand something. You and Makeda-Angel are free now, in my eyes. And soon, you will be legally free."

Ember pressed her lips into her child's hair and eyed Gallatin, the one who she thought had bought them.

"Gallatin helped to free you, but I signed the papers. All of that is just legality. I don't own people," Twilight said. "I don't believe in it. But for now, until we can get your freedom formalized, you'll have to come with me to my parents' home. There, you can work for wages."

Ember whispered, "No Rich-tone is free in the South. Some may think they are free, but they are not. Though those who aren't enslaved are freer than those who are."

The blood from Ember's wound was soaking through her shift. Twilight said, "We need to tend to your wound immediately, Ember. You and Makeda-Angel can ride my horse. Spirit will be easy and sweet. Gallatin and I will lead the horses and walk home. I live nearby. Is that agreeable, Gallatin?"

Gallatin said, "Ember shouldn't walk after that beating, but if she rides, we might be harassed, attacked, or worse." To Ember, he said, "I can carry Makeda-Angel, with your permission."

With an expression dry and determined, Ember said, "I will walk. I will carry my child."

"You're bleeding, Ember," Twilight implored, hoping Ember would let Gallatin carry Makeda-Angel.

Ember repeated, "I will walk. I will carry my child."

Twilight nodded. "I live just a few blocks from here."

As they walked, Ember moaned softly from the pain but held fast to her child, refusing Gallatin's offers to carry Makeda-Angel.

Gallatin said to Twilight, "You have some serious considerations to face." She knew to what he was referring: Tennessee law required, after Ember's and Makeda-Angel's liberations, that Twilight provide for them to be sent to Africa, typically Liberia, the country created for that purpose. She'd ask Ember what she wanted to do. If Ember wanted Africa, then Twilight would pay for their passage there. If Ember wanted to stay in the United States, they'd have to figure out how to make that happen. State laws seemed to change nearly every year, and sending away someone who'd been granted manumission wasn't required to be immediate. Ember would have to register as free. Her registration certificate would be renewed every three years, subject to her character as deemed by the county court. Twilight could petition for Ember and Makeda-Angel to stay within the state. She'd heard such petitioning was sometimes successful in Tennessee.

But she knew there was more to Gallatin's concern—he was also wondering how her parents would react. *Deep in my heart, I believe Father will be proud of what I've done. But he'll act upset because Mother will put on such a show. She'll swoon, and Cara will run for her salts. Rachel and Sarah will be ridiculous as always, or worse. And when Mother learns that I bought them just to keep them together and to provide their freedom, she'll be unbearable. I mean, after all, that is against Southern social practice. If only she knew her own lineage.*

As the four turned from Main Street onto Adams Avenue, they passed the Worsham House Hotel. Gallatin said, "It was just a year ago that John Able shot and killed John Everson in cold blood here. In the spirit of vigilante justice, many wanted to promptly and directly string up the shooter."

Shaking her head, Twilight said, "Cold-blooded shootings, vigilantes wanting public hangings. People enslaved, whipped, beaten, and worse. Can't we do better?"

The enslaved from Forrest's Mart circled inside the yard bordering Adams Avenue, eyes diverted toward the ground. A guard watching the captives glared at Gallatin, Twilight, Ember, and Makeda-Angel. Twilight whispered to Gallatin, "That guard looks so angry and mean."

"My dear, it seems you always draw attention."

"Unwelcome attention," Twilight said. "It would be odd if he could sense that I'm going to emancipate Ember and Makeda-Angel. Hang me from the highest gallows, for I surely have sinned." She laughed weakly.

"Twilight, never joke like that. With the South's sickness for slavery, actions like yours might be regarded unfavorably."

Twilight clutched Gallatin's hand. Her trespasses had always been against social norms; never had she crossed legal bounds. "Gallatin, I've done nothing wrong—legally, I mean. Buying people feels so wrong, even if for the right reason: to free them. But, here, though wrong, it is legal. There's no law against freeing them, either."

"Not this year. The laws go back and forth on that."

"You don't think I'll be noosed, do you?"

"No. But I don't think you should joke about the dangers. Vigilante 'justice' is real—some individuals and mobs think they can kill others by what they call 'taking the law into their own hands.' The South is teeming with misguided vigilantes becoming overly suspicious about anyone against slavery. I steer away from such types."

"They are overly suspicious?"

"Yes. And fearful that anyone who doesn't own people or at least support enslaving people is a threat to the livelihood and, thus, the existence of the South. Many think the South is special, different, and not even a part of the United States—and that slavery should exist, no matter who suffers or dies."

GrandMama warned me. I must be careful while being bold. "Surely I am not in any danger for my actions." Saying the words somehow made her feel they were true. Glancing under her lashes at the man she loved, she said, "Besides, if anyone wants to hang me, I'll just stow away on the *North Star* forever with Gallatin at the helm."

Making no reply, Gallatin considered her with a pained smile.

Twilight wished she really could stow away with Gallatin. Forever.

Chapter 12
Family and Kin

Saturday, June 19, 1858
Early Afternoon
Memphis

Sarah's mouth dropped with her teacup when the four entered the parlor.

Cara, who listened to and for everything, ran in to pick up the cup and blot the tea from the carpet.

Rachel jumped up from her chair then clapped her hands. "Enslaved servants. We have enslaved servants. That little girl can bring to me things I need." She giggled like a spoiled child with yet another toy. "Little enslaved girl, get me that pillow over there. I need more comfort."

Makeda-Angel pressed into her mother. Ember, holding her baby, recoiled to the door.

"Rachel! Shut your ugly mouth!" Twilight yelled. *If only you knew of your ancestry, Rachel, would you behave so terribly? Probably you would. You'd deny the knowledge, even to yourself.* To Ember, she said, "You never have to listen to a word Rachel says."

Harley placed his hand on the arm of his chair and pushed his torso straight and forward as if readying and steadying himself for anything. Elizabeth acted peculiar, not at all like herself—for once, she wasn't swooning or calling for salts or becoming hysterical. Instead, she sat quietly, smiling oddly at Ember.

Gallatin bowed to Twilight's family, saying, "Good day, fine family."

"Mother, Father, and Sisters," Twilight said. "This is my friend, Ember, and her daughter Makeda-Angel. Cara, please prepare some warm water and dressings and take them to my room. A horrible man lashed Ember. We'll tend to her wound there."

Rachel said, "Twilight, whatever *are* you saying? Your friend? She's Rich-tone, Twilight. She's enslaved and a servant."

"Not all Rich-tone people are enslaved, Sister."

"In Memphis they are."

"That's not true. There are free Rich-tone people here. Some were born free. Some have been manumitted. Gallatin and I are providing Ember and Makeda-Angel manumission as soon as possible. During that process, Ember will work for wages here. After she receives her freedom papers, she can stay as a paid servant or she can leave; that is her decision."

"Such absurdity! Now we are to be disgraced and ruined forever! Whoever heard of anyone in the South having a Rich-tone for a paid servant! Everyone in the South owns their laborers, Twilight. Everyone." Clenching her fists by her side, Rachel addressed the family. "What's wrong with us? We are Southerners, yet we've never owned a Rich-tone laborer. Here is our chance, and Twilight wants to pay her. How humiliating! Father, as you've so proudly reminded us, you came to Memphis with your family when you were only four years old. Memphis itself was barely a year old and not even incorporated as a town. There were few residents, you and your parents being three of them. You helped this tiny lawless bluff grow to a civilized city of twenty thousand. And yet, you, a true son of Memphis, have never owned a Rich-tone! Why?" She stomped her foot. "I want to know why!"

With an uncharacteristic firmness, Harley said, "It's true, Rachel. You all know my heritage, and I am proud to be one of the first residents of this fine city. Memphis and I have grown up together, so to speak, and I love the city like a brother. But we may love our brothers even though they don't always do what is right. And slavery is wrong. Owning people is reprehensible."

It was the first time Twilight had heard her father speak his opinion of slavery directly to the family.

Rachel continued, "So, Father, you think you're right about that? Are you saying you know more about right and wrong than anyone else in Memphis? What about our friends and neighbors? They are fine upstanding families. They love their captives and consider them family."

"But they are not free."

Even though the words were a whisper, they were spoken by the young woman Ember, thus carrying the effect of a cannonball at the Independence Day celebration. Everyone stared at her. Ember stood unmoving, but her head and gaze were directed ahead of her, not focusing on anyone. Then, beyond the boldness allowed the enslaved and even most free Rich-tone people, she looked directly at Rachel and stated, "Loving someone and owning that person—both can't be true."

"You were not ordered to speak or to look at me," Rachel spat as wickedly as a frightened cat.

Twilight said, "Rachel, speak to Ember as my friend, or don't speak to her at all. Actually, just keep your mouth shut so no more ugly words can come from it."

"Fine! I wouldn't know how to speak to a friend of yours anyway, for you've never had any," Rachel replied.

"I am Twilight's friend," Gallatin said.

And then miraculously, Elizabeth spoke in an unfeigned manner. "Rachel, Twilight is right. You will accept this woman and her daughter in our household, and you will speak to them as you speak to Cara."

The moment was as intense and dense as a triple meteor shower. No one said a word, as no one knew what to say after a moment that none had ever experienced. For the dueling sisters, the moment was especially potent. To Twilight, it seemed a dream; to Rachel, a nightmare—their mother, for the first time, had supported one of Twilight's actions. Again stomping her foot, Rachel ended the instant of wonderment, then screamed in frustration as she marched out of the room. Sarah shuffled behind her.

The familiar amused expression returned to Gallatin's face. He approached the doorway and said, "Rachel, stop a moment. I want to add that your claim that everyone in Memphis owns their laborers is incorrect. Many people are hired, though I'm not sure how many hired laborers are Rich-tone. But, I'm guessing that possibly one-fourth of the population of Memphis are enslavers. Still, that's one-fourth too many."

Everyone heard Rachel's clear reply from the hallway: "Well, if that's even true, then most of the three-fourths who aren't enslavers probably can't afford to buy Rich-tones and envy those who do own them. The very few who don't want enslaved workers for themselves? Well, they nod their heads to slavery, don't they? And others—like some in this family, and like you, Gallatin—turn their faces, pretending they don't see the slavery that is everywhere. It's the Southern way."

With a nod, Gallatin said, "She has a point."

Elizabeth placed a hand over her eyes and said, "Please leave now. I feel fatigued."

Harley moved closer to his wife as Ember picked up Makeda-Angel and left the room with Gallatin and Twilight. At the base of the staircase, Twilight whispered, "By the full moon, Gallatin, did you hear my mother say that I was right?"

"I did," Gallatin whispered. "It's a shame you had to wait sixteen years to hear a bit of approval from her. And your father made an anti-slavery statement. I'd say you and Ember shook this household today."

To Ember, Twilight said softly, "Thank you. For what you said." To Gallatin, she said, "Now, sir, if you will excuse us, we three ladies are going to my room to dress Ember's wound and help her find something to wear."

"I'll see you at supper," Gallatin said, taking Twilight's hand and lifting it to his lips. As he placed a lingering kiss there, his eyes gazed into her eyes with an intensity that went inside her. Her cheeks started to burn, then the sensation moved through her entire body.

Chapter 13
Games and Love Potion

Saturday, June 19, 1858
Afternoon, Evening, Night
Memphis

Intrigued with the heavy curtains at Twilight's bedroom windows, Makeda-Angel hid behind one, then peeked around it at her mother and giggled.

Cara brought warm water, clean cloth, ointment, biscuits, three glasses of lemonade, and a doll made from a sock with brown yarn for hair.

After eating a biscuit, Makeda-Angel looked at the tall bed, then at her mama for permission. Twilight smiled and Ember nodded, then Makeda-Angel climbed on the bedside stool and onto the bed.

With the doll clutched in her hands, she fell asleep. Ember covered her with a quilt and kissed her temple. Then she went to sit on a chair next to the basin. Obviously in great pain, she lowered her head on her arm, flinching and holding back tears as Twilight carefully washed and applied an ointment and a dressing to the broken skin on Ember's back.

"I stopped wearing cotton dresses when my gentleman caller made me aware that I was supporting slavery by buying goods made by enslaved laborers," Twilight said.

"Mr. Gallatin?" Ember, hurting, asked through choked breath.

"What about him?"

"Your man. Mr. Gallatin. Made you aware."

Twilight blushed. "No. Gallatin is my friend. My gentleman is Mr. Canon, Jackson Canon."

"Oh," Ember said. "I thought Mr. Gallatin is your man since you two are so in love."

"Ember, you can call him Gallatin. And what are you saying? You've only just met Gallatin and me. How can you think we're in love?"

Ember looked at her sleeping child, then back at Twilight. "Maybe I was born enslaved. Maybe I've never been to school. But I know love."

Pensive, Twilight finished the bandaging, then walked to the nightstand, sipped her lemonade, then opened her wardrobe. "Well, Gallatin and I are just friends. As for Jackson, we'll see, but he does have an effect on me. I think it could be the buds of love. So, as I was saying, your community worked hard to produce the cotton that went into these dresses. And I don't wear them anymore. Would you like them?"

Silent, Ember considered. Then, she said, "Wearing them speaks words I would never speak."

Twilight nodded.

"No person should be enslaved," Ember added.

"That is true. It's madness that enslavement is even discussed, the supposed pros. Slavery arguments are all cons. No need for debate. It is simply wrong." Twilight thought a moment, then said, "I do have a linen frock for chores that I can give you. I think it will fit you well enough for now. Some items of clothing are not as comfortable when not made of cotton, but the enslaved have worse discomfort."

Handing the linen frock to Ember, Twilight said, "We'll get some gowns and more chore frocks made for you immediately. As you know, there's more than enough to do to keep a household. Cara, Sarah, Rachel, and I will welcome your help. There's clothing and bedding to wash then hang to dry, windows to open every morning during the summer to let in the cool night air then close before it gets hot. Sweeping, dusting, milking the cow, making cheese, watering and weeding the garden. Vegetables to pull and fruit to pick, then clean and preserve. Eggs to gather. Cara does the baking, and she cooks most meals. Father buys meat, which our family seldom eats. I don't eat animals at all; I detest the thought of them being killed. Father and the twins build the fires in the winter. But we women do most chores, except Mother, and Mother pretends we do none of it. But all that is for later. For now, I'll take you to our pump and then to the kitchen where we heat water so you and Makeda-Angel can wash. We don't have a water closet. We each, of course, empty our own chamber pots. But, we women have to wash the outhouse. If there are spiders or other peskies, I ask the men to help." She laughed, then continued, "There's a bed for you and Makeda-Angel on the top floor. Also, I rarely enjoy meals with my family, but tonight I plan to, with Gallatin here. Do you and Makeda-Angel want to join us for supper, or would you prefer to eat in the kitchen? That's where I usually eat."

"The kitchen."

With a child now living in the house, Twilight decided to keep her Deringer unloaded, hidden, and out of reach—high at the top of her wardrobe.

At supper, none of the women were speaking, so to break the strained silence, Gallatin and Harley discussed river travel and the postponed christening of the *North Star* to prior its departure the next day. Afterward, Harley, Gallatin, and Twilight retired to the library. Rachel and Sarah waited in the parlor for the coppersmith brothers they had met at the ball. Elizabeth disappeared; everyone assumed she had gone to her room.

In the library, Gallatin relaxed in a leather chair and opened *Leaves of Grass* by Walt Whitman. Twilight placed her fingers over her mouth, feigning a shocked expression. "My, my, good sir. Reading Whitman? You should take more care with your reputation." They laughed.

"You know you enjoy Whitman's verse, too," Gallatin said.

"I do," Twilight said. "Very much. He's a star shining on us."

Harley said, "Chess?" Twilight took his challenge. Forty-five minutes later, Harley won.

Gallatin said, "Finally, I get a chance. I thought I might have to board the *North Star* before you two would finish."

"Twilight is tough competition," Harley said, chuckling.

"In many ways," Gallatin said.

Smiling at Gallatin's comment, for his pride in her always cheered her, Twilight pulled an ottoman up to the table to watch every move of the game between her father and Gallatin. This was her customary place. Once, a couple of years before, when Harley had jested that she was disturbing him with her breathing, she replied that if he didn't want her at the edge of the chess table, she would have to lounge and smoke as he and Gallatin did. Harley had laughed and told her to stay put.

Gallatin won against Harley in twenty minutes, then against Twilight in fifteen. At nine o'clock, Cara served tea and sherry. With one swift move of his bishop, Harley gave Gallatin the second game they were playing as he was ready for a sherry break. After pouring a sherry for himself and one for Gallatin, he poured a third in a teacup and handed it to Twilight, saying, "You're entitled to this for your actions today. But never let Mother know."

Surprised, for her father had never before offered her a drink, Twilight sipped. Immediately she liked its lush, sweet taste. She moved from the ottoman to a thickly-fluted wing chair. Snuggling deep into the leather, she slipped off her slippers and pulled her feet under her, letting the warm feeling of sherry relax her body as the oil lamps played romantic games in the deepening night. Harley and Gallatin talked and smoked. "My last cigar, Gallatin," Harley announced. "They are gone after these two, and I'm not buying more."

Gallatin nodded. "I'm also boycotting tobacco after this and having some trouble enjoying this last one."

The two men looked at their cigars, then at each other. Gallatin set his cigar in the tray. Harley did the same. The smoke of their last cigars slowly died away.

Refilling the sherry glasses and adding another splash in the teacup, Harley said to Twilight, "You're quiet, dear. So unlike you. What is roaming about that prodigious mind of yours?"

Maybe it was the sherry, but Twilight felt she could speak openly about her feelings for Gallatin. "I'm sad that Gallatin leaves tomorrow."

"We all hate to see Gallatin leave," Harley said, patting her arm. "He's family. But I'd have no one else be chief pilot of the *North Star*." Silently, they sipped their sherry. When Harley finished his, he said, "I must check on Elizabeth. Good night, Twilight, Gallatin." After kissing the top of Twilight's head and patting Gallatin's shoulder, he left.

Relaxed and sherry-warm, Twilight snuggled deeper into the large leather chair and into a cozy silence. After a few moments, Gallatin moved to the ottoman in front of her. Pulling money from his pocket, he said, "I'd like to pay for the freedom of Ember and Makeda-Angel. You shouldn't have to."

Sherry-spelled, Twilight reached and stroked Gallatin's clean-shaven face. "Thank you for offering, but I want to pay half at least. I could pay all, but I know you want to be part of helping them."

"I do. But also, Twilight, that's your dowry money. You shouldn't use that, even for freedom. Let me pay you back so you can deposit that in the bank."

It took a second for Gallatin's implication to sink into Twilight's diluted mind: Gallatin wanted her to have an ample dowry and, thus, be prepared to marry. To marry someone. Not him. Irritated, Twilight straightened and said, "So I see, Gallatin. Well, don't fret; I don't need a large dowry to lure a man into marriage." Placing her feet on the floor and leaning toward him, she continued, "Let me tell you an item or two. I'll never need a man so desperately that I'll have to settle for one who wants money from me. I'll only marry for love. I will love him, and he will love me. And he won't care if I spend all my dowry freeing the enslaved because he'll love me for who I am. And he'll want me—an emotion of which you are incapable. You are foolish, Gallatin. The Mississippi River will never keep you warm at night."

Her candid comparison that included her body—their bodies together—surprised Gallatin. Even outspoken Twilight had never openly mentioned such private matters that happened at night, matters reserved for a husband and wife. Her words released a feeling building inside him at the reference of his beautiful, spirited Twilight warming him in bed. He reached for her, putting his arms around her and pulling her close until she was seated on his lap. He kissed her eyes, her ears, and her mouth, his lips brushing every curve of her face, then angling down the bend of her neck. He whispered "I love you" more times than all the lovers of history could ever have said it.

Her hands cupped his face. One slid to caress his neck, then moved to the top of his chest, fingers lingering there. Her mouth and his mouth moved together with the artistry of impassioned creativity. In a place she'd never imagined existed and loving this more than she ever thought possible, Twilight lingered, fully with it while somehow hovering above it. Then reality jarred her mind. *My head can't be clear, nor his. Surely that sherry has acted as a love potion. This is not the time to succumb to the pleasure of kissing.*

She pulled away from Gallatin's lips, from his body. With her hands on his shoulders and her arms stretched out to keep distance between them, she said, "Let me go." They breathed deeply and unevenly; Gallatin moaned. He held onto her arms. She whispered, "I hate you. You are teasing me. You don't want me, but you will kiss me. After you leave tomorrow, Friend, I hope I never see you again as long as I live. All your business dealings can be with Father from now on."

She pushed herself from the chair in a fluid motion; Gallatin kept hold of her hand and said, "Twilight, please—wait. You're right. And you're wrong. I'm not teasing. I truly love you. But we both have things we must accomplish. Even after we do those things, I can't promise I'll leave the river."

"So you've said. Repeatedly." Then she was gone from the library and, she decided, from Gallatin's life forever.

Chapter 14
Trying to Forget

*Saturday, June 19, 1858, Night
and Sunday, June 20, 1858, Morning to Twilight
Memphis*

In bed twenty minutes later, Twilight tossed as misery crowded the place in her heart reserved for loving Gallatin.

She'd lost her best friend and the hope that they, someday, could be companions in navigating the river of life. *But by Heaven's moon, how I love that man! Gallatin. My river prince. My pilot. Already, I miss him.*

"Oh, this is no good," she said to herself, wishing for that detached feeling from the warm wonders of sherry she'd experienced earlier that evening. "I need to get that sherry feeling back." Slipping from her bed, she donned her night jacket and velvet slippers. Then, remembering that her slippers were cotton velvet, she kicked them off. Maybe Sarah would make her a pair of linen or wool velvet; after all, Sarah had been relentlessly reading that book *Every Lady Her Own Shoemaker*, supposedly authored by an anonymous woman. Twilight didn't believe it. *A man probably wrote it. He and the publisher are in cahoots to keep women thinking they should be thrilled to do even more work in the home than they already do.* Barefoot, Twilight crept downstairs.

Being nearly eleven o'clock, everyone was asleep, including Gallatin in the guest bedroom. In the library, she found the sherry decanter was gone. *Where does Cara keep it?* In the dining room, she opened a curtained door at the bottom of the buffet, where she knew her father kept brandy. *It's not sherry, but it will have to do.*

Not wanting to leave evidence of her iniquity or to bother washing a glass at that hour, she tipped the bottle to her lips. The brandy was much warmer and harsher than sherry, not nearly as sweet and tasty. No matter; with a second sip, it tasted better. With the seventh sip, the clear vision of Gallatin that defined her dreams started to blur.

⇢⇢⇢ ⇠⇠⇠

"Twilight. Missy. Wake up."

Lilting across the fog of her mind, Twilight heard a familiar voice.

"Missy, are you ill? Your father says you must get ready for church."

Comprehending very slowly that the voice was that of Cara, Twilight tried to open her leaded eyelids. When she succeeded in actually seeing Cara standing over her, a pain wracked her head. She tried to speak, but her mouth was so dry no words would come. Braving the agony of moving, she lifted her arm and limply pointed to the water pitcher beside her bed, then let her weighted arm fall. Each movement exploded through her head. Cara poured a glass of water then helped Twilight sit up. She took a sip from the glass, which instead of making her feel better, immediately made her nauseous.

Speaking with effort, for her lips failed to work correctly, Twilight whispered, "By the full moon, Cara, I am so sick. Tell Father that I'm sorry, I can't attend church today. I'm such a fool. How much did I drink, anyway?"

"Drink, missy? You're ill from too much drink? Lands a mercy. No lady should drink."

Twilight laughed with a slow hmm hmm hmm. Then, she said, working to correctly pronounce each word, "Cara, you've known me long enough to know that I am no lady. But I am no lushy, either. Anyway, it was simply too much brandy. And I hope I never see brandy—or even the color amber—again as long as I live. I just hope that I live past this morning." Feebly grabbing Cara's sleeve, Twilight pleaded, "Oh, Cara, you won't tell on me, will you?"

"No, dear. Now rest. I'll inform your Father that you're experiencing a slight illness," she said, then bustled from the room.

Though she tried, Twilight couldn't recollect how much she drank or of returning to her bed. Drinking too much was certainly poor judgment, but she wasn't angry with herself when she realized that she'd experienced two phenomena exclusively for men: being loaded and being sick the morning after from being loaded.

Cara entered with a tray. "Twilight, I brought you something to chase away your illness. I had to sneak it up here," she said, holding an item covered with a napkin. Cara removed the napkin to reveal a snifter of brandy.

"No! Cara! Are you trying to kill me? I told you I never wanted to see brandy again as long as I live, which, honestly, the way I am feeling, might not be much longer. Ooooo. I think I am going to be sick all over this bed."

"Hurry, missy. Drink it. Believe me, it will relieve this katzenjammer."

Frowning, Twilight grabbed the snifter, closed her eyes, and downed the drink. Certainly, it must work, for Cara's remedies for other illnesses had never failed her. Wild coughing overtook her for a few seconds; then, she felt some relief. "It's a miracle, Cara. How does that work?"

"A little hair of the dog that bit you," Cara stated. "Your body got accustomed to having brandy in it last night. And now that it is wearing off, your body wants more. So, we gave it just a little to help your body ease out of this. After this, I'd suggest you not touch brandy again."

"What looks good to me right now is some of that tea you brought up."

"I'll return soon with dry toast," Cara said, then left.

Soon there was a timid knock at the door. Sitting up, Twilight grabbed her night jacket draped on her bed. "Come in," she said as she finished slipping, with pained effort, into the jacket.

The door opened just a bit, and Ember peeped in. "I'm here to see how you are feeling."

"Ember, come in. I'm feeling somewhat better." The door was pushed wide open, and in ran Makeda-Angel, her hair bobbing, her feet bare. She scrambled up on the comfy bed and sat cross-legged beside Twilight.

"Makeda-Angel. You didn't ask first. Where're your manners, child?" Ember said.

"I left them in my room," the tiny girl said. Twilight, Ember, and Makeda-Angel laughed.

Patting the bed, Twilight said, "You might as well join us, Ember. How are *you* feeling?"

Choosing instead to sit on a chair near the bed, Ember answered, "My back is sore."

"That man lashing you. Brutality," Twilight said. *Where are the Champion Men? GrandMama's letter implied there are some, other than Frederick Douglass.* She noticed that, while Ember was not shy to speak, her eyes held a reserved look. No, not exactly in her eyes. Rather, behind them, as if she was holding back the treasure of her truest self. Twilight didn't expect them to be instant friends, and maybe they'd never be confidants. She might never know what was kept hidden behind Ember's eyes. *After all, the enslaved or formerly enslaved are wise to protect themselves by not trusting too soon anyone Pale, or thought to be Pale.* Makeda-Angel scrambled off the bed, crawled onto her mama's lap, cuddled into her mama's arms, and twisted her hair while she watched her mama and the older girl talk.

Ember kissed the top of her daughter's head, then continued, "Cara has given me some duties. I hope you don't mind me disturbing you while you are in your room and ill. But I came to thank you for what you and Gallatin did yesterday for me and my child—keeping us together."

At the mention of Gallatin's name, Twilight fought her confusion about the rugged, charming river tamer. "I suppose he left this morning?"

"Yes, early, or so I heard Cara say."

"Oh, I missed the *North Star* christening." Tears formed in her eyes, then Twilight said, "So, you think we are in love, do you, Ember?"

A slow smile spread across Ember's face as she nodded.

"Then tell me, why would a man who loves a woman leave her as Gallatin leaves me?"

"He has no choice," Ember said.

"Of course he has a choice. The man has free will to do whatever he wishes."

"Not if he is in chains."

"What are you saying, Ember? Gallatin's not enslaved. No one owns him—" Twilight's voice trailed. "You are wise. In his mind, the Mississippi River owns him. He feels he can't make a decision that doesn't include the River. If he marries me, he would have to resign his position as a pilot, that is, if he wanted to see me more than one overnight every week or two. And, of course, that's what I would expect. It makes sense."

"When you are enslaved, you can see the bondage of others. Maybe they seem happy, but the pain of being trapped shows in their eyes. It's not the same as the cruel bondage of the legally enslaved, but there are subtle similarities."

Both women were quiet, Twilight attentive to Ember's gaze into the space of the room. Then Ember sighed. "My sweet, handsome husband, Manuel. He was enslaved by the Pale and enslaved by choice. He cared too much for the enslaver, so he couldn't see the truth."

"Your husband? Why, of course, you've had two children. I'm sorry; I hadn't thought of your husband."

Ember nodded. "It's the way Pale folks think of us, that we have no husbands, no wives, or families, or any love or loyalty to another soul. That we are supposed to love and serve *their* families while *our own* families are taken from us."

"I'm trying to learn," Twilight said, her finger under Wondrous Ring softly twinging. "I'm trying not to be mindless and insensitive. I know, at times, I am, from ignorance. But please know I don't think of you in the way you just described. At all. I just get self-absorbed sometimes."

Searching Ember's eyes, Twilight received a steady look. "Ember, if you don't mind telling me, what do you mean that your husband cared too much for his enslaver?"

After three beats of quiet, Ember said, "I suppose I can do that. It's this way: no one wants to be enslaved, do they? I think most will always fight it, even if you never see the fight—except sometimes it shows in their eyes or in their tensed muscles, even when they try to hide it. Some can keep the fight out of their eyes and bodies so no one will see, but it's there. The fight for freedom is always there, inside them. Who wants to feel as though you're always living in the bonds of evil? Some do what they can to accept their lives in some way, which is also resistance to living in the bonds of evil."

Twilight listened.

Taking a deep breath, Ember's chest rose and fell. She continued, "That's the way it was with Man. He was born and grew up in his enslaver's house. He resisted living in the bonds of evil by trying to believe that his life was good. The enslaver actually insisted Man call him 'Uncle' instead of Master or Enslaver. And Man always insisted the enslaver did act more like an uncle, not an owner. But he knew better. Still, Man wanted his enslaver to be proud of him, so he always did as he was told. And he wasn't afraid. Man and I met when I was thirteen, when my little sister and I were taken from our mama and daddy. The enslaver's daughter chose my little sister and me to serve only her. Man and I fell in love the minute I entered the big house. The enslaver, well, he didn't want Man giving any time to anyone but him, so Man and I had to hide our love and then our marriage two years later. We'd sneak into the forest at night when all in the big house were asleep. Loving me confused Man. Though he loved me with all his might, he'd say it bothered his head, doing something Uncle wouldn't like. Then I became big with our child, Men. His name is actually Menelik." With a smile, she added, "I know; when I speak of them, it sounds like the loves of my life until that point had been Man and Men." Twilight smiled at the wordplay.

Her smile fading, Ember continued, "The enslaver wanted to know who did that to me. Always honest, my Manuel told him that we'd been married for months. Furious, the enslaver grabbed a big brass candlestick off the dining room table and right there smacked it against my Man's head. I saw it happen. I have nightmares about it. Every night."

Taking another deep breath, Ember said, "I'm sure I always will. As Man lay dying, that horrible person said, 'Man, you serve one—me. Now get up and do your chores.' He walked out of the room. Man died. Man's blood soaked the carpet. I cleaned the carpet; I cleaned Man's body for burial. He was only sixteen. Some said we should have jumped the broom on a Tuesday instead of a Wednesday. But I know it wasn't the day of the week we married or our wedding broomstick that made Man's life short. There's no evil in those. There's no evil in things." She thought, *Evil lives in people who accept it as a welcome guest—or a permanent occupant.* She said, "It was the evil of the mean master, the destroyer, our enslaver." A faraway look shrouded Ember's eyes. She added, "Such a kind, beautiful person Manuel was. Soon after my Man's death, they sold me to a man with the last name of Clayton. When Menelik was three, Enslaver Clayton died, so his family sold us all for the money. That's the last I saw of my son."

"Oh, Ember! What a tragedy. How terrible he killed your husband. How terrible they took Menelik from you." Twilight lightly touched the back of Ember's hand. "Your son is alive? I thought, from what you said, how you look to the moon to feel close to him, that he had passed on."

Ember said, "He's alive."

Glancing out the window, Twilight said, "Maybe your husband didn't really care what the mean creeper thought. Maybe Man was afraid of telling him, because he suspected what would happen if he did."

"I was afraid of the master. Man wasn't." With an indignant look, Ember added, "If Man had seen clearly about living in captivity, he would've been afraid. Fear exists for a reason. Fear keeps us alert. Fear helps keep us alive. Anyone enslaved by anything, especially another person, *should* be afraid. But who wants to live in fear? Man didn't want to. Man didn't accept that when you're a captive, you have to keep fear for protection."

Neither spoke for a moment. Then with that guise of her eyes glinting and opening slightly the chest filled with the treasure of herself, Ember said, "There's a world of difference between caring what the master thinks because you want to please him and not caring about the master, but obeying him to survive." Ember ran her fingers lightly over her daughter's hair. "I'd been carrying Makeda-Angel seven months when Enslaver Clayton died. His wife needed money, or so she said. First, she sold Men away from me when I was birthing Makeda-Angel. Then, a week later, she sold Makeda-Angel and me together to a neighbor. Two years later—yesterday—the auction." Tilting her head, she said, "You're curious to know who is Makeda-Angel's father?"

"That is none of my business."

"Enslaver Clayton's son is Makeda-Angel's father. John Clayton. He said he didn't want to sell me because he said he loved me, and he knew the child I was carrying was his, and he hated to sell his woman and his child."

Quiet, Twilight listened carefully.

"I was fifteen, almost sixteen, when John's father bought me. John was seventeen. He started bringing me flowers when I first arrived. But it wasn't until a year had passed that he sneaked into my room. My room was in the big house, in case I was needed during the night, but it was downstairs, separated from the family's rooms upstairs. So no one heard him in my room. He came in and said he loved me and that he knew I loved him. He said he'd waited so long he couldn't wait for me any longer. I told him I didn't love him. I told him to leave me alone. I told him to get out of my room. I fought him. John told me if I ever said any of those things again, or if I fought him again, he'd have his father sell Menelik. And then John got in my bed. I hate John. I stayed silent to keep my child."

Twilight had never talked to someone who'd been through such horror. Her world was expanding further into the twisted ways of men who believe themselves superior to all other humans. *They must be the men who make up the Society of Supremacy that GrandMama warned me about. The ones supporting the Dominion of Men.* She said, "How terrible, Ember."

"As I said, and I'll say it again, I hate him." Placing her cheek against Makeda-Angel's head, Ember added, "But I love my Makeda-Angel. Looking at her takes the hate from my chest, at least for a heartbeat."

"I'm so sorry. You returned to this memory to tell me. I'm sure it hurts to remember," Twilight said. "I can't even imagine what you, your husband, all of the enslaved, and also the free Rich-tone people endure."

"Bravery fills each breath of our lives," Ember said, surprising herself again that she spoke so candidly to Twilight, revealing so much about her life, thoughts, and distrust of Pale people to this young Pale woman. Twilight was not her friend. Not yet. And maybe never would be. She thought, *Why am I compelled to reveal the pain of my life to Twilight?* She knew she must heed her own belief that trust does not result in safety.

"How old are you now, Ember?"

"Twenty-one; just turned."

Twilight said, "Remember, you're a free woman now in this home and will be soon in the eyes of the law. The manumission process takes some time. But please know that you're free to choose who you want to love and who you don't want to love; you are free to live where you want to live and work for whom you want to work. You can stay here doing housework for wages as long as you like. But if you ever want to leave after you have your freedom papers, that is your choice. What you want to do with your life is your choice."

Nodding, Ember was thinking: *She's naive. Even with freedom papers, I will never be truly free in this country. And I won't go to Liberia without Menelik. For all her confidence and outspokenness, Twilight is quite an innocent one. What is it about her that does seem different from other Pales, possibly even trustworthy? Should I trust my instincts telling me that Twilight has no desire to hurt me or Makeda-Angel? Or is Twilight playing some perverse game and will sell us still?*

While enslaved, Ember had seen all kinds of people, many with sick ideas, and she believed that no one who condoned slavery could be in their right mind, which apparently was just about every Pale person in the South. And, tragically, even some Rich-tone people. Yet, she had witnessed Twilight speaking against slavery in front of her family, a family that owned no one. Having a trustworthy Pale ally could be helpful. So, with time, maybe she could believe Twilight. Until then, she would be careful.

Cautiously, Ember said, "Here is what I want to do with my life: I want to find Menelik. I want to learn reading and writing and numbers. I want a garden."

"Of course! An education for both you and Makeda-Angel. I can help you with that. We'll begin looking for Menelik. And you'll have a patch of the garden for yourself. Now, why don't you tell me the full name of the Clayton woman who sold Menelik, and maybe I can find out some information about your son for you."

Again Ember wondered, was this a trick? Did Twilight want to try to sell them back to John Clayton? She wanted to find Men, of course, but it was too soon to confide in Twilight. She'd told her too much already. She evaded answering Twilight by saying, "That would be a gift, to know about my Men. I miss him so much. My son. My child." Cradling Makeda-Angel in her arms, Ember stood. "Also, I wanted to tell you that I've decided on the surname I want. Free. Our names will be Ember Free and Makeda-Angel Free and Menelik Free."

Twilight smiled, nodding. "Perfect."

"We should leave so you can rest." Ember set Makeda-Angel on her own two feet, then, holding hands, mama and child walked to the door. "I came to see how you were feeling, to say thank you, and to say that your mama has been very welcoming to Makeda-Angel and me."

Truly surprised, Twilight said, "What? My mother?"

"Yes. After supper last night, she came to my room. She talked with me a bit. She's very nice."

"Mother visited you in your room? By the full moon and its mysterious shadows. I've never seen that woman act this way before."

"Act what way?"

"Well, so nice. So accepting. Just talking to people rather than swooning all over the place."

Just then, there was another knock on Twilight's door. "Who can that be?" Twilight whispered to Ember. Being unpopular in the household, Twilight seldom received guests in her room, even when ill, except for Cara and the twins. Thus, Twilight deduced that it must be Cara at her door, for the twins were visiting a friend's plantation in Nashville. "Come in, Cara," she said.

The door opened, and in walked Elizabeth, who had never once stepped foot into Twilight's room. Upon seeing Ember, Elizabeth beamed a smile and said, "Hello, dear. If you and your daughter will excuse us, I'd like to talk with Twilight."

As they left, Makeda-Angel turned, smiled, and waved her hand. Twilight smiled and waved back.

Awed that her mother was in her room and was actually going to have a conversation with her, Twilight sat silently for a second, then asked, "You didn't go to church with Father?"

"Not today. I was feeling too good, and preachers have a way of making me feel ashamed that I was born human. Well, anyway, Twilight, you needn't say a word. Just rest; I know you are ill today. I'll sit here in this chair. I just want to tell you how grateful I am that you've brought that wonderful Rich-tone woman here."

Was she dreaming or was she still loaded? It had to be one or the other because her mother's visit, statement, and manner could not be reality.

"You see, I want to tell you a story about a special friend of mine, Cherish. She was my closest friend. I haven't seen her in years, and your friend is so like her. I guess you'd say that seeing your friend is like having a bit of my youth returned to me. Cherish was a Rich-tone, and she and her mother lived with us in England. You did know that your grandparents lived in England, didn't you?"

Twilight nodded. *I know more about your mother than you do.* "Grand-Mama spoke of it at times."

"I'll tell you the whole story," Elizabeth said.

You don't know the whole story.

Elizabeth began: "My mother was British, and my father is German. They met when my father went to Great Britain to test his fortune in various business opportunities. None were highly successful. Hearing that America is the land of opportunity, we moved to this great country, then made our way to Indiana when I was fifteen. We settled in Evansville because, as you know, it is situated on the Ohio River and has opportunities for products and trade. My father opened a general store and started an Evansville-based packet. There, he's been very successful. We'd lived in Evansville just a few months when my father contacted Captain Harley Adams of the Memphis Star Packet Line and suggested they do business. Harley traveled to Evansville and came to supper at our home. Immediately, Harley fell in love with me; we married. I was sixteen. Then we moved here, and I love Memphis as if it were my home. Though Southern customs differ from what I've always been used to, I think I have adjusted well."

Twilight suppressed a choke at that comment, for she'd never considered her mother well-adjusted to anything. Further, her mother preached Southern customs to her continually, as if they were her first nature. So the thought that her mother had to adjust to them was odd.

"Anyway, before moving to this country, back in England, my parents had hired a wonderful maid, Hannah. Slavery was allowed in England at the time, but, as you probably know, my mother was a devoted believer in equality and human rights and would never have owned anyone. Slavery was outlawed in England the year we moved to America."

"Yes. It was made illegal in 1833 but not put into effect until 1834—and then not throughout the entire empire. And they certainly buy American cotton."

"Yes. Hypocritical England."

Twilight shook her head sharply, then blinked deeply, still unsure this was real, for her mother was speaking without swooning and patting her head with her handkerchief. Her voice was confident, without distress. And her conversation points were making sense.

"Are you all right, Twilight?"

"Yes. Yes, Mother. Please continue."

"You did appear as though you might have a fit just then. Anyway, about my special friend. Our Rich-tone maid Hannah had a daughter my age, Cherish. Hannah and Cherish had their own room, but it wasn't long before I asked Mother and Father to move a bed into my room for Cherish as she and I had become like sisters. Cherish and I grew up together. We were tutored together in piano, literature, numbers, and the French language. Then when I was nearly fifteen, a beau, Archibald, my dear Archie, began calling on me."

Elizabeth blushed a bit, then continued. "He was nineteen, and we were in love. He called every evening and on Sunday afternoons. Straightaway he told me he didn't like that I treated a maid's daughter as my sister. After all, he explained, we were worlds apart, as my family was of a higher class, and Cherish would never be more than a servant. Archie was so important to me that I immediately began shunning Cherish. I told her to move back to the room with her mother. I stopped speaking to her, and whenever Archie was there, I would order her about. Why, once, as Archie and I returned from a stroll, I called her to come wipe my slippers. I didn't even remove them; I stood as the Queen, having Cherish bow before me and rub my slippers with her handkerchief. Then I ordered her to wipe Archie's boots. She certainly didn't have to do it. My parents would have been upset had they known I was ordering her. But I ordered her, and she did it. I treated Cherish poorly, and I have regretted it ever since. And here's that lovely Rich-tone young woman you brought home, who reminds me of Cherish." Elizabeth sighed. "But Cherish got even with me. That very night, she eloped with Archie, my beau! She was kind and beautiful, but I had no idea Archie would marry her. It was all an act, I suppose, the way Archie berated Cherish and the way he insisted I treat her. An act to hide their love affair. Archie's family was quite wealthy, so I am sure that today Cherish has many more servants than I do. That was the last I heard of her. Soon after, we left England. I should let you rest. I need rest, too."

Elizabeth stood and left the room. The entire story with nary a breath, and then, poof, her mother was gone, just like that.

This is the strangest day I have ever known. Even if it was a rather disturbing delivery—a narrative almost entirely devoid of her mother's typical staccato speech and, in fact, no pauses—it was more of a visit than Twilight had ever had with her mother. And it was the only detailed information she'd ever heard about her mother's life. This was an entire chapter of emotional life and basic family history that her mother just confided to her, making Twilight feel that maybe she was special, after all, to her mother. And somewhere in the story was most likely the mystery of why GrandMama had not confided the secrets to her daughter. Was losing her best friend to the boy she loved the reason Elizabeth wasn't emotionally strong enough to carry the knowledge of her lineage or of the Sisterhood of Gifts?

While wiggling around in the covers for a new position, there was another timid knock at the door. *Who in the world, now?* "Yes?"

Her father looked in. "I just wanted to check in on you, dear. How are you feeling? You missed a fine sermon today."

"Father, it's good to see you, but by the full moon, I have received more people today than the Pope does in a year! Please, come in. I feel a bit better."

Harley entered, kissed his daughter's forehead, then walked back near the doorway. "How do you know what the Pope does? We're Episcopalians."

"Oh, you remember, even though we had little in common, I sometimes visited with the Magevney girls when I was younger. They discussed Catholic customs. And, of course, I read."

Harley nodded and mumbled, "Oh, yes." Then he said, "So, several visitors? Who has been to see you today?"

"Father, I've had quite a guest list. Cara, of course. And Ember and Makeda-Angel. And—Mother. Now, you."

"Your mother visited you? Why, how nice." Harley smiled oddly, visibly surprised.

"Yes, and she told me she is grateful I brought Ember here." *Though she doesn't say Ember's name and refers to her only in a tonal way, as if to emphasize Ember is different than her. Mother even referred to Ember as "that" Rich-tone young woman.*

"She has been acting livelier," Harley said, eyes searching around the room as if hoping he'd see an answer to Elizabeth's puzzling behavior.

"Father, last evening after supper, when you and Gallatin and I went to the library, Mother didn't retire to her room."

"No? She was in bed when I checked on her."

"Well, first, she went to see Ember."

"This is news. I wonder what intrigues her about Ember?"

Twilight shifted under the covers. "I think she was confiding in me, but you *are* my father and her husband. Certainly you know about her closest friend."

Harley closed Twilight's barely-open bedroom door, then said, "She told you about her?"

"About Cherish? Yes."

"Interesting," Harley said. "She's never told me, or anyone, about Cherish. I learned the story from your grandparents when I was courting your mother. They thought I should know, that it might make a difference to me."

"Make a difference to you? About marrying her? Why? Just because the mother of Mother's friend was a servant and Rich-tone? That shouldn't matter if you want to marry someone, and I know that wouldn't matter to you."

"No, not that your mother had a friend who was a servant's daughter and a Rich-tone girl. Of course, that's of no consequence to me. What your grandparents thought might make a difference to me is what Cherish did the night your mother made her polish her slippers."

"Ran off with Archie?" Twilight said, smiling. "Father, you should be glad of that, or Mother would have never married you."

"What? Ran off with Archie? Your mother didn't tell you?"

"What, Father? What didn't she tell me?"

Harley hesitated before answering. "Your mother found Cherish that night, hanging—by a winter scarf she'd knitted for her one Christmas—from the rafters in the attic."

Rubbing her head as if she could rub away the confusion, Twilight said, "No." Then she reached out her arms, wanting to hug her father, who'd married the lies as well as the woman.

Her father approached her, leaned for a quick hug, then straightened and said, "Seems she wanted to apologize to Cherish. So she went to her room, didn't find her there, then went to the attic, where, when younger, they'd created their secret clubhouse. She found Cherish—dead. Your mother hasn't balanced her emotions since."

"But that happened before you met her. So she must have been"—Twilight paused, searching for the right words—"terribly delicate when you met her. Why did you marry her, Father?"

"I loved her. Her frailness attracted me. She was in need; she was, and is, so lovely. I thought my love could ease her guilt. I was wrong," Harley sighed. "She does seem better with Ember here."

Twilight wasn't sure about that.

Chapter 15
More Surprises

Sunday, June 20, 1858, Evening
Monday, June 21, 1858
and Tuesday, June 22, 1858
Memphis

Reading or sleeping was impossible as Twilight contemplated how far from reality her mother must be to have created and convinced herself of such a lie.

Just as the sun was setting, the door shook with a succession of sharp fast knocks.

More visitors? What an unusual day. She called, "Come in."

Swinging open the door then bounding into the room were a couple of playful pups in the form of Jed and Jesse, her seventeen-year-old twin brothers. Constantly laughing and yapping, the twins were medium height with unkempt looks and shaggy brown hair, making Twilight see two adorable puppies scampering and yipping.

"You rascals! By the full moon! You're home at last!" Shifting herself out of bed—still in her night jacket covering her linen chemise to just above the knees of her ankle-length pantalettes—she swayed on bare feet from Jesse to Jed, then from Jed to Jesse, kissing and hugging them, ruffling their hair. They absorbed the attention, making Twilight imagine that if they had tails, they would wag them. Ever funny and frisky, maturing was not something that interested Jed and Jesse. In any other male, Twilight would find that unattractive, but in her ever-loving brothers, she found it endearing. Opposite from her—as she thought deeply, delving into all concerns—there'd never been an issue the twins had given serious consideration, except for what Cara should fix for meals, as they were voracious eaters. For Twilight, being with the twins was a holiday.

"Why're you locked away in this room, Twilight?" Jed said.

"You're not sick. You don't look sick. She doesn't look sick, does she, Jed?" Jesse said.

"Naw. She looks great. Twilight always looks great," Jed said.

"What's wrong, darlin'? Tell brothers Jesse and Jed all about it," Jesse said, taking her right hand.

"Yes, what's wrong, darlin'? Tell brothers Jed and Jesse all about it," Jed said, taking her left hand.

Feeling silly with a lanky brother on each side of her holding her hands, she laughed, then said, "Oh, nothing's wrong now that you two rascals are home."

"Then come out of this little room and join the family for supper," Jed said.

"Yes, Cara said you're eating in your room tonight, but we just got home and we want you in that dining room with us," Jesse said.

"Please, please, please?" Jed said.

"Please, please, darlin', please?" Jesse said.

"Cara is fixing vegetable stew, collard greens, fresh corn, biscuits, and two big apple pies," Jed said.

"Umm, umm, a feast," Jesse said, licking his lips.

"Enough!" Twilight continued to laugh, shaking their hands off hers. "Yes, I'll be down for supper since you two are back." Returning to her bed and snuggling under the covers, she asked, "But now, tell me about your visit with the Johnstons."

"They bought the plantation from a descendent of an original Virginia family, an FFV," Jed said.

"A 'First Family of Virginia,'" Jesse said.

"I know—*everyone* knows—what FFV is," Twilight said. "Tell me, what's it like?"

"It's named Clover Hill, and sure enough, the big house sits right on top of a hill in the middle of clover. They must have six horses," Jesse said.

"Then all around the clover for miles and miles are brown fields. Of course, they'll look white in September and October as cotton bursts its bolls," Jed laughed, then continued. "In front of the mansion are rows of apple trees. I want to go back for the harvest to see the Riches everywhere, gathering apples and cotton. The plantation was more lovely than any painting you've ever seen."

Jesse grimaced, and Twilight noticed. He said, "They are people, Jed. Call them people. Enslaved people. Enslaved people everywhere."

"Yes," Twilight agreed. "Or say Rich-tone people. Not Riches. They are not our riches; they are people, as Jesse said."

Jed said, "They are the riches of America—they create the wealth for this entire nation. Everyone knows that. Anyway, we'd spend each morning riding and each afternoon relaxing on the veranda drinking mint juleps and watching the Riches work. We even saw a duel between two other planters. Bloody mess. Now I know what I want to do with my life. I want to own a plantation."

At this, and despite the tension on this subject and her feelings about enslaving people, Twilight laughed, for neither of the boys had expressed an interest in their futures before this. "I'm not joking, Twilight," Jed said. "In fact, I'm going to find out if any plantation around here needs an overseer. That will show Father I'm serious; then he'll have to let me have my inheritance money to buy a plantation."

Her heart twisted. Jed wanted to work on a plantation, then someday own one? Because she loved him, she decided that for now, she'd simply listen to his dreams. Later she could help him see that the price of his plan was human lives. "By the full moon! You, Jedediah Adams, are standing here in my room saying you want to work. I do declare, miracles can happen. Just don't get into any duels." Then Twilight looked at Jesse as if to say, "And you?"

Jed and Jesse had always been nearly identical in every way, in appearance, thoughts, and actions. So it was natural for Twilight to assume that if Jed had decided on plantation life, then that must also be Jesse's decision.

"I don't know what I want yet. But I do know that life on a plantation does *not* suit me. And losing Jed to one won't be easy for me. You know we've been almost one person for our entire existence." Upon openly admitting his feelings for his brother, Jesse appeared just a hint awkward. Agitated, Jed paced between the two bedroom windows, looking out one, then out the other. Jesse added, "I hope Father will allow me to work with you at his packet business."

"Jesse, I can tell you right now that Father would be very pleased that one of his sons wants to work with him," she said. To Jed, she added, "Father loves you, so he will support your decision, most likely. How did he respond when you told him? I'm curious, since plantations are built on enslaving human beings, which is a concern of Father's—and of mine."

"Well, there is debate on whether the Riches are human beings in the same way we are. As for what Father thinks, I haven't told him yet. And with Jesse wanting to work for Father, he'll probably want me to work at the packet business, too. He won't understand why both his sons don't want to follow in his footsteps."

"Jed, your language about Rich-tone people is callous." *What would he think if he knew what I know—?* "The 'debate' you mention is vile."

Jed didn't respond.

Twilight added, "I think Father gave up on the expectation that either of you would become interested in working."

"Are you implying, little sister, that our Father thought we'd be scampers our entire lives?" Jesse said, taking one of her pillows and bopping her on the head with it.

"Us? Scampers our entire lives?" Jed echoed, grabbing the other pillow and bopping her on the head with it.

Twilight laughed harder. Then, changing her expression to seriousness, she said, "Father will be pleased that you two want to work, finally."

"Hey, you hold her and I'll tickle her," Jesse said to Jed.

"No, you hold her and I'll tickle her," Jed said to Jesse.

"No, no!" Twilight screamed, laughing. "If you tickle me, I might die. My head feels like it's made of dynamite on the verge of exploding. I need to dress. So, please leave or supper will be served late if the family has to wait for me."

"She has a point," Jed said.

"A good point," Jesse said. "Let's go sneak in the kitchen and sample some of Cara's cooking."

"Right. The Clover Hill cook was good, but not as good as Cara," Jed said. "That's one reason we came home early."

"I'm so glad you did." Twilight smiled. "Would one of you tell Cara to ask Ember to come to my room, please?"

"Ember," Jed said. "Is that the Riches you bought?"

Twilight replied, "Don't use that term, Jed. I never want to hear you say it again. And I didn't buy Ember. I bought her manumission. See you in half an hour."

In a few moments, Ember arrived. "Where's Makeda-Angel?" Twilight asked.

"She's already sleeping."

"My darling brothers are home. I'd be so pleased if you joined us for supper. I have a silk gown you can wear. What do you say?"

"Oh, I couldn't. I'd not be at ease eating with your family."

Twilight suggested, "We can go to the dining room together. Would that help?"

An array of thoughts collided in Ember's mind.

Twilight said, "Father likes you, Mother adores you, and so do I. Who cares what Rachel and Sarah think?"

Ember nodded, pursing her lips.

A half-hour later, two lovely young women—both in silk—descended the staircase. The rest of the family was standing in the dining room, waiting to take their seats. Elizabeth smiled when she saw Ember. Harley glanced at Ember, then watched his wife closely. Sarah grabbed a handful of her skirt and twisted it nervously. Rachel frowned. Jed's eyes widened. Jesse, expressionless except for a light in his eyes, walked over to Ember, bowed, and introduced himself.

Rachel stomped her foot. "This must stop!" she said. "Father, I will not have our name disgraced. And I refuse to eat at our dining table with a Rich-tone."

"Then you will dine in your room, Rachel," Elizabeth said.

"What? Mother?" Aghast at being banished from the family dining table by her mother, Rachel flashed a stare at Twilight and said, "Just who do you think you are? The disgraceful Fanny Wright?" Beseeching her parents, she said, "Mother, Father, she is trying to turn our home into another Nashoba, the shame of Memphis and all of Tennessee. First, she refuses to wear cotton, then she brings two enslaved servants to live here and plans to free them! Father, even you are catching this disease. Ever since I can remember, I've smelled the lovely fragrance of your cigar. Now, you won't use tobacco? Please, don't let this happen." Then to Twilight, she said, "Not even wealthy, determined Fanny was successful in freeing and educating the enslaved. She tried to help them live in *our world*, and it just didn't work. She failed in just a few years and moved to that commune in Harmony, Indiana." Rachel paused for a heartbeat, then said, "Isn't that commune near Evansville, where you grew up with Grandfather and Grandmother? That area must be thick with rebels like you, Twilight. Why don't you go back there and live in Harmony with that Rich-tone loving rebel?"

Taking a deep breath, Twilight answered, "It would be difficult for me to live with someone who died several years ago." Rachel glared at Twilight. Thrilled that she could use her mother's wishes for once against Rachel, Twilight added, "Why don't you do as Mother expects and go to your room."

Turning sharply, her skirts circling around and behind her, Rachel swooshed out of the room and stomped up the stairs.

To Ember, Elizabeth said, "Won't you sit next to me, dear? Cara, Rachel will be taking her meal in her room. Cherish will take her place next to me."

Stunned, Harley and Twilight stared at Elizabeth. Uncomfortable, Ember wrapped her arms around herself. "Mother," Twilight said, "You mean Ember will sit next to you."

Cocking her head, Elizabeth looked at Twilight strangely but didn't reply. Jesse pulled out a chair next to his mother for Ember, then the one next to her for Twilight. After taking a tray to Rachel, Cara joined the family. Mealtime calmed as Jesse dominated the conversation by asking his father question after question about the packet business. Whenever Jed would interject with vivid descriptions of their antics with their friend George Johnston at Clover Hill, Jesse would interrupt his brother as he took shy glances at Ember. And then she understood: Ember wouldn't want to hear about plantation life from Jed's perspective. Twilight marveled at Jesse's compassion. She had expected Jed to fight for conversation dominance, but, oddly, he didn't. Acting nearly starved, he ate voraciously—and brooded.

With that secret, guarded expression behind her eyes, Ember watched Jesse and Harley speak. No one addressed her; she ate little and spoke not at all. Elizabeth, also quiet, smiled considerably, making everyone uneasy. Always Rachel's echo, Sarah said nothing, as her keystone had been removed from the room. After supper, Twilight asked Ember to join her in the parlor. Sarah's face crinkled as if the ceiling was falling in on her. She looked at the stairway, then approached Twilight and whispered,

"My beau is calling tonight. So is Rachel's." Twilight considered timid Sarah's implied request.

"All right. Ember, let's go to the library then. No one except Father will know we are there."

After she and Ember settled in the leather chairs, Twilight said, "Ember, I hope supper wasn't too uncomfortable for you, but I'm glad you joined us."

"I must get used to being among the free as Ember Free."

"I just hope you won't do something, like having supper with us, just to please me."

"I won't," Ember said.

Twilight smiled, nodded, and said, "Good." Then, after telling Ember of all the visitors she'd had that day, Twilight commented, "There's only one person who didn't call—Jackson. Because I haven't heard from him, I'm going to ask Father to inquire about the town, just so I know he hasn't come to harm."

Elizabeth peeped into the library, smiling ridiculously. "Oh, there you are," she said to Ember. "I am retiring for the day. Good night, Cherish." Then she bustled away.

"Why does she call me Cherish?" Ember asked.

Shaking her head in dismay, Twilight answered, "I'll tell you another time."

Jesse entered the library, saying, "I need not ask if I may join you since women are not supposed to be in this room." Laughing, he added, "This is a *man's* room."

"All I care about is that this is the room with books." Twilight surveyed the room, hugging herself. "It's so cozy in this room, with its comfortable chairs and fragrant pages and redolent bindings. Since it's hidden from the main hallway, Sisters' beaux will never know that I am sitting in this room with, heaven forbid, another woman!"

Choosing the chair next to Ember, Jesse sat, leaned forward, and said, "I want to tell you more about how I felt at Clover Hill, Twilight. I couldn't tell you earlier in front of Jed."

Standing, for this appeared to be a private conversation, Ember said, "I'll check on Makeda-Angel."

"No," Jesse said, smiling tenderly at Ember then blushing. "I mean, if it's time to check on your daughter, then by all means, please do. But if you can and wish to stay, I'd like that. I'd like for you to hear what I have to say." With her eyes protecting what lived behind them, Ember didn't answer. He repeated, "Please stay, Ember."

Curiosity, with the hint of something more, graced Ember's expression as she sat. Jesse smiled at her. "Twilight and Ember," he began, then took a deep breath and let it out slowly. "Not only did I not enjoy life at Clover Hill, I found it revolting. Jed knows I'm bothered, but I can't tell him what it is that's disturbing me. It hurts that I can't be honest with him for the first time in our lives, but he wouldn't understand. Our views on plantation life differ because," he glanced at Ember, "our views on enslaving people differ. Since our family has never owned people, I've always overlooked this 'peculiar institution,' as they say, which isn't really peculiar. It's blatantly evil. But I couldn't avoid it at Clover Hill. Each evening we sat on the veranda of the large, wonderful home. Enslaved people served us tall, cool mint drinks. The fields encircling us were lined with enslaved people who'd been there since way before we arose each morning. They never stopped working, even past dark if the moon was bright enough. Their only break from hard work was a fifteen-minute small dinner of bread, and sometimes bacon, which they'd carried out to the fields tucked in their shirts or pants. Nothing more to eat than that. Moreover, if someone accidentally snapped one cotton plant branch, a driver or overseer would whip that person soundly, for a broken branch won't produce bolls. Children as young as ten were working the fields. And the children were nearly naked, wearing only very short breeches—"

"Even the girls beginning their blossom," Ember said, her eyes holding an edge.

"True," Jesse stated, looking away from Ember and Twilight, red tingeing his cheeks. "A lot of the men and boys shared clothes, it seems, because I'd see some wearing only breeches and some wearing only shirts.

The animals were treated somewhat humanely; the enslaved people were not treated humanely at all. There is no empathy on a plantation. What is a place with no empathy? It's Hell. I hate it. But Jed likes it. In fact, he practiced with the whip every day. It's so odd. For the first time, what repulsed me attracted Jed. What can I say about my twin who thinks a place that thrives on lack of empathy—Hell—is Heaven?" Pausing, Jesse dropped his head and stared at his interlocked fingers, then said, "Jed and I are—different now."

This was a tragic time in the otherwise joyful, playful life Jesse had always led. Before, Jed and Jesse had acted like two halves of one person. Now, here was separation, and with that, loss. Twilight felt she was witnessing in Jesse a death and a struggle for rebirth.

"Jesse, you know how I despise slavery. We've always ignored it here in the Adams home. Even with Bedford Forrest as a neighbor, friends who own people, and enslaved people living and working near us, we as a family have avoided the issue." Reaching to rest her hand on his arm and leaning toward him, she continued, "But once you become aware, you can no longer ignore what is all around you that hurts others. People say I'm outspoken. Rachel equated me with Frances Wright. Forrest himself called me a rebel. I don't think of myself as outspoken or rebellious. I know slavery is wrong, and I will not sit by and watch."

"Nor will I," Jesse said.

Has Jesse joined the Band of Champions? I know I can't just sit by if I am to honor my heritage and my place in the Sisterhood of Gifts. To bring justice to all women and children, to all people who are oppressed is part of the secret society's mission, GrandMama's letter said.

And then Twilight realized that it wasn't her heritage or the mission of the Sisterhood of Gifts that made her want to do what she could about ending slavery. It was her chosen wild conviction.

"It's a crime, even if our laws don't state that, and I will not be an accomplice," she said.

Ember said nothing, but stood and left the room. Jesse watched her walk away.

Having enough of bed for that day and knowing her help was needed for the *Pennsylvania* victims, Twilight returned to Exchange Hall and worked throughout the night.

Dawn was christening the new day of June 21 when Henry Clemens was taken to the death room. Twilight, on Spirit, nearly flew home to tell her father, who, with coffee cup in hand and standing at the kitchen window, was watching the day's first light fill the sky. Together, they rushed back to Exchange Hall, to Sam.

An hour later, Harley took heartbroken Sam, who had not left his brother's side, to the Adams home. After a few hours of sleep, Sam returned to Exchange Hall. He thanked the kind women of Memphis who'd cared for the much-adored and terribly-suffering Henry and, after his suffering had ceased, prepared his body for travel.

The next day, Sam, distraught beyond words and accompanied by a young friend of Harley's, boarded the steamer *Hannibal City* to take Henry home.

Chapter 16
Visitor

Tuesday, June 22, 1858, Evening
Then, November 1858
Memphis

The knocker sounded on the huge oak front door, breaking the quiet.

Cara answered, then hurried to the library where Twilight and Jesse were reading. "Twilight. It is Mr. Canon."

"Jackson? Thank goodness!" Twilight said.

"Oh, and who is Mr. Canon, Sis?" Jesse asked, his eyes teasing.

"A beau," Twilight said. "My beau." Even though it wasn't true, Jackson, when he'd called, had hinted at being her beau. So, she said it, because she liked how it sounded, saying those words. *My beau. I have a beau.* Standing, she smoothed her dress and her hair and went to the parlor to greet Jackson.

He was standing tensely with his silk top hat in hand. Upon seeing Twilight, he bowed deeply, drawing his top hat in front of him.

"Hello, Jackson," she said, holding out her hand.

Straightening, he kissed her hand, then held onto it as he said, "It's an unusually cool evening, perfect for sitting on the porch or taking a stroll around your home. Would you join me?" He smiled as he put on his hat.

"I would be delighted." Hearing their plans, Cara scurried to Twilight, carrying a linen shawl and silk lace gloves. Lifting the shawl from Cara's hands, Jackson placed it around Twilight, tied it at her neck, and adjusted it on her shoulders. Twilight shivered at his touch, for a man had never done what Jackson was doing, and it seemed as if he were dressing her.

They strolled to the side garden. Twilight said, "You missed the ball, Jackson. That was four days ago. I wondered if maybe you had returned to Magnolia Bay or if you were ill or worse. But if that were the case, I thought surely I would be notified."

"I have been worse than ill."

"What do you mean?"

"I didn't miss the ball," Jackson said.

Surprised, Twilight said, "You were there? How can that be? I was there, and I never saw you."

"You saw only the man with whom you were dancing."

Jackson was there, watching Gallatin and me?

"You two were quite involved. It's no wonder you never noticed my presence."

Twilight pondered the exciting time she'd had with Gallatin and how she'd thought they were finally in love. And then she thought of how Gallatin reminded her that they would never be a couple.

"Who is he, Twilight? Are you in love with him?"

To avoid looking at Jackson, she instead looked at her hands. "No," she said. "I love him, but only as a brother." She believed that if she repeated those words enough in her mind, they would surely become true. *So, I'm not exactly lying to Jackson.*

With a light touch, he directed her face to his gaze, then said, "Watching you two together, I felt sure you were in love. I didn't know who he was or where he came from." Jackson dropped his hands, palms up. "I thought the evening at the ball was to be ours. Yet, you were dancing with another. So, I left and stayed away. I thought I could stay away forever. I thought I could forget about you. But, Twilight, you are unforgettable." His eyes gleamed from trapped tears.

He cares so much for me that he is nearly crying?

"I had to see you. I've done much thinking since I saw you with him, and I know now that I love you more than anything. I want you and need you." Putting his arms under her shawl and around her, he pulled her close and kissed her. With ease, he picked her up and cradled her in his arms, then kissed her again.

Kissing Jackson was different from kissing Gallatin. Different, yes, but still very nice. Twilight liked the kisses. And she liked being in Jackson's arms. Yet— "Jackson, put me down. What if someone were to see us?"

"You don't care what people think," Jackson whispered. "And neither do I if it means having you." He carried her to a wooden bench hidden by tall hedges and sat with her in his lap; then, they kissed again.

She scooted off his lap to sit next to him.

"Is he still courting you?"

"No. He has never courted me."

"Good." He caressed her fingers with his. "Why were you dancing with him?"

"He's the pilot of one of our steamers. He's a member of our family."

"You two didn't act like siblings."

Twilight thought of Gallatin, of how they danced together. She thought of him holding her to him and kissing her on the stairway. Her first kiss. She thought of how they kissed again and again in the library. Kissing Gallatin was like nothing she'd ever experienced. No, they weren't like siblings. But it was over between them before it even began. To Jackson, she said, "That is because you were looking through jealous eyes, Jackson. There is nothing between him and me, and there never will be. He has other interests."

"And you?" Jackson gently pulled the glove off her left hand and placed her fingers to his lips. "What are your interests?" he whispered, his lips caressing her fingertips as he spoke.

Twilight smiled up at him. "You, Jackson. You are my interest."

Yes, she liked being kissed. They'd already kissed in the garden, so she didn't see how it could do any more harm if they kissed again. Placing her hands—one gloved and one not—on Jackson's neck, she kissed him.

"My darling," Jackson said. "I don't want another man to touch you, to dance with you ever again. I haven't yet spoken with your father, so forgive me, but I can't wait." Kneeling on one knee, he held her hands and said, "Will you be my betrothed?"

When Jackson said the words that would map her life, Gallatin's image flooded her mind. *But why wait for someone I can never have and lose a man as wonderful as Jackson? Still, this is so sudden, and just days—too soon—after we met. Of course, the worst of it is that his father is an enslaver.* She didn't answer.

Jackson said, "I know this is sudden. But it is real. And, darling, think of this: you will be the mistress of Magnolia Bay. I assure you that as master and mistress of Magnolia Bay, we will make changes to better the lives of the enslaved."

Here was her chance to be loved *while* acting against slavery. *This must be an opportunity provided by the mystical ways of the Sisterhood of Gifts.*

After three heartbeats, she said, "We will free them."

"Of course," Jackson said. "In the last few days, away from you, I devised a system of the enslaved working for wages that will buy their freedom after one year. Upon their liberation, if they stay, they work for their own wages."

"Why can't they receive manumission now? Then stay on to work for wages if they wish?"

"Darling, you know much about business, but you don't realize how suddenly paying wages that don't support the plantation to two hundred people will run Magnolia Bay into the ground. That won't help anyone, not even the enslaved. We will pay them. But they must use this year's wages to buy their freedom. From this year's profits, we can pay our workers next year. Next year, they can leave or stay. If they stay, they keep their pay as hired laborers. That also gives us a year to hire other workers, in case some decide to leave, and to balance the sheets with the expense of wages."

Twilight frowned. *I guess this is a feasible plan. Even Fanny Wright had the enslaved work to buy their freedom.* Wondrous Ring glinted piercingly in the faint rising moonlight.

Jackson pulled her closer and kissed her. And kissed her. And kissed her, clouding her thoughts into a thunderstorm of passion.

She whispered, "By the rising moon, Jackson."

"Imagine kissing like this every evening, my darling," he said.

She could imagine it. It was thrilling. She said, "Before I step foot on your plantation, you must promise that your workers will immediately receive wages that will give them freedom in one year. And they will get better living and working conditions. And, for those who desire it, education in reading, writing, and numbers. Also, never call me a plantation mistress. Maybe, in time, I will be your wife. But I will never be a plantation mistress."

"Of course, my beautiful Twilight."

In anticipation of more kissing, Twilight said, "Yes, I will be your betrothed, Jackson Petigru Canon, after you ask for my father's blessing. However, I will not marry you until a decent interval of time has passed. And after I've seen for myself the changes to benefit the enslaved at Magnolia Bay, all of whom will be free in one year."

"Done. I'll speak with your father about you visiting Magnolia Bay as my betrothed. My parents, of course, will be our chaperones." He smiled. "You can visit until our marriage. That way, you can be sure you're making the right decision and can witness the changes."

Twilight nodded slowly.

⇢⇶⇛ ⇚⇰⇠

By mid-November, Twilight and Jackson had been betrothed for nearly five months. Jackson said his father wrote that the changes were in motion, so Twilight going to Magnolia Bay sooner wouldn't have expedited the improvements for the enslaved. She didn't want to rush their departure date for the plantation, but Jackson insisted it was time for him to return and that he would not go without her.

She was still trying to push from her mind all that she would miss when she went to Magnolia Bay for an extended visit—or forever. She would miss working at the packet office with her father. She would miss Jesse. Jed, however, would be going with them to be an overseer on the plantation, and she hoped Ember and Makeda-Angel would go with her, too, as her friends. She would miss city life, with its balls, plays, and concerts. She would miss seeing the riverboats at the wharf. She knew the part of her life she would miss most of all—Gallatin. As Mrs. Jackson Petigru Canon, Twilight would never be able to ride with Gallatin again. Or talk to Gallatin again. Or laugh with Gallatin again. Or kiss Gallatin again.

However, she had become adept at reminding herself that she would never see Gallatin again even if she didn't marry Jackson: she'd told Gallatin she no longer wished to see him. Ever. And, the fact was, she hadn't seen Gallatin for five months. Once a regular visitor to their home, he'd not appeared at their doorstep since she told him goodbye. *Just as well. Each time I think of Gallatin kissing me but telling me not to wait for him, that he might never leave the river—meaning he will never marry—I want to scream. I'll show him—I'm marrying Jackson.* Her heart skipped a beat. *Maybe.*

Whenever images of Gallatin filled her mind and heart, which was almost always, she skillfully guided her thoughts to what she would *not* miss about Memphis. She would not miss her mother. She would not miss her sisters. She would not miss people staring at her and commenting about how she rode Spirit. She would not miss her neighbor Forrest and his mart, where he imprisoned, paraded, and sold people. She would not miss Atrocity Square. She would not miss the slavery—everywhere—she could do nothing about.

Twilight trained her thoughts: *Maybe I need to go to the plantation for my Sisterhood gifts to emerge. Nothing really seems to have changed since I opened GrandMama's letter. Supposedly, I have gifts—even a power—but I feel no different. The only power I'm feeling is Jackson's love. Besides, the enslaved are as much in Memphis as they are at Magnolia Bay. In Memphis, I can do nothing for them. However, as Jackson's betrothed, I am doing something, acting against slavery, fulfilling my pledge. Changes are already being made, Jackson said, because of me. The enslaved will receive their freedom there next July. At Magnolia Bay, I'll be accepted for who I am, adored by my betrothed and his family, and effective in working against slavery.*

Every time she saw the look of disdain from each sister directed at her, every time she thought of her mother who ignored her, every time she thought of her gone-forever best friend Gallatin, she imagined Magnolia Bay as paradise, provider of purpose, the answer to her every dream. A place where she belonged. Her home.

There, I will be understood. There, I will be loved.

Chapter 17
That's Final

*Tuesday, June 22, 1858
to Thursday, November 25, 1858
Memphis*

With Twilight and Jed leaving for Magnolia Bay at the end of November, Jesse felt betrayed.

Although he'd avoided facing the truth, he knew he'd lost Jed during the summer at Clover Hill. But Twilight? He never thought he'd lose his feisty, fiery, determined sister to a plantation; she, his only comrade against slavery. Less than delighted and very confused by Twilight's sudden betrothal to a plantation owner's son, Jesse tried to talk sense to her: "Twilight, don't you see that you, by marrying Jackson, are marrying a plantation that is successful because of the enslaved? You will be the wife of an enslaver."

"No, Jesse, *I* will be reforming the plantation. A plantation built on education and wages and freedom for the enslaved. *If* I marry Jackson, I will be marrying only Jackson. Not the plantation. Jackson's father won't be an enslaver for much longer. So, *if* I marry Jackson, I won't do so until *after* all of the enslaved have been manumitted. Jackson has promised changes are already being made. Don't you see, Jesse? Here is a chance for me to actually *do* something about educating and freeing two hundred enslaved people. Instead of merely talking against slavery and boycotting goods made by the labor of the enslaved, I am taking action." Twilight inhaled deeply, exhaled slowly, then continued, "I believe in reform. And, I believe in love." She smiled, "It's nice, feeling loved."

Then Jesse knew—Twilight was lost to Jackson. He wasn't sure what it was all about, and it had been strange that Gallatin no longer visited the family home on his infrequent but regular overnights in Memphis. But, somehow, Jackson apparently provided the love Twilight needed in her life. And Jackson promised Twilight a purpose. Jesse wondered if having a purpose could be more powerful than love. The two combined? Maybe as beneficial—or as destructive—as dynamite touched by a lit lucifer match.

Feeling lost in his own life, Jesse's most enjoyable moments were when he watched Ember play with Makeda-Angel; she, filled with love for her child, cuddling and kissing her tiny daughter often, speaking to her in what seemed to be a secret speech—a coded, personal language and vocabulary with lyrical sounds and words he could not understand. Until recently, he and Twilight had shared the instruction time of reading, writing, and numbers with Ember. Now, Twilight's busyness with her plans for an extended visit, likely leading to marriage, meant he was meeting with Ember usually by himself, and he completely enjoyed that time with her. In fact, he savored every moment.

One night, a week before Twilight's day of departure, Jesse saw Ember enter the side garden. The night was slightly chilled, clear, and star-filled. Ember strolled among the bushes and trees, stopping occasionally to gaze at the heavens.

"Ember," Jesse called, hurrying to join her. "Is Makeda-Angel asleep?"

"Yes," Ember sighed. "She does look like an angel when she sleeps."

Looking at the millions of stars above them, Jesse said, "It's awesome, isn't it? All of those suns. All of those worlds. I like to wonder what is happening in the lives of the people in other worlds." Turning his gaze to Ember, he asked, "What do you think about when you look at the stars?"

Without hesitation, Ember answered, "I wonder about my son. Menelik. I wonder where he is and what he is doing. I like to think he is looking at the sky just when I am, for then we are looking at the same thing at the same time. It makes me feel close to him somehow. And when it is very late and I gaze up there, I pray that he is sleeping soundly in some warm, clean place." Wiping her eyes with the back of her hand, she said, "I'll never know what he is doing, where he is sleeping, if he is well." She added, "I do know he is alive." As if a plea, she looked to Jesse, shook her head, and said, "But he's alone. Without his mama. He's only five."

"You have a five-year-old son, and you don't know where he is?"

Ember nodded. "Does that seem strange to you, Jesse? That is how captivity works, separating us from our families. We ache to hold our loved ones. We are tormented and grieving, for we know we will never see them again."

With a combination of genuine sorrow and pain, Jesse said, "I'm sorry, Ember. I am—a man who doesn't know a damn, forgive me, darn thing."

"Thank you. I shouldn't have turned my torment on you. I know you don't mean to sound ignorant about the lives of captives. But I thought you knew about my son. I thought Twilight had surely told you."

"No, she hasn't told me. She doesn't talk to me much anymore. She doesn't seem like Twilight since her betrothal."

Ember nodded, thought a moment, then responded, "She's a fine young woman. I want happiness for her. I wish she'd wait awhile before leaving with Canon."

Jesse nodded.

Then Ember said, "When you gaze at the stars, Jesse, you have many wonderful thoughts."

Directing his attention again toward the stars, then back to Ember, he said, "Lately, though, the stars and I share other thoughts, like how I will miss Jed and Twilight when they are gone." Quietly, he added, "And how I will miss you, Ember. Twilight says you and Makeda-Angel are going with her?"

Though she didn't answer, she was thinking, *I will not return to a plantation. And I will never put Makeda-Angel back on one. Never.*

Gently and very briefly, Jesse caressed the edge of her fingers. She didn't draw back. He looked at her and said, "May I touch your face?" She nodded. Slowly, he touched her chin lightly with a forefinger and searched her eyes. Jesse whispered, "I'll miss everything about you, Ember."

Ember stared at Jesse, then said, "I should go in." Hurriedly, she left him in the garden.

He didn't see Ember the entire next day. By nine o'clock that evening, everyone had retired except Jed, who was at a tavern. Jesse, in the library, paced in a circle and thought of Ember. The more he thought of her, the faster he paced. He stopped and clutched the reading table. But his mind continued, his thoughts a mad dance. He had to see her. Quietly, he walked out to the side garden. She was there, gazing at the moon. Seeing her, he calmed. He knew she could hear his approach, but she didn't turn. Composed, he stood behind her and whispered into her ear. "Are you thinking of your son?"

Still concentrating on the night sky, Ember answered, "Yes. Always, I think of my Menelik." After a moment of quiet, she added, "Tonight, I'm also thinking of you."

Jesse asked, "May I touch your shoulders?"

At first pensive, quiet, she then whispered, "Yes."

Placing his hands on her shoulders, he gently turned her to face him. "Ember, maybe there is a world up there among those stars where all people have the same skin tone. Or maybe they don't, but no one cares. Or maybe you and I were born at the wrong time. Maybe, someday, on our planet, love will be love. Maybe someday, we can be who we are—persons, with no restraining definitions, where what is allowed is what is true—that a person loves another person." Jesse took a breath. "In our wicked time, as we know, it is against the law for a person with my tone and a person with your tone to marry. But if it were different, and if you would have me, I would marry you. I love you, Ember."

Ember frowned, then smiled very slightly. *How odd that I am having deep, good feelings about Jesse,* she thought. *True, his kindness seems to be real. And he is such a gentle teacher during our lessons. But—Mama said loving a Pale man is more than a risk: doing so could conjure harm.* Twilight had told her that when it wasn't illegal, the first mayor of Memphis, a Pale man of course, and a Rich-tone woman married. So Ember supposed such love, though rare, was possible. Ember loved her mama, but she didn't believe everything her mama said. *I believe that true love always conjures good.*

Yet—maybe my feelings for this seemingly kind man are because I've been lonely, and I feel odd living in the home of Pale people, supposedly as their equal, supposedly as their friend. But I am their servant. While I miss the plantation not at all, of course, I do miss my community of women, my sisters, who live there. We have our customs, our beliefs, our songs, our language. Here, I am so alone, except for my child. Memphis makes it hard to find Rich-tone friends. I don't want to navigate the curfews and other restrictions on moving about or worry about penalties for accidental violations of arbitrary injunctions. So, I stay here mostly, in this house. I've come to like Twilight, but Twilight lives only in her own world lately. It is Jesse who somehow makes this house feel more like my home. Maybe loving Jesse could conjure good. Still, I must continue to be cautious.

As if in reply, somewhere within her, a thought responded, jarring her: *I loved Menelik's daddy. But Man is gone. Forever. Now, looking at Jesse, I see that I will never know love again, for he and I will never be free to love.*

Very lightly, Jesse caressed her arms, bringing her thoughts back to him and only him, standing before her.

She said, "Oh, Jesse, if only the whole world were blind, then no one would see that you and I are different tones."

Placing his forefinger lightly under Ember's chin, he gently tilted her face so he could look into her eyes even more deeply and directly. "My lovely woman," he said, "the whole world *is* blind."

Then he bent his head and brushed her lips with his so slightly that it was as if he had touched only the space between them. "It can never be for us," he whispered. "But know this: I love you. I ache for you. And because I can't be with you in that love, I will live in torment for the rest of my days." Abruptly, he turned and strode into the house.

Ember watched him walk away. Her mind stopped resisting what she knew to be true. Her heart spilled to fill her entire being.

※※※ ※※※

The next day, Ember approached Twilight. "I am free, isn't that so, Twilight?"

"Why, yes, Ember. I have always made that clear. I should have the papers, my dear friend Ember Free, to give to you before we leave for Magnolia Bay."

Ember continued, "That is wonderful. Thank you. You're special to me. But I need to tell you something. We'll not go to Magnolia Bay. My child and I will stay here."

"Here? In our home? Forever?"

"Well, I don't know how long. But it frightens me to step foot on a plantation again. I should've told you when you first asked if Makeda-Angel and I would come with you."

"I just assumed—I was wrong to do so."

"The thought frightens me to my very core. The truth is, I've never planned to go with you."

"Ember, you are good at hiding your emotions. Or am I just too self-absorbed right now to notice? Of course you can stay here. Mother will welcome you in our home as long as you like, that's certain. I will miss you. You're the only friend I have. I thought you might want to leave because, if you leave, you can get away from Mother always jabbering at you and calling you Cherish."

"I thought you'd know, or finally realize, that I will never return to a plantation. Compared to a plantation, your mother is an enlightened angel."

After considering for a moment, Twilight said, "I do understand why, even being free, you want to avoid any plantation. But I would protect you. Changes are happening there. It is a reformed plantation. Wages. Education. Freedom for the captives in less than a year."

"Twilight, I'll be bold and mouthy. Here it is: you've had it rough with your sisters and mother not showing you love. But that lack of love is nothing compared to the wicked goings-on at a plantation. You don't know plantation life. Despite what you say or do, my child and I would be captives again. You might be Pale, but you're a woman. You have privileges, but not as many as a Pale Male. You'll have to obey Jackson's whims. In the wrong place, you won't be able to protect us. Or yourself. Be careful. A plantation is always the wrong place. Nothing good happens on a plantation. Ever."

Twilight was thinking about how Fanny Wright accomplished changes on her plantation. She'd also been doing her research. She discovered that in the late 1840s, Quakers had bought Woodlawn, a Virginia plantation formerly owned by a relative of George Washington who had enslaved ninety people. The Quakers, being avid abolitionists, changed the plantation into one without enslaved workers, making Woodlawn a communal agricultural area for Rich-tone people and Quakers. *Aren't those steps good? However, convincing Ember that reforms could be made is not my mission. My mission is to get freedom and wages for those now enslaved at Magnolia Bay. Workers being hired for wages—not being enslaved—is the first step.*

Ember continued, "I think Jesse will be glad of my decision."

"Jesse?"

"Yes. He'd feel alone here without one of us to talk to. He seems very caring. He even came to me this morning and told me he would find my Menelik."

"Oh, Ember, forgive me! How rotten of me to neglect finding Menelik. I've been so absorbed in myself, and by the full moon, all I can think about is Jackson and the improvements I'll make at his plantation." Twilight closed her eyes and rubbed her forefinger on her forehead. Then she added, "I can be oblivious to others when I focus on my cause. What an irony." She shook her head while grasping her frailties. "I truly am sorry. Yes, let's find Menelik now. I *will* help. And remember, I might not stay at Magnolia Bay. I plan to marry Jackson, but I haven't yet. This will be a visit, only. Maybe it will become an extended stay. Maybe a marriage. Regardless, if we marry, we will do so in Memphis. So, if you come with me, we might be returning home for good anyway, and certainly, we will for visits."

"Twilight, what has happened to you? Are you not listening? I'll never change my mind on this," Ember said. Then, her face softening a bit, she added, "But, I do think I might miss you, Twilight."

Twilight smiled. "You are truly being free by telling me this, choosing what you want for your life. Of course, it is natural, and smart, for you to fear returning to a plantation. I suggested you come with me because I know I can make changes so you'd be safe. Jackson promised I can make the changes I think are right. Something has happened to me, Ember. Love has happened to me."

Ember was thinking, *Sweetie, you love Gallatin, not Jackson. If you take off with that enslaver, you'll ruin your chances for real love.*

After a brief hesitation, Twilight asked, "You have a strong relationship with Jesse?"

Ember hesitated, then said, "A kind relationship. Not strong. Not yet, anyway. A strong relationship is what you and Gallatin have."

Startled, Twilight said, "You mean what Jackson and I have."

"I mean one that lasts forever, like what you have with Gallatin."

"Gallatin again. Ember, I don't want to talk about Gallatin. I haven't even seen him in months! Besides, I love Jackson. I love Jackson more than anything in the world."

Ember sighed.

"Just be careful, you and Jesse. You know that almost everyone everywhere is prejudiced. Even in the North." Twilight said nothing for a moment, then added, "It is against the law, as you very well know, for you and Jesse to ever become involved. Maybe you should come to Magnolia Bay with me, away from Jesse; you might be safer there."

"Twilight, I can see your fingers are not in your ears. Why aren't you hearing me? Magnolia Bay will never be safe," Ember said with a bit of edge. "I can spell it out for you if you need me to," she added, "now that I can spell." She smiled at her young friend who had first helped her to spell. "And, are you suggesting I escape to Magnolia Bay to avoid love? Is that what you are doing, thinking you'll be safe, forever away from Gallatin?"

"Stay here, then, Ember, of course. But don't talk to me like you are my conscience. You don't know how I feel inside about Gallatin."

"I've seen you with Gallatin and with Jackson. And I think you should wait to marry until after you've seen Gallatin again."

Twilight nodded, thoughtful. Then, she looked at the mirror on the wall and watched her reflection say, "I'm leaving with Jackson. And that's final."

Chapter 18
Magnolia Bay

Tuesday, November 30, 1858
Late Morning to Early Afternoon
Memphis to Magnolia Bay Plantation

After five months of visits with Twilight's parents—for with time comes trust—the day came when Jackson whisked Twilight away in his carriage for a leisurely three-hour trip to Magnolia Bay, nine miles south of Memphis.

Jed followed, riding Spirit. When they neared his home, Jackson relayed to his betrothed details of the plantation home and the family.

"My father named me after Andrew Jackson, his personal friend and, as you know, one of three men who bought the first tracks of land that became Memphis."

Twilight had suspected Jackson was Andrew Jackson's namesake, but she always pushed the thought away. Diverting her concern from something more troubling—that she might soon be entering an even stranger place than Memphis—she asked, "When did your father and mother marry?"

"Father was thirty-nine. Mother was getting a bit old, seventeen. Father was one of the first town officials of Memphis, and he sold his land for new businesses. It was during a winter visit in 1827 to the Hermitage, Andrew Jackson's home in Nashville, that Father met Mother.

Mother had been visiting with Jackson's wife, Rachel, since the previous summer. Mother and Father designed Magnolia Bay after the Jacksons' plantation mansion, with a few changes. We own one thousand acres, the same acreage as the Hermitage. But while Andrew Jackson was the enslaver of one hundred who worked two hundred acres of cotton, we are the enslavers of two hundred who work three hundred acres of cotton."

"Jack, why didn't you tell me this before?"

"I suppose it's because when we were in Memphis I just wanted to talk about you and our future together. My parents' pasts didn't seem important then. But now that we are on our way to live at Magnolia Bay, I thought you would like some history about our home and Mother and Father."

"I'm a bit nervous about meeting them, Jack." The farther they drove away from Memphis and toward the plantation, the more naive she was feeling.

"Don't be, my dear," Jackson replied, patting Twilight's arm. "Since all of her daughters have married and moved away, Mother enjoys the company of women in the mansion. My parents will adore you."

Soon Jackson pointed to a grove of magnolia trees near the river and said excitedly, "There!"

Twilight couldn't see the mansion for the trees. "You're acting like a boy, Jackson." She laughed tightly. "As much as you love Magnolia Bay, I can't believe you ever left to pursue your dreams."

He squeezed her hand. "I'm glad I did, for I came back with you. Together, we'll own the plantation."

"You know that's not true," Twilight said. "Legally, a woman doesn't own diddly, except for what her father gives her. And then, when she marries, her money and possessions become her husband's. In fact, upon marriage, *she* becomes her husband's possession. So, you will own Magnolia Bay and me. I will own nothing."

"Twilight, what a way to talk." He glanced at her, gently smiled, then faced the road ahead of them. His smile changed to devious when he added, "You'll find out on our wedding night what you own."

Twilight blushed as she concentrated on her gloved hands. Jackson didn't notice. "Look now," he said. "Isn't my home magnificent?"

Her face still warm, Twilight looked up. Peering in the distance, she could just make out a huge white house with stately columns looming behind the grove of winter-stark magnolia trees. To the west ran the river. The house, a mansion, sat on a hill and overlooked a cove formed by the Mississippi River edging into the land. Lining the cove and the slope to the home, weeping willow trees arched, their delicate bare brown branches billowing softly in the breeze as nature's ancient lace, swaying like curtains at the open window of the sky. The enchanting scene reminded her of her own beloved Willow Land, with its densely-gorgeous magical willow grove.

"Breathtaking," Twilight said. *But not as lovely as Willow Land.* She felt homesick for her childhood home.

"Now you can see why Father named it Magnolia Bay."

"Yes. There are dozens of magnolias. Another nice name could have been Willow Cove, as it is actually a cove, not a bay. The willows leaning over the cove create the most serene scene God ever painted." *And Willow Cove rhymes with willow grove.*

"Dream all you like. It doesn't change a thing," Jackson said with an edge. "The name is Magnolia Bay."

"I agree. Magnolia Bay is a beautiful name, the best name," Twilight replied, laughing, then nudging him just a bit in the ribs.

"Don't do that."

"Jackson? Are we having our first quarrel?"

"We are not quarreling. The name of the plantation is Magnolia Bay. End of discussion." He paused, then said, "Stop talking for a while."

"Yes, darling, I said I agree it is the best name, a beautiful name. My, Jackson. It seems the closer we get to seeing your parents, the moodier you become," Twilight said.

"This has nothing to do with my parents. You annoy me sometimes," Jackson said.

By the blood moon. "You've never told me that before," she said.

"Quiet," he said. His tone was sharp. His word was imperative. She was confused.

They drove through a long row of towering magnolias, regal trees that held onto their leathery leaves in even the coldest months, and then through a long archway of moss-covered oaks with limbs that curved and touched. It was as if they were wandering through a cool, dark, mysterious forest into a faerie tale. So densely grew the trees that the sky was nearly blocked.

Then, suddenly, sunlight appeared, and in the center of it stood the Magnolia Bay mansion, shining in the light. It was an immense, two-story building defined by six large fluted white columns spanning the height of the house. A front porch with chairs surrounded the massive front doors. Above, a second-story veranda spread across the entire façade. A one-story wing commanded the north, and another commanded the south. Facing west, the mansion viewed the Mississippi River and the America beyond, and beyond that, the America-to-be. She couldn't see what was hidden behind the mansion.

"It is magnificent," Twilight said breathlessly, the scene blotting out Jackson's admonishment. "I have never seen a house so large. Or so white."

Jackson pulled the horse to a halt, stopping the carriage in front of the mansion, and helped Twilight step down. Spirit and Jed stopped next to them. "Would you look at this place?" Jed said. "It makes Clover Hill seem more like Ant Hill. Lordy, I'm going to like being an overseer here."

Hugging Jackson's arm, Twilight thought, *I'm going to be happy here,* as the majesty of the place gave her a sense of euphoria.

What she pushed to the back of her mind as she gripped Jackson's arm was that this was the kind of euphoria she'd felt only once before—from drinking too much brandy.

Chapter 19

The Canons

Tuesday, November 30, 1858
The Rest of the Day
Magnolia Bay

Still clinging to Jackson's arm, Twilight crossed the double-door threshold into the stately, whitewashed mansion.

A man in a white suit hurried to them. "Why, Master Jackson, sir. You've come home." He bowed, then held out his arms to receive their wraps.

"Hello, Billy. This is my betrothed and her brother, Mr. Adams," Jackson said, nodding at Jed behind them, "a new overseer. Where are your Lord and Lady?"

"In the back parlor, having tea, sir. An honor to meet you, mistress."

"Please, call me Twilight."

A very slight smile quickly crossed Billy's face. He bowed, then hurried down the foyer hallway to hang the wraps on a great mahogany hall tree.

Jackson said, "You should be called Mistress Twilight by the captives, as my mother is Lady Canon."

"I told you, Jackson. I will *not* be a plantation mistress; I will never be called that," Twilight said.

Jackson gave Twilight a harsh look.

Twilight ignored Jackson's reproof by absorbing the space of the hallway. It was so high, wide, and deep that it could have been two rooms. They walked through an open doorway and into a parlor. Sitting opposite one another by the windows and holding teacups were a handsome couple, Jackson's parents, James and LaDonna. Their faces boasted deep wrinkles. Both appeared to be rather tall, as their legs seemed much too long for them to be comfortable in their chairs, with the seat height, as typical, being just a bit over a foot from the floor. Seated in the high-backed velvet Victorian chairs, they appeared as a king and queen. A tall, slim woman in a gray dress, white apron, and blue head wrap stood as a sentry behind LaDonna, her arms folded, a frown pulling down her face.

"Hello, dear," Jackson's mother said, holding out her arm to Jackson. "Come give Mother a kiss."

Jackson obeyed, regally kissing the back of his mother's hand, then shook his father's hand. He walked to the woman standing behind his mother and kissed her cheek. "Hello, July-May." July-May gave him a thin smile.

Turning and motioning to Twilight, who stood at the threshold, Jackson said, "Come here, dear. I would like for you to meet Father and Mother, Lord and Lady Canon."

Taking her place next to her betrothed, Twilight curtsied. LaDonna, frowning, examined Twilight from hair ribbon to shoelace. James grinned.

"It's wonderful to meet you, Mr. and Mrs. Canon. And you, July-May," Twilight said, smiling to each person as she said their name. July-May, mouth closed tightly in a line, made a sharp, deep noise in her throat.

"Welcome to our castle," James said with a booming voice. "But, make no mistake, you must call us Lord and Lady. Now, Son, sit and tell me all about what is happening in my city."

"Yes, tell us about all of our friends and their children. Your father wants to know all about the new businesses and about that fine friend of yours, Mr. Bedford Forrest," LaDonna said.

"And I would—," Twilight began, her stomach churning at the mention of Forrest.

"Later," LaDonna interrupted, holding up her hand, palm facing Twilight.

With his hand on her elbow, Jackson maneuvered Twilight to a settee. She listened to the conversation that didn't recognize her presence in any way: it was as if she didn't exist. After an hour, they went to supper.

In the fabulous dining room, Twilight felt unkempt after their trip. Annoyed that she hadn't been shown to her room to freshen herself or to change into a dining gown, Twilight whispered to Jackson, asking where she might wash. Billy appeared, saying, "Please, follow me."

When Twilight returned and all were seated, in swooshed a lovely blonde young lady wearing a stunning pink dress. She walked straight to Jackson and kissed him, lingering for three full seconds, squarely on the mouth. Twilight was so stunned she just stared. She noticed that Jed stared, too, and she thought he probably wished he were Jackson at that moment. Jackson's parents didn't seem to notice.

The young lady looked at Twilight. "I'm Victoria DeWitt Canon. Jackson's cousin," she said.

"I'm Twilight Wild Adams. Jackson's betrothed."

"Charmed," Victoria said, tilting up her nose and swirling to her chair next to LaDonna and across from Jackson.

Maybe at another time, not so fresh after she arrived at Jackson's home, or maybe if the kiss had not been so solid and deliberate and passionate—and three seconds too long—on Jackson's lips, Twilight might have tried to ignore the trespass. But at this time, the thought of ignoring the kiss never crossed Twilight's mind. She said, "Never kiss my betrothed on the lips."

Everyone except Jed looked sharply at Twilight.

"Don't look at me like that," she said. "I'm not the one who kissed someone else's betrothed."

"Dear," Victoria said. "You are new here. You have some things to learn, such as the fact that I have been related to Jackson for fifteen significant years. You are not related to him at all. Earn the right before you speak to me in such a disagreeable manner."

"As Jackson's betrothed, I have the right."

"Ladies," Jackson interrupted. "There's no contest for," he paused and dabbed his lips with his napkin, then resumed, "my lips." Twilight noticed a hint of a smile crinkling the corners of his eyes and mouth. Addressing Twilight, he said, "Victoria is my cousin. It was simply a kiss of greeting. A custom. But if it upsets my betrothed," he turned his gaze to Victoria, "I want you to not do so again." Looking back at Twilight, he said, "Try to get along with everyone. We are not your enemies. We are your family."

"Oh, James, isn't this fun?" LaDonna said, clapping her hands. "I think I'm pleased after all that our boy brought this girl here. At least it is entertaining."

Twilight didn't feel one bit comfortable with her prospective family. She ate little. No one addressed her during supper, though they often asked Jed questions. After supper, she followed Billy upstairs to a large room. Her trunk and carpet bag had been unpacked, surely by the efficient and unseen captives who cared for the home. A fire blazed. Warm water filled the pitcher on the washstand. Twilight poured some into the basin.

Gazing at herself in the washstand mirror, she, seriously and intently, studied her image as if she was seeing for the last time the person reflected. She felt a little scared and even, oddly, homesick. No one here was being friendly to her, not really. Billy was nice. Everyone else, though, was pretty mean. Even Jackson had taken an odd turn. Maybe it was all just a transition away from Memphis into country life, where families had to depend on each other in ways they might not in the city. Their closest neighbors were miles away, not just next door, like in Memphis.

So maybe that made the family members act excessively bonded to each other and strangely toward her, an outsider. Regardless, she didn't like it.

She reached into her right hidden pocket and took out her secret Deringer, which she carried only on rare outings since Makeda-Angel began living in her parents' home. At Magnolia Bay, she would be safe, so she need not carry it any longer. Besides, Jackson would surely discover it at some point if she continued to carry it, as she had promised. Promised Gallatin. She must keep this part of herself hidden. She knew just where to hide it. She lifted the empty carpet bag from the floor. Within it, she carefully placed her Deringer and the small box of items from Grand-Mama's shrine. She pulled loose some of the stitching of the carpet bag lining. She took from her left hidden pocket her most important secret, GrandMama's letter, then tucked it inside the lining of the carpet bag.

"What am I doing? I feel as if I am putting away myself," she said to her reflection. *Well, I must do this. I must truly uncouple myself from Gallatin. And I must hide GrandMama's secrets. My secrets.* Turning from the mirror, she put the carpet bag on top of the wardrobe. Placing the organza bag of the three tiny stones in a drawer, she decided she would place it in her pocket each morning when she dressed.

She would keep those gifts from GrandMama, along with Wondrous Ring, with her.

Chapter 20
Another Vow

Wednesday, December 1, 1858
Morning
Magnolia Bay

The following morning, rapid knocking on Twilight's door ruined her dreams.

Slipping on her bed jacket, she answered and saw Jackson smiling and wearing a suit. "Dress in one of your finest dresses," he said. "Then come to the parlor. I have a surprise for you."

When she entered the parlor, she saw a man standing by Jackson.

Taking her hand and smiling, Jackson said, "We're getting married, darling."

"Yes, we are, someday," she said, laughing. "Probably."

The man cleared his throat and said, "I am Reverend Samuels. Please continue to hold hands and stand before me."

"Wait. Reverend Samuels, you are here to discuss our wedding, is that right? It's not any time soon, so we should continue this conversation later." Neither man spoke. Twilight laughed nervously, then said, "Jack, I'm hungry. I'm not sure what's happening here, but can it wait until after breakfast, at least?"

"We must do this now," Jackson said, grinning like a boy with a new toy.

"Do what?"

"Darling, we are getting married. Here. Now."

She jerked her hand from his. "No, Jackson, we are not."

"Yes, dearest. It's time. You know that." He sank to one knee and held her hand. "Marry me. Marry me. Please, my beauty, marry me." He stood, and the reverend quickly pronounced them "man and wife."

Neither had said "I do." Twilight had not said a word. Jackson started to slip a ring on her finger. Shock led her consciousness into a locked closet, but she retained enough of herself to pull back her hand. Jackson tugged her hand back to him and pushed on the unreasonably tight band. "Oww," Twilight said, rubbing her knuckle. While Jackson signed a paper that the reverend held to him, Twilight managed to swear, "By the damning absent moon!" Abruptly, the reverend left as Twilight said, again swearing, "Jackson, what the hell just happened?"

"My darling wife, do not speak with such language in this home," Jackson said, kissing her forehead and caressing her hair. Then, holding her hand, he led her into the dining room. Only the two of them were there for breakfast. She didn't eat. Her hunger had vanished the moment they wed. The house was too quiet. The room swayed. The awful wallpaper print reached out to grab her. Twilight clutched her chair, confused, and said nothing. *What just happened? I'm not ready to be married. But, isn't this why I came? To marry Jackson? Jackson must love me so much he couldn't wait. Was it romantic, what he just did? I don't know; this feels wrong—.* She felt dazed into nowhere.

"Go to our room," Jackson said. "I'll meet you there momentarily."

Twilight went up the stairs. In her room, she looked at her hands. On the right—the mysterious Wondrous Ring from GrandMama that fit perfectly. On the left—the ill-fitting wedding band from Jackson. She gagged into the washstand basin. Then, she slid downward, sinking to the floor, sitting lopsided like a rag doll. She felt no sensation, not even numbness. She felt nothing.

Jackson entered, carrying a tray with a decanter of sherry and two cut crystal glasses. He called to Billy, who took away the wash basin then returned with a clean one and a glass of minted water. Billy poured water from the pitcher into the fresh basin. He left. Jackson closed and locked the bedroom door. He lifted the subdued sixteen-year-old and sat her on the bed. With the fresh water from the basin on a clean, embroidered cloth, he blotted her face and lips. He gave her a sip from the glass, telling her to swish the minty solution then release it into the basin. Wordlessly, she moved to his instructions. When she was seated back on the bed next to him, he leaned and kissed her shoulder. "Are you happy?"

Twilight nodded—because that was what he expected. Besides, what could she do now? It had happened. She was married. To Jackson. Now, Gallatin was definitely out of her life.

"It should comfort you to know that Mother and Father confirmed they will be moving."

For the first time in her life, she didn't care. About anything.

Jackson said, "To Woodland Manor."

Woodland Manor, Jackson had told her soon after their engagement, was the smaller mansion a quarter mile northeast of Magnolia Bay that James had built for his wife's parents. After the death of his grandfather when Jackson was three, his grandmother had lived there with a few enslaved servants. When Jackson was six, she died. That had been thirteen years ago. Vacant since then, James had promised to move there after Jackson married and took his place as master of Magnolia Bay.

She mumbled, "I am unwelcome. I am uncomfortable. I miss home."

"This is your home, dearest. I will make you comfortable," Jackson said, pressing his bride to his chest and stroking her hair. "And your brother is here. He will make a good overseer. Good ones are hard to find. Too often they become unreliable, even drunkards. I know I can trust Jed. In that way, he is like you." He kissed her; then he pulled her onto his lap. Cradling her, he stood, gently laid her down on the bed, and fluffed pillows behind her.

After pouring two glasses of sherry, he carried them to the bed, where he sat on the side. Giving her a glass, he said, "Here's to us, my lovely wife," touching her glass with his, making a quiet click.

A strange time to drink. Twilight was especially reluctant after her experience with too much brandy. And it was early morning. She'd not eaten breakfast. But all of her feelings were blunted into nothing. *Maybe the sherry will help.* She felt caught in an odd vague puzzle with no clues on how to find a solution, a maze with no way out. *Did I really marry Jackson? I didn't even say "I do." I didn't sign anything. Maybe on a plantation, women never sign anything, not even their own marriage papers.*

The unspoken consequence of marriage further froze her mind: women frequently were dead within a year after loving their husbands. A child, she would welcome, someday; childbirth, she would not welcome, ever.

Wasn't she herself still a child? Why had she thought she was ready for marriage and the hopeless trunk of troubles marriage might hold?

It was an overcast wintery day, so even though it was morning, the room was dark except for the soft firelight. The wood crackled merrily. Jackson again clinked his glass to hers, and they sipped the aromatic drink in the snap and glow. The last time she'd sipped sherry was with Gallatin. But, she reminded herself, it was Jackson she loved. She pushed her thoughts of Gallatin back into her mental dungeon.

Sip after sip. Jackson poured a bit more. Sip after sip. With the spell of the sherry, Twilight's mind moved from vacancy toward her hopes of fulfillment as Jackson's wife. Taking her empty glass and setting it next to his on the nightstand, Jackson leaned over her, unbuttoned her dress, gently slid it off her, then unbuttoned her chemise. She saw in his eyes both desire and vulnerability.

With his touch, she tensed; with his kiss, she relaxed.

And then, with more kisses in their shared, and sherried, near-nakedness, a new, dynamic sensation carried her away: she wanted nothing but this. Again and again and again. Their actions, like agonized thrill, stopped the sun, sealed their bond. At Jackson's culminating reaction, she wondered if—contrary to what society dictated—men, even rich men like Jackson, were truly all-powerful.

Intertwined, resting together, they were innocents, together in a new land.

Chapter 21

Makeshift Honeymoon ~ Two Months in One Room

December 1858 to February 1, 1859
Magnolia Bay

Winter weaved icy days into cozy nights.

Doing her best to avoid the unpleasant weather and the even more unpleasant LaDonna, James, and Victoria, Twilight spent each day and night entirely in her room. In fact, her doing so was Jackson's idea. He insisted they celebrate their marriage with a "makeshift honeymoon."

He arranged it so that she would be relieved of her chores and that all meals would be brought to their room, where the newlyweds devoted much activity. Twilight thought she'd found a secret paradise: she relaxed in the solace of the huge, comfortable room where she read in front of an ever-burning fire—and then roused to the magical appearance of Jackson, cold from working outdoors and ready for her to warm him. Tossing aside the book he forever carried, Thomas Affleck's *Cotton Plantation Record and Account Book*, he joined her in bed, reveling in the blend of their bodies. The action and thrill of their lovemaking was all the diversion she needed from her Shakespeare, Dickens, Wheatley, and Whitman.

Always sleepy after their tossing voyage to yet another undiscovered place, she struggled to stay awake, for that was when Jackson told her everything she wanted to hear. Lying in his arms, her small body cradled against his broad, muscular chest, Twilight felt more love and security than she'd ever thought possible.

"Stay here, in our warm utopia, darling. You're right, my parents were mean to you. There's no rush to try to make them happy. They'll move soon; then you can leave this room. Besides, it's freezing outside. I'll keep you safe, warm, and loved," Jackson would croon as if a lullaby. "This room is our Camelot, my dear Guinevere." Sometimes, as his fingers traced along her body, he'd softly say, "We are living in God's light, here in our Garden of Eden."

Each day, she asked Jackson if the enslaved were getting their wages for manumission. Each day, he said yes. Each day, she asked if their discussed improvements in clothing and meals for the enslaved were being made. Each day, he said yes. When she'd say she needed to get out of the room and see the conditions of the enslaved for herself, he'd say they were staying mostly in their homes for the winter, so there was really nothing or no one to see. She talked about her plans to start lessons when it was warmer. Jackson told her he was having a small cabin repaired to be a warm, welcoming schoolhouse. Each day, she asked about Spirit, saying she wanted to see her and that she missed her. Each day, he told her Spirit was in the best of care. He repeated between kisses, "Stay in the room; it is the best thing you can do right now. You'll be busy with the enslaved soon enough."

Thankful not to have to face his family, she buried herself in her beliefs that Jackson was doing all he could for the best interest of the captives and of her.

Occasionally, when Jackson was gone, Twilight gazed out the window to the river. The Mississippi was freezing in places, so river traffic would cease for a time. Out of habit, she pondered on the effect of the freeze on her father's packet line. She wondered if her father had ceased trafficking people. *I must write to him and ask.*

And she wondered in which river port Gallatin was stranded, awaiting the thaw so he could return to his beloved river.

One odd thing kept happening: soft rhythmic creaking sounded through the shared wall of the room next to theirs. The room was vacant—or was supposed to be. Then, very late one night, after hearing the creaking—*it must be a rocker on the old floorboards?*—Twilight heard the room's door opening and closing. She tried to wake Jack to ask him about it, but he only mumbled two words that sounded like "Grandma Ghost."

She lay awake for what seemed hours, listening. Then, she heard the door again. Finally, she slept. She dreamed of a total eclipse, but instead of it being a wondrous natural event, people shrieked and ran. Twilight reached out to those who raced past her, hoping to calm them, but upon seeing her, they screamed more loudly and pointed to where the sun once was; then, the people exploded into dust as the sun exploded around the moon. She woke, shaking, and moved closer to the stability of Jackson's body. The next morning, she told him that she'd had a nightmare, then asked him about "Grandma Ghost." He looked at her strangely and said, "What weirdness are you reading now? Hamlet?"

"Jack, where is your grandma buried?"

"She and grandfather are buried near the home they loved, Woodland Manor. We'll ride there together one day to pay our respects."

The rocking in the next room and Twilight's exploding-sun total eclipse nightmares continued.

On the first day of February, eight weeks after she'd retreated to their room, warm sunshine flooded the cove, signaling an early spring and, she decided, the end of their makeshift honeymoon. Twilight was tired of the room.

Wanting to meet the enslaved, missing Jed, and aching painfully to see Spirit, she ventured outdoors. Not sure where to find Spirit, she went looking for her brother, as Jackson had told her the direction of the overseers' cabin. Jed was there. Seeing him, she realized how profoundly she missed him. Then, she started missing Ember, Makeda-Angel, Jesse, her father, the packet line office—and the *North Star* pilot. Suddenly, she realized she missed her old life. Immediately, she shoved her emotions behind her creed that Jackson was her world now, and who could ask for more than the sensually sensational world of Jackson?

"Twilight! How wonderful to see you, Sis!" Jed hugged her. "I'd almost forgotten we lived at the same plantation. I never see you."

"You're so busy, Jed. Working day and night, Jackson tells me. You're different here. You don't seem like the same person."

"Odd," Jed said, squinting his eyes. "That's what I've been thinking about you."

"What do you mean? I'm no different."

"Of course you are, Twilight. You've transformed from a lioness into a cub."

"You mean I've lost my fight?" she said, thinking about Gallatin's advice to never lose her fight.

"Not exactly. I still wouldn't want to tangle with you about something you really care about. Maybe it's that your beliefs are changing. You, living on a plantation? You, retreating into your room for two months? That's not the Twilight I know. You seem to have accepted that I oversee two hundred enslaved laborers. I really can't believe it."

"Nonsense. I haven't accepted slavery. I'll never change on that point. They are working for their freedom. And, it's winter anyway, so most of the time the enslaved are keeping warm in their homes," she said. Jed looked confused. She considered for a moment, then added, "As a newly married woman, I redirected my passions for a time. I have been," she paused, "busy."

Either missing the point or not wanting to think about it, Jed pulled out two simple wooden chairs from the table, whacked a cloth against the seats to dust them, then said, "No matter. Please, Sis, sit down. What a terrible host I am, making you stand so long."

"Oh, Jed, Jack is wonderful, perfect. And love is—fantastic!" she said, wrapping her arms around herself.

"I'm glad you're a happily married woman. But tone it down a bit. You're making me want to have some of that marital joy, and I'm not married. Yet," Jed said, laughing now.

"Yet? Why, Jed, is there someone you're sweet on?"

"I have my plans."

"Yes? Do tell."

"James says I'm doing the best job ever done here. He says he would hate to lose me, but he knows my intention has always been to have my own place. I can't live much longer sharing this cabin with John. He drinks too much and stinks to high heaven."

"I know you, Jed, are a good and kind overseer. When it gets warmer, I will be starting a school. And, in five or six months, the enslaved will be free."

Jed studied her, then continued, "I'm moving to my own place and will share half of my profits with Jackson for a period of years as payment on my house and land. It's what I have to do, as Father would not allow me to use my inheritance for payment on a plantation."

"You're buying some of Jackson's land? Where are you building?"

"Not building. I'll be buying the fifty acres around Woodland Manor."

"Woodland Manor?" Twilight frowned. "Not building? Where will you live?"

Jed, smiling and bouncing to a stand, reminded Twilight of how she'd always thought of him and Jesse—as a couple of pups bounding about her. "Woodland Manor! I'll live at Woodland Manor. It's to be mine. They don't want it vacant any longer." He took her hands. "Twilight, soon my dream will come true! I'll own a plantation and be the master of my very own mansion."

"But Jackson's parents promised to move there."

"I guess they reconsidered."

"Jackson didn't tell me."

Jed dropped her hands and sat again at the table, now with a dejected look. "You *are* happy for me, Sis?"

"Oh, certainly, Jed. Certainly, I am, as long as you hire your laborers, when that day comes," she answered, rubbing his arm lightly, then patting it. "I'm just surprised. And not a bit happy that ole LaDonna and James will be living in the same house with us. I don't much like Victoria either, but she's only on a visit, so she'll be leaving soon."

"Not if I can help it."

"What do you mean, Jed?"

"I love that beautiful young woman. I want her to marry me."

Twilight began to fan her face with her gloved hand, then stopped abruptly when she realized the action as one of her mother's favorites, one that Twilight detested. "By the full moon, today is a day of news." Then, in the exaggerated drawl that Jackson enjoyed—and had insisted she employ during their honeymoon—she added, "Jackson just doesn't tell me a little ole thing." *Actually, Jackson has told me different things than I'm hearing from Jed. Maybe Jed has it wrong.*

"Well, Jackson doesn't know about my feelings for Victoria." Then stretching his legs in front of him and locking his fingers behind his head, Jed said, "But Miss Victoria knows my intentions."

"You've already spoken to her of them?"

"Yep. I have."

"And what did she say?" If Jed *was* going to Woodland Manor, at least he could take Victoria there and get her out of Magnolia Bay. Then she'd have to deal only with the two old people who, she thought with a mixture of guilt and relief, couldn't live forever.

"She said that she's in love with someone else and that she'll wait for him until the day she dies."

"By the full moon, Jed, don't you think you had better forget about her, then? I think that sounds rather final."

"She's just teasing me."

"Oh?"

"For one, there is not a beau for miles around. Besides, if he does exist, why hasn't he been calling on her? I certainly haven't seen any gentleman callers in my eight weeks here."

Twilight shrugged. "It's winter."

"Weather would never keep me from the woman I love."

"Spoken like a smitten man," Twilight said. "Maybe he's waiting for her in her hometown. She's here on a visit."

"Twilight, surely you know what 'visit' means on a plantation?"

Twilight was silent.

Jed said, "It means staying for a very long time. Even years. Miss Victoria has been visiting since she was twelve years old."

"Since the age of twelve? Jed, that means she has been here three years!"

He nodded.

"She could be here three more years?" Twilight said.

Jed nodded again, smiling, then said, "Or forever."

Chapter 22
Let God's Children Live Free

Tuesday, February 1, 1859
Afternoon
Magnolia Bay

Finding it difficult to believe that his ever-curious sister had never explored behind the mansion where the fields began, Jed went with her as she ventured there.

"I can't wait to see Spirit," Twilight said. "And I can't believe I haven't been to see her." *Jackson is amazing, but what the moon in Hades happened to me?*

"I can't believe it, either," Jed said. "You love that horse, almost as if she is half of you."

Twilight, holding back tears, became quiet and contemplative as they walked.

Along the back of the mansion ran a covered porch. Attached to the end of the porch was the cookhouse, a kitchen housed in a separate building from the main house but connected by the covered porch so that food could be carried into the dining room without exposure to much weather.

They walked past the smokehouse directly behind the kitchen. Immediately behind the smokehouse, the fields began, running for acres behind and to the south of the mansion. Bordering the east fields were stables, corrals, barns, and forest.

Stretching before them were the fields. Twilight was surprised to see captives working. Though it was a warmer day, it was still quite cold. Jackson had assured her the winter was too cold for the captives to work the fields and that they rarely left their homes. But they were there, whacking at the ground with heavy boards. What surprised her even more was that they all looked very young. She went closer to get a better look.

"They are all children and youths," she said to Jed, who'd walked up next to her. "Jed, they are all very young, probably my age to maybe six years old." She furrowed her brow in confusion and said, "Where are the older captives? Where are their parents?"

Jed didn't answer.

"What are they doing, Jed?"

"Cleaning up."

"Cleaning up what?"

"The cotton land. They are finishing the clearing of the stalks left from last year's crop. Because the weather is warmer now, they have to quickly chop down the last stalks before it warms even more. The colder it is, the better for this job. Cotton stalks break off easily when they are frozen. Those mornings when the ground was frozen, if you'd looked back here, you'd have seen them with those bludgeons knocking down the stalks, just as they are doing now. They've been hard at work all winter."

"What?" Twilight was confused. This was not at all what Jackson had told her.

Jed pointed to two Rich-tone men, carrying whips and walking with the young field workers. "Those are two of the drivers," Jed said. Then he pointed to a Pale man on a horse. "That's John Bratton, the other overseer and hopefully my not-for-long cabin mate." Chuckling, he added, "If I'm going to share a room with someone, I want it to be either Jesse or Victoria. Not John."

John Bratton called to an older youth several feet away who'd stopped and was wiping his forehead with his shirtsleeve. "Get going, Jeff, before God himself punishes you!" The young man ignored Bratton and stood for a moment. Bratton rode to the young man, then slashed him once with his whip. A driver also whipped the boy once. The young man fell to his knees and put his hands to his face.

Twilight clutched Jed's arm. "Do something, Jed. Do something!"

Jed assessed Twilight, cocking his head slightly. "Sis, you really have been hiding out. This is what we do."

Twilight stared daggers at her brother. Then, she ran to the atrocity, screaming, "Stop! Stop!" She reached to grab Bratton's hand. Bratton snarled and moved his horse against Twilight, pushing her to the ground. The whipped young man watched, then stood and returned to work.

Jed ran to Twilight as she stood. "*You* stop," he said. "This isn't your business."

"It *is* my business!" Twilight screamed. "This is why I am here. To stop this cruelty! I'm married to Jackson."

Gently, Jed said, "Go ask your husband just what that means."

"He told me. It means I can do whatever I wish."

"That's what he told you? You had better check with him again on that." Then nodding toward the field, he said, "As you can see, the whipped one is working even harder now. And all the Riches are singing."

Twilight did see. And heard. The youth who'd been abused sang loudly, "God's children must live free. Let God's children live free." The field of children worked, echoing the words in hypnotic, mournful voices. "God's children must live free. Let God's children live free."

On sang the singers. A deep voice leading with two hundred higher-pitched voices echoing as one. "God's people must live free. Let God's people live free." Their bodies a visual rhythm, they smacked the cotton stalks in unison, punctuating a beat to their vocal music. "God's people must live free. Let God's people live free."

Two hundred children. Working a field in the winter. Without parents. Twilight stood in disbelief.

Breaking into Twilight's shocked observation, Jed said, "We're good overseers, Twilight. We don't whip often. Just when we have to. And hardly do we whip the youngest ones. That particular dissident is Jafaan; we call him Jeff. Story is, he has always been trouble and just downright hard to break. Untamable. But he's nearly seventeen. He'll be sold then unless he turns out to be the winner."

"I cannot believe what I am seeing," Twilight said, eyes locked on the unforgiving scene. "Whipping children? Jed, are there only children enslaved here?"

Jed nodded.

"By the disappearing moon in Hades," she whispered. Then she said, "And what do you mean the winner? The winner of what?"

"The winner of freedom," Jed said.

"And how does one become the winner of freedom?"

"You'll see."

"They should all have freedom, Jed! They are *people*. And here, they are all *children*! There doesn't need to be a winner of whatever game you're being so secretive about. As you know, they all are buying their freedom with their wages. In July, all will be free."

Ignoring her, Jed said, "James has his reasons why he owns only children for field hands. He buys them when they are typically six. No younger. He sells them when they turn seventeen. If they don't know their birthday, we give them one."

Moving her eyes to glare at her brother, Twilight said, "That practice is over. Freedom for all this July. And I hope Victoria does marry you. You deserve her." She stalked away.

⇢⇢⇢ ⇠⇠⇠

As she headed for the corral, she muttered, "What am I doing here?" Spirit nickered the moment she neared. Running to the gate, she quickly unlatched it; Spirit, waiting for her, vigorously tossed her head and pawed the ground. They ran to each other. Twilight threw her arms around Spirit's neck. "Oh, Spirit, I've missed you. Why haven't I been to see you? Why?" She leaned into Spirit. Deeply, she cried. Then, she rubbed her companion's nose, singing quietly, "Soft is the velvet of a rose, but, my oh my, there's nothing, no nothing, softer than a horse's nose."

Twilight stepped back, then took a forward step and leaped. But for the first time in her life, mounting Spirit in her usual leap wasn't so easy to do, and she landed on her stomach across Spirit's back. Moving her right leg over and against Spirit's side, Twilight leaned and cried into her mane. "What has happened to me? Something dreadful has happened to me. I gave up everything I am to be Jackson's wife. He is so tender and wonderful. But he's been lying! I wandered away into Jackson Land. Now I am lost. Oh, Spirit." She wiped away her tears of baptism. She slid off Spirit and began brushing her. Wondrous Ring quietly hummed a melody.

After spending hours with Spirit, her thoughts, and the hum of Wondrous Ring, she kissed her horse's nose. "I don't want to leave you, Spirit, but I have to. I will visit and care for you every day." Spirit rubbed her nose against Twilight's face.

※※※

It was twilight. As she walked in the nightfall to the mansion, she saw a shadowy gray scene darker than the dusk. As fast as it had come, it was gone. It seemed the scene was showing ghostly figures of hanged dogs. Tears flooded her eyes. Shock, sadness, and fear gripped her. She sprinted to the trees, but thankfully, no pets were hanging from them. She stood shivering at the sinister plantation that was now her home.

From behind a tree, a rare antlered doe appeared. Her rich brown eyes searched Twilight. She walked closer. Twilight held her breath. The doe tilted her head, touching Twilight's forehead gently with the tip of her antler. Then she turned, flicking her white tail, and sauntered away.

"Wait," Twilight said, raising her hand, but the doe paid her no heed. Wondrous Ring glinted.

Confused by the appearance of the doe and sickened by the mirages and the realities, Twilight's mind was a blur when she entered the mansion through the back door.

⇝ ⇜

LaDonna and Victoria were waiting for her.

LaDonna grabbed Twilight's elbow and led her to the back parlor. July-May appeared and stood behind LaDonna's chair. Billy poured two cups of tea—one for LaDonna and one for Victoria—none for July-May or Twilight, then glanced at Twilight and left. LaDonna perched herself onto the chair, draped her arms on its arms, lifted her head, and appeared as a queen on her throne. Victoria, seated in a chair on LaDonna's right, said through smugly curled lips, "So, she decides to appear after two months in her room. Obviously, you have no desire to be a member of this fine family."

"Sit, Twilight," LaDonna commanded.

"I'll stand," Twilight said.

LaDonna shot Twilight a wicked look, then said, "Victoria and I heard about your disgusting outburst concerning that unruly captive Jeff."

Between gritted teeth, Twilight said, "Jafaan is a person. Further, he is a youth. He is sixteen. I've learned that besides Billy, July-May, the drivers, and an artisan, the two hundred enslaved people here are children. What the hades—no—what the hell!"

LaDonna gasped, putting her hand over her mouth. "Watch your mouth, young lady! Listen and learn—captives are captives; age doesn't matter."

"The enslaved are all children anyway, regardless of age," Victoria said. "They need us to care for them."

Twilight winced. "You love your brainless and cruel beliefs, don't you?" she said, looking at both women. "In fact, you are married to your brainless and cruel beliefs! The enslaved, of any age, have more maturity than any of their enslavers."

LaDonna said, "Twilight, dear, if you wish to remain Jackson's wife, you must learn to be a proper lady and mistress. *Never* speak in that manner to us. Furthermore, we must *never* hear of anything again like what you did today. What you did was disgraceful. And his name is Jeff." July-May punctuated each of LaDonna's sentences with her specialty, the gruff throat sound, sharp and deep.

"Just what do you mean, 'if I wish to remain Jackson's wife'? I am Jackson's wife, and nothing can change that."

Giggling, Victoria glanced at the carpet, then rolled her eyes upward to stare, grinning, at LaDonna.

"You are too confident, my dear," LaDonna said. "I don't know why you are so sure of yourself on so many things, but staying married to my son is one thing you cannot depend on. If he wants to dismiss you," LaDonna waved her handkerchief in the air, "he will." Placing the handkerchief back on her lap, she continued. "Here are the facts. Jackson may think that he loves you, but it is important to him that his wife supports his work." Pausing to take a dainty sip of her tea, then dabbing her lips with a napkin, LaDonna added, "You are a poor excuse for a wife. As his helpmate, you should be dependent, gentle, affectionate, pious, pure, nurturing, benevolent, and sacrificing."

"And subservient, devoted, sweet, and prudent," Victoria said, shifting her adoring stare from LaDonna to a disgusted stare at Twilight.

"You should never question your husband, nor should you bore him," LaDonna said. "You are to be ever available to him and never expect more from him than what he already gives you—a home, food, clothing, and children. He works hard to provide, and he must be respected for that. He is your lord and master. Remember that. Above all, you are to be silent in most matters, never speak of politics, never read novels, and you must be submissive. By being submissive, you ensure your husband's love and thereby ensure your security in life. This is a woman's existence and purpose."

After another dainty sip, LaDonna added, "My dear, it is the greatest privilege of all to be a woman, to give unselfishly to your husband, to his enslaved, and to his children. An unselfish woman is a virtuous woman. God smiles at selflessness and rewards us in Heaven. Others might fear death, but we look forward to it, for when we die, we are rewarded for dedicating our lives to our lords." July-May continued her punctuating gruffs. Though perfected so as to not distract from LaDonna's words, the gruffs were nonetheless annoying.

"Sounds like your life will begin at your death," Twilight said. "Let me guess. You two are devoted followers of *Godey's Lady's Book.*"

"Along with many practical books for female instruction in behavior, we enjoy the sensible views of that periodical," LaDonna said.

Inside, Twilight felt the glorious snap and burst of herself returning. "I use it to fuel my fire," she said, then walked toward the staircase.

"Twilight!"

Twilight turned to face her mother-in-law. LaDonna said, "Such spirit doesn't become a woman. So let me be clear, in case you think otherwise—you *will* be broken."

Twilight said, "I won't even bend."

Chapter 23
Gifts and Names

Late January to February 1, 1859
Memphis and Magnolia Bay

Ember was digging in the frozen garden and thinking how it surprised her that she missed Twilight.

She knew she liked Twilight, but her mind told her that Twilight couldn't be considered a friend. Yet, what Ember felt within her heart was, quite simply, that her friend was gone. Certainly, it wasn't the same as missing her own community of women friends with their sharing of joy when a sister fell in love or had a child, the sharing of grief when a sister's man was sold, beaten, or killed by the Pale and when a sister's child was sold by the Pale or became ill or died, the sharing of caring for the sister who'd been beaten and violated, the sharing of potions and spells for love, protection, and remedies, the sharing of tending to their children, the sharing of celebrating self, community, beliefs, and spirituality with storytelling, singing, dancing, shaking, chanting, drumming and gourd rattling in hidden spaces in the woods and near the river, and even their disagreements and spats. Ember missed those friends deeply, but not the plantation to which she had been chained.

And now, she was missing Twilight.

She pondered: *What do Twilight and I really share? True, even though I'm not considered or treated as such in America, we share being human.*

And true, we share being women, though, in America, how Twilight is viewed as a woman is superior to how I am viewed as a woman—I'm viewed as female, not really as a woman, except in my own community. For me, missing Twilight is a new feeling—that of missing being with someone with whom I have essentially nothing in common, but who, so far, has acted with a good heart.

Twilight wrote often to Ember. Her letters included her search for Menelik. When Twilight talked to Jackson about the neighboring planters and their enslaved, she did so strategically, to appear that she was merely interested. However, she was trying to glean from his answers if someone nearby had Menelik. So far, she'd provided three leads for Jesse and Ember to follow up on. They had, but none of the boys had been Menelik.

Whenever Ember received Twilight's letters, she carefully but swiftly pulled up the doe and tree seal. She asked Jesse to read the words that she hadn't yet learned, though she was learning quickly and would soon be able to read the letters entirely by herself. Twilight's intense enthusiasm for knowledge and for questioning everything, Ember realized as she pondered, was something they did share.

Twilight had told Ember about her own education. Living with her well-educated GrandMama and Grandfather and after learning how to read at age four, Twilight found no shortage of books for her to absorb, for they had an extensive library in their home. As well, two prominent teachers of the Evansville Female Seminary were their neighbors, so books were lent between the families. The teachers enjoyed talking with young Twilight and were sad to see the avid future pupil leave in 1854 at the age of twelve.

When Twilight had arrived in Memphis, her mother would have preferred that she be sent to a boarding school. But she had pleaded with her father to let her stay and learn about his business. Harley knew that there was nothing Twilight could learn at a boarding school, which would offer instruction for proper female behavior more than expanding the intellectual knowledge that Twilight already had amassed.

Harley and Twilight agreed that she was educated enough to be a teacher, rather than a student, at the public school, which allowed only Pale children aged six to sixteen as students. But, at twelve, she'd never be allowed to be a teacher. So, they decided that Twilight would not be sent to boarding school or public school and that she would continue her education independently by reading books and newspapers, which she did avidly. Gallatin contributed books for the Adams' library from his travels to the various Mississippi River ports and "acquired through other means," as he had once said.

"Ultimately," Twilight had said to Ember, "once one learns how to read, write, and work numbers, the most valuable aspects of education are reading widely and discussing with others educated opinions—opinions based on research, and opinions that might change when more facts are discovered."

Twilight had two copies of her prized book—*Poems on Various Subjects, Religious and Moral* by Phillis Wheatley. Wheatley, an expert poet, was the first American woman to earn a living by writing. She was the first American Rich-tone person and the second American woman to publish a book. Twilight cherished the copy passed down from Grand-Mama. Her second copy, she gave to Ember.

In the garden, Ember found what she'd been looking for—the twisted root of the black walnut tree that, Jesse had told her, the twins had cut down a few years before. Around the stump, a small root peaked through the ground. It was dry, and, with a rock, Ember could break it into the piece she wanted. Black walnut was perfect. She knew why the tree had been cut down before Jesse had explained the reason: while the tree's wood was beautiful and its nuts delicious, its roots were powerful, halting the intrusion of plants that grew too near. Black walnut protected itself.

Carefully, she dusted the dirt from the root that, twisted nearly in a knot, rather resembled a heart. She threaded a soft piece of twine through one of its spaces then tied it around her neck. She touched where the root lay. Perfect. Right at the base of her throat, where speech began. She would send this to Twilight with a letter she had written herself. As she removed the amulet necklace and slipped it into her pocket, she reflected on this gift for Twilight and also on her gift to herself—her growing ability to read and write.

By learning to read and write, she had found the key to unlock all locks. Even and especially the ones in her own mind.

In her room, Twilight opened the letters and the small package that had just been delivered from Memphis. She had a letter from Jesse, which she placed aside to read later. First, she opened the small package and pulled out a piece of beautiful root threaded with soft twine. The note that came with it was written by Ember, telling her the protective power of the root. Deeply moved, Twilight held Ember's gift to her heart.

Going to the mirror, she tied it around her neck; it lay against the base of her throat. This was more than a gift from Ember, which alone would make it special. This was an honor. With this, Ember was sharing with her some of her beliefs and heritage. Touching the root amulet, Twilight felt blessed. She said, "I will call you Precious Friend."

She took the organza bag of tiny stones from her pocket and spoke:

"Lapis lazuli—for receiving and speaking my truth. Black obsidian—for clarity and for protection. Rose quartz—for love, compassion, and for my quest of love to honor my Great-Great-GrandMama Rose. I will call you Power Gems."

She slipped the gems back into her pocket.

Then, she turned a chair to face the window so she could watch the Mississippi as she turned Wondrous Ring on her finger.

A cat appeared at the window. She'd seen him before, scampering around the yard. Solid deep gray except for four fluffy white paws, he looked like a shadow walking on four little clouds. He must have climbed up the vine that, even though it was not yet Spring, had been stretching quickly closer to her window. Cats—or mousers, as LaDonna called them—were forbidden in the mansion. Mousers had a specific purpose on the plantation, LaDonna said, so they were never to be loved.

Twilight opened the window and took the cat in her arms. His fur was as cool and sleek as frost. He purred at her touch. After closing the window, she settled back into the chair with the cat on her lap. He immediately became comfortable, closed his eyes, and purred loudly, as if announcing his good luck to the world.

"Shhh, shhh," Twilight laughed. "Don't let LaDonna know you are here, little boy. You and I both would be thrown out." She laughed again, then said, "Hmmm, actually, that might not be a bad idea. So, go ahead, purr away." He opened his large eyes and blinked slowly, lifted his chin to her, closed his eyes again, and settled into his purring. Twilight said, "I will call you Taboo."

Caressing the sleeping Taboo with one hand and touching the gift at her throat with the other, she contemplated as she watched the river. *I lost myself somewhere in loving Jack. Jed is right; I have mellowed. Frightfully so. But those days are over. It felt good to scream at that John Bratton, and it felt good to state my place with LaDonna and giggly Victoria. The worse part is, Jackson lied.*

Aloud to Taboo, she said, "Taboo, this is a thorn in my heart. I love loving Jackson. But he's a liar. Is anything he promised true? His lies were a ploy to get me here. In his bed. At this plantation—a plantation of enslaved children."

Footsteps in the hall stomped on her thoughts. "Sorry, Taboo," she said, sure Jackson would admonish her and possibly tell his mother about her adorable guest. Taboo blinked his large, sleepy eyes at her.

Quickly she opened the window and put him out on the vine just as Jack walked in. Turning from the window to Jackson, she said, "Jackson, there are some important issues we need to discuss."

"Can this wait until after supper? If we don't go down now, we'll be late."

"We're dining with your family?"

"Our family. And yes, it's time. I hear you visited with Jed. I think you are ready to visit with everyone. We'll talk after supper."

"Before we go, I'd better tell you that your mother and I had a bit of a disagreement today."

"What? Look, Twilight, I forbid you to argue with my mother. She's my mother, after all. You must learn to get along with everyone here."

"It wasn't my fault, Jack. She told me that if I didn't become her idea of a proper wife, I would lose you. Our marriage is none of her business. Nor is it her business how I act."

"Unless you act improperly."

"Improperly? Jack, what do you mean? You, of all people, know that I've never acted properly concerning what I believe, which almost always goes against what society teaches. So are you implying I must change now just because I am at Magnolia Bay? And what about you? You lied to me. Numerous times. That, mister, is improper! It is worse than improper!"

"Lied to you? What are you referring to?"

"You said the enslaved don't work the fields in the cold winter. And you didn't tell me that all the field laborers are children!"

He took her hands in his and smiled. "Darling, are you dreaming? I said they rarely leave their homes. They might do *some* field work in the winter, but they certainly don't work the fields during the winter months. And they are not all children."

She pulled her hands from his. "I saw them today with my own eyes, all children and youths, clearing the field of cotton stalks."

Jackson nodded. "Maybe your vision is the liar. I'm not lying. They are not all children. And today was the first day they went back into the fields because it was sunny and warm. They only worked the warmest part of the day today."

She didn't want Jackson to get angry at Jed, so she was hesitant to tell him what Jed had said. But, she knew she must: "I heard from an overseer that they worked all winter, even in the coldest months. That the freezing temperatures are best for breaking the stalks."

"What? My overseers wouldn't lie, so this is news to me! They worked this winter? They never work the fields in the winter. I don't know why, but John Bratton must have made them do it. I'll have a word with him to get this straightened out."

"Jack, you're so chilled when you come to our room on winter afternoons. I know you were working outside. How did you not see them?"

"Twilight, I was outside each afternoon taking care of Spirit. You didn't seem interested in seeing her, so I groomed and fed her, exercised her, and gave her water, which meant breaking the ice in the trough. I know how much you love that horse, so I would let no one touch her but me."

"I did want to see her, Jack. I said many times I wanted to see her. But you said she was getting excellent care, and it was best for me to stay in the room. I thought you wanted what was best for me in this new place with your unfriendly family, so I did what you said."

Jackson shook his head. "You said one time that you wanted to see her. That's all. Once. I do want the best for you. I cared for her each icy day."

"I said every day I wanted to see Spirit."

He caressed her cheek. "Darling, you said it once. Your mind is muddled due to the many recent changes you've experienced. It has been only a short time since you left Memphis. We needed these two months for us. Believe me, we'll never have that expanse of time again to enjoy one another, learn one another. It's going to get busy from here on. Spirit is fine. It has been only two months. I thought you would appreciate my efforts at ensuring we had this makeshift honeymoon together. If we had left home for a honeymoon, we would have been gone for the same amount of time, and neither of us could have cared for Spirit during that time. You wouldn't have seen Spirit, or the laborers, until now either way. A honeymoon is a honeymoon—couples take time away from life's routines. Please don't ruin our special two months together now with your unwarranted concerns roaming your confused mind. You haven't even thanked me for caring for your horse."

"Thank you." *His words make some sense, but they feel all twisty, too. I know I asked every day about Spirit and the enslaved. I know I did. Is it possible Jack is a constant liar? He loves me. I know he does. I need to sort this out—.*

"I love you, Twilight. I want the plantation to be successful, profitable. I've just begun to run it myself, and I want it to be noticed that I'm doing a good job. Can I have your support in that?"

"I'll support you in whatever you do if it is humane. So don't expect me to accept what I view as improper treatment of another human being. Your mother thinks she is the one who decides what is proper behavior? And she believes that beating human beings is proper behavior? I don't care what your mother says   beating and whipping someone is improper behavior. Even more than improper, it is wrong. And cruel. It's abuse."

"You saw a whipping today? Whipping is not allowed at Magnolia Bay."

"Your overseer said differently. And he confirmed they are all children."

"This is crazy! Bratton must be off his nut! Don't worry. I'll get this all straightened out."

Though she purposely avoided naming a name, Twilight realized that Jackson had to know it was Jed who'd informed her. But Jackson would be speaking with Bratton about all she'd heard. Twilight wondered how that would work out.

"Will you speak with your mother, too? That's what our confrontation was about. She agrees with the whipping. And she didn't deny it when I said all the captives were children."

"This is confusing. Mother doesn't agree with whipping. Yes, I'll talk with her, too. None of this is adding up. I'll get this figured out." Jackson put his arms around her and kissed her neck. "Have I answered your questions, darling?"

"I'm not sure. Listen, Jackson, I admit I was subdued for a couple of months, very subdued. But that's over," she said. "Twilight Adams is back."

He kissed her, then whispered, "God, you make me crazy."

Chapter 24
Canon Fire

Tuesday, February 1, 1859
Evening
Magnolia Bay

James, LaDonna, Victoria, and Jed sat quietly at the table, watching the newlyweds enter the dining room.

Billy served the meal. July-May, so obvious everywhere that she'd almost become invisible, stood in the corner.

"Billy told me you would be joining your family to dine. Finally! And then you arrive late to the table, having a pleasant time at our expense," LaDonna drawled. "We have waited so long that this fine meal is surely ice cold."

"We apologize, Mother," Jackson said, bowing. He pulled out Twilight's chair. After she was seated, he gave her a quick kiss on the cheek, then added, "Our apologies, everyone." He sat and gazed adoringly at Twilight.

"Twilight, what is that horrid thing on your neck? It looks similar to what some of the captives wear," LaDonna said.

Everyone looked at Twilight's neck. James grimaced. Twilight didn't answer, so LaDonna turned her attention to Victoria.

"Victoria, dear, please say grace," she said. "You always speak originally to our Lord in Heaven. We tire so of those memorized prayers of the pastor's, don't we, James?"

James grunted. "We go to church three times a year, and ole Reverend says the same words every time."

Nodding to Victoria, LaDonna said, "Please, dear."

After everyone had bowed their heads, Victoria spoke: "Thank you, Lord, for the morning light; Thank you, Lord, for the day so bright; Thank you, Lord, for men, our kings; Thank you, Lord, for all these things. Amen."

Suppressing her laughter, Twilight felt Jackson's knee knock lightly against hers under the table. She glanced over to see his smirk smother the laughter that pulled at his lips.

"You honor us, Victoria, with those words of pure poetry," LaDonna said with a look of rapture on her face. Then, turning her gaze, which faded rapidly into disgust, to Twilight, she said, "Speaking of 'kings,' haven't you heard, Twilight dear, that Cotton is King?"

Oh, no, around we go. Spreading her napkin on her lap, Twilight said, "My dear husband made me aware, when we first met, that I, though always an avid reader, could read even more widely." She smiled at Jackson. He kissed her hand. Turning her attention to LaDonna, Twilight continued, "Since then, I've been reading whatever I can, especially about what is happening in Washington concerning slavery. My understanding is that 'Cotton is King' is becoming a popular—even overused—phrase, ever since Senator Hammond of South Carolina used it last year in his speech to the United States Senate advocating that future states admitted to our nation should allow slavery. In this case, I think it was concerning Kansas. He also advocated the eminence of the South and its cotton production. It seems Hammond took the phrase "Cotton is king" from the title of an 1855 publication written by an unnamed author." Twilight looked inquiringly at Jackson.

Jackson said, "The first edition stated the unnamed author as 'An American.' A second edition carried the name of this 'American'—David

Christy. He's from a state in the North, I believe. The entire title is absurdly long."

James said, "We own a copy of that publication. It is authored by 'An American' because the publication's views are American views. We don't need a lecture from you, Twilight."

Twilight said, "So if one does not agree with the views of this 'American,' then one is un-American? That's preposterous. Are we to believe that, as a nation, we will always uphold economics—specifically economics that serve to make the wealthy even wealthier—above all other considerations? Over freedom? Over humane actions, treatment, and care? Over equality? Over education for everyone? Such thinking is against a democracy built on liberty. Such thinking is regressive."

"Regressive? The South is progressive. What is economically progressive is always right," James said. "The poor planters, the ones without enslaved laborers, which are most, don't care about education. They need their offspring in the fields, not in the classroom becoming the next Shakespeare or our illustrious Sir Walter Scott. They lead practical lives."

Trying to weigh her words, Twilight redirected the conversation toward logic. "It seems that new territories and states in the West are leaning toward not allowing slavery, thankfully. Still, Westward expansion has its crimes against humanity, such as forcing this land's first people from their homes where their families have lived for centuries, enslaving many, and killing many. And they lived here before anyone else did! Westward expansion, even past California to the Hawaiian Kingdom, oppresses immigrants from Asia, most of whom are from China, with terrible working conditions and paying next to nothing. Westward expansion means people who were once living in Mexico are now living in America; Mexican Americans, who are living where their families have lived for decades, sometimes even centuries, are also treated as if they don't belong. For those who believe that people with African heritage should return to Africa and that people with Asian heritage should return to Asia and that people with Mexican heritage should move away from their homes that used to be Mexico into what is now Mexico, what is their equivalent statement about this land's Indigenous people? That would mean they get back what we call America, all the way from the Pacific Ocean to the Atlantic Ocean. And what does this line of thinking mean for people of European heritage? It means Pale people should get back on boats and return to Europe."

James replied, "Bah! We Pales should not and would not return to Europe. The difference is that the others are not us. Pale men are superior, and our wives and children live under the protection and with the advantages and privileges of our superior status. We Pale men with Anglo-Saxon ancestors are the most superior. We are the pure-blooded pristine Pale of nobility. Even one drop of blood from any other heritage or class dilutes our blood. That is why a pristine Pale procreating with anyone other than another pristine Pale should never happen. If it does, the offspring are inferior. Skin tells us what is pristine and what is not."

James breathed deeply, puffed out his chest, then continued, "Twilight, so that you understand how the law of our land works, I'll explain. Of Pale men, there are two classes. First, the most superior are the pristine Pale—we noblemen. Second, the less superior are the peasant Pale. For this to be a great nation, it must be we pristine Pale men who are in charge. Everyone else is a laborer, inferior, and of the lower classes, which includes two groups. One, the peasant Pales with skin sullied by soil; and two, those with inferior blood that stains their skin in varying tones. Only pristine Pale men are supreme. We reign supreme. We are lords."

Twilight's revulsion at James's "law of our land" made her heart palpitate; she suddenly felt ill. With her wedding ring hand, she clutched the Power Gems in her pocket. Precious Friend warmed at her throat. She touched this special gift lightly with her right forefinger.

LaDonna looked toward the window as if to see a reason for the quick flash at Twilight's right hand. The sun was setting. "Close the curtains," she said. Billy complied. Turning her attention to Twilight, LaDonna said, "So, you seem to understand, Twilight, where the phrases originated that we so dearly adore here in the South—'King Cotton' and

'Cotton is King'—but you do not seem to understand the truth that cotton *is* King."

Twilight leaned over and took a few deep breaths. Clutching the Power Gems more tightly and concentrating on the amulet at the base of her neck, she sat straight, then answered, "I would not call cotton 'king,' but I understand that many believe cotton production is essential to economics, and I know that Southern cotton is exported worldwide."

"Then what is your distaste for our finest of Southern crops, and I might add, the crop that supports Magnolia Bay and puts food in your mouth, young lady?"

Twilight glanced at the food on her plate, which she had not even touched, as the attack on her began before she'd taken a bite. "To what exactly are you referring, Mrs. Canon?" she asked.

"You must refer to me as Lady Canon. And don't play naive, dear. You wear beautiful silks and linens. But Jackson told us you never wear cotton. We must assume it is because of your distaste for cotton," LaDonna said.

"My distaste is not for cotton," Twilight stated. "The forced, unpaid labor of the enslaved is what I find more than distasteful. Enslaving people is evil."

James jolted, sitting severely erect, as if a rifle barrel had been suddenly shoved up his spine. Jed rubbed his forehead. Jackson groaned. Victoria giggled. Unusually quiet, July-May didn't gruff. LaDonna smirked and said, "I see."

Why is James being so adamant and dramatic about this if he is now paying wages to the enslaved so they can buy their freedom? He hasn't mentioned the changes Jackson put in place. Twilight's heart skipped a beat. *Unless—*

With eyes nearly bugging out of his head, James strained toward Twilight, jabbing his fork in her direction, and shooting words. "Then just what are you doing here, girl? I won't have a child, an abolitionist girl at that, criticizing my livelihood. You eat my food. You sleep under my roof. Without labor by the enslaved, you would not have these fineries."

He smashed his fist on the table. "To Hell with not wearing cotton! That is nothing. Captives maintain this mansion. Captives serve your food. Captives clean your room. You might as well not eat this food, and you had better sleep outdoors!"

Interjecting, LaDonna said, "Our enslaved servants do most chores in the mansion. We could *not* manage without them." Billy entered with steaming bread, fresh from the oven. "James, as you expect," she added, smiling at her husband and reaching to hold his hand, "while Billy does serve our food, we do not allow any captive near food preparation and cooking—our hired Pale cooks do that. And we, the fine women of the mansion, do the gardening and many household duties."

James nodded, calming a bit at LaDonna's touch. He continued: "There must always be the poor and the enslaved who labor for those of us with wealth who pay them or provide their care. Just as Hammond stated in his speech of last year to the Senate that you referenced, the lower classes are necessary to do the work so the higher class, as leaders, can create a civilized world."

"His mud-sill theory," Twilight said. "Frightening."

"God decided what skin and what class a person is born in. You disagree with God's design?" James said.

Twilight merely looked at him. *How does one reply to such twisted, self-serving, inhumane statements? No doubt, James Canon is an Egoman—an Egomaniac—a leader of the Society of Supremacy.*

James continued: "God is a Pale man. We know this because his son, Jesus, was a Pale man. Pale men are closest to God; therefore, we deserve all legal rights. The Pale man is the only true person."

Jesus probably wasn't Pale and definitely was not James's definition of pristine Pale. But if I say that, a civil war will ignite right now at this table. Though revolted by James's corrupt reasoning, Twilight sat quietly, wishing the entire conversation would end.

James looked at LaDonna. She nodded. Turning to Twilight, he continued: "Women, as you do not seem to understand, are not men, so they are not in the line of being near God. Women are inferior. The

Pale woman is less inferior because she is under the control of her Pale husband or father, who is her lord. No woman is in God's line. Woman is in Eve's line, and as we all know, Eve was man's downfall. As are all women, whatever degree of tone or Pale. So, man must keep woman obedient because woman listens to the devil serpent, as Eve did in the garden. Under man's rule and tutelage, a woman is trained and her nature restrained so as to not be disobedient or a seductress. Being under a man's control is her salvation from her evil heritage and nature. Woman exists to help man and to breed. Women of the lower classes—from Rich-tone to peasant Pale and all in between—breed more laborers to serve the pristine Pale man and, by extension, his family. Because of him, his family benefits. Our country is built by people of many heritages who labor for America with little pay or with no pay. It is a system that works. Keeping them poor will eventually do away with many of the varying tone groups and the peasant Pale. That's fine, as we only need a certain number of those in the lower classes to labor for us. It's been calculated."

Taking a quick breath, he added, "For providing our country with laborers, the system of slavery—unpaid labor—works best. We take care of our enslaved, so they benefit because they, like our wives and children, do not need to worry about anything. Since they are provided with what they need, the enslaved population grows, and thus, labor without pay grows. That is good economically."

These statements of James's are immoral and horrific. I wish he'd stop talking!

Taking a deeper breath, James clasped his hands, then inverted and stretched them in front of him, cracking his knuckles. He continued: "What about the place of the pristine Pale woman? Though she herself is inferior, she bears superior Pale sons, elevating her status. Also, she bears Pale daughters, who then bear more superior Pale men. Like Jesus's mother, Mary. Mary existed to bear a superior Pale man—God."

James continued: "Jesus was born Jewish, but he became the first Christian, then started Christianity as the supreme religion. Pristine Pale men, such as we who own and rule the Southern plantations, are of

God's heritage. We are lords. The supreme religion is the Pale man's religion. Because we are noble and magnanimous, we share our religion and salvation with anyone, including women and all other inferiors."

Quickly, Twilight said, "His entire life, from birth to death, Jesus was Jewish. He didn't create Christianity."

"Jesus was the first Christian!" James yelled. "He was Christ; hence, his religion is Christian!" Imploringly, he tilted his face to the ceiling and said, "What is wrong with this child?"

Then he stared at Twilight and continued: "Woman was not created to have the rights of man. No woman was created to have the rights of any man within her tone group or Pale group, pristine or peasant. Woman was created to help man, serve man, create more men, and create more women who then serve men and create more men. That's how it is. That's how it goes. It's simple: you are born with the blood and into the skin—and thus the tone—and the male or female body you are born into. And that is God's decision. If you aren't happy with that, then talk to God about it. See where that gets you."

"Your diatribe is appalling," Twilight said.

James yelled: "If you do not honor God's plan, God's men, and the South's King Cotton, then leave my table! Leave my plantation! You're the disgrace of your family. You're a disgrace to the virtuous, genteel Southern lady! You mock the honor of the supreme Southern gentleman who provides for you and protects you! Your parents should have lashed you into submission! But it's not too late." His stare bore into her eyes. "I am your parent now."

"Calm yourself, dear," LaDonna said, patting her husband's arm.

"How can I be calm with that—that—girl at my table!" James shouted. "Jackson, control your wife! She's a child. Discipline her! If you don't, I will! I've never heard of any female acting in this manner! Muzzle and rein her! Lock her in her room!"

Muzzle and rein me? Lock me in my room? That'll never happen. James has lost his mind, if he ever had one.

"Father," Jackson said firmly. "As unusual as her behavior is, I feel she learned to be so from the unladylike women in the North, where she lived most of her life. And, though ladies should never state opinions on topics only for men, such as politics, Twilight is entitled to her beliefs. Still, I do agree, she should keep them to herself." Twilight's chest froze, then relaxed a bit as Jackson continued. "However, she is here at Magnolia Bay because she loves me. She has had to look away from some of her beliefs to be with me, for she knows of my devotion to you, Mother, and Magnolia Bay. She is to be commended for suppressing her wit so that the man she loves can entertain his."

Applauding lightly, LaDonna said, "Bravo, Son, well-delivered. But you admitted that Twilight does not want to be here. Don't you think that having her here, feeling as she does, will continue to put a strain on our happy home?"

"I know I am only an employee here," Jed said, "but I must say something. Twilight is a wonderful person. I love her very much. The world is made of all kinds, and we as Southerners must accept that there are some, unfortunately, who do not endorse our peculiar domestic institution." To LaDonna, he said, "Lady Canon, my sister was merely answering your question honestly. It might help to know this about your daughter-in-law: she is always honest, and her honesty may be blunt as the spine of a knife, but she is not malicious."

Surprised that he was taking a stand for her in the company of his employers, Twilight smiled, nodded approvingly at her brother, and said, "Thank you, Jed."

Chuckling, Jackson said, "I remember a time when her remarks could cut to the quick."

At the memory of her first two meetings with Jackson and how angry at him she'd been, she said, "I was outraged." Leaning near her husband and gently squeezing his arm, she added, "I did realize, afterward, my hypocrisy, thanks to you."

Jed continued, "Sister, I do think you misunderstand the importance of the South to the entire world."

"Oh?" Twilight replied, taking a sip of water and readying herself for the next round of word whipping and verbal firing balls.

Jed said, "Although the entire world may not endorse slavery in *word*—after all, it is the peculiar domestic institution of the South—it is true that the world does support and endorse slavery in *deed* by the mere fact that everyone buys our cotton. A lady in Britain and a lady in Boston might say slavery is immoral, but they certainly buy cotton, our cotton. The Northern states use huge quantities of cotton in their textile factories. They're all using cotton, our cotton. Thus, we have the truism that Cotton is King. We may not always like what our King stands for, but as King, we all need him."

"Right. Right. That's right," James said, nodding deeply.

"Jed," Twilight said, "when the United States of America won our freedom from the British monarchy, we vowed to never bow to another king. If what you are saying is true, then what we fought to win only eighty years ago, our freedom, is a sham. Because if what you are saying is true, then we all bow to the economy." Looking around the table, she said, "You all bow to the economy, to enslaving, and to a plant."

"Not just a plant," James boomed. "Cotton! Cotton!"

"Lest we forget, not everyone living in our thirteen colonies supported the revolution," Jed said. "Some prefer the traditional government, meaning people united under an authoritarian leader—even if that means he is a monarch. Or, if not a monarch in title, then a president who has the dictatorial characteristics of a monarch, a president who is essentially an unchecked tyrant."

Jackson, who had said very little, added, "There are still those who see the United States as, yes, a democracy, but are more comfortable with it being ruled, so to speak, by the strongest."

"You mean the wealthiest, don't you?" Twilight said.

"Of course. The ones owning the most Riches are the richest," James said. "We are the strongest and the fittest, which is why we are rich. And that is how a nation should be governed. By the richest, the strongest, the fittest."

"Who are the greediest," Twilight said. "Those who know how to get the votes, swaying a democracy to essentially an oligarchy."

"So? It works. The nation is strong because of the decisions made by the richest—men like me," James said.

Twilight said, "A popular stance in politics is that the Federal government should have limited decisions in individual rights. This would be wise *if* everyone had liberty, equal rights, and safety. Yet, the reality is that the Pale Males who are property owners and typically the only voters have all the rights. Where are the individual rights in that?"

"I've already stated, Miss Annoying-Know-It-All, no one other than the Pale man is a true individual. Our rights are individual rights because only we are individuals! Being superior, we know what is best for all. Don't you listen? Don't you understand?" James said.

Not sure where to begin to refute his multi-spiked anti-human scourging word whip, Twilight said, "Exploitation, Mr. Canon. Everything you've stated results in the exploitation of others—for your benefit, for the benefit of the men you deem to be supreme, those you call pristine Pale men. You and others like you don't care about anyone's rights but your own," Twilight said. "Everything you say is no more than an excuse to ensure that you and others like you will have all the rights, prosperity, and pursuits."

"Yes, Pale men have all the rights, prosperity, and pursuits. As we should. Because only we are people. We, the people, are superior," James said.

Twilight stopped her foot, the sound of frustration and resistance resounding from beneath the civilized appearance of the dining table. She said, "Not paying wages to the men, women, and children who ensure the production of cotton is an economic asset for plantation owners. Further, owning people is an economic asset for any enslaver. Profits are made from the selling of people that also defines American slavery."

"You think running a plantation is cheap?" James said. "There are processes! You think keeping enslaved laborers is cheap? We may not pay them, but we provide for them. We give them food and homes and clothes. And we buy them. I spent five hundred dollars for each captive I own, so I have invested at least one hundred thousand dollars to have enough laborers for my fields. Then another several thousand a year to keep them fed, clothed, and healthy. I ensure their needs. They cost fortunes! They have no worries. They've got it good."

They have no worries? They've got it good? Stunned at the lies James profusely spouted, Twilight sat silent, shaking inside.

"Don't feel too sorry for the Rich-tones, Twilight," Jed said. "They don't know any different. Most were born enslaved in America or in Africa, so what else do they know? Their parents or their grandparents in Africa were owned by other Africans. So if they'd been born in Africa, they might have been born enslaved. So what is the difference if they are enslaved here or enslaved in Africa? They likely would be captives no matter where they lived."

"That's an excuse—and unsubstantiated—to allow cruelty!" Twilight shouted.

"Shut up, girl!" James said. "Jed, I'll tell you what the difference is. They are better off being enslaved here in America than being enslaved in Africa. They've got a better life here. If it weren't for we enslavers of the grand South, they would never have known this great land."

"That's absurd!" Twilight yelled. "This is a great land only when you are free. And the promise of having one's feet on American soil is freedom."

"The Riches know no different, girl!" James yelled, pounding his fist on the table. "Don't you have ears? Their people were enslaved in Africa so they are enslaved here. They were born to be enslaved. They will always be enslaved. It's in their blood. It shows in their skin! Why do you think they're Rich-toned to begin with? It's the mark of Cain's curse. We enslave them to provide their protection and salvation. And food, clothing, shelter."

"That is ridiculous! What is wrong with you? No one should be enslaved. Anywhere. And certainly not in America," Twilight stated.

"Many die trying to obtain their freedom. But all are fighting for their freedom in some way, even if that means not fighting anyone at all, but staying alive one more day."

"Whose side are you on, girl!" James shouted. To Jackson, James said, "This girl of yours riles me."

LaDonna looked worried. "James, please calm yourself."

"I am on the side of freedom," Twilight said, "for every person."

"Every person does have freedom," James said. "Because only Pale men are people. Anyone else is not a person."

James leaned back in his chair and continued: "Women of any tone or Pale, rich or poor, are not truly people. That's why all women, like children, are owned by their superiors—men. You, like our enslaved, need us superior men. You, like our enslaved, need our protection and salvation. And, out of the goodness of our hearts, that's what we give you. Protection and salvation. And food, clothing, shelter. We are called fathers, guardians, husbands. Those words are niceties. The reality is—we are your lords. We are your masters. We own you. We own all of you."

"Wives, daughters, and the enslaved are owned for good reason," LaDonna said.

"Each individual who is not a Pale man *is* a person. I am a person," Twilight said.

"That's your opinion," James said. "You think everyone should believe as you do? Who are you to decide for everyone? You live in my home, the world I created. Without me, you can't survive. I make the decisions at Magnolia Bay. You are not a person to me, so you are not a person."

Feeling the gentle pressure as a kind caress at her throat from Ember's gift, Twilight stood and said, "Owning people is heinous. There is nothing you can say, no excuse you can give that can justify enslaving people. Slavery is an atrocity. It is evil. The truth of it is as simple as that." She stomped her foot. "From what you say, it is the practice and system of slavery, not cotton, that is king. From what you say, in America, ownership is king."

She stared at James, adding, "And, by the way—you don't speak for all men. Many men don't believe as you do." *Like Grandfather.* "Even some Southern men don't believe as you do." *Like Gallatin, my father, Jesse. They must be Champions.* "Many men aren't driven by your false yet dangerous beliefs of superiority, supremacy, and dominance. Maybe you and those like you"—*the Society of Supremacy*—"don't care about others, but many men do. And many women know we—meaning *all* girls and women—are not inferior." *I hope more Champion women and men realize who they are and come out of hiding to champion humanity, freedom, and equal rights.* Precious Friend warmed. "No one is inferior or superior. Just as each state in America is unique with rights protected under our created-equal stars and stripes, everyone our flag waves over is unique and should have freedom, equal rights, and humane treatment."

James, crimson with anger, glared at her.

Twilight said, "I'm leaving this firing squad of hypocrisy," just as James shouted, "Get her out of here!"

Chapter 25
Bedtime Conversation

Tuesday, February 1, 1859
Night
Magnolia Bay

Jackson, disturbed and agitated, ran his hands through his hair while watching Twilight with rising need.

Seeing her seated on the bed so terribly sad, desire overtook his conflict.

Twilight responded to what she thought was Jackson showing kindness. Afterward, Twilight snuggled in Jackson's arms and said, "Jack, we really must talk."

"What's on your mind, my Twilight?"

"Jack, you know what's on my mind."

"Dining was difficult," Jackson said. "I don't mind you questioning my father at times; it might be good for him, actually. But you two turned the dining table into a battleground."

"What he said was worse than horrid. And he didn't mention the changes—that he was paying wages to the enslaved and that they will be free within months. I don't think our changes are really happening."

Jackson said, "What? You doubt me, dearest? You are accusing me again of lying to you? I would never do that! Father was simply on one of his tirades—mouthing off a fierce stream of pro-slavery rationalizations that are impressed in his mind. He often behaves like that. He's made changes, though he won't admit it."

Twilight wanted to believe Jackson. But her mounting doubts were real.

He tightened his arms about her. "Darling, if only you could conform more, for harmony in the family—. And yet," he kissed her, "I find your defiant ways incredibly arousing."

Twilight gazed into his earthy blue eyes for a moment. "So you want me to stay as I am?"

Jackson didn't answer.

Kissing his lips lightly, Twilight pulled from his arms and sat up against the pillows. "Why did you marry me?"

"Because I love you."

"But why do you love me? I'm not like your family or your friends. I simply don't fit into your life."

"Fit?" Jackson laughed. "Honey, if I want something to fit, I'll buy riding boots."

"According to your father's definition of women, I am no more than riding boots. Well, a bit more than riding boots, I suppose. Maybe I'm almost as important as your horse, if your horse is a mare and produces offspring."

"My family will adjust. You're right and they're wrong. Eventually, they'll have to see that."

"I don't know. Traditionalists I've met think their beliefs are bolts from Heaven."

Eyes focused far away, Jackson said, "Traditional Southern blood truly is molten lead lightning." Looking at Twilight, he added, "But I see a new age coming, Twilight. People like you won't be so rare in the South. True, those of the Old South, such as my parents, will never see life as anything but cotton and captives. They will always revel in being enslavers. But there is awareness among the younger Southerners. Youth questions its heritage, and with all the anti-slavery rumblings in Congress, I think we'll see a gradual change in the attitudes of the South. And I think the gradual freeing of the enslaved through their earning of wages, as you and I are doing, will be an overall evolution in the South through the awareness of our younger generation. Further, if it's done gradually, it can be done without war, without killing."

Twilight thought Jackson's rationale made some sense. But everything seemed twisted. Quietly, she pulled the quilt around her, retreating into her thoughts.

Jackson gazed at his child bride, then at the quilt covering them. His finger traced the connecting triangular silk pieces that fit like a map, a chronology, and a heritage. He could remember his sisters wearing the dresses from which the cloth fragments came. It was an old quilt; July-May had pieced it together at night for at least two years when he was a young child. He would watch her work, and together they would play a game of "Whose dress was this?" He'd touch a silk piece and call out the sister's name. July-May would nod or frown to signal if his answer was correct or not. He kept score of his right answers. By the time the quilt was complete, he could call each of the five hundred pieces correctly. He'd chosen this quilt for the bed he shared with Twilight because it was made of silk, not cotton. And, now, he realized there was another reason. He'd been a happy boy, receiving much attention from his sisters. He was their young master. Lying each night next to Twilight, it could be too easy for him to forget who he was. This quilt reminded him. He could still call each of the five hundred pieces.

"If I move too quickly with reforms, Father will be displeased. Possibly he might take Magnolia Bay from me. Then how could I help anyone? Let me change things gradually so that Father can adjust. Just like our discussion concerning our nation, change should happen gradually."

"So you have made the primary changes—the enslaved are working for wages for manumission by July? They have good food and clothes? I will have a cabin schoolhouse?"

"I've told you. Yes. Yes. And yes." He turned on his side, then wrapped his arms around her, pulling her back to his body. He kissed her neck. "After supper, while you were preparing for bed, I talked with Bratton.

He said the captives did break the stalks during some winter days—because they wanted to. It is colder, but the freeze makes the job much easier. It was their choice to do it when it was less work."

Makes sense, I guess. "And the whipping?"

"Bratton should wear his trousers on his head; that would be more fitting," Jackson said.

Twilight laughed. "Very punny, Jack."

"Such an asshead sometimes. What he did was wrong. No more lashing. Ever," Jackson said.

"The driver did it, too."

"Only following Bratton's lead. Won't happen again."

But Jed said, "This is what we do." Though, he added that they don't whip often. I'll talk with Jed again. I think he's confused about his role here. They should not be whipping at all.

"Jack, they are all children. With no parents. That is so wrong. Why did you say they're not all children?"

"I didn't know. I asked Bratton about that, too. I discovered that was Father's doing in the last year. Remember, I was away on my Grand Tour for a year. While I was gone, Father turned this into a plantation of child captives. He kept the children he had, then bought two more for each older captive he sold."

Twilight tensed against his encircled arms.

Jackson continued, "We're right. Father is wrong. You need to help them plan for freedom in the South, Twilight. As children, once free, where will they go? It would be hard to reunite them with their parents. Their parents are enslaved somewhere, probably on someone's plantation, someone who isn't paying them wages for manumission. The children would become enslaved again if they chose to be with their parents. Here, they will be free within months. But if you don't have a good plan for them in place, they will be taken into slavery again by someone. No one can protect a child."

Closing her eyes, Twilight felt she was swimming in a sea of sickness. "I know you were away a year. But we've been here two months, Jack. How did you not know? Your father said nothing? You saw nothing?"

Jackson shrugged. Then he kissed her neck again. "I've been busy. My darling, we've been busy. You've been my focus."

"Focusing on me means focusing on my concerns. And my number one concern? No slavery on this plantation."

"I understand," Jackson said, kissing her shoulder.

Twilight squirmed. Then she turned to him. Speaking softly into his warm chest, she said, "I thought your parents were moving to Woodland Manor soon."

Jackson groaned.

"I'm happy for Jed, but not for us. I don't think I can live here with your parents. They want to lord and lady over us, Jack."

"Twilight, it's a mansion. There's plenty of room for us all to live here together."

"Does 'us all' include your cousin?"

"Victoria? Well, yes, of course. Victoria is always welcome."

"Obviously. She's been visiting for three years."

"That's not uncommon on a plantation."

Sitting up and pulling from Jackson's embrace, she said, "Three years, Jackson? I don't know if you realize this, but she's not leaving. She's waiting—for you."

"Waiting for me to do what?"

"To marry her."

"What?" Jackson laughed. "Twilight, you and I are married. Your imagination is going wild. You need to stop reading. Why don't you go for a ride on Spirit tomorrow? We have many lovely unfarmed acres where you can ride. You love to nearly fly bareback on that horse—something Memphis residents think is appalling but that I find very attractive." His arms tightened about her. "But never ride in the fields. Never. It is forbidden. Only my trained Tennessee Walkers know how to never trample the plants."

"I'm not joking, Jack. Victoria loves you. That is why she is here. Just how closely are you two related anyway?"

"She's my cousin."

"I know that. But how?"

"How? Let me think. It is something like this—her great-grandfather, Sharpie DeWitt Canon, and my great-uncle, George Davison Canon, were half-cousins. The fathers of Sharpie and George were half-brothers who had the same father but different mothers. I think."

"And you call her your cousin?"

"Yes. Why not?"

"By the full moon, Jack. I could be your cousin if we look that far back. You two are distant relatives. She's here because she wants you."

"And I want you," he said, pulling Twilight's bare body back to his, kissing her everywhere his lips could find.

In the middle of the night, Twilight heard a slight scraping. Sitting up, she saw that a piece of folded paper had been slid under their door. Near the fading fire, she opened it. In an awkward scrawl, one word was written: *Leave*

Probably from Victoria. Twilight started to throw it in the fire, then instead, placed it on a table. She walked to the window. On the grounds, in a ray of moonlight, stood a stark white figure. She wore a long white chemise. Her head was covered in what appeared to be white gauze. She was looking up at Twilight. Then, she walked away. Twilight shivered. Getting back in bed, she tried to wake Jack to ask him about it. He said in the slur of sleep, "Grandma Ghost."

The next morning, when she told him what had happened and what he'd said, he looked at her like she was spinning off her spindle. "Why would I say something strange like that? You need to get out of this room more," he said. "And I'll say it again, stop reading. It's ruining your mind."

Chapter 26

Warning Signs and Threat

Wednesday, February 2, 1859
Day and Night
Magnolia Bay

The next day, after finishing her designated household chores and caring for Spirit, Twilight rode her adored horse down the mansion lane and onto the road.

With Spirit's hooves lightly touching the ground, they explored the surrounding woods. It was lovely riding Spirit again in the beautiful countryside. But she missed the city. She was homesick. And she needed to talk with her father.

That night, Twilight said to Jackson, "I want to go to Memphis."

"Twilight, you've just emerged from this room after two months. You've contributed nothing to this plantation since your arrival. Finally, by doing your chores today, you're a giver, not a taker."

"A taker? That is not why I came to Magnolia Bay. I came to help."

"Exactly right."

"You told me to stay in our room for the two months, our makeshift honeymoon."

"I did. But that time is over, and you've just begun the real life of being my wife. A honeymoon is a fantasy. A plantation needs a mistress, which is what you are. Prove yourself first; earn your right to visit your family in Memphis," Jackson said, pushing himself to a sitting position in their bed. "You have your household chores. After chores, a mistress sews, reads her Bible, paints, plays the piano."

"I am not a plantation mistress. Oh, Jack, can't I go to Memphis? I miss my father and Jesse and Ember. I want to see the riverboats at the landing. I want to visit the Memphis Star Packet office and see my old desk."

"Twilight, you knew what you were leaving. Here, you can be important. You wanted to spend time with the enslaved. That is what you should do. What about your plans for their education?"

"Will that day ever come, Jack?" Leaning back against her pillow, she sighed. "Those plans won't work until you shorten their work day. I've been watching them. They're so busy. You said they barely work in the winter. But all I see is them working. They'll have no time for lessons in reading, writing, and numbers. You haven't even shown me the school cabin yet. You keep saying it is under repair and that you want to surprise me when it is finished."

"You're so impatient," Jackson said.

"Your favorite word has become 'gradually,'" Twilight said.

What she wasn't telling Jackson was that she wanted to go to Memphis to consult with her father on the issue of only children being enslaved at Magnolia Bay. She wondered if there was a law against a plantation run entirely on child labor. Due to her better sense, she had serious doubts about everything Jackson had told her. She was sure James would not free the children as Jack said he would. She had to find a way to make it happen. There were two hundred children, so finding homes for them all would take some doing. She thought her father and Jesse could find them homes with free Rich-tone people in Memphis and surrounding areas. She hoped Ember would help. But, if she wasn't careful, and if there were any questions asked of James, he'd probably buy a few adults. For him, the issue would be solved. But she would have jeopardized any hope of their manumission. She could write her father a letter, but she really wanted to hear his advice. Should she stay quiet and continue to follow Jackson's lead in the hope he hadn't lied about everything? Was that best for the enslaved? She wanted to talk to her father.

"I want to go to Memphis."

"No." With one quick motion, Jackson threw back the covers and rose from the bed. Naked, he walked to the window; placing his hands on each side of it, he leaned and gazed into the night.

"Well, then, I'll start spending time with the captive children, even if that means late into the night since they stop working at dark," she said, pounding the bed with her fist.

"Twilight," Jackson said, turning from the window to her. "You are a spoiled child. You'd be satisfied with plantation life if you gave me a son. Are your monthlies still on time?"

"Jackson! You're so blunt."

"Mother and I are wondering. You and I have spent much time in our bed and, yet, no child conceived? It seems strange."

Twilight left the bed, walked to the window, stood next to Jackson, and gazed out. Calmly she said, "You and your mother are discussing my monthlies? How humiliating. You're starting to sound like her. It's becoming rare that you speak like you. I've been wondering what has happened to my darling Jackson?" Her eyes searching the grounds, she said, "Where has that man I love gone?"

Jackson looked at her and took her hand. "If I didn't know otherwise, I'd say you're having your monthly now, making such an odd comment."

"Women don't start making odd comments when they have their monthlies, Jackson. Anyway, my comment wasn't odd. You don't seem like the same young man who courted me or spent a honeymoon with me. And why is it so strange that I carry no child? Maybe God doesn't want us to have a baby at this time."

"Mistresses are known for bearing many children. It keeps their lives full."

"I'll bet."

"Mother had six children, you know."

"I'm not your mother."

"I wish you were more like her."

"I know you love your mother, Jackson. But to me, you could not have said anything worse." She pulled her hand from his.

Jackson eyed her. "I'm going down for a smoke." He walked behind her, put his arms around her, then pressed his lower extremity to her bottom with a thrust. "Get used to plantation life—and conform," he said. Shoving again, he whispered, "To be continued." He released her, pulled on some pants and a smoking jacket, then walked barefoot out the door.

No way will I conform, Mr. Husband. And I don't like how you pressed yourself against me just now. Instead of doing that, why didn't you hold me and apologize for saying I should be like your mother?

A few minutes later, Taboo appeared at the window. Twilight opened the window and scooped Taboo into her arms, then heard a sound at the doorway. She turned. There was another folded paper on the floor. Reaching for it, she heard the quiet closing of the door to the adjoining room. Then she heard soft knocking through the wall. Placing Taboo on the bed, she opened the note. In the same script as the last note, one word was written: *Or*

She went to the room next door and knocked. She waited, but there was no answer. She pressed her ear to the door. There were no sounds. In the hallway, Billy appeared. "That room is empty," he said urgently.

"I hear sounds from this room, Billy."

"It is empty," he repeated.

They looked at one another for a moment. Twilight walked back to her room with Billy watching until she shut her door. She looked out the window, but no one was outside. She sat on the bed, cuddling Taboo. Then she reached into her pocket and held the Power Gems.

In the middle of the night, when Jack was snoring, she went to the window. She could see more clearly this time: there was the woman covered in white gauze, with a face so white it might have been powdered, looking up at her. As quietly as she could, to not wake anyone, Twilight hurried outside. No one was there.

When she returned to her room, another folded paper was waiting under the door. Opening it, she watched a feather fall from its folds—a Downy Woodpecker wing feather, black dappled with white. Twilight read in the same scrawl: *Die*

The three notes together: *Leave Or Die*

Chapter 27
The Rider

Wednesday, February 2, Night
To Friday, February 4, 1859, Afternoon
Magnolia Bay and the Road to Memphis

S omeone wanted her dead!

She didn't even bother trying to wake Jack. He'd only mumble "Grandma Ghost" then deny it in the morning. Who she was seeing was not a ghost. Twilight was sure of it. Especially if those poor hanged doggies she had seen were ghosts; they were shadowy gray figures, and fleeting. This woman in white had a solid look, and her face was stark white, not gray. It had to be Victoria. Was she entering the room next to theirs, making noises, and rocking in a rocking chair just to try to scare Twilight? And was she covering herself in white gauze and her face in white powder as a sick way to frighten Twilight into leaving? Victoria had to be off her spindle. Or brainless. Or just mean. Or all three. Twilight crawled back into bed and curled next to Jackson's warm broad body, which made her feel safe.

But later, she had a dream in which all was dark. She could see nothing. People were screaming all around her. She woke with a start, and a thought came to her: are the notes—*Leave Or Die*—a warning rather than a threat? If a warning, the woman wasn't Victoria. And why the lovely feather from the Downy Woodpecker? The woodpecker, which needs trees to thrive. The woodpecker, which persists with its noise.

The next afternoon, Twilight rode with care into the forbidden fields. When she could barely see the mansion's back porch, she felt she had entered a different world. In monotones, the enslaved sang loud and slow. John Bratton cracked his whip with ease across the backs of children. Nodding his approval over it all was Jackson.

As there were no cotton plants to accidentally trample, she raced Spirit back to the paddock. "Spirit, I feel furious and numb at the same time." Spirit shook her head and nickered. In her room, she held Taboo and said, "Taboo, I feel furious and numb at the same time." Taboo lifted his chin to her and said, "Mhrrr."

She spoke not a word at supper, then later in their room, she said to Jackson, "Jack, Bratton whipped them, the children. You were there."

"I forbade you to ride in the fields."

She glared at him. "There are no cotton plants yet. I harmed nothing going back there."

"You disobeyed. The result? You saw what you didn't want to see. That's the harm. Your disobedience is the problem. My rules are to protect you. Your obedience is essential for your bliss."

She said nothing.

"You know we don't want to lash the laborers on this plantation. It's not our way. We have better, kinder methods of ensuring captive compliance. But Bratton heard of unrest among captives at the Taylor plantation. Nothing serious, no revolt. Still, two Taylor laborers are missing. Running for freedom. Somehow word spreads quickly among captives between the plantations. The lashing is just to remind our laborers of their proper place. No one escapes Magnolia Bay."

"Are all your promises to me simply words with no meaning? Will the enslaved be freed by July? That's a year from when you said your father started paying them wages."

"You believed that? We'd be broke if we paid wages or freed them."

The love she once held for him lost all gravity and, without an anchor to keep it secure, slipped down and over the edge of her life, far away and deep into a void.

Later, in bed, she was relieved when Jackson turned his back to her. He said, "Not everything I said to you was simply words with no meaning." She didn't reply. They didn't touch each other the entire night. After all the joy of their union during the winter, she no longer wanted the liar to touch her. *Everything he promised must have been a ploy to get me to come to Magnolia Bay with him, to marry him, which he forced on me.* She couldn't sleep. She was floating in the too-familiar sea of sickness.

The next day, which was the fourth day since she'd left her room after her makeshift honeymoon, she wandered about the quarters of the captives. In the last three days, she'd seen the enslaved in their community of shanties from a distance, but she'd not entered their community until now. She found shocking the terrible conditions but was moved by the improvements the youths made with little time and materials. Above most doorways hung bundles of herbs or branches or roots. Behind each shack stretched a long, narrow garden. The sun shone warmly.

The long row of clapboard shacks stood tightly together. She counted forty, meaning five children shared one shack. Wide holes and thick cracks punctured the clapboard walls. After knocking on a few doors that were merely propped against the opening, and no one answering, she glanced in. What she saw in the small one-room shanties was that, despite the children's best efforts, their basic needs were not being met. The children had insufficient food, insufficient clothing, insufficient medicines, insufficient warmth, and insufferable living conditions. After hard labor in the fields—working longer than the farm animals were made to do, even in terrible weather—they returned to homes that were cramped, bare, and cold. She had no one to blame but herself for the dereliction of her promises to help the enslaved. She had believed Jackson, and that was naive.

In one home, she peeked around the broken door to see a baby lying on a cloth on the floor and kicking at a thick cloth atop him. Twilight knocked on the broken clapboard door. "Hello?" No one answered. Feeling awkward, as if she was trespassing, but also being pulled to the baby, she stepped inside the threshold, sat on the dirt floor, picked up the baby, and, tucking the cloth around him, held him close. He was only a few months old, yet, alert, he stared up at Twilight and started to whimper. Instinctively, Twilight placed her knuckle in his mouth for him to chew and suckle.

Suddenly, softly, Twilight began to cry. Closing her eyes, she saw herself in the middle of a wide river, swimming, swimming wildly for shore but getting nowhere. *How did I get here? How did they get here?* Opening her eyes, she saw the drafty shack and the tiny owned person in her arms. "How did we get here?" she whispered to him. After a few minutes, a girl about her age came to the door and, upon seeing Twilight, stopped, crossed her arms, and glared at her.

"Please excuse my intrusion," Twilight said.

The girl said nothing.

"I'm Twilight. What is your name?"

She said with a tone of disdain, "The Canons call me Nancy."

"May I ask, what is the name your mama gave you?"

"My name is Ifeoma. It is not Nancy. It will never be Nancy."

"Ifeoma, what is this child's name?"

"Jimmie. I found a root I cleaned off for him to suckle." Reaching for Jimmie, Ifeoma continued, "He's mine now, now that his mother—Jasmine, my twin sister—died after you sent her back too soon to the fields."

"I didn't send her back to the fields."

Ifeoma gruffed, reminding Twilight of July-May. "You didn't stop it," she said, taking Jimmie from Twilight. Jimmie made sweet baby sounds.

"No," Twilight said, shaking her head. "I didn't stop it. I didn't even know about Jasmine and Jimmie. Jimmie was born before I arrived. Is he about four months old?"

"Five."

"I'm so sorry your sister is gone."

"One way to be free," Ifeoma said.

I've got so much to learn. Addressing the baby, Twilight said in a singsong, "Hello, Jimmie, hello." Jimmie smiled. Ifeoma frowned. Twilight said goodbye and went outside. Shading her eyes with her hand, she searched the fields. All she saw, far away, were bending bodies. Whose hearts of those bending bodies were breaking? She knew the answer. All.

All hearts breaking.

All stomachs gnawing.

All muscles snapping.

All torsos shivering.

All backs blistering.

And she hadn't done a damn thing about it. Nor had Jackson.

The ocean of human bodies moved as waves to the command of the demanding man pale as the moon, always above everyone, even when unseen.

"I hate this place." Twilight scanned the fields again. *Listen to what you just said. Listen to yourself.* Letting her hand drop, she decided. She went to her room and stuffed her carpet bag, then she found Spirit, took two steps and leaped onto her back.

At the mansion lane, Twilight turned toward the road to Memphis. A flicker of white flashed at the window next to her bedroom, then disappeared. *Leave or die. Well, Grandma Ghost, if you're the one who wrote that, I'm leaving. There's just too much to be changed here. It's overflowing with meanness here. Nothing I do will make a difference. Jack won't let me do anything. He's been lying to me this whole time. I hate him. I hate being his wife. I hate living here.* Under the giant trees arching to lock limbs over the lane, they trotted to the main road, then galloped. Despite what Jackson said, she was going to Memphis. She would escape Magnolia Bay. Spirit's hooves reached into the air, moving them away from the plantation.

When they slowed to a trot, a strong sense jolted her—that what she was doing was wrong. Not because Jackson would fire off the Canon catch hound if she didn't go back. Terrifying, but not the reason. This was wrong because she felt that at Magnolia Bay she was needed. *Many* needs must be met, but I haven't even tried to help the enslaved yet. *I can do something about the lack of warmth, lack of clothes, lack of food, lack of medicine, and lack of education for the captive children. Besides, the enslaved can't just up and leave, so why should I? I have the resources in the mansion, so surely I can do something to help them. I am no older than many of them. We are children. We are kindred.*

Then, as if comprehending a poem, an epiphany entered her chest. *I need them.* They, stoic, endured. She, spoiled, received. Instead of running away, she needed to see her deluge of privileges against the drought inflicted on them. True, she was being treated terribly at Magnolia Bay. But they received not one drop of fairness, rights, respect, or humane treatment. The more she learned about their lives, the more she could do something about the injustices. *Awareness, GrandMama always said and had written in my letter, opens the heart's passage to Epiphany, Change, Freedom.*

Spirit stopped and stood stock-still. Twilight spoke aloud: "I hate Magnolia Bay, but hating doesn't have to mean running away. It can mean being brave and making changes. It can mean being one who loves in the wasteland of hate."

A breeze caressed her face with a soundless motion. Tiny tips of tender leaves peeked at her from a solitary tree standing straight as a sentry near her path. Moments broke like buds. Breathing deeply, she knew: *Now isn't the time to run like the doe. Like the tree, it's time to grow where I stand.* Yet, before heading back to Magnolia Bay and a life of slavery, she hesitated. Jackson's lies were the truth that scorched her love for him. His behavior had pushed her love over the edge to its death. Someday, when the captives were free, she would map the way to free herself from Jackson, from Magnolia Bay, from the place of no love. For now, she must return.

Behind her, she heard a horse approaching from the direction of Memphis. *What bad luck. I hope it's not someone who'll tell Jackson how far on the road to Memphis I am.* She turned off the road to hide in the woods. But it was too late. The horse began running and was upon her.

The instant she saw the rider, she knew without a doubt that marrying Jackson was worse than a mistake.

Chapter 28
Meeting

Friday, February 4, 1859
Afternoon
Off the Road to Memphis

"Gallatin," she whispered with released breath.

Spirit and Charger whinnied.

What she'd dammed for so long came rushing back with full force—the feeling that being with Gallatin was all she had ever really wanted. Nearly losing themselves in one another's eyes, Gallatin said, "Some things are eternal."

Then, cocking his head slightly and squinting, he said, "I didn't know if I should come. You told me you never wanted to see me again. I stayed away from the office when you were there and from your home for months. I got a feeling a few days ago that it was time to see you. After all these months, I went to your home. They told me you were at Magnolia Bay. I had to see you, so here I am."

"Gallatin. I am—I am married."

"I know. Harley told me today when I asked about you. He said he's worried. Let's dismount and talk."

"No. We can talk just fine, right where we are."

"Maybe you're right, because if I were nearer to you, I'd take you in my arms and never let you go."

"Oh, you'd let me go. Soon enough. Whenever it is time for you to return to the river, which will be tomorrow unless the *North Star* needs repairs or the water is low."

"Is that what this is all about? Is that why you said you never wanted to see me again? Because I won't leave the river?"

"You know that's the reason! Why else? And you were teasing me! You kissed me then said not to wait for you. That you probably wouldn't leave the river. You wanted me to have a dowry to entice someone to marry me. You might have well been kissing me then shooting me with the mate to my Deringer."

Gallatin shut his eyes, squeezing them together for a moment. Wiping his eyelids with the back of his gloved hand, he shook his head, then gazed at her with deep gentleness. "I boarded the *North Star* the morning after you said you never wanted to see me again and headed down the river, wishing every second that I would just jump off and swim back to you. But I thought I had time. I thought I could make it up to you after some time had passed and your anger had cooled. But when I went to your home to make things right between us, I found you were married." Taking a deep breath, Gallatin clenched his fist and asked, "Why did you marry? You feel it, what we have together. How could you marry anyone but me?"

"You don't want me to marry you! And you *told* me not to wait for you!"

"And you do whatever I tell you to do?"

"Not anymore."

Silence. Gallatin's expression was pained. "I didn't say I would never marry you. I said to not wait for me because we both have things to accomplish. I didn't mean you should write me out of your life completely and marry another man."

Twilight said, "Oh. Damn." After three broken heartbeats, she added, "By the odd moon. Well, actually, all of this is weird. *I* didn't marry Jackson. I came here for a visit, to decide if I could go through with the marriage. He forced me to marry him as soon as we got here. It was weirder than the Weird Sisters of *Macbeth*. I didn't like it, but I didn't know what to do. So, after, I tried to convince myself that I was fine with being married. What else could I have done? For a short while, I thought I was fine. But not anymore. I want out. And yet, now is not the time to get out."

"Did you sign the marriage document?"

"No, I didn't sign. I didn't say 'I do.' But I doubt that matters. The Canons are a powerful family. If Jackson says we are married, we are married."

Gallatin nodded, then said, "When I left Memphis today, I didn't know how I would find you; obviously, I couldn't just go to the mansion and ask for you. And if I did see you, I didn't know what I would say. But I had to try to get a glimpse of you, at least. And here you are, on the road, riding Spirit. It was meant for us to meet. Yet, you are married, newly married, so custom dictates I shouldn't say what my heart feels. But here we are alone, where no one can hear us. So, custom be damned. I love you. It's my fault you are with Jackson."

"Oh, Gallatin," Twilight shook her head.

"Why are you so far on the road to Memphis?"

Twilight rubbed her temples with her gloved fingers. "I was running away—running away from slavery. I don't belong on a plantation. And I was running away because Jackson lied to me. I was going back to Memphis for good."

"So. You were leaving Jackson. But now, you're headed back to him."

"Not to him. To Magnolia Bay. Gallatin, all of the enslaved laborers at Magnolia Bay are children."

"What the hell?" Gallatin said. "Slavery is evil no matter who is enslaved. But a plantation of only children?"

"Exactly. I mean, as we know, children are enslaved on all plantations. Many away from their parents. But at Magnolia Bay, of the enslaved, only the two drivers, one craftsman, and the two who work in the mansion—July-May and Billy—are adults. I left because I wanted out of this evil place. I want to see if Father knows of a way to free the children.

Then it occurred to me that the children could use a friend from the mansion. I'm needed there. I'm returning to help them. I want to be their friend, disguised as Jackson's wife. That way, hopefully, I can help. And also because I think I can learn from them, too. So, discreetly, because I don't want Jackson's father to retaliate, would you talk to Father about the situation?"

"Of course." After pulling the gloves from his hands, Gallatin dismounted and walked over to Twilight sitting above him on Spirit. He rubbed Spirit's nose and neck and whispered some words to her. Then, he placed both hands on Twilight's lower leg and rested his forehead on her skirt-covered knee. After a quiet moment passed, he looked up at her. He stepped back. Twilight glided from Spirit's back to land directly in front of him. Charger nickered. She reached to Charger and scratched his ears.

"Hello, Charger; I've missed you," she said, pressing her eyelids closed to dam her tears. Then, opening her eyes, she looked at Gallatin. It was true. This was real. Gallatin stood before her as her dream realized.

Charger and Spirit touched noses.

"Don't get angry with me," Gallatin said, placing his hands on her face. "Don't tell me to go away," he whispered in her ear, which he kissed. Gently he kissed her forehead, her eyelids, her nose, her chin. He placed his face next to hers, pressing his nose against hers, and breathed. "I want to breathe the same air you breathe." He touched where the ruffle of her blouse met her chin. "May I?" he whispered.

Twilight's chin lifted slightly, a cautious consent. He unbuttoned her blouse just enough to reveal the skin of her neck. Tenderly, he pushed her amulet necklace aside, then pressed his face into her neck and breathed deeply. "I want to breathe all of you—into me."

This felt like the only right thing she'd ever done. "This is wrong," she whispered, holding tightly onto him with her hands, her body rigid.

"What is wrong is that I didn't tell you sooner how deeply and thoroughly I love you before you had a chance to marry someone else. I even told you to not to wait for me, which you interpreted as me telling you to marry someone else." He pulled her closer to him. "I am the biggest fool God ever created."

"Yes, you are." She allowed herself to relax, then leaned onto his chest and said, "And so am I."

"Every time we part, it feels as if my soul is being ripped from me. And whenever I see you, I feel like I am together again. I came today hoping to find you alone so I could say these words: Come back with me, Twilight. Leave Jackson and marry me."

After finally hearing the words she'd longed to hear, and feeling caught in a desperate situation, she started to lightly cry.

"But I know now that you can't, in all good conscience, leave enslaved children if you think you can do something to help them and hopefully free them. Can you continue to live without me?"

Twilight didn't answer.

"I can't live without you. I will return. Hopefully, we can help the children. I'll talk with Harley. Do you have other thoughts on how to free them?"

"Not yet. Jackson had told me he was paying them wages so they could buy their manumission by July. That was our plan; it was my requirement for becoming his betrothed and visiting Magnolia Bay. But he just admitted that he isn't doing that. There must be a way to free them."

"After they are free, you'll come to me. We'll be together." Caressing her face, he tilted her head back slightly and searched her eyes. "Are you going to tell me to stay away again?"

"I can't do that."

"Where can I find you when I return?"

After thinking a moment, she said, "I'll be spending most of my time, after finishing my chores and caring for Spirit, at the quarters of the captives."

Gallatin pulled Twilight to him and held her as the moments drifted. Then he said, "I hate to leave you. But I've seen you, held you. That's more than I'd imagined would happen. Unless the Mississippi freezes, I'll be back in a month at the latest."

"Take care when you approach the plantation. There is a wicked tracker catch hound penned up always but will bark if someone gets near its pen. And Jasper, a sweet little dog loved by everyone, runs loose and 'sounds the alarm' for the plantation. Jasper barks at anyone or any sound different from Magnolia Bay. You never know where he might be. Watch for him so he doesn't alert anyone of your presence."

Gallatin lost his fingers in her hair, his left hand moving down her neck and along her back. Her hair ribbon loosed from its tenuous hold and fluttered on the soft wind. Gallatin caught it, then put it to his nose and lips. It was fragrant with the lavender scent of her hair. Looking at her, he kissed her ribbon. "A hair ribbon, Twilight?"

"Jackson insists that I tie my hair back with a ribbon."

"May I keep this?"

"Please do," she said.

Tucking the ribbon into his breast pocket, he kissed her forehead. He strode to Charger, then turned to face Twilight. He stared at her long and hard and said, "I'm going to miss you." Keeping his eyes on Twilight, he mounted Charger, tipped his hat, and joyfully smiled. Then he galloped away.

She watched until he was out of sight. She touched her lips. He hadn't kissed her mouth. She'd wanted that. And she knew he, too, had wanted that. But that would have pushed her over a line on which she was precariously balanced. Gallatin, kind sir that he always was, would not expect too much too soon: he would wait for her to choose to cross that line, or not.

Feeling her heart expand, she took two steps then leaped onto Spirit and headed for Magnolia Bay, feeling as though the sun had exploded and an eternity of cold surrounded her.

Chapter 29
The Fire Gathering of Girls

Friday, February 4, 1859
Evening and Night
Magnolia Bay

When the blooming-too-soon mansion magnolias loomed imposingly before her, Twilight's confusion heightened.

Because Jackson had lied to her—and since seeing Gallatin—she couldn't ignore the turmoil brewing like a twister inside her. She rode through the line of trees that arched to hang their heads over the entry road.

Then, in the dusk, she saw, for a fleeting moment, Magnolia Bay in decay and the children marching away. Then, a band of horses, led by Mystica and Spirit, raced across the sky. The shadowy sights went by so quickly that she wondered if she had merely imagined them. But no, she was sure she saw them, though faster than two blinks.

By the mysterious moon, what is happening to me? It must be my subtle gift GrandMama mentioned in her letter, but it isn't subtle, and it doesn't feel like a gift. GrandMama, where are the Wise Ones? Where are others in the Sisterhood of Gifts? The women here are all Deniers. And the men, without a doubt, are leaders of the oppressive Society of Supremacy and the Dominion of Men. Gallatin is a man of goodwill, a Champion—I know that must be true. Jesse, too. And Father. But where are the others? Why are weird things happening to me? And why must I be so alone, with no one to whom I can confide? Against Spirit's reins, Wondrous Ring flashed.

When she entered the mansion, Jackson was waiting for her. She said, "The magnolias are already blooming. Doesn't that seem strange?"

He eyed her carpet bag and her loose hair. "Why is your hair not tied back? Where is your hair ribbon?"

"It flew off when I was riding. That will always happen when Spirit and I nearly fly with the wind. Jack, you used to like my hair free. Now you insist I tie it back. I don't want to tie it back any longer."

"You'll tie back your hair. And never ride away from the grounds again," he said.

"You told me to ride Spirit."

"Not with a carpet bag. And not off our land. We own plenty of property for you to have a vigorous ride. I repeat, never ride away from the grounds. If you do, I will forbid you to ride Spirit."

"I am not your captive."

"That's exactly what you are, Twilight," Jackson said. "My captive."

With a toss of her head, Twilight retorted, "Ridiculous." Then, at the top of the stairs, she said to Jackson, "Make your bed in another room, mister." She went to her room to change for supper.

After supper, during which Twilight hadn't said a word nor eaten much, Jackson retired to the back parlor to smoke and talk with his father and Jed. LaDonna and Victoria were in the front parlor. July-May, forever her enslaver's sentry, stood with her hand on the back of LaDonna's chair. Twilight started up the steps to her room. Then, as unobserved as a ghost, July-May vanished from the room.

When Twilight reached the top of the stairs, she suddenly became curious as to what the family might be thinking about Jackson and her, so she decided to join LaDonna and Victoria—surely the women would pounce on the chance to comment about the obviously estranged newlyweds. There, Victoria sewed a sampler. LaDonna read aloud from the Bible, softly, so she wouldn't disturb the men in the adjoining room. Both women gave Twilight an odd look when she entered and took a seat near the open doorway, a vantage point for hearing what the men were discussing.

"We have a surprise, Victoria," LaDonna said. "Twilight has joined us. Would you like to needlepoint a sampler, Twilight?"

"No thank you."

LaDonna inhaled deeply, raising her torso abruptly. Then she resumed reading, a bit more loudly, passages about her house being overtaken by thieves, punctuating each word and looking at Twilight.

Purposely ignoring her mother-in-law, Twilight tapped her foot on the floor to the tune running through her mind, the popular Stephen Foster song entitled "Jeanie with the Light Brown Hair." LaDonna read a bit louder, then glared at Twilight. "Stop that!"

Twilight leaned nearer the open doorway to hear what the men were saying:

"The South will secede." *Jed*. "Congress simply is not giving us respect. It's more than the slavery issue. Though, why our peculiar institution should bother the Northern representatives, I can't say. As long as *they* don't own laborers and as long as *we* are providing the cotton, why should they care if *we* enslave our laborers or not?"

"We know that Cotton is King." *Jackson*. "And the North knows it, too. I don't think they will wage war even if we do secede. They need us. They may have the factories, but we have the crops *and* the laborers for the vast demand for our crops. In addition to the North's dependence on us, the British Empire needs us. As we are their major supplier of cotton, even above India, the United Kingdom will certainly support our cause in war. The North won't want to fight us *and* the British."

"You never know; Northerners are ignorant." *James*. "They think they are superior because they have factories and large cities. They see us as mere farmers. Bah! I'd invite any one of them to visit Magnolia Bay or any of the fabulous plantation estates we've built in the South. They'd see then that we are superior. Farmers! Bah! We are landowners of manors with expansive acreage, descendants of nobility. We are new world lords, earls, and thegns, carrying on the finest British traditions. Our sons take the Grand Tour and attend military academies. They have the talent and refinement of knights and cavaliers. They marry young ladies of fine aristocratic families."

A pause. Twilight imagined he was looking at his son with reproach.

"The poor planters who depend on our aid and all the peasant Pale look up to us, wishing they were us." *James continuing.* "They are the audience of our elite lives, which are the finest theater. Venerating us, they are loyal to the hierarchy, wanting to believe *our* world is *their* world—and calling it Southern pride. They would fight for *our* Southern cause, which, ironically, keeps them in their lowly place. But why not venerate us? We have the ancestors, horses, and foxhounds of the finest blood. While the entire country has golden fields of grain, only the South has white fields of gain. We have true gold—white gold, cotton. The North would be foolish to fight us. We are lords. To cotton, our king!"

You are bores. Twilight left the parlor. Grabbing a wrap from the hall tree and a lantern from a table in the foyer, she escaped into the quiet night. "I've had enough of Supremacy conceit for one evening," she mumbled, then walked toward the children's quarters. She knew they'd be awake, for they had much to do before dawn, when their field work would resume.

Candlelight and firelight flickered inside the shacks, their homes. The full moon brightened the night. Twilight walked behind the row of clapboard shacks. Many children sat in the darkness, adeptly sewing, washing, repairing tools, gardening, grinding corn for their noonday flatbread, attending to cuts or injuries, and applying mud on the holes of the clapboard homes.

Still feeling as if she were intruding, Twilight kept her distance as she walked through their community, saying "hello" to several children and youths as she passed. Hearing her approach, they looked up, and some stared briefly at her root amulet necklace, visible in her lantern light. Then they turned quickly back to their work.

She decided to walk a bit more before returning to the mansion. The moon was so bright she blew out her lantern. In the cool evening, she wrapped her shawl over her head and across her mouth. Only her eyes peered out. She must do something about how inadequately dressed the captives were for the chill in the night. She walked farther into the trees near the river. And then, in a clearing, she saw firelight. About thirty feet away, girls were gathered in a circle around the fire. They didn't notice their observer hidden by the trees.

Girls—chanting in hypnotic, magnetic tones. Girls—dancing in ways Twilight had never seen anyone dance, with a freedom of the self, as if releasing their bodies from bending all day, as if releasing their bodies from being captive. Exuberantly, girls danced, their bodies becoming a celebration. Thrilling music—drums with deep beats and gourds with shimmering sounds—rose up around them as the fire rose up in the heart of their vibrant circle. Instinctively, Twilight's foot tapped and her torso swayed. Hearing and feeling this music rushed her away into a new exhilaration.

In her life, while singing could be heard at any time, instrumental music was rare: stringed instruments and a piano in the homes of those who could afford them, some stringed and wind instruments and the piano at the dances, and the organ at the Episcopal church. But this! This music, with its repetitious beats and rich rhythms, shot her soul into the sky as if she were made of fireworks. Ecstasy engulfed her. In their enslaved lives that trapped them in a living hell, the dancing, singing, shaking and drumming girls created a numinous threshold and, at least for a while, crossed over it and set themselves free.

※※※※ ※※※※

July-May was extremely cautious. Lives depended on her reputation in the big house as being aloof to the children and completely dedicated to the destroyers, the Canons. So, she never took chances. What she did take—assiduously and only when no one would ever suspect—was food, cloth, medicines, and other provisions for her two hundred children. Her bundles of gifts were small but coveted—and greatly appreciated.

Some of her community of captive children were still alive due to her ability to sneak out what might help them to survive. Dividing her offerings fairly, she left no one out—each and every child received her care. So far, her attentive benevolence had ensured that not one of the few Pale-favor-seeking-snitches among her children had given away her secret to the destroyers.

July-May was extremely clever. Her entire purpose in winning the trust of the Pale on the plantation was to help her children. With each single-syllable gruff sound she made to emphasize LaDonna's statements, which she detested, she simultaneously sent a plea to any spiritual entity that might be listening to free her and her children from the destroyers. July-May expertly wore the mask of submissiveness and obedience and, thus, invisibility. She had mastered the art of stealth.

July-May was extremely caring and careful. But, being human, for the first time ever, on this night, she had been careless. She had seen Twilight go up the stairs. She had not been in the parlor when Twilight came back down and then left the big house, so she thought Twilight had stayed in her room, as was her after-supper practice. Usually, July-May didn't make assumptions. And even though Twilight only had been attending supper for four nights, July-May felt sure—due to how badly the girl was being treated by the destroyers—that her routine of retiring to her room early in the evenings was as set and unchanging as the opinions of Southerners on enslaving people. And, this night, there was a baby who urgently needed a blanket. July-May had found an old one, ripped and moth-eaten, that would not be missed.

Intent on her mission for the night, she didn't notice the tree-cloaked Twilight, who saw her furtively walking in the shadows to the shacks.

Chapter 30
The Voice

Friday, February 4, 1859, Night
Saturday, February 5, 1859, All Day
Magnolia Bay

Snuggled in her bed with the silk quilt piled around her and pillows bolstering her back, Twilight felt warm, cozy, protected, and not at all alone there without Jackson.

She held GrandMama's Bible. Her mind was brimming.

Tomorrow, first thing, I am getting the children more blankets, clothing, and food. She felt terrible she'd waited so long since her arrival to actually *do* something for them. But, she'd believed Jackson when he'd assured her that their agreed-upon improvements were happening. Further, she hadn't truly been herself for several weeks.

She, in her comfort, was thinking of the needs, terrible treatment and conditions the captives were forced to endure.

She was thinking of Jackson and his repeated lies.

She was thinking of how she'd believed him.

She was thinking of her meeting with Gallatin and how it was him, not Jackson, she ached to hold.

She was thinking of July-May and her secret that Twilight would forever keep: she'd seen July-May walking to the captive quarters, carrying a sack that was undoubtedly filled with basic necessities denied the children. Twilight smiled, incredibly impressed with the chameleon abilities of the sly woman. With her feigned devotion to LaDonna and punctuating gruffs to LaDonna's every word, July-May had fooled her. And undoubtedly had fooled the Canon family all these decades.

She was thinking of the stunning music, ecstatic dancing, enchanting singing, gorgeous stories, and lovely language of the young women and girls around the fire she'd witnessed that evening. She giggled, thinking of how, when she'd returned to her room, she tried to dance as they had, though she'd had trouble making her body move in that way. How lovely and fluid they looked; how awkward and erratic she looked. Maybe, with time and practice, she could dance with such freedom.

She thought again of how both Frederick Douglass and Sojourner Truth spoke boldly concerning rights for all, including women. The right to be seen as people first, not always less-than-the-man. The right to vote. Equal rights for all people. She was awed by the expansiveness of the passion of Douglass and Truth, their love for people being treated as people. And by how they both spoke of true equality after escaping the murderous bonds of enslavement. It was humbling to her, someone whose life was comparatively so easy.

Then her thoughts returned to the girls dancing, drumming, chanting, and telling stories. She had begun to realize that their language included special words and inflections for speaking only to each other, in ways the enslavers wouldn't understand, which also was an element of their identity and of their resistance against their oppressors. Each amazing person was contributing to resistance against their mistreatment. Enslaved and thus unable to speak out publicly as did Douglass or Truth, they achieved their resistance work where they were—and creatively. *What they do to resist and protect their identity shames my feeble efforts to work for justice for all.*

At the fire gathering of girls, she'd heard a delightful story about Cain being the first Pale man.

After a quick rap on the door, Jackson entered and sat on the side of the bed near her, smelling of tobacco. "Reading the Bible, Twilight? That's different."

"I am researching, reading the Cain and Abel story. Your father says the mark God put on Cain is being Rich-toned, making Cain the first Rich-tone person. But I'm sure you know that Rich-tone people have a different version. In their story, Adam, Eve, Cain, and Abel were Rich-tone. After killing Abel, Cain saw how angry God was about the murder, scaring him so much that he lost all color—and voilà, the first Pale man." Twilight laughed.

"That's not funny. It's blasphemous. Where did you hear such a story?"

"Why Jackson, it's a common story," Twilight said, thinking how, once, Jackson would have laughed with her in the enjoyment of this tale.

"I've never heard it. Anyway, I'm not here to talk about the origin of races. I want to talk about us, Twilight." Leaning close so that his mouth nearly touched hers, he said, "We need to be close like we were just days ago. We've been married a short time, and so soon we are fighting, and you are requesting we sleep in separate rooms."

Resting his cheek against hers and stroking her hair, he said, "My darling, I've loved you from the minute I saw you, guiding Spirit through that crowd in the square during the auction. I needed you in my life so much that I terminated my work with Forrest—in fact, that very hour. Remember, darling?"

Lightly rubbing his clean-shaven cheek against her cheek, he whispered, "You're every man's dream. But I'm the one who wanted you enough to marry you. I'm the one for you, Twilight." He kissed her neck. "No one could ever love you the way I do," he said between kisses moving along and down her throat. He said no more as his mouth found other interests. He grabbed the large Bible from her lap and flung it on the floor, then fully stretched atop her.

"No!" Twilight yelled, trying desperately to push him off her.

Jackson stopped. His eyes hot flames burning through her, he stood and said, "No other wife in the South would dare order her husband as you do. No other wife in the North would either, I'd wager. If I didn't love you so much, I'd hate you." Then he stalked from the room.

※※※

The next morning, Jackson entered, his eyes glinting as highly-polished knives. "I'm sick of your smug attitude, Twilight. You are my wife. It's your duty to lie with me. It's your duty to obey me. It's your duty to bear my children."

Twilight glared at him.

Smiling smugly, Jackson said, "You, like my enslaved, are my chattel, my rightful property. Don't ever forget it. I'll see you. Tonight." Then he strode from the room, slamming the door behind him.

※※※

That evening, LaDonna said to Jackson, who had just entered the parlor from his day of work, "I was telling James and Victoria earlier about the Gilberts."

"Yes, Mother? What about them?" Jackson replied in what Twilight considered to be a disgustingly attentive manner.

"It seems that their son and his wife have been married for two years, and she still bears no child. And she's nearly seventeen! Of course, they're all terribly upset, especially their poor daughter-in-law Helen. She so badly wishes to be a mother, and she's so ashamed that she's not a complete woman. Sometimes I think I can hear poor Helen's shrieking and weeping all the way from their mansion to ours."

"A shame, true," Jackson said, shaking his head. "Excuse me, Mother. I must make a few entries in the finances log before supper." Taking his mother's hand, he kissed it, then left the room, ignoring Twilight.

Ducking a bit, Twilight prayed that they wouldn't continue to speak of the private, personal matter of conceiving. But LaDonna did continue the topic of the poor childless Helen Gilbert. "Of course, we all know it's a woman's fault if a couple is childless, just as a woman is to blame if she can't bear a son. That was the cross I had to bear until our Jackson was born. I had five girls, can you imagine? Then, finally, Jackson came along. I was quite embarrassed producing only girls for so long. James was disappointed in me, and I was ashamed of myself. What a tragedy if a woman cannot bear her husband a son, but, of course, a worse tragedy if she bears him no children at all."

Nodding, Victoria said, "Blessed indeed is the woman who bears many sons."

"Though it took me a few tries before I produced a son, at least everyone knew I was a complete woman. Producing and carrying a child was never my problem, though they were all girls until Jackson." LaDonna laughed. "But girls can be a blessing, too, if they are like my daughters, or like you, Victoria."

Victoria blushed. "Thank you, Auntie LaDonna. You are as a mother to me."

Twilight stood, whispered, "Excuse me," then nearly bolted away, grabbing a wrap from the hall tree and escaping through the back door. *I bet I'm one of those women who can't carry a child.* The idea saddened her somewhat, for she wanted to have children someday to love just like her GrandMama had loved her. Yet, she was relieved that she wasn't with child. After all, she wasn't quite seventeen.

Even if that ole LaDonna thinks seventeen is the prime age to be a mother, it seems too young to me. There are plenty of women who marry older than sixteen. There is time, later, to be a mother. Anyway, the last thing I want is to be carrying Jackson's child. The way he spoke to me this morning confirms again what I know to be true—I no longer love him. And the terrible fact remained: being married to Jackson meant she was trapped forever at Magnolia Bay. That is, unless he'd grant her a divorce.

According to LaDonna, if Twilight continued to be herself—bold and rebellious—Jackson, someday, just might divorce her. She could only hope.

Suddenly, as she walked near the trees, she heard GrandMama's voice. It was a voice she heard within her, and not as a voice in her mind, but—there was no other way to describe it—a voice in and through her soul. GrandMama's voice said, "I named you Twilight because twilight is your time."

She whispered, "GrandMama?"

She listened and heard again, "I named you Twilight because twilight is your time."

Twilight whispered, "GrandMama. I hear you!" *Incredible! Am I finally hearing the language of the Sisterhood?* "What does that mean, GrandMama? That twilight is my time?"

And she heard, "Always at twilight, listen. It is twilight now. Listen. Listen as you did when you were a baby."

Twilight stopped walking, lifted her face to the night sky, and listened with her soul. Her heart swelled, and it seemed to radiate energy. At first, she experienced feelings she'd never known, sweeping feelings radiating large, as if she were vibrating into electricity. It seemed her heart had been a mere bud, and now it burst into full bloom, expansive in infinite petals of eternity.

And then she seemed to understand something larger about her world. Free-flowing words—coming from somewhere other than Grand-Mama—poured through her mind:

There are always people who rigorously follow the ancient, classical traditions of exclusivity and expect everyone to do so. Those traditions can be cruel. And then, some people challenge those traditions to create new ways with rights for all. But challengers never have an easy time of it. Yet, without them, there would be no progress in how to think, in how to care. In how to love.

A society based on dominance stays static until it falls.

Weapons warning! If the nation wars against itself, America will become armed to the blood-dripping incisors. Armed America, a threat to its citizens, will allow crimes against humanity with rampant murders by guns. No place in America will be safe.

Twilight, stay your course. You are a Challenger. You are a Champion of the Sisterhood of Gifts. If you get lost, look into the evening-budding sky and find yourself. Stay alert. Listen. Look for the Wise Ones, the doe, the tree. And remember, privilege can carry a lack of vision.

Then, silence settled her mind. Taking a deep breath, she lingered in the void of the clear, strong words of what she, at that moment, began to think of as the Voice. Looking for a map among the emerging stars, she began to understand the Voice as intuitive revelations—tiny lights that would coalesce to guide her as her own personal North Star, helping her to pilot her place in the swollen rivers of inequality and cruelty flooding all of America.

Chapter 31
Let Me Speak So I Can Fly

Saturday, February 5, 1859
Night
Magnolia Bay

While darkness settled, flickering stars sparkled their lights brightly above her as flitting fireflies wound their loving lights around her.

Though she sat on a patch of grass, most of the earth about her was bare, loose, soft, and smelled rich, enticing her to do the unthinkable—she removed her shoes and her stockings. Then, she worked her feet into the cool soil, covering them, and imagined she was a tree, drawing the life force from her grounded place, patiently expecting sun and rain. A silent hour passed. The night chilled, reminding her she was only human.

She brushed the earth from her feet, then pulled on her stockings and shoes, and reluctantly, stood. Silently she made her way to where the gathering had been the night before. But no one was there. She saw a fire farther away. Shying in the shadows and walking wistfully, she neared as close as she could without being discovered. Circling tonight's fire sat girls and boys.

Ifeoma, with Jimmie asleep on her lap, was speaking. "We can fly. We've forgotten our ancient, powerful language holding the words that can send us soaring." Then she dropped her voice to a whisper. "Someday, we will remember. Believe it. We can fly."

They sang. Jafaan led them in the refrain: "Let me speak so I can fly."

Melting to the ground, Twilight cried with all that had ever been inside her. She didn't try to stifle her tears or to cry quietly, because she couldn't. She knew she was being rude, intruding on their gathering with her extraordinary emotion, but these were forceful tears, persistent and unstoppable.

Finally, when her crying decided to cease, she wiped her eyes with her handkerchief; the children and youths around the fire silently watched her. Standing, she walked a bit wobbly to the circle, then said, "I apologize. I know I'm intruding. I won't tell anyone about your gatherings. I promise."

No one spoke.

Most looked at her; some looked away. Ifeoma glared. Jafaan glanced at Twilight. Did she detect a very slight smile?

As if on some mysterious cue, everyone stood and threw dirt on the dying fire. Gently, Ifeoma handed Jimmie to Jafaan, who cradled Jimmie against his chest with his left arm, then with his right hand, held Ifeoma's hand. Together, they headed to their shack, Ifeoma leaning her head on his arm. Then, they stopped, and Jafaan turned, asking Twilight, "How is your fine horse?"

Surprised, Twilight said, "She's wonderful, Jafaan. How do you know about my horse?"

"I cared for her in the two coldest winter months, each day before and after working the field. She's special."

"Oh. Oh, thank you, Jafaan," Twilight said, understanding that this was one more thing Jack had lied about, and something that made Jafaan dear to her. In addition to all of his other work, Jafaan had cared for her Spirit in the cold when she was being gullible and lounging in a soft bed. Those two months had been really odd and felt creepy to her now. She was pretty sure she'd had some kind of illness defining that time. Some sort of weird illness twisting up her mind.

When Twilight returned to the big house, she found Jackson draped over her bed in his dressing gown. She stopped in the doorway. Then, she retreated one step back into the hall.

"Twilight. It's late. What have you been doing? You missed supper. I want to tell you something. I spoke terribly to you this morning, and I'm sorry. I don't know what happens to me sometimes. We both need to think over our marriage, darling. I want you to want me back in this room, back in our bed. I could force you. It is my right. But I won't force you. I know you, my darling. If I return to our bed, you'll simply leave in the middle of the night and sleep elsewhere." He chuckled. "That's the way my girl behaves." He chuckled again. "So, I'll continue to sleep in the guest room across the hall until you ask me back. I hope it won't be too long." Then he left her room.

Chapter 32
Secrets, Sacred

March and April 1859
Magnolia Bay

In March, Twilight received a letter from, of all people, her sister Rachel, filled with a litany of complaints about "how strange Mother acts with the Rich-tone in the house."

The letter ended with shocking news: Sarah was getting married. Rachel announced she was coming to visit in June and that she, Jed, and Twilight would return to Memphis for the wedding in early July.

Oddly, Sarah, who Twilight thought would never marry, found a husband before Rachel had. Probably due to envy, Rachel didn't give any more information about Sarah's beau, but Twilight supposed it was the coppersmith brother she'd met at the ball the previous June.

Twirling about in her room, Twilight hugged the letter to her, for she'd be going to Memphis! She had to wait until July, but now she had a valid reason to go. Certainly, Jackson wouldn't stop her from attending her sister's wedding. Finally, she would see her father, Ember, Makeda-Angel, and Jesse! She'd be able to speak with her father in person about the possibility of freeing the children of Magnolia Bay. And the possibility of freeing herself from Jackson.

However, once again, she was starting to believe her life would not be as Gallatin claimed it would be—with him. He hadn't returned to see her as he so convincingly had promised. The river had frozen in places, but not around Memphis, so she didn't understand why Gallatin had lied to her. *Do all men lie? Certainly, Champion Men don't lie. And Gallatin, even if he doesn't know it, must be a Champion Man.* The awful ache of living with infrequent visits with Gallatin never lessened, but she was getting used to the longing.

What she couldn't get used to was living on a plantation. She didn't know how much longer she could last at Magnolia Bay—or as Jackson's wife—but she was also starting to believe her life there did hold purpose. In the evenings, she sewed by hand simple clothing for the children. She began adding straw and corn husks to the corncob stuffing in their mattresses. She bought blankets from a neighbor who handmade and delivered goods to Magnolia Bay. Jackson allowed her to purchase four blankets a month, but at that rate, it would take forever to get much-needed blankets to all of the enslaved. So, she resorted to something she thought she'd never do—sneaking into Jackson's room during the day to steal one dixie a week from his thick stash in the top drawer of his dresser—then making covert purchases from the enterprising neighbor.

As Spring warmed the earth and sky, and after completing her growing list of LaDonna-assigned household chores, she spent long hours visiting with and caring for Spirit. Sometimes at night, Jafaan would walk by, nod to Twilight, and say hello to Spirit. Spirit would neigh.

Afternoons, Twilight tended to her garden. From Ember's letters, she was learning about the riches of nature, the growth of plants, the healing properties of herbs, vegetables and flowers. She enjoyed simply observing the natural world, becoming adept at absorbing its messages:

> The industriousness of worms working the gardens. The internal intimate light of the firefly. The gentle flight of the butterfly. The soft touch of the ladybug. The invisibility of the walking stick. The hum of the June bug. The method of the bee. The dance of the dragonfly. The agility

of the grasshopper. The confidence of the praying mantis. The resilience of the beetle. The craftiness of the spider. The focus and strength of the ant.

She started to notice the mystical in all of ordinary life:

Tree leaves wave. Sunrises and sunsets gleam. The air and the earth smell sweet. Geese seek. Owls warn. Whippoorwills enchant. Patterns abound in flowers, in stars, in tree branches, in water fall and flow.

She learned lessons from every bird, insect, flower, tree, rock, and raindrop. Attentive, she sensed their currents, like the flow of the Mississippi, except this was the flow of everything together as one grand life river.

Often at twilight, she listened. As the canopy of dusk transformed into night, she heard nothing. The Voice remained silent. But her surroundings began to pulse with energy. On occasion, in the gloaming, she'd see fleeting bluish-gray mirages. They looked like vibrations in the air. Sometimes she could make out images—thankfully, none were disturbing. Still, they disappeared so quickly she couldn't quite grasp what she was being shown.

She spent so much time outdoors that she decided to wear trousers, donning a dress only for supper. Unencumbered, she moved through her day with more ease and breath; she found herself more productive in all her chores. Strangely, her new attire caused no stir with her husband or her in-laws.

She discovered why at supper one April evening. Always they spoke *about* her and never *with* her, as if she wasn't seated with them. She'd been relegated to the role of the audience of the family's one-act plays.

That April evening, which she thought of as "The Trousers Debate" play, the conversation went:

LaDonna: How lovely it is that Twilight is now wearing trousers and getting so much outdoor air. Good for the blood.

James: Reminds me of the days when the women rode in the fox hunts for their health. Restart the fox hunts soon, Jackson. And the jousting tournaments.

Victoria: I think Twilight looks ridiculous. Tomboy.

LaDonna: Oh, don't be mistaken, my dear. Twilight's not a tomboy. When a lady dons tomboy attire or hairstyle, she also dons a stricter attitude to the enslaved. More dominant, similar to the attitude of our fine Southern gentlemen. Sadly, this is not the case with Twilight.

Victoria: Well, then, if she's not going to *be* a tomboy, why does she dress like one?

Jackson: It's just trousers; wearing them aids her in outdoor work. At all other times, her attire is quite feminine.

Victoria: At least she's not wearing the horrid Bloomer costume—part dress, part children's clothes.

LaDonna: The fresh air and vigorous outdoor work she's getting in those trousers will help her breed strong Southern boys and also strong Southern girls, who will then breed more strong Southern boys.

Victoria: I'll have many strong Southern boys and girls without ever wearing trousers.

Many evenings, Twilight read GrandMama's letter, absorbing the words into her. Such strange concepts it held, and yet, those concepts were becoming more familiar with each read and with each day. Her mystical gifts seemed to have heightened at the place of captivity, Magnolia Bay.

One day, following Taboo's romp through the grounds and gardens, Twilight watched him vanish behind—no—*into* a wide oak. Rather, he vanished into what Twilight saw as a shadowy bluish mirage—it barely outlined the mildly-vibrating trunk as the branches and leaves shimmered with light. Circling the tree, Twilight couldn't spot him. And then, as if from nowhere, he leaped from the tree, landing at Twilight's feet.

She scooped him into her arms; his fur felt cool and silky. "Hey, little mister, where out of this world have you been?" Taboo jumped from her arms and scampered up the tree, looking at her from the lowest branch. She pressed her body next to the tree, her heart against the trunk, and she felt the current of her heartbeats in rhythm with a pulsing that emanated from the tree.

Closing her eyes, she thought of only the tree. Touching its trunk with her fingers, she suddenly understood that the tree held more wisdom than all the books in her father's library. "Tell me what you know, dear old wise one," she whispered, feeling as if she were falling into the tree, her body disappearing into the shadowy mirage that appeared thinly around it and into the tree itself. It was as if she were falling into tree mysteries, knowledge she couldn't articulate but filled her with ease. Then she knew: trees were GrandMama's Wise Ones.

Twilight learned more about plantation life, some of the history of Magnolia Bay, and some tales of the captives. From a fifteen-year-old named Ava, she learned "The Tale of Jafaan and Ava." They'd been found in the woods near Magnolia Bay two years before. The Canons thought they were siblings, though Jafaan and Ava never said they were. After about a week, James went to the field, thrust a whip into Jafaan's hands, and ordered him to be a driver. Jafaan dropped the whip, crossed his arms, and, though only a boy of fifteen, stood as solidly as an ancient oak. He said, "I will never drive any of my brothers and sisters." James picked up the whip and lashed young Jafaan with one mean crack. Then James said to Bratton, "Get him out in the field. He does good work there, leading them all in a work rhythm with his singing." Twilight knew that James cared only that the songs created a "work rhythm" and that the lyrics, always about the ache for freedom, meant nothing to him.

The children who shared a shack called themselves a family. Many families wanted pets, but that was forbidden. Twilight discovered from Jackson that, when found, the captives' dogs were hanged. *Those are the doggie ghosts I must have seen. How disturbing that the Canons kill them! I hate this place!* Regardless of the death threat to dogs that hung over Magnolia Bay, the previous year, a secret doggie had chosen a family of children as his own. Named Fearless by the family, he was loyal, loving, and smart. Fearless seemed to understand there was an imminent danger to his life if he were to be seen by certain people. So before dawn, he left his family and hid in the surrounding woods. At night, when no one threatening was around, Fearless trotted to the shack of his family and lovingly settled in with them for the night.

What no one on the plantation, captive or free, knew was that July-May and Billy cared for another wily night roamer—who the Canons intentionally blotted out of mind. Someone who, during the day, stayed "dead" and locked in the room adjoining Twilight's. Someone who rocked at night. Someone who'd slipped notes into Twilight's room, hoping the resplendent girl would understand the message.

Chapter 33
Secrets, Sacred and Profane

*Late Afternoon and
An Evening in April 1859
Magnolia Bay*

Often when visitors arrived and sometimes when captives left, the plantation's two dogs sounded the alarm, as Twilight had warned Gallatin.

The Canons permitted one dog—and only one—to be the plantation pet, Jasper. The other dog, the Cuban hound known only as the catch hound, stayed behind the overseers' cabin in a small fenced kennel area.

One late afternoon, walking nearby the kennel area, Twilight saw John Bratton order a young man named Zvi—whom the Canons called Steve—to run yards away and then up a tree as Bratton set loose the snarling, vicious catch hound. In horror, Twilight watched the cruel crazed creature snarl and growl, trying its best to scale the tree as Zvi climbed higher and higher into the branches. If the hell demon caught Zvi, it would kill him.

Finally, Bratton walked to the barking, scratching, jumping hound, spoke a word, threw it a morsel, the demon calmed, and he leashed it, taking it back to the kennel. Zvi remained in the tree. After a half hour, Zvi crept down the tree and ran back to the field.

Twilight gripped her stomach, panting in anxiety for Zvi. Sweating and nauseous, she ran deep into the woods. Among a dogwood patch, she saw a cabin. *Is this the cabin Jackson had, maybe once upon a time, intended for my schoolhouse?* But as soon as she'd wondered, she knew it couldn't be true. Jackson had told her, after she again refused him in her bed, that there had never been plans for a schoolhouse.

Twilight went to Jackson's room and asked him about the cabin. Not looking up from his account book, he answered that no one lived there, but "it has its purpose." When she asked about the vicious scene she'd witnessed, Jackson tore his gaze from his book and explained the training for track and attack:

"Bratton trains the hound, as he's done from the time it was a pup, in chasing, tracking, then attacking captives. Never does it see an enslaved laborer except for the training in track and attack. However, we never set the hound because we don't have to: no one escapes Magnolia Bay. Every enslaved laborer is part of the training, so they know better than to try it. The track and attack training is really a measure to keep the enslaved from leaving." He looked back to his accounts book. "That fact, as well as our threats-made-good that we'll sell their best friends or siblings if they try to leave, keeps them here." He looked at her. "No one escapes Magnolia Bay."

Agitated, she walked back to the cabin. When it was in view, she saw a girl run out the door. Twilight hid behind a tree to see who it was. The girl vomited, then sprinted away toward the shacks. Twilight recognized her—Ava! Then a man emerged and walked toward the big house. It was James.

What was James doing in that cabin? Why was Ava there?

The purpose of the cabin was a strike of lightning in a twisted night.

In the hurricane of anger rushing within her, Twilight suddenly understood that Jackson—and probably thousands of Southern Pale people—must have enslaved brothers and sisters. She wondered just how many sons James Canon really did have, though LaDonna had borne only one. And how many daughters did James have in actuality? More than five, no doubt. Cringing but furious, she thought of how James must keep some of his own children enslaved and working harder and longer than the plantation animals. Breathing deeply, she hurried up to her room. Pausing at her door, she turned and went across the hall to Jackson's room. Wearing a smoking jacket and still holding the accounts book, Jackson said, "Back so soon, my dear?"

She stepped inside. "Jack, I know the purpose of the empty cabin. And you do also, don't you?"

Nodding, he said, "Of course I know. Well?"

"Well? Doesn't the violence that happens in there bother you?"

Jackson's face was expressionless.

"Your father uses that cabin. Doesn't that bother you?"

"He bought those captives. They're his property. He can do with them what he wishes."

"Oh, Jackson. I know what you have been taught to believe. But think with your heart for a moment. What do *you* feel? How do *you* feel about girls being hurt? That's ra—"

Jackson put his hand on her mouth. "Don't use that disgusting word! Females are our property."

She pushed his hand off her mouth. "Oh! You make me so angry!" She stomped her foot. "What a sick mind you must have to think that everyone is your property and you can be as cruel to them as you want to be. I want an answer. What do *you* feel about the probability that you have brothers and sisters living out in those shacks, enslaved, working for you?"

"I don't have any brothers or sisters here."

"By the gibbous moon, then, Jack. Half-brothers or half-sisters."

"I don't have any half-brothers or half-sisters living here."

Puzzled, Twilight said, "You don't? But how? Surely over the years, at least one girl has borne a child of your father's."

"There have been eleven that I'm sure of, though Mother, appropriately, shows no awareness."

"Eleven?"

"Yes. Eleven. Four boys. Seven girls."

"Then where are they?"

"Soon after their births, Father sold them, along with their mothers. He made at least one hundred dollars for each child and much more for the mothers."

"What? I can't believe what I am hearing! And how does that make you feel?"

"My father can do whatever he pleases with his property."

"That isn't what I asked. I asked, 'How does that make you feel?' How do you feel, Jack, about your father doing that to girls, then selling the girls and his own children?"

"Twilight, it doesn't matter how I feel about it. It's an accepted custom. All masters do so. I'm sure all mistresses know of this natural occurrence."

"Natural occurrence?"

"Yes, that's right. Of course, it's never discussed. Plantation wives would never question or discuss it, for unlike you, they are proper Southern ladies, and they know it is a master's privilege."

With the glare of a noonday sun in the middle of July, Twilight said, "I hate you." Turning, she marched out of the room, slamming shut the door, wishing she could shake the entire plantation, wishing she could wake the entire nation.

※※※

After marching out of the mansion and to the river's edge, she saw Jafaan, with Jimmie cradled in a cloth sling against his chest, and Ifeoma fishing in the closing dusk. She went to them and stood quietly. Jafaan said, "You're troubled."

"I'm so troubled, Jafaan. About something that angers me so much I can't talk about it right now." They stood in silence. Then Twilight said, "What do you know about this plantation before James turned into one that enslaves only children?"

"Always, the Canons of Magnolia Bay have been enslavers of only children. Because of that, Magnolia Bay is notorious among Rich-tone people from the Gulf of Mexico into Canada. Jackson grew up among hundreds of enslaved children," Jafaan said.

Telling me that James changed to enslaving only children while Jackson was away on his Grand Tour was another lie. Her disgust for Jackson was surpassing bounds. "On a different matter, do you know anything about a ghost who wanders around the big house at night?"

Ifeoma turned her head away in her typical lack of acknowledgment of Twilight, but Jafaan kissed the top of Jimmie's head and replied, "We have our own ghosts, dead children from our community, but I've not seen or heard of a ghost of the big house."

Looking at her fishing line in the river, Ifeoma said, "There is a rumor about a Pale ghost."

"Yes?" Twilight asked.

"Just that one exists. That's all I know about the Pale ghost rumor. But I'll tell you a real story." Pulling a handful of dirt from her pocket, Ifeoma turned to look into Twilight's eyes and said, "This is from the grave of Jimmie's mother. Jasmine dances on her grave, then crumples atop it and weeps. I see her dancing and weeping for Jimmie. Dancing for the child she loves and weeping that she cannot hold him." She put the dirt back into her pocket and focused on her line.

Twilight blinked back a tear and asked, "Is she a white ghost or a gray ghost?"

Eyes steady on her line in the water, Ifeoma said, "She's a black ghost, of course; a beautiful black ghost. Jasmine's ghost shines the blackest, dimming the night around her."

In wonder at not only of what Ifeoma had said but that she had actually talked to her, Twilight stood, thoughtful. *Jasmine is not the one. I'm sure the one haunting me is not a ghost at all.*

Ifeoma said, "Don't even think of trying to find Jasmine's grave in some feeble attempt at honoring her or whatever you faded folk do to feel better about yourselves for the terrible treatment and deaths of the enslaved. We keep hidden the places where we bury our dead."

Shaking her head, Twilight whispered, "I won't." *That's the Ifeoma I know.* Twilight smiled. Then she said, "Jafaan and Ifeoma, I want to begin lessons in reading, writing, and numbers for whoever can take some moments from their chores once leaving the field."

Ifeoma turned to Twilight, put a hand on her hip, thrusting it forward, and said, "What do the big house people say to that idea?"

"Jackson's parents forbid teaching the captives," Twilight said, "but I'm ignoring them on legal grounds: in Tennessee, it's not illegal—as it is in several other Southern states—to provide education for the enslaved. But, I'll never speak of my plans with them. They won't know."

Dropping her hand off her hip and standing straight, Ifeoma said, "We don't need your help. We don't need help from any faded folk. We need our freedom. And a fair chance. We can do the rest."

"Don't you want to learn reading, writing, and numbers?"

Ifeoma made an exasperated, pushed-from-the-throat, sharp "awh" sound, then repeated, "I just said—didn't your faded ears hear me say it?—we don't need your help. Just give us our freedom. Until you do that, we have nothing to talk about." She set her fishing pole on the ground, took Jimmie from Jafaan, and walked away.

Ava, holding the hand of a nine-year-old girl named Glory, approached.

Oh, Ava. Twilight wanted to reach out to hug her, but she didn't.

Jafaan said, "Ifeoma thinks you can help us by staying out of our lives. But I say that we need food, clothing, bedding. You are helping us by getting those for us. You have been more helpful than the other big house faded folk."

Ava said, "We can use some books, too."

Twilight nodded. She was beginning to understand.

Chapter 34
Independence Day Plans

Wednesday, June 1, 1859
Afternoon to Evening
Magnolia Bay

June brought the arrival of longer days and of Rachel, who made the days even longer in Twilight's opinion.

Upon her arrival, Rachel chattered: "Twilight, your Lord Jackson has become even more charming! He's quite the prince! But you're certainly no princess. Who would *ever* have thought that all of this wonder would happen to you, a distasteful little snip who always does just what she pleases and rides astride, bareback—lands a mercy!—nearly flying on that horse! And now? Wearing trousers like a man? Appalling. I, for one, am certainly delighted to be a guest of Jackson's here at Magnolia Bay. I think I will call it Magnolia Bay Castle. Where is that enslaved servant? Billy Billy's his name?"

"His name is Billy."

Ignoring Twilight, Rachel continued, "I simply must have a tall, cool drink. My throat is quite parched from that dusty road. Oh, Billy Billy!"

Magnolia Bay hosted one barbecue a year, on July 4, to celebrate Independence Day with the Annual Freedom Games and the Freedom Barbecue and Ball. The Freedom Games included the Freedom Race, and while Twilight was glad one youth, the winner of the race, would gain manumission, she hated that it was a spectacle and that the children had to compete for freedom. Twilight didn't plan to attend any of it.

Upon hearing about the event, Rachel actually jumped for joy, giggling and clapping her hands. "Oh, barbecues! I've heard about the fancy barbecues the planters have. And a spectacle to watch! The Freedom Games! And there's always a ball after the barbecue. There is a ball afterward, Twilight?"

"That's what Jackson told me," Twilight said.

"My, my. This will most certainly be much more exciting than the dreary old dances we have in Memphis. Why, there's so much wealth here. So much nobility. I feel I must be in a dream. Or in Europe. Or both."

"You act so empty-headed, Rachel," Twilight said. "So I am sure you will catch several beaux at the barbecue."

"Oh, I will because I am pretty. And I'm fun, unlike you," Rachel said, pouting, batting her eyelashes, and jiggling her open fan.

"Save it," Twilight said, "for the barbecue and ball, where it will be appreciated and coveted."

Though she tried several times, Twilight could get very little useful information from Rachel about the family. The only interesting information that Rachel shared—on the second night after her arrival and in the parlor in front of LaDonna, Victoria, and July-May—was how strange Gallatin had acted when he'd docked at Memphis in February.

"You'd have thought his best friend had died. Why, when he heard you were married, I thought he was going to cry. You two always were so close, like brother and sister, that I surmised he was hurt because you didn't wait to get married when he could attend the wedding. But we told him that none of us were invited."

Obviously, Rachel hadn't even noticed Gallatin didn't visit for months. Typical. If something doesn't concern her, she doesn't notice.

LaDonna peered over her needlework at Twilight, as did Victoria. July-May seemed unconcerned; there was no gruff from her. "Who is this Gallatin?" LaDonna asked.

"A family friend," Twilight said. "He's worked for my father for years, piloting a riverboat." The fear that he had reconsidered his proposal to her grew each day as a consuming disease within and around her heart.

"If he is such a good friend, maybe he will come for a visit," LaDonna said.

"He's always on the riverboat," Twilight answered.

"He docks sometimes," Rachel said. "Sometimes for days."

"The *North Star* docks only overnight, Rachel. Rarely is it in port longer, just for repairs," Twilight said.

"We should invite him anyway. Surely he'll find time to visit his good friend," LaDonna said, emphasizing the words "good friend."

Twilight prayed to see Gallatin, but not at LaDonna's bidding.

Chapter 35
Freedom Games

Monday, July 4, 1859
Afternoon
Magnolia Bay

When the guests—planter families within five miles of Magnolia Bay—began arriving for the Independence Day celebration and Freedom Games, Rachel, nearly faint from excitement, fluttered her hand about her face for air.

Twilight, dressed in her trousers and work clothes, tried to find solace with Spirit. Jackson found her, and he was beaming with pride, for none of the neighboring planters had yet met his beautiful, very young wife. Also, he had special plans as, at this event, they were celebrating her June birthday.

On June 16, 1859, Twilight had turned seventeen years old.

"This day is a gift to you, in honor of your birthday and our marriage. You are stunning. I will be the envy of all my neighbors," he said. He took her hand and pulled her to her room, then took her bright blue silk dress and bonnet from her wardrobe. "Get out of those trousers and dress like the breathtaking lady you were when I met you."

If she refused, they would fight, and he would win. So, she complied, deciding she'd make herself scarce when the games began. When she appeared before Jackson, who was waiting outside the bedroom door, she wore lace gloves and carried an embroidered handkerchief, a blue silk parasol, and a blue silk fan.

"Don't flirt with that handkerchief or fan," Jackson teased—or warned?

"Of course not," she said.

Rachel, radiant and intent on luring suitors, flitted her fan about her face as she flitted about to meet everyone. Twilight, her hand on Jackson's arm so he could lead her in meeting all the planters in his niche of the county, caught her husband glancing frequently at Rachel. Between those glances, Jackson was busy introducing his bride. Beneath her smiles and her playing the part of the happy wife, Twilight repeatedly thought, *I feel like such a liar.*

Serving the free parents and children who reclined in shaded seats around the yard were five of the captive youths—three boys and two girls—all finely attired. "Jack, where did those clothes come from?"

"They aren't new. We keep those suits and dresses just for this occasion. They've lasted for years, so they are not proof that we can afford more clothes for two hundred captives. Get that thought out of your head," he said.

After the meal, Pale men sat on the long veranda, smoking, and the Pale women chatted under nearby trees as their Pale children ran around. Soon, the Pale families walked to the yard where the games would be played. Not wanting to be a part of any of it, Twilight strolled to the river, took off her bonnet, and stood near the bank, watching the Mississippi flow, enjoying its serenity, and starting to feel its pull, the magnetism so attractive to Gallatin.

Freeing her curls from a ribbon, she combed her fingers through her hair, letting it billow in the breeze that clipped over the river. The sun hovered hot.

"Twilight—" A man's voice. Turning, she saw a handsome man of about forty standing near her. "—is such a lovely part of the day, don't you think, miss? But twilight is elusive, passing by so quickly. I try to see the sun as it sets on the river whenever I can, and being here at Magnolia

Bay is the perfect chance to do so. I'll return to this spot at twilight. I hope to find you here to enjoy the scene with me."

With a laugh, Twilight said, "We haven't met, have we? I am Mrs. Canon. But my given name is Twilight. I thought you were addressing me."

A broad smile lifted his black mustache. "This is the magnificent moment of our meeting. I wish to know better such a becoming young woman with such a wonderfully unusual name." Bowing, he said, "I am Clairmont McCay, owner of Ivy Falls and enslaver of fifty. May I escort you back, Mrs. Canon? The games are about to begin." McCay touched Twilight's elbow. "Or, perhaps you should walk first to the mansion. I'll follow later."

Pulling her arm from McCay's touch, Twilight said, "We've done nothing wrong, sir. We've simply met and have barely spoken. I'm sorry that I didn't meet you earlier at the barbecue with my husband."

"I arrived within the last hour, met a few young ladies blossoming under trees, went to the stuffy veranda of men, left the stuffy veranda of men, and came here for some fresh air," he said, smiling at her, "which I found." He paused momentarily, then added, "Please say nothing to your husband, but I truly am sorry that you are married, for you certainly are the loveliest creature at this event."

"You are bold to say so, sir. Apparently, you've not met my sister Rachel or my husband's cousin Victoria. Both are unmarried and, I'm sure, much more in keeping with your fancies," Twilight said, hiding her fan and handkerchief in the folds of her dress to not appear flirtatious.

"I did meet them, but I am bold, and I daresay you are more beautiful than both of those women together. You are stunning, dazzling, enchanting, bewitching—"

"I'm a married woman," Twilight said, interrupting his list of adjectives cast as creepy lures. "I'm sure my husband is wondering where I am. Good afternoon." She hurried up the slope and toward the big house.

In leaps, McCay was upon her, grabbing her arm and tugging her next to him. "I certainly forget my manners when you are about," he said, panting, and not from the short sprint to catch her. "You entrance me. I want your company, madam. If you ever wish a secret liaison—"

"Sir!" Twilight exclaimed. "Remove your hand." McCay complied but leered at her.

She hurried ahead of him and found Jackson talking with his father. Seeing McCay trailing Twilight, James squinted his eyes, shook his head, and clicked his tongue. "Do something, Son," he said.

Taking Twilight's elbow, Jackson led her to the games.

Forming a wide circle, the adults sat. Those who were, as James designated, the peasant Pale sat on blankets. The adults of James's designation as pristine Pale nobility—the richest—sat on chairs. Jed stood at the "front" of the circle, where the Magnolia Bay Lord and Lady sat on their high-backed Victorian chairs brought from the mansion. Jackson led Twilight to two chairs next to James, LaDonna, Victoria, and Rachel. Inside the circle, at the far end, the Pale planter children and the Rich-tone captive children were standing in a horizontal line, all facing Jed. He cracked his whip. Twilight winced.

Children ran, finding potatoes lying in the grass, picking up as many as they could hold or stuff into pockets, if they had pockets, or carry in aprons, if they had aprons. Thus, the clothes worn by the Pale planter children meant more potatoes. Regardless, all children smiled as they found the hidden treasures that would mean a meal. There were only two skirmishes over the last potatoes. After this game ended, the Rich-tone children carried their bounties to their shacks. The Pale planter children carried theirs to their parents.

Soon, again near the far end of the circle, planter children and captive children gathered, laughing as they put themselves inside large burlap sacks. Jed cracked the whip. Children hopped, laughing, falling, standing, hopping again, falling, standing, hopping. Hats from Pale heads flew; the captives had no hats. The Pale audience laughed, clapped, and shouted as children hopped past Jed's outstretched arm. Jed, laughing, called, "Every child wins this game! You all can keep your burlap sack! You will find many uses for it! Now, for our next game!"

The games continued with a handkerchief hanging outside the back of each boy's trousers and girls running to pull as many "tails" as they could, getting to keep the handkerchiefs for sewing clothes or other needs.

The games continued as children threw bags filled with beans and sewn shut toward Jed. The winners were the ones whose bean bags landed closest to Jed, though none came closer than several feet from him. The winners got to keep the bags of beans, providing more much-needed food.

The games continued as children, a small board atop each head, walked carefully toward Jed. The three who got the farthest before their boards fell were the winners, keeping the boards to cover holes in the walls of their homes or for other household repairs.

The games continued with the two tallest children holding the ends of a broomstick, and the other children bending backward, hopping under the stick. The youngest children won this game, their laughter loud when the youngest five each got a bag of cornmeal.

The time came for the final game—the three-legged race. Children gathered in twos, tying their legs together with two knitted scarves per duo. Because there were many more children enslaved at Magnolia Bay than Pale planter children visiting, mostly Rich-tone legs were tied together. However, a few Pale children and Rich-tone children gravitated to each other. They tied their Rich-tone legs and Pale legs together. Leaning to Twilight, Jackson said, "Friends. They get to see each other at this event every year."

Jed called, "The winners of the three-legged race are the two who work best as one! Ready. Set. Go!" Each duo ran, and, as Jed had called, those who couldn't keep their tied legs working as one, fell. First-place, second-place, and third-place winners kept the knitted scarves that tied their legs. In the winter, the scarves would be better than gold.

The prizes benefitted the enslaved children more than the Pale planter children. However, the six families—whom James called, behind their backs, the "peasant Pales, sullied serfs, low-class Pale chaff packs"—hid their thrill at the sight of the potatoes, burlap sacks, handkerchiefs, beans, boards, cornmeal, and knitted scarves their children brought to them.

The remaining four families—whom James called, to their faces and publicly, the "planter aristocracy, the nobles, the pristine Pales"—might let their children keep the prizes to play with or, sometimes, gave them to the six less fortunate Pale planter families, or, rarely, to an enslaved child.

Then Jackson stood and announced, "Congratulations to all of our winners here today. All children certainly had a joyous time! After a break, we will commence with the Freedom Races. Today—Independence Day—one lucky enslaved youth will win his independence! Within weeks after winning today, that youth will leave the hallowed land of Magnolia Bay, holding freedom papers!"

Clapping filled the air. Twilight knew the applause was not that freedom would be won but instead for the spectacle of the race.

Standing, Twilight said to Jackson, "I'm not going to watch."

"My dear, you won't have to."

Twilight turned to go.

"Put on your beloved trousers."

"What?"

"You won't have to watch because you'll not be a spectator."

"I understand. So what does that have to do with my trousers? I'm dressed for the ball."

Jackson smiled. "You don't understand, it seems."

"By the full moon, Jack. You can't be thinking—"

"You turned seventeen, my dear. You spend more time with the enslaved than with me. You are in the race today."

At first, Twilight glared at him. *He can't be serious. By the full Hades moon.* Then, she felt Wondrous Ring warm, and she said, "Good! We should all experience something of the humiliating life you impose on the captives. I wish I could win so that I could be free from Magnolia Bay and from you, my twisted husband. But even if I could win, which I am sure is impossible, I'd not take that place from one enslaved child."

Jackson smiled and nodded. "That's right. Freedom from me is not for you. But there are other incentives for you to do your best in the race. Change into your trousers and return here if you know what's good for you."

※※※ ※※※

When Twilight returned in trousers, several women planters gasped. Most laughed. The men whistled. One yelled, "Jackson! You know how to rule your roost!"

She joined the other children who'd turned seventeen—Sally, Alfred, Hank, and Jafaan—who were waiting at the fenced race field that once had been the area for jousting tournaments and a hunter-jumper obstacle course used to train horses for fox hunts.

John Bratton was seated at a table, taking bets on the winner. Hands down, the bets were on the two strongest-looking boys—Hank and Jafaan—with the bets leaning more toward Jeff, as they called Jafaan. A planter called out to Jackson, "This isn't fair! None of the captives will beat your girl for fear of the lashes! She can't be strong or fast enough to win! But she will win! None will take their chance at beating her! We'll all have to bet on her!"

Jackson paced for a moment, then called out an announcement: "Twilight will not race with the captives. She will race on her own. Make your bets on the child you think will win freedom!"

The racers were studying the obstacle course. They could see the white cloth flags tied to sticks in the ground that showed the circular route. It stretched about 350 feet. They were to maneuver the route of hedges, jumping fences, incline boards, rock walls, and a long jousting list field divided down the middle with the tilt rail. The route then disappeared into the forest, where, the racers were told, white flags would mark the way, circling back into the open, over two more rock walls, then finally, through a pond. The finish line was the same as the starting line.

Jed walked to Twilight. "I won't watch this, you racing. It's wrong."

"Why, Jed? Because you're seeing me humiliated?" Twilight said. "Why is my running any different than the captives having to race for a chance at freedom?"

Jed looked at her with a softness in his eyes she hadn't seen in a while. "I love you," he said, then walked to Jackson. "I won't start this race," he said, then walked toward his cabin.

Jackson nodded to one of the drivers, who walked to the front of the obstacle course.

Without looking at the driver, Twilight walked to stand eight feet in front of him.

Jackson faced the spectators and announced: "Women must learn their place. Since my spirited wife enjoys trousers more than gowns, I've decided that today, she'll get her wish and wear her trousers. And she will celebrate her seventeenth birthday by demonstrating her skill in obedience." He turned to Twilight, speaking loudly, "You'll have an incentive to go as fast as possible. If you obtain the goal by finishing before I shoot my pistol at the seventeen-minute mark, you will be saving something important to you. And you must vow to never disobey your husband again."

The onlookers clapped.

Twilight had no idea what Jackson was referring to—the saving of something important to her—but, like the enslaved, she had to face whatever was before her.

With the crack of the driver's whip, Twilight was running, following the white flags of the obstacle course. She scrambled over or through hedges, crawled under jumping fences, and leaped, in what appeared to be near flight, from incline boards to balance atop stone walls, jumped down, raced down the jousting list field, and circled around trees in the forest. The onlookers, at times gasping, walked and sprinted to follow her progress.

And then, just inside the forest, twelve feet above her on the limb of an old tree, stood Taboo, crying in a terrified howl. A short rope tied to his neck was also tied to the branch. If he tried to climb down, the rope would tighten on his neck. If he fell, he would hang, breaking his neck or strangling to death. Below the branch was Bratton with a pole, ready to push Taboo.

For a split second, Twilight stopped in horror. Then she screamed and ran with full force, bumping into Bratton, pulling the pole from his hand, and smacking his head with it. From somewhere long forgotten, a knowledge filled her: like a cat, she scrambled up the tree and onto the limb, balancing perfectly, pulling Taboo to her. She untied the rope from the branch, but the knot was too tight to get off his neck and still finish the race before Jackson shot his pistol to announce her time was up. If she didn't finish the race in time, who knew what Jackson might do?

Holding tight to Taboo, she leaped from the limb. The spectators screamed. Jackson fell to his knees. Twilight glided, landing softly next to Bratton stretched on the ground, moaning and holding his head. Hugging Taboo to her, she ran, then leaped, gliding over the last two rock walls. The onlookers gasped at her ability to accomplish what seemed to be impossible.

Her last task was through the pond. With Taboo protectively cupped in her hands and high above her head, she waded in. It was shallow enough to walk most of its length, but when the water reached her chin, she kicked her legs, moving across the pond like a swan gliding. Taboo screeched and, unable to claw, bit her hands. Remaining steady, she walked the last few feet out of the water and lowered her arms to cradle Taboo, the rope trailing them, moving past Jackson.

Jackson shot the gun into the air.

Twilight had won. Just barely, but still, her win. She knelt to untie the knot on the rope around Taboo's neck. The knot had tightened, and she couldn't loosen it. Taboo was yowling and wriggling, making it impossible for her to get the rope off him. She concentrated, and as if by magic, the knot slackened. She untied it and pulled the rope off Taboo.

Holding him close, she walked to the big house. She heard Jackson call, "You won. This time. Now, clean up, put on your gown, and meet me to dance."

She was happy to not watch the enslaved run the course. But, after running it, she suspected something—maybe some of the captives, like her, had tree-climbing, leaping, gliding, swimming, or similar abilities, unknown or unremembered until direly needed.

She suspected something else—while the obstacle course provided entertainment for cruel people, during full moon late nights it might also be serving as a training ground for escape by the freedom champions.

Chapter 36
Dance with Stale Mate

Monday, July 4, 1859
Evening and Night
Magnolia Bay

Upon the entrance of Jackson and Twilight to the improvised dance floor, three Rich-tone men, enslaved musicians from a neighboring plantation, played a rousing tune on their fiddles.

The furniture had been moved aside in the front parlor and adjoining dining room. Jackson took Twilight's hand and began the first dance of the evening. Planter couples swirled around them.

She leaned to his ear and whispered, "By hell's blast to the moon, Jackson. How could you be so cruel to a little cat? But then, what am I saying? You treat children worse."

He leaned to her ear and whispered, "No one escapes Magnolia Bay."

Their dance was a ruse she had to endure for hours.

When the dancing ended and the men started talking of the imminent secession of the Southern states, Twilight fled to the grounds. All of the children and youths, free and captive, were there, talking and playing. Some were dancing to the music still being played inside the big house. Sneaking around buildings and through trees so the children wouldn't see her, Twilight wandered deeper into the forest until soon finding herself near the dogwoods. She stared for a while at 'that cabin,' wondering if she was bold enough to burn it to the ground. She pondered the oil lamp she was holding. She was so tempted. But, as a summer fire, it could get quickly out of control, which could cause devastation. Regardless, destruction couldn't find a place within her soul. No matter what. She turned to leave.

Then she heard a man say, "Twilight." Stopping cold in her tracks, she thought, "Oh, no, that awful Clairmont McCay followed me." Bristling and prepared to run, she heard the voice again. "Twilight."

And she knew it wasn't McCay, for she recognized the voice as the one she heard speaking continually to her heart. With a pivot, she whispered, "Gallatin."

Stepping out from behind the cabin, he stared at her. "Damn, I love you," he said.

She ran to him. Pulling her inside the night shadows and close to him, he kissed the top of her head and breathed into her hair. "Will we be seen here?" he asked.

"No. The children are in the yard surrounding the big house. And the adults are inside."

Taking her hand, he led her behind the cabin. His attention fully on Twilight, Gallatin ran his hands firmly down her arms. "I've missed you so much that I ache with every breath." He stroked her hair as she rested her face against his chest.

"I hoped you would be back to see me months ago," Twilight whispered.

"I did come. Twice. Once in May and once in June," he said. "Weather kept me away until May. I waited in the woods near the quarters, as close as I could get without being seen or without Jasper noticing me, for an entire evening and into the night. You never came that way. It is just by chance I saw you tonight. What if you hadn't come out walking? You're the hostess of a ball, it seems."

"You were here and I missed seeing you? Twice? Oh, Gallatin, I wish I'd seen you!" She hugged him. "Gallatin, I need to say things to you that my heart screams."

"Tell me. And marry me. You must come with me tonight. I'll sneak Spirit from the paddock, and we'll be off. Then it will be just you and me forever."

"I don't think Jackson will grant me a divorce. He says no one escapes Magnolia Bay. He says it to me so often that I know he means I also will never leave. Besides, I can do good things here." She took his hand and said, "Let's walk more into the trees, away from this cabin of evil."

They walked to where Gallatin had left Charger, too far from the big house for the aging Jasper to roam. Shaking his head, Charger nickered softly to Twilight; she hugged his neck. "I wish Spirit were here to see you, Charger," she said.

Among the trees that reached toward the heavens, Gallatin said, "Come with me. I promise I will marry you."

"What would I do until my divorce, *if* it were approved?"

"Stow away with me on the *North Star*."

"Oh, it sounds so romantic. But it wouldn't work. It's just not possible for a married woman to take off in the night with another man and stow away on a riverboat until her husband grants her a divorce. That's plot for silly novels."

"Then talk to Jackson. And when you are ready, I'll be there for you."

Pushing her fists to her eyes, she said, "That's just it—you won't be there for me. You'll be somewhere on the Mississippi River, your first and greatest love." Letting her hands fall, she continued, "It all seems impossible. With your life on the river, with my life here. Don't you see, Gallatin? Even if by some miracle Jackson grants me a divorce, the problem between you and me will still be there: I want you with me; you want to be on the river."

"So what do we do?"

"I don't know." Twilight sighed. "I'm trapped here, it seems. I could try to leave, but I'm not sure if I'd be forced to return to Jackson or if my father could intervene to keep me in Memphis. But, also, for now, I need to be here. Besides, I can't be a woman who waits for her man's steamship to come in every few weeks. I don't want an occasional husband."

Motioning toward himself with his hands, Gallatin said, "Look at me. Who do you see?"

"Gallatin, let's not play games."

"Just talk to me. Who do you see?"

"Gallatin. I see Gallatin."

"And who is Gallatin?"

"Gallatin is—the pilot of the *North Star*, lover of the Mississippi, and the impossible man with whom I fell in love the first time I spoke with him."

"There, you said it yourself," Gallatin said. "I am Gallatin of the Mississippi. It's me, Twilight. Don't you see? If I leave the river, I tear out my soul. I betray—myself."

"Why doesn't it tear out your soul to leave me?"

"It does."

"I cannot count the number of times you've left me since we met."

"But you know I always return."

Taking Twilight's face gently in his hands, he stared hard at her. And then, he leaned toward her, his mouth moving to hers. She moved toward him. They kissed. Their second kiss. With this kiss, they both felt its rousing power to body and soul. Then, Gallatin lifted Twilight into his arms, held her to his chest, and said, "I can love you better in just one night than Jackson could in a lifetime of nights."

"Don't do this to me. Don't make me love you more than I already do."

"And how is Jackson treating you now?"

Wickedly. Twilight didn't answer.

"You must leave him. Leave him and go with me tonight. I want to marry you," he whispered. "And after we've married, I will love you so completely that *every* day, even the days I'm on the river, you will never wonder again about my commitment to you." Carefully placing her feet on the ground and stepping back from her, he held her shoulders and said, "There's not a man that God Almighty could create who can love you like I do. Twilight, you know you are my mystic princess. Use those abilities. Listen to your heart. You know I will always return to you."

Twilight shook her head. Grieving over the stillborn conversation, she sighed deeply. "I don't know. This all seems impossible. I *am* doing good work here. And the fact remains, I'm trapped at this plantation by my marriage. Maybe if you go away, and I know you're not coming back ever again, I can get on with my life."

"Maybe you are afraid of being loved so completely." He placed his hands gently on the sides of her face. "Does that frighten you, darling? Does the thought of being loved so deeply and completely frighten you?"

Twilight felt a jolt. It was as though a cryptic door had been opened somewhere inside her, offering her to venture into a place she hadn't known existed. Strangely, her chest tightened in anger. Then, breathing deeply and controlling her anger, she felt intrigued. Tears gently washed her eyes. "Does love scare me?" Moving into the warm feel of his hands on her face, she said, "Maybe it does. I think I want complete love, and yet maybe I completely fear it." Searching his eyes, she said, "Maybe you should leave me forever."

"Is that what you want? For me to leave and tell you I am never coming back?"

"I don't know. At least it's a move. As it is, we're in a stalemate."

Dropping his hands from her face, Gallatin stood quietly for a long time. Then he held her hand, and they walked to a tree where he sat with his back braced against it and held her in his lap. She snuggled into him. After a river of clouds passed before the moon, it sounded to Twilight like Gallatin was softly crying. She looked up at him; he was gazing at her with tenderness through misty eyes.

Finally, he stood, still holding her in his arms. He kissed her, set her on her feet, and said, "I've been unfair. I can't be what you want. You will never see me again." He gazed at her as if absorbing her every feature into his memory. Then, he turned to go.

Torn in agony, Twilight watched in horror as he walked to Charger. Gallatin stopped and stared at the saddle. Long seconds passed as he continued to stand by Charger. Relieved that he had not yet mounted and galloped away, Twilight, barely breathing, waited. Time stopped. Everything stopped.

Finally, he turned. "I'm lying like a New Orleans lawyer. I can't do this. Even if I tried, I couldn't stay away from you. And I don't want to try. I'll be back the next time we dock in Memphis."

Twilight laughed and ran to his arms. "Oh, good! Good! I love you so, Gallatin of the Mississippi."

Chapter 37
Invasion Averted

Monday, July 4, 1859
Late Night
Magnolia Bay

When Twilight entered the big house, the guests were leaving.

Annoyed to distraction, Jackson said gruffly, lowering his voice, "Where have you been, Twilight? Can't you at least, when we have guests, behave as a wife and lovely hostess? I thought your birthday run would cure you." Then he yanked her by the arm to the door to bid everyone a good night.

When Clairmont McCay approached his hosts, he bowed, lingering over Twilight's hand after he kissed it. "It was the *deepest pleasure* meeting you, Mrs. Canon," he said.

Twilight flushed with anger, for McCay was acting absurdly, as if they had an attraction—or, worse, had had an encounter. And right in front of Jackson.

"I see you've enjoyed our brandy tonight, Mr. McCay," Twilight said, hoping that would put him in his place.

"Just another of Magnolia Bay's pleasures worth savoring," he said, staring at her. Shaking Jackson's hand, McCay said, "You lucky devil, finding such a combination! A very young, spirited wife, full of vigor, who can run the course, and who, at the same time, strikes with her loveliness and femininity."

Jackson smiled at McCay, but his eyes were dangerously brooding.

After the guests were gone, Twilight hurried to her room and locked the door to be alone with her thoughts of Gallatin. She couldn't sleep—all she could think of was how wrong it was that she and Gallatin weren't together. She kept reminding herself that she was married to Jackson, which seemed so strange, for she felt married to Gallatin.

She heard a gentle rapping at her door. Covering herself with her night jacket, she answered. There stood Jackson, looking forlorn.

"Jack?"

"Twilight, I can't sleep. We need to talk. May I come in?"

Nodding, Twilight opened the door wider so he could enter, then shut it. "I agree. We need to talk."

He waited.

"Well, Jack. We haven't been getting on too well. I'm not the right person to be a planter's wife." She paused.

"What is it you're saying?"

"Grant me a divorce. Please."

"You've spent time with someone else! And I know who it is."

Twilight held her breath. How could he know? Had he seen them together?

"You were with him tonight!"

Twilight's chest clenched around her breath.

"You've dallied with Clairmont, haven't you? Clairmont McCay. I'll challenge him to a duel and shoot his ass into the ground!"

Surprised and relieved, she burst into laughter and waved her hand at him. "By the eclipsed moon, I am not interested in Mr. McCay. I just met him today, and I don't even like him. McCay was acting idiotically when he left. Too much brandy, I'm sure, gave him a ridiculous, loose, and terrible tongue."

Jackson stared hard at her. "Not McCay? Then, tell me, who is he? Who do you fancy?"

"This is not about someone else," she said. "It is that you and I are not suited for one another."

He smiled menacingly. "Oh? We were quite suited not so long ago. We could hardly leave our bed, don't you recall, my darling?"

"Jack, it has been a strange marriage. I should have said these words weeks ago: I've lost my love for you."

"You act as if you don't need love. Well, I know just what you need." Forcefully, he kissed her.

Pulling back from him, she said, "No, Jack."

"You want me," he said.

"No! Stop, Jack!"

He pushed her face to his, again kissing her roughly.

She tried to say "no" again, but he pushed his weight against her, his mouth firmly against her, pressing so hard against her mouth and nose that she couldn't speak—she couldn't breathe!

She struggled, both arms pushing at him, but her strength was nothing compared to his. *I can't breathe!* Panicked, she tried to raise her knee sharply into his groin, but he caught it before it hit him. *I'm suffocating! I'm going to die!*

At that moment, a rapid succession of thumping sounded through the bedroom wall. Loudly and consistently it continued, causing Jackson to jerk his face away from Twilight's to listen. "What the—," Jackson cursed between clenched teeth.

Twilight gasped for air, coughing and panting. Her eyes were wild with fright. Rapid breaths throbbed through her nose and heaved her chest. She fought to pull air into her lungs.

Jackson went to the hallway and saw Billy. "Billy, what is that noise?" The noise stopped.

"I'll check, sir." Billy opened the door just a crack to the adjacent bedroom from where the noise had come, looked in, and saw the aged, nightgowned occupant armed with a copper chamber pot—what she'd been using to bang on the wall to stop Jackson—and poised to, if necessary, bang the wall again. She winked. Billy stifled a smile, closed the door, and said, "I see nothing out of the ordinary, sir."

"Odd," Jackson said, then went back into the room and stood next to Twilight.

Scared to death and beyond, Twilight cowered against the wall, her eyes focused away from the phantasmagoria of horror named Jackson. "You had no right," she whispered so softly there was almost no sound.

"I'm your husband; I've been very patient waiting for you. I've been patient for months, for far too long. No husband has had to endure such separation from his wife. Being with you *is* my right."

"What about my rights?" she whispered, terrified.

"Young woman, you have no rights."

Twilight's hand blasted across his face. She didn't know where that came from, for she felt far too frightened to do anything but cower. It was as if her hand had acted on its own. She braced herself for his counterblow.

Instead, blinking, Jackson seemed truly surprised. She saw a thin red mark on his cheek from Wondrous Ring. He said, "I thought when you resisted you were teasing. I thought making love would remind you how much you love me."

She said with full voice, "We weren't making love. You were going to take me against my will. You would have ra—"

He put his hand on her mouth. "Don't say that vulgar word. Being with you in any way I want is most definitely my right." Taking his hand off her mouth, he added, "But I won't come to you again unless you ask."

"I'll never ask. I want a divorce."

"No, you'll ask. Sooner or later, you'll want me. I will not grant you a divorce." He stood, studied Twilight, who was staring anywhere that was not him, turned and left the room.

Chapter 38

The Importance of Stories and Names

Tuesday, July 5, 1859
Evening and Night
Magnolia Bay

After working late into the night in her garden with Twilight and Glory, Ava said, "Twilight, why don't you join us tonight? We're meeting in the forest."

Twilight had avoided the community fire circle gatherings, as she knew it wasn't her place to intrude on what was sacred, secret, and not hers. Simultaneously glad yet reluctant, Twilight nodded, said "thank you," and walked with Ava and Glory into the dense land of trees.

A group of eight had already gathered. Ifeoma gave her distinctive glare directed at Twilight and said, "Just because you ran the race and just because Ava invited you here tonight, don't think for a moment you are one of us."

Twilight, an outsider everywhere, dipped her head and looked sideways at nothing.

Squinting her eyes, Ava said, "Who knows? Maybe she's a distant cousin."

Shocked, Twilight smiled at Ava.

Ava continued, "Or a friend."

"She's neither," Ifeoma said, arms crossed.

Three people told hope-filled stories about Moses leading his people to freedom, faith-filled stories about the compassion and suffering of Jesus, and horror-filled stories of family members being stolen from their lives in Africa, shoved into tight spaces on the ships, and the ensuing illness and death of children, parents, and grandparents, and for the survivors, torture and captivity.

Twelve-year-old Ben spoke: "My mama told me our family is of royalty." He straightened; determination lined his mouth.

Softly Jafaan sang, "Only God knows, only God knows, only God knows my sorrow. God cares, God cares, God cares about my pain. God sends soothing Love." Then, all sang the words together. After everyone had finished speaking, Jafaan asked Twilight if she had a story to share.

Surprised at his invitation, she glanced into the night, then said, "I'm so sorry for the devastation and pain inflicted on your families." She looked at Wondrous Ring. "I don't have a story."

Jafaan asked, "Nothing to share with us? A story about your GrandMama?"

"I do have a story that GrandMama used to tell me."

"Tell us, if you will," Jafaan said.

Twilight smiled. Taking a breath, she began. "GrandMama said that when she was a girl, on her ninth birthday, she received a new pair of shoes made for walking in the rain." Immediately she realized her insensitivity and wished she hadn't begun the story, as the captives had one pair of flimsy shoes for rain or shine. "Actually, I don't have a story."

While she'd been speaking, Jafaan had leaned toward her, cocking his head to the side, his left ear facing her. "I'd like to hear your story," he said, leaning slightly closer.

Then she realized, Jafaan must have trouble hearing. She wondered if he was perceived as ignoring the drivers and overseers at times because, when working or even stopping to take a quick breath, he didn't know they were talking to him. Defiant if told to whip someone, yes. That would be Jafaan. But, maybe some of what was perceived as his rebelliousness in the field was actually that he had difficulty hearing.

Everyone was looking at her, so she continued, "As is usual in England, where GrandMama lived, it started raining that day. So, trying out her birthday gift, she sloshed around in her new shoes, watching her feet splash the water. When she finally looked up, she couldn't see her home, for she'd splashed so far that she didn't know where she was. It started raining harder, suddenly becoming a horrible, scary thunderstorm. At first, she huddled against a building and cried; then, she heard a tiny voice inside her saying, 'Don't give up. Never give up.' So she stopped crying, held up her head, and looked around. Nothing seemed familiar at first. But then she saw a light shining from a house down the way. She followed the light to her home. Her mother had left the drapes open with a lamp shining in the window."

Jafaan nodded, then sang low, "Shine, shine, shine, keep your light bright, so I can find my way home." Then he said, "Tell us about your freedom."

After thinking for a moment, she said, "I'm sorry, I have no idea what to say. Freedom should be a birthright. I wish I could give you freedom. But here, I have no power." Twilight considered again what it must be like to be owned by another human. And, while it couldn't be the same as how the enslaved people were owned, she felt as if the Earth had opened to Hell as she realized the truth of her marriage.

"I can tell you about when I was younger. Until I was twelve, when my GrandMama died, I lived at Willow Land, my grandparents' home with a few acres. Willow Land is on the banks of the Ohio River in Evansville, Indiana, one of the southernmost towns in Indiana, across the river from Kentucky. That makes Evansville an interesting place to live, for it is a border town. The enslaved people in northern Kentucky would be free if they lived just across the river in Indiana. But it's not that simple. With the horrid Fugitive Slave Act, if they cross the river and stay in the area, they are hunted to be returned to the South and enslaved again. I remember that some people from Kentucky and even farther South did come to our home for an overnight visit. Most arrived after swimming the river. Some said they had help crossing on the boat of fishermen. We'd give them food, wash and dry their clothes or give them new clothes. The next day, they'd vanish in the dark before the dawn on their journey to Canada."

The ten listened attentively. Continuing, Twilight said, "My grandfather still lives at Willow Land. When you cross the Ohio River from Kentucky, you can see the house standing just two blocks southeast of the wharf. It's painted white, with green shutters and a veranda above the front door facing the street, Water Street. I always loved walking on the veranda to watch the river laze by. Surrounding the house are several black willow and weeping willow trees. They stand so closely together it's as if you need to pass willow sentries to enter our land. Behind our home is a grove thick with them, as dense as a small forest. I loved escaping under the draping branches of the weeping willows and within the clusters of black willows. It was magical. I loved Willow Land. It hurt so much to leave." She paused, then added, as if to finish her story about GrandMama, "At night, as her mama had done, GrandMama always kept a lamp lit at the side window near the back of the house."

It seemed as if a thin light from Jafaan's and Ava's fingertips sparkled so quickly that Twilight imagined it. She stopped talking, trying to recall more about her childhood in Indiana, but the fuzzy precious memories skittered away like tiny darling barn mice caught in the light.

A girl named Dove asked Twilight, "Could you tell us how you were named? Sometimes we tell how our mamas named us."

Ifeoma interjected, "My mama said to me, 'Honey, your name means all that is good and precious and beautiful.'"

Twilight nodded, whispering, "And you are all of those, Ifeoma."

"I'll never be Nancy," Ifeoma added, then petulantly pushed forward her determined bottom lip.

Everyone was quiet for several heartbeats. Then Dove asked Twilight again to explain her name's origin. She did, then asked Dove, "How were you named?"

Dove smiled. "My family is related to the Ethiopian woman who married Moses." With her finger, she drew a snake in the dust, saying, "Do

Pales know Moses married an African woman of power? Some say hers was hoodoo power. Her father had the power, too, and helped Moses develop his great power, particularly the power of words." She looked up and continued, "My mama believed that the name given to a baby has power and that the name should be what the mama first sees after bringing that child into this world. My great-grandmama told that belief to my grandmama, and my grandmama told it to Mama, and Mama told it to me and my sister. Mama said that when I was born, she saw a dove fly. 'With a dove you came to this world,' she said, 'and as a dove you will leave.' I think that is so pretty and comforting. Were you born at twilight?" Dove asked.

"I don't know, but I think GrandMama believed that twilight is a special time for me," Twilight said.

Dove continued, "Mama bore my sister late at night, just as the fire died away. Mama saw the fire embers, so she named my sister Ember and said, 'By an ember you came to this world; by an ember you will leave.' Maybe it just means my sister will die as a warming fire dies. I think it is true, what Mama told us, but my sister never gave it a thought."

"You have a sister named Ember? I have a friend in Memphis named Ember. Could my friend be your sister?"

"I doubt it, if your friend Ember is free."

"I took Ember and her little girl from the auction block in Memphis so they could stay together; they are free. They live at my father's home in Memphis. She's twenty-two years old."

Dove smiled and said, "I'm fifteen, and my sister is seven years older. We were together until the enslaver sold her. I was sold a year later. That's when I came here. I don't know where Ember went."

"Was Ember married to Manuel when you were together? And she was with child?"

"That's her! That's my Ember!" Dove laughed, clapped her hands twice, then clenched her clasped hands to her heart. "Ember is free?"

"Yes. I had the power to do something there, at my Father's home. Here, I am powerless. But yes, Ember is free! And she took the surname

Free. She is wonderful! She has two children: her son, who was sold from her, but we are working to find him, and her daughter. I'm returning to Memphis soon for my sister's wedding. I can't wait to see Ember, and I'll take you, too, Dove."

Dove's smile faded, but Twilight didn't notice, as she was lost in her thoughts: *Gallatin is needed on the river, and I am needed here. And I need those who are here; they are teaching me how, even as a captive, to craft a meaningful life.*

As she stood to walk back to the big house, she touched within her pocket the feather Gallatin had found under the tree the night she'd seen him, a light black wing feather of the female American Goldfinch, which, usually monogamous, might switch mates. And she builds the nest mostly by herself.

But, someday, Gallatin and I will be together. I just know it.

While walking the opposite direction to the captive quarters, Jafaan sang, "Shine, shine, shine, keep your light bright, so I can find my way home."

Chapter 39

The Large Mystical ~ Tensions and Mysteries

Tuesday, July 5, 1859, Evening and Night
Magnolia Bay and Mississippi River
Friday, July 8, 1859
Memphis

Jackson's thoughts trailed his disobedient gaze, which wandered into the adjoining parlor, away from the political conversation between his father and his brother-in-law, then rested on the serenity of the women seated there.

The evening was nearly perfect: the men were smoking in one room; the women—with one exception—were sewing in the other. Being a married man, he should be admiring his wife, who should be properly seated by his mother, both contentedly sewing. Instead, he was admiring Rachel, who was sitting in Twilight's place doing what Twilight should be doing.

He assumed that again, as with every evening, his wife had chosen to be with his captives rather than with his mother. Suppressing his annoyance, Jackson clenched his fists and vowed to make her into a pristine Pale nobleman's wife before the harvest. His parents would be pleased. Twilight would *not* be pleased, of course, but pleasing both his parents and his wife was impossible. Twilight would have to adjust.

But Rachel. Plantation life agreed with her perfectly. Adjustments of any sort would be unnecessary if he'd married Rachel. With Rachel, arguments, demands, problems would never happen.

When he'd first met Rachel, he thought her gorgeous but not nearly as exciting as Twilight. In fact, when compared to Twilight, Rachel had seemed, like most females he'd met, boring. And often ridiculous. After having been married for a while, Jackson noticed that what he formerly found attractive about Twilight—her fiery determination and unbridled conviction—he was now finding troublesome and tiring. If only she would be like her sister, they could live harmoniously.

To Twilight, Magnolia Bay was Hell; to Rachel, it was Heaven. Twilight argued, stomped, and fumed about everything. With serenity, Rachel absorbed plantation life. Now, Rachel no longer seemed boring. *And Twilight not wanting me in bed?* Jackson thought. *That is man's ultimate rejection. She is my wife, after all. She is not complying with our world, which is, as Father calls it, the Dominion of Men.*

He thought back to the first day he met his wife, realizing that he should have seen then what he knew now: *Twilight is a bothersome witch.*

⋙ ⋘

I wish I could dismiss Twilight as a bother and leave it at that, Gallatin thought as he steered the *North Star* up the Mississippi away from Memphis. But he knew he couldn't. Twilight wasn't a bother. She simply knew what she wanted and wasn't afraid to voice it. He shouldn't expect a woman to want the type of life he led, to live entirely in *his* world, and yet, that's just what he'd been expecting from Twilight.

But now he was worried about her. A slightly built young woman anyway, she had lost considerable weight and was looking spindly and spent. The wolf she was married to was abusing her. She'd told him about the obstacle course run and her overall treatment by all of the big house.

He'd repeatedly asked her to leave with him. For her health. For her life. For them. But, even withering away as she was, she'd refused. She kept insisting she had work to do at the plantation. That she cared about her friends there. That she'd made a vow.

He'd made a vow, too. Thus, he could relate to how a promise could be a deterrent to considering other possibilities in one's life. But how much was he to blame for her commitment to staying at the plantation? If he agreed to leave the river, would she leave the abuses of her plantation life?

The bigger question was: could she leave? Now that he knew Jackson was abusive, he understood that her life could be at stake. And he left anyway, not even challenging Jackson. The truth was, Jackson was well-positioned with the judges. Challenging him might only make Twilight's situation worse.

What kind of man am I? He feared he'd turned their love into a duel and that he might kill what they had if he didn't decide soon to leave the river. His attraction to her was greater than reason, stronger than self-control, more powerful than any emotion he'd ever known. Except for the call of the Mississippi.

What kind of man am I? He'd left the woman he loved to the whims of a mean man on a plantation run by a family of abusers.

What kind of man am I? Three years prior, the strange couple on his riverboat—Miss Summer and Mr. Fall—had said he was a man of goodwill and a river prince. They even called him a Champion Man. It all, he realized now, was more intense and profound than it sounded. At first, he thought they were just being a sweet older couple, saying nice things to the young pilot.

But their words had started to resonate. He piloted, they said, the spiritual river of life, having a flow countercurrent to the prevalent expectation of a man being dominant and unemotional. He was, they said, a prince against the Society of Supremacy and Dominion of Men. They'd told him he would someday meet a mystic princess. If he fell in love with her, he must vow not to marry her until she discovered on her own the spiritual river that "flows within us all," as Miss Summer had described it. "Only a few have a strong current; only a few are part of the Large Mystical," she added.

"You should not tell her what you know until she learns who she is on her own," Mr. Fall had said.

Their words had sounded simultaneously odd and authentic. Somehow, strange as they and their words were, he knew—he felt—what they said was true.

Since meeting them, he'd been learning about piloting his spiritual life, which now seemed to be a tributary to a new world. When he met Twilight, he knew immediately she was his mystic princess. Over time, with his elders' repeated visits and "trainings" on the riverboat, he agreed that he must allow Twilight to live her life, learning independently—until a certain point, and he would know when that was. And Twilight would know, too.

He'd thought meeting her on the road in February had been the "certain point." But, Twilight said "no" to leaving Magnolia Bay with him. Then, upon hearing of Jackson's abuse, he thought that would be her "turning point." But, she'd insisted on staying at Magnolia Bay. It's true; she was trying to do good work for the children trapped on the plantation. If she were in Memphis, she probably could do nothing for them. Harley had said he wasn't having any luck in how to legally challenge the Canons so that the children would be freed. In the meantime, Twilight was sacrificing her own life and making little progress in aiding the children due to the Canon traditional mindset carved in classical stone.

Apparently, Twilight still had no idea who she really was, because, according to the strange couple, as soon as she did know, otherworldly tasks would fill her life. As horrific as it sounded, she had to face more before understanding her actual place as a mystic princess.

He suspected Ember, too, was a mystic princess. "Most are unaware that the Sisterhood of Gifts exists or that they are part of it," Miss Summer had said. "Regardless, those of the Large Mystical often find each other, gravitate to one another. Finding each other helps make life in this physical world of money-mongering, greed, and meanness a bit more tolerable."

The shoreline curved, becoming Twilight's soft cheek and delicate lips as she tilted her face to him, smiling. His body flamed. He wanted to see her, had to see her. Even if Twilight didn't know, *he* knew it was time. He had to stop the abuse by Jackson. He had to stop the pain to which he subjected her.

"Starboard!" he yelled to the watchmen at the helm, then turned the wheel to the right, directing the riverboat 180 degrees to head back to Memphis, back to Twilight.

The riverboat had barely begun turning when the captain charged into the pilot house. "What in blazes are you doing, Mr. Gallatin?"

Gallatin shook his head as if to clear it. "I'm not sure."

"Do you need rest, man? Are you sick? This is strange behavior, especially for a pilot of your reputation and ability. No more tomfoolery."

"I'll set her straight," Gallatin said, gently turning the wheel, guiding the steamer back on course. The captain said, "You're the best pilot I've ever known. You're a true professional. Don't worry—this incident won't go on your record. You must be extremely tired, young man, to do something so odd. After your shift, get some rest, son." The captain lightly smacked Gallatin's back and left. Gallatin tried to concentrate on the river. With the *Star*, he was confident, in charge. He'd made a pledge to the couple who were more than they seemed. He would abide by it. Piloting the river, for now, is where he belonged.

Yet, what if his leaving the river was the "certain point" when Twilight would realize it was time for her to leave the plantation? How could he subject her to more abuse by doing nothing?

Running his hand through his hair, he thought about Twilight's hand doing that very thing.

This is no good, he thought. Vowing to make a move soon, Gallatin decided: he must leave the Mississippi River to be with Twilight.

But what of my other vow?

※≫ ≪※

Another night alone and angry, Jackson headed to his room. Twilight was already in hers, with the door locked, for he'd heard the sound of the key turn as he climbed the steps. With a punch, he opened the door to his room. The guest room door in the adjoining hall opened quickly, and Rachel whispered, "Jackson."

He turned. She was standing just inside the threshold in a white, floor-length dressing gown pulled closed and belted around her. Her hair was lying about her shoulders, and she was lovely.

"Rachel," he whispered, his voice low and deep.

"I have a problem the size of Tennessee," she drawled. "I *must* have, simply *must* have, a strong gentleman to help me."

The desire to be near her, to help his sister-in-need, overpowered his annoying marital conscience.

"That incompetent enslaved servant filled my pitcher too full, and I do declare, I cannot lift it to fill my basin. My arms are so terribly fragile," she said. She stepped to the side of the doorway, opening a space for Jackson to enter.

Without a word, Jackson crossed the threshold. He walked to the washstand, poured water into the basin, replaced the pitcher, then turned to leave. Rachel slipped between the door and Jackson. She closed the door behind her, pressing her back to the door, then stretched her arms out and placed them firmly against the door, barring him from leaving. "I know you are my sister's husband," Rachel breathed. "But Twilight doesn't know how terribly lucky she is to have a wonderful, heavenly man like you. She treats you horribly, not at all with the respect you deserve. Why, if you were my man, I would thank God on my knees every morning, noon, and night until the day I died." With an exaggerated flutter of her eyelashes, she said, "I think you are simply too magnificent, too godly, for words."

Smacking his hands on both sides of the door to encase Rachel, Jackson pressed his body against her, penning her against the wood barrier, his manliness aching for her, then abruptly straightened, released her, and whispered huskily, "I *am* married. To Twilight."

"And yet, sleeping in separate rooms? Please stay," she whispered.

Moaning, he grabbed her and buried his face in her neck. Rachel sighed, flinging her arms around him and kissing his hair. Crazed, he tore himself from her, paced the floor like a caged lion, shoved her away from the door, and left. Crossing the hall in two strides, he pounded on Twilight's door. "Let me in, Twilight."

Fearful of what he wanted to do to her, Twilight closed her book and decided: *I'll not make a peep. He'll think I'm asleep. He'll go away.* Taboo was lying in her lap. With her fingertips, she combed his silky fur. Though LaDonna often had the vine to Twilight's window cut, it grew so fast that, each day, Taboo could climb up to and through Twilight's window. As Jackson pounded, Twilight thanked God for the seemingly magical vine and for Taboo as she simultaneously pleaded to God that Jackson would leave her alone.

Jackson wrenched the doorknob. His voice sounded an octave deeper than usual. "Let me in. Let me in!" Taboo jumped from the bed, disappearing through the window. Without waiting to see if Twilight would answer, Jackson raised his leg and firmly kicked the door with the bottom of his foot, breaking the lock and knocking it off its hinges, sending it with a thud to the floor of the room. Determined and strong, Jackson strode atop the door, across the room, and right up onto Twilight's bed. Standing above her, he saw she was shaking, but she stared at him in defiance.

He knelt next to her. Gently, he stroked her hair and said, "You are consistent, Twilight. No matter what, you cower to no one. I can only admire someone like you." Pacific as a sunlit autumn hill, he nestled beside her and whispered, "I won't do what I did last night. When I tried to love you last night, you know you wanted me, just not fully. I want you to want me fully, as I want you. I love you. I've been wrong to keep you here in this house with Mother and Father. We need time alone. Just you and I, and of course some enslaved laborers, will move to Woodland Manor soon. We'll live there together, without Mother and Father, until Jed can purchase it."

Twilight said nothing and felt nothing but fear. She had started to heal after Gallatin's tender, comforting care—he only holding her, not pushing anything on her, not expecting anything, just holding her. But now, with Jackson here, she was falling back into oblivion flanked by terror.

"Honey, I want to make you happy. I want us to have a happy marriage," he whispered. Finally, he walked to the broken-down door. Picking it up off the floor, he leaned it against the frame enough so they would have some privacy. Then he returned to the bed, pulled off his house boots, and took off his evening jacket. "I just want to be near you tonight. I'll just lie here next to you. I won't even undress." In his trousers and shirt, he again lay next to her. "I miss you. Tonight, I want to know you are next to me."

After he was quiet for a time, Twilight noticed he was asleep. Hearing a noise near the broken door, she caught a glimpse of Rachel peeking through a gap in its placement against the frame. Twilight grabbed her pillow and, with the precision that comes only from practice, threw it at the door, hitting bull's-eye where Rachel spied. Twilight heard Rachel scurrying away.

Next to Jackson and his snoring, Twilight couldn't sleep. Suddenly, she saw a face peering through the crack. This time, it wasn't Rachel. It was an extremely ashen face of an aging woman. *Grandma Ghost?*

"Hello?" Twilight said, leaving the bed. Moving the heavy door to the side, she squeezed through. The door to the room next to hers shut. She knocked lightly. She heard the faintly-spoken words: "Leave, or die."

Shivering at the words, Twilight said, "Hello?"

Billy came out of his room. "May I help you with something, Miss Twilight?"

"Billy, there is a woman in this room. Who is she?"

Shaking his head, Billy said, "There is no one in that room. Please, miss, time to rest."

"Tell her I am so grateful that she stopped Jackson last night. Tell her I said thank you. Good night, Billy." She returned to her room, whispering, "No one in that room? This is a house of lies."

The next two days confused and frightened Twilight more than ever. Jackson continued to talk about their move to Woodland Manor and returned to being somewhat like the man he'd been when courting her. He spent time with her in conversation. But he dared do no more, he told her, until she was ready.

"I'm not ready. I never will be," she'd tell him.

Jackson would smile, lightly placing his hand on hers.

Only Jed, Rachel, and Twilight drove to Memphis for the wedding.

Jed had invited Victoria to join them, but she refused, saying she was needed at Magnolia Bay. Being summer, Jackson had much to do on the plantation, so he didn't accompany Twilight, much to her relief. Though Twilight had planned for Dove to come with them to visit Ember, Jackson wouldn't allow it.

In Twilight's secret pocket was GrandMama's letter.

Chapter 40
Twin Tensions

*Friday, July 8, 1859
and Saturday, July 9, 1859
Memphis*

Memphis! Around every corner, an event awaited.

In one direction—people, horses, carriages. In another direction—markets, churches, shops. A wedding outside a home, an argument in front of the jail, singing in the marketplace, and a puppet show in the park greeted Twilight's plantation-agitated eyes. When they approached the Adams home, Twilight nearly leaped from the carriage and ran to the side entrance. She pushed it open, calling, "Ember! Mother! We're here!" Rachel pushed by her, rushing inside.

Soon, Makeda-Angel, her curls bouncing, ran to Twilight, followed by her mama. "Hello, darling," Twilight said, lifting Makeda-Angel and kissing her cheek. Balancing the child in one arm, she hugged Ember with the other.

"It's good to see you," Ember said, returning Twilight's hug.

Just then, Elizabeth appeared with Rachel behind her. "Twilight, my dear," said her mother, putting her arms around Twilight and patting her back. Twilight stiffened severely—this was the first time her mother had ever touched her. "How have you been, dear?" Elizabeth continued, stepping back but still holding onto Twilight's arm. "And how is wonderful, charming Jackson? I'm proud of my daughters, marrying such fine men. Where is Jed? Your father and Jesse will be home soon." Elizabeth released Twilight's arm and walked away, chattering to herself.

"See?" Rachel said to Twilight. "I told you she is acting stranger and stranger." Then, directing her stare at Ember, she said, "For Mother's health, we should really get rid of *that* Rich-tone."

Looking directly back at Rachel, Ember said, "I am not a 'that.' I am a person. My name is Ember."

"Rachel, will you ever stop saying such mean things?" Twilight said, adding, "I think Mother is acting somewhat better."

"You would," Rachel said, walking away, then turning her head to add, "The more Mother spins off her spindle, the better you like her, I'm sure."

After unhitching the horse and carriage, Jed found Twilight and Ember in the parlor. Addressing Ember, he asked, "How fares Jesse?"

"He is busy at the Memphis Star office," Ember answered. "And he's happy."

Pensively, Jed nodded. "I'm looking forward to seeing him again."

"And he is eager to see you, Jed," Ember said. "You're all he talks about."

"Oh, I bet he talks about more than me," Jed said, staring at Ember. "I'll wait for him and for Father on the front porch."

After Jed was out of earshot, Twilight asked, "And how are you and Jesse?"

Ember whispered, "I wish we were free to be in love. But as it is, we are very good friends." She sighed, then said, "How are you and Gallatin?"

"Gallatin? You mean Jackson, Ember. About those two men, you're as mixed up as the ingredients in Cara's famous Whacky Cake," Twilight said, laughing.

Ember said, "Gallatin is a baker's window when it comes to his emotions. Anyone can see what's inside. And inside? His favorite Whacky Cake—you!" The two young women laughed. Ember continued, "I thought he was going to die when he came here and learned you were married. Then no sooner than he'd heard, he asked your father for Charger and was gone for some time. He loves you."

Twilight sighed. "I'm married. What can I do?" Whispering, she added, "Jackson scares me."

"You're not looking well," Ember said.

Twilight paced the room, shaking her head, and said, "I don't feel well." Then she stopped and said, "I know I no longer love Jackson. I love Gallatin. How could I have agreed to be Jack's betrothed, knowing how deeply I love Gallatin? If Gallatin didn't exist, I can see why I might have wanted to marry Jackson. I mean, the way Jackson was back then, before he became so mean. But Gallatin *does* exist—he's the blood rushing through my heart; he's the breath that fills my lungs; he's the colors that flood my eyes; his voice whispers continually in my ears. He exists in every way, in me. You're right, I'm confused about my behavior and decisions."

Ember said, "You're human."

"We all have that excuse, don't we?"

"We all should be *allowed* that excuse and that existence," Ember said.

Twilight nodded. "Yes, Ember, you are right; perfectly stated."

"Besides, you only agreed to betrothal. Jackson forced you to marry. You remember, of course, the letter you wrote to me in distress right after it happened. Don't blame yourself. It's Jackson who causes confusion. Jackson strikes me as a man of the wind."

"What does that mean?"

"One day, he blows this way; the next day, he blows that way," Ember said. "Sometimes a calming breeze, sometimes a killer tornado."

"Sounds like Jackson. What type of a man would you say Gallatin is?"

"You know the answer."

"A man of the river."

Ember nodded. "A current in him runs strong and swift; if he would heed it, it would take him to his home."

"Gallatin of the River," Twilight whispered. "My river prince."

"You are a woman of fire, Twilight," Ember said. "Forever burning bright, a light for all to see by. And yet, with power so fearsome, most want to keep it contained, as in a hearth."

"Or they throw dirt on it," Twilight said wryly. "But it is a nice analogy, Ember. And Jesse? What is Jesse?"

"A man of the night," Ember said. "Gentle. Cool. Secret. Romantic."

"By the full moon, Ember. You two had better be careful."

"We do nothing to harm one another. We know we can be only friends."

"Friends. Yes. So, Ember, what are you a woman of?"

"What would you say?"

Twilight thought, then said, "A woman of the sky. You have wisdom, as if you fly high above everyone else, seeing all around us, seeing better than we can see."

Ember smiled.

"I like these analogies. Are they some of your ancestry with lovely beliefs and possible hoodoo power?" Twilight asked, smiling.

Ember pursed her lips. "How do you know about my ancestry?"

"Well, I've saved the best news for last. Ember, would you like to see your sister, Dove?"

Ember's face lit. "Little sister Dove? You know Dove?"

"She's a wonderful person."

"You know Dove. How amazing! After we were sold apart, I thought I'd never hear about her again as long as I lived," Ember said. "I suppose Magnolia Bay is where—she is?"

"Yes. I was going to bring her with me to visit you. But Jack wouldn't let me. Someday, I will bring her to see you."

Ember frowned and wiped her eyes.

They heard loud, happy voices. Through the open front door, they saw Harley, Jesse and Jed standing on the porch.

"Hey, hey, twin!" Jesse said.

"Hey, hey, twin!" Jed said.

They hugged, pounding each other on the back.

"Let me look at you," Jesse said, stepping back from his brother and giving him the once-over. "You haven't changed a bit. You still look like me!"

Jed said, "Yep, you're as handsome as ever."

Twilight, Harley, and Ember laughed, but they were clearly the audience, as Jed and Jesse seemed absorbed in their game. The brothers and their father walked into the parlor.

"I sure don't miss your snoring," Jesse said.

"You snore just like I do," Jed said.

"No. You're worse. Much worse," Jesse said.

"We snore the same," Jed said. "But I've got to tell you, no one snores as bad as my cabin mate at Magnolia Bay."

"Oh, yeah? Who is she?" Jesse said, poking Jed in the ribs.

"You ole dog. I wish I did have a wife for a cabin mate, even if she snored as bad as you. But, for now, my cabin made is an overseer, John Bratton, and whew, not only does he snore sounding like a million ailin' cattle, but he stinks like a million ailin' cattle!"

"It's true about Bratton's smell," Twilight said. "I've never known anyone to refuse a wash like that John Bratton."

Redirecting the conversation, Harley said, "I sure miss my companion down at the office, Twilight; though, Jesse is a fine associate."

"You'd better not mess things up," Twilight said, pointing her finger at Jesse.

"Awww, come here, Sis," Jesse said, pulling her to him with a big hug. "Darlin', you are wasting away to nothing. You're not ill?"

Twilight shook her head. Then nodded. "Maybe a little ill."

Jed looked at Twilight, concerned. Then he said, "Hey, Jesse, would you take time away from work tomorrow so we can go fishing?"

"Yes to that!" Then to Ember, Jesse said, "Good evening." He walked to her, his expression revealing unabashed love. Ember gazed at him, also obviously in love.

Jed's smile disappeared. Scowling, he said, "On second thought, Jesse, we'd probably have a bad time. Nothing is like it used to be."

"We've grown up," Jesse said.

"But I never thought we'd grow apart," Jed said. Slapping his father's back, he said, "Let's go to the library for a smoke before dinner; what do you say, Father?"

"Let's make it a brandy instead of a smoke, Son." To Jesse, Harley said, "Won't you join us, Son?"

Jed walked down the hall toward the library, motioned to his father, and said, "Just you and me. Father and reasonable son, what do you say?"

"Oh, Jed, knock it off," Jesse said.

Jed stopped and said, "You knock it off, Jesse. Just what can you be thinking, anyway? What has gotten into you? Look at her. She's a Rich-tone."

"Yes, I'm a Rich-tone woman," Ember said. "I'm a person."

"Jed, though I don't agree with your life, I don't question you on it," Jesse said. "So don't question me about my life. We've chosen different paths."

"How can that be? We're twins. We've never thought one single thought that wasn't shared by the other. How could this have happened? One of us is wrong, and it is you, Jesse. Wake up and look around you. You can't go on with her," Jed said, pointing at Ember. "You'll end up on the noose end of a rope. It's against the law, what you're doing. Don't you understand that?"

"No, Jed. You're the one who doesn't understand. Whose law? The law of narrow-minded people? But what about a higher law?" Jesse said.

"What higher law? Come back to Earth, man!" Jed said.

"I'll tell you what higher law," Jesse said. "The law of God. And the law of humanity. Ember is a person, a special person, a unique person. Everyone who is enslaved is a special, unique person. But not one is allowed the dignity of living as a person should live."

"I was looking forward to spending time with my twin. But we'd better forget it, Jesse. We're too different on important issues. We're too different now." Jed turned, walked a few steps to the library, then stopped and said, "You'd better move North, man. It's dangerous here for people who think as you do. Especially now, with ideas of secession assembling in a true Southerner's head. But listen to me, my brother. Even in most states of the North, becoming involved with a Rich-tone is illegal. You may vex me, but I don't want you to die." Then Jed walked into the library.

Harley shrugged his shoulders. "You're my son, Jesse. Jed's my son. I love both my sons." Then he followed Jed into the library.

"Oh, Jesse. I'm so sorry," Ember said. "I want the relationship to be good between you and Jed. But he's wrong. He's wrong. And you'll not hang. We've done nothing and will do nothing to deserve that."

Jesse smiled at Ember. "Damn. That guy is my flesh and blood. But you're my heart and soul, Ember. You're right; we'll continue to keep our relationship cool to stay alive." Jesse sighed and gazed at her. "But you know, it would be worth hanging just to love you one night."

"Jesse, don't speak such words. Hangings happen," Ember said.

Surprised that Jesse would speak so boldly in front of her, Twilight backed out of the parlor. She felt ashamed that she was holding the secret that could allow Jesse and Ember's relationship: if Jesse knew of his blood lineage, he and Ember could marry. But he would have to claim to be Rich-tone for that to happen. What would the knowledge do to her entire family? Their freedom would likely be in jeopardy. She caressed the letter in her pocket; not wanting the chance that it could be found while she was away, she had decided the safest place for it was on her person. *I must never be ashamed of keeping the secret; I made a vow at GrandMama's shrine.*

The next morning, the Adams home bustled with activity, readying for Sarah's wedding. The wedding, held in the garden, was simple with few guests. After the vows, everyone enjoyed cake and punch. Harley found Twilight and said, "I still cannot believe Jackson didn't let you have your wedding in Memphis with your family. And looking at you, I see that his control extends much further along harm's way." He hugged Twilight. "Daughter, do you have some things to tell me? I'm your father. I can help."

She said, "Jackson forced marriage on me."

"My dear! That is disgraceful. Why didn't you tell me?"

Twilight shrugged slowly. "I'm not sure. But I wasn't ready to marry him. It's been horrible. Someday, I'll need your help getting away from him for good. For now, I'm helping the enslaved children at the Bay, so I need to stay. Have you discovered anything that can help free them?"

Harley shook his head. "The Canons would be formidable foes."

Twilight nodded. "Yes, they are."

Harley said, "Children are taken from their parents as it is, so no one with authority cares what the Canons are doing."

"So, I will stay," Twilight said. "To help from the inside."

After the refreshments, Twilight and Jed prepared for the trip back to Magnolia Bay. Twilight dreaded going. Rachel, however, was panting to go. She begged her father repeatedly to let her return. In an unusual stand for Harley, he told Rachel definitely no. Twilight had prayed Rachel would stay home, but she'd said nothing to her father about it. Though he often appeared unaware, in fact, Harley was insightful and attentive to details. He must have understood that Rachel, with her presence at Magnolia Bay, added draining strain on the disappearing Twilight. Harley kissed Twilight's cheek, then said, "Buck up, Daughter, and take care of you." He searched her eyes and said, "I mean it—buck up and take care of you."

Ember pressed her right cheek to Twilight's right cheek. Whispering in her ear, Ember said, "I haven't told you. I'm the descendent of Makeda, the Queen of Sheba. You, too, descend from ancient wisdom. Somehow, I know it."

Twilight wanted to talk so badly with Ember about the Sisterhood of Gifts. But instead, she lightly squeezed Ember's hand, stepped into the carriage, and left Memphis with Jed. Pensively, as Jed drove, Twilight watched the road, her heart wrenching.

When captives planned to run for their lives, July-May was ready. She'd cover two large turkey legs in her calming herbs and tonics. After giving one to her beloved Jasper, he'd be so sleepy he wouldn't hear or smell escape. Then she'd sneak to the catch hound pen and throw in the other treated turkey leg so, in case the wicked hound was released, its dulled sense would make it track more slowly. The destroyers typically employed the neighboring tracker with his bloodhound track pack. She'd give the freedom champions herbs and tonics to alter their scents, which helped to keep the track hounds off track. On the night of each run for freedom, she'd chant and pray.

Usually, her intervention worked. But not always. Still, regardless of destroyer Jackson's repeated statement that "no one escapes Magnolia Bay," what July-May knew, as did many of the enslaved at the Bay, was that by risking everything, freedom champions could, and did, escape. But to do so, they had to leave their families and friends behind.

And, they might die.

Chapter 41
Flight

Saturday, July 9, 1859
Late Afternoon
Magnolia Bay and Away

One of the captive girls had vanished.

"Damn!" Jed yelled. "I leave, there's a freedom runner. I should've been here!" In one fluent motion, he stooped, picked up a stone, and pitched it at a tree. When it hit the tree, Jed flinched as if he'd been hit. He stood confused momentarily, then added, "Bratton hired the nearby tracker with his bloodhound pack *and* set our catch hound, so they'll get that runner."

In her room, Twilight, on her knees, prayed that the girl would be imbued with cleverness, stealth, energy, resilience, luck, and, ultimately, freedom. She wondered at the girl's courage and her steps away from Magnolia Bay, risking it all for her freedom, even against great odds of success.

No one had mentioned the girl's name. *Could it be Ava? After what James did to her, I bet she wanted to get away. She's much braver than I am. Has my belief that I must stay at this plantation to help the enslaved become an excuse for my hesitation, my fear of flight? Is my captivity of my own doing?*

She went to the quarters to see if she could discover who had fled. She found Ifeoma and Jimmie. Eyes flashing, Ifeoma said, "They sold Jafaan."

"What?" Twilight's body stiffened. "What? Jackson sold Jafaan? Jafaan won the contest. He was supposed to get his freedom."

Ifeoma clenched her hands into fists. "Then we all heard this morning that Ava was gone, escaped."

Jimmie crawled to Ifeoma. She picked him up and wrapped her arms around him; he started crying, saying over and over, "Jaf—Jaf—Jaf—" Since Jimmie was not even a year old, Twilight knew he, being so young but still understanding that something had happened to Jafaan, had to have an extraordinary connection with Jafaan. Ifeoma looked at Twilight. "You want to help us? Well, here's your chance. Get Jafaan back. Then get him his promised and earned freedom."

Twilight stormed to the group of men who were standing in a nearby field. Jackson was talking with John Bratton; his whip hung limply. Twilight screamed, "Jackson! You sold Jafaan? He'd won his freedom!"

Jackson smiled. "No good businessman would set free that amount of riches. Got a good price for Jeff. Besides, I don't trust him. He'd try to get Nancy and others to run. He's probably the reason we just had a runner. So no winners this year. Hank, Alfred, and Sally have also been sold."

Spinning, Twilight grabbed Bratton's whip from his lax hand, then jumped back several paces. "You're a horrible man, Jack," she said calmly.

Amused at his spirited wife, Jackson smiled his now-frequent smug smile and walked toward her.

Twilight cracked the whip at Jackson, pivoted and cracked it at Bratton. With shocked expressions, the men jumped back from her. Cracking the whip again, she whispered, "Being a sharpshooter and an expert leaper aren't my only talents." With the sound of the third crack of the whip, forgotten vignettes of "GrandMama training" filled her mind, coalescing into a picture of magical and martial abilities.

"Stay away from me," she ordered and cracked the whip. Neither man moved. She cracked it at each of them again. Neither man was smiling their smirky-arrogant-good-ole-boys-club-smiles now.

But the memories redirected her focus from the men to the no-longer-forgotten fantastic images. *Until I was eleven, when Grand-Mama got too sick, she taught me so many fun things! GrandMama taught me how to crack a whip with accurate placement. And to develop my power to leap as if my feet have wings. And to climb a tree as if I were a cat. And to kick effectively. But Gallatin taught me how to shoot.*

Behind her, James lurked. Before she knew it, he was on her, grabbing her arms, pinning them to her sides. She struggled, and if he'd been in front of her, her knee would have disabled him. But he was behind her, and her training was rusty. Though aged, his arms were strong, and her body had withered into a reed.

Jackson walked to her, pulled the whip from her hand, and broke the handle across his knee. He wrapped the broken parts of the handle together with the whip's thong and fall. Throwing it back to Bratton, he said, "Have a Rich-tone fix this." Then to Twilight, he said, "Go to your room. You'll stay there until you learn to be a proper lady and obedient wife."

"So, that's your method, is it? First Jafaan, then me. If you can't break us, you put us away—any of us with spirit."

"I only want to tame your defiance and your tongue. If I must break you to do it, then so be it."

Shaking the loosening hands of James off her, she straightened. Glaring at her husband, she said, "Break me? I won't even bend."

Jackson stared at Twilight, seemingly undecided about how to reply. Then he nodded to Bratton. "Escort my wife to her room. Then saddle up two Walkers. We'll ride out to check on the progress of the Riches on the back perimeter. Jed can continue to oversee the group closer to the quarters."

What is Jackson doing having that grimy, smelly John Bratton follow me to my room? Once there, Bratton stood at the doorway, watching her with his gritty, half-mouth-open-broken-tooth grin. He had to step back to avoid being hit by the repaired door when Twilight slammed it shut. She locked it.

Within minutes, Jackson pounded on the door, his voice demanding she open it. She didn't. He kicked it. With hinges weakened from the first time he had kicked it in, it fell from its frame, and he entered, holding a cloth bag tied with a bow. "Sit down, Twilight," he said gently. "I have a gift for you."

She stared at the bag, wondering what he could possibly have in there. She sat on the edge of a chair.

"I love you. All I have wanted is for us to have marital bliss. It is your responsibility, as the wife, to ensure that. But you don't even try. My gift will change that. So we both can be happier; so we can enjoy our marriage."

Twilight said nothing.

He handed the bag to her. She pushed it away. He put it in her lap. "Open it," he said.

She shook her head. Trepidation crawled through her body like fire ants.

"Open it. It's a gift." He leaned to kiss her. Blocking him, she kept her lips pressed firmly together.

He untied the bow, opened the bag, and pulled his "gift" out of the bag for her to see. A rough iron contraption. She had no idea what it was. *A weird mask or a small cage?*

Jackson started to put it over her head.

"No!" she screamed, standing. Roughly, he encircled her body with his left arm, pinning her arms against her body. Then, he lowered the contraption onto her head. Two vertical flat iron pieces curved around her nose, and one horizontal flat iron piece pressed into her mouth. He released her arms so he could use both hands to fasten and lock the cage.

"What are you doing?" she tried to say, the flat iron piece cutting into her face. She shoved him hard with her body to knock him off his feet. Barely moving, he quickly regained his balance, pushed her against the wall, and ordered, "Open your mouth so no teeth are damaged." She did and screamed. He clicked the padlock, dangled the key before her eyes, then slipped the key into his pocket. She gagged. "You can't scream now. Or talk."

Tears poured from her eyes as the piece of iron in her mouth trapped her tongue and shot pain throughout her body. Held down tight, her tongue began to swell. She couldn't breathe. Panicked, she gasped for air.

"Breathe through your nose, Twilight," Jackson said evenly. He walked behind her and began rubbing her shoulders. "Try to relax, or it will hurt more, which makes breathing difficult."

Frightened for her life, terrified he would not take it off even if she choked on her tears and saliva, she obeyed and tried to calm herself. Still rubbing her shoulders, Jackson said, "You'll get the hang of it."

When she was breathing slowly through her nose and open mouth, he moved to stand in front of her and said, "Father insisted. It'll only be for a few hours. But you don't want me ever to have to put it on you again, for next time, it would be for much longer. You'll learn to restrain what you say and how you behave. You'll learn to obey. Father said it's time you become a Denier."

What? James used the word Denier! Now there is no doubt he is an Egoman of the Society for Supremacy. He must know about the Sisterhood. Does Jackson?

Jackson caressed her hair. "I feel sadness that you have pushed your bad behavior to such an extreme, but since you have, it is my duty to make you obey, to curb your tongue, since you will not do so of your own volition, even with multiple warnings."

Horrified, her eyes pleaded for her release.

"We've not even had to use this on our enslaved in quite some time, since '56, in fact. It's a scold's bridle, but we call it a bit or a gag. It was made in Europe to bridle the tongue of disobedient wives, though from what I hear, they're seldom used in America for that reason. I don't know why, as this appears to be an effective tool for wife training."

He began pacing, talking as if he'd memorized his words as a speech: "Father has this bit and some iron collars for the enslaved. However, as you know, we don't believe in punishing our enslaved. Unlike many enslavers, we use humane methods of keeping order. We've found it effective that the captives be brought here as children and that they create close bonds with their friends. Bonds so close that the threat of being sold dictates their compliance. More than anything, they don't want to be sold from their loved ones. Therefore, they don't run; they don't escape Magnolia Bay."

He stopped pacing, leaned and kissed her right shoulder, then resumed pacing. "We leave them alone in their quarters. We rarely patrol. This has proven effective. We warn them that they or their loved ones will be sold if they misbehave. One warning. They always behave so that they can stay with their friends. Jeff is lucky; he isn't that far away. I sold him close for a reason—so that maybe, in time, when he learns to obey, he'll be allowed to visit Nancy and Jimmie on Free Sundays. I could've easily sold him downriver into the deep South. But I didn't. I gave him special consideration. You should thank me for that."

Her mind and heart were screaming, but she breathed evenly. Jackson continued, "The only times we resort to collars and the bit are after captive uprisings. Father started using these methods after Nat Turner's slaughter of Pales. For one month after we hear of a revolt, we choose captives randomly to wear these devices, changing wearers after a day or two. They get the message. We've never had a revolt."

Never had a revolt? They're children. What is he thinking? A bunch of children will revolt?

"Our catch hound also deters any thoughts they might have of running. We've not had a freedom runner for years. And it will stay that way. The very odd situation of the disobedient who just ran *will* stop; she *is* being hunted; she *will* be caught; she *will* serve as an example. The catch hound *will* tear her to shreds."

Please, God, don't let that catch hound catch her! He wants Ava to be killed, and so brutally! How could Jackson have become so cruel?

Jackson droned on: "Even without our deterrent methods, I can't understand why anyone would want to run away from Magnolia Bay. As Father says, at Magnolia Bay, they've got it good. But, since some of them don't seem to understand that, we have our effective methods. No one escapes Magnolia Bay."

Tears shone in Jackson's eyes. *False tears—tears of blood.*

"Not even a rabble-rouser named Rex had this put on him, though we did try the collar with him twice. Twilight, why did you not listen? After today, you will listen. And you will be happier. This day—your day of wearing the bit—is my gift to you."

Twilight looked from him to the mirror. Out of the mirror, her caged face stared at her, her eyes still pleading for her release from the iron-clad agony.

His hands slid down her arms, then onto her bottom, which he rubbed, then moved his hands along her hips. Wanting to scream, she did her best to breathe evenly. Then, there was the slight crinkle sound of paper. *Oh no!* Twilight panicked. His hand found the open seam that made her secret pocket; he reached in and pulled out the letter from GrandMama. *By Heaven's moon! Why didn't I burn it as GrandMama directed?*

He peered at Twilight, then opened the letter. After quickly skimming each sheet, he nodded, pulled one page, folded it, tucked it in his front pocket, threw the other pages on the bed, then took her hand and tugged her down the stairs and out to Ifeoma's shanty. At the unexpected appearance of the destroyer Jackson with his wife gagged by the bit of a head cage, Ifeoma kept her face expressionless and directed at Jimmie.

"Nancy, watch over my wife. Calm her if she needs it so that she doesn't suffocate." To Twilight, he said, "I must leave now, my dearest captive. I'll be back in a few hours to take this off. Understand, Twilight, understand the message: watch your tongue, or you will be bridled. You will live here with Nancy and her family group for an unspecified time. Maybe forever. This is where you belong, with my enslaved. Because, my dear, you *are* one of my enslaved. Here, you will obey me. Here, you will always be mine, the way I want you." He left.

Frantically, Twilight's eyes pleaded with Ifeoma. Closely, Ifeoma examined the torture device to see how it was put together. "The key is the only way," she said.

Twilight's tongue burned, and her eyes welled with tears. She sat, taking controlled breaths, trying to ease her fear and panic. Then, through the slightly-open door, Taboo appeared and leaped onto Twilight's lap. Twilight petted Taboo. Gently, Ifeoma patted Twilight's back. She said softly, "Troublesome faded folk. And I'm not talking about you."

When Twilight could breathe evenly, she put Taboo on the ground, touched Ifeoma's shoulder then Jimmie's cheek, trying to communicate with her eyes by looking intently at their eyes. Then she left.

With each step, the head cage torture device sawed with its rough iron edges against her face, so she walked softly and slowly to the field. She approached Jed, whose back was facing her. Intent on watching the enslaved, he didn't hear her behind him. Reaching out, she touched his shoulder. He turned, then jumped back. "Dearest Twilight! What in God's land?"

Her eyes filled with tears.

"Oh, darlin', no," Jed said. The enslaved continued to work, but Twilight knew they noticed what was happening even when focused on their tasks. Jed took Twilight by the arm and deftly led her to his cabin. "Thankfully, I have a key, though I've never used this—punishment device—on our laborers."

From a drawer, he took a key. He unlocked and removed the padlock, then carefully lifted the iron cage off her head and threw it on the floor. The heavy thud and clank made a glorious sound. She fell into Jed's arms and pressed her face to his chest. "Oh, darlin', darlin'," Jed repeated, stroking her hair as his shirt became stained with her blood from where the iron had rubbed.

Then, she stood on her tiptoes and kissed his cheek. "Thank you, my dear brother."

Jed said, "Releasing you, I might lose my position and my chance for my own place, and even my chance for Victoria, because, I suppose, this was Jackson's doing."

"Yes. He said James told him to do it."

"Well, I'll probably get the boot, but darlin', my dear little sister, it's all right if I do."

Taking both his hands in hers, she squeezed them lightly. "Promise me, never use that wicked thing. Ever. No torture devices, no whipping."

He nodded.

"Thank you for saving me." She hugged him tightly and said, "I love you."

"I love you, my little sis."

"I know you do. I've always known that. But you have proven it a million times over just now."

He smiled, bent, and softly kissed a place on her cheek that had not been rubbed raw.

"And, Jed, there's more at risk here than your job—your life is now threatened because of me, something Jackson knows about our family. You should leave."

"What are you talking about?"

"Just leave, Jed. Go home."

"Whatever it is, I'm not worried. Jackson has never been happier with an overseer than he is with me. He probably won't give me the boot. But fine if he does."

"There's something else, though. Something that might make Jackson enslave you."

"What are you talking about, Sis? You sound crazed."

Twilight shook her head. "Be careful. And leave this place." She wrapped her arms around him, hugging him again, then quickly released him and left.

Twilight sprinted stealthily to her room. Taboo was lying on the letter where Jackson had thrown it on her bed. He looked at her and lifted his chin, saying, "Mhrrr." She took the Deringer from its hiding place in the carpet bag and put it in her pocket. She picked up Taboo, cradled him in her left arm, and with her right hand, gathered the pages together and tucked them into her other pocket. She returned Taboo to her bed.

At her door appeared the ashen woman she'd seen before. Billy stood behind her. Dressed in a white dressing gown, she walked into the room. *Grandma Ghost?* She was, of course, a real woman.

Her voice was very soft. "I am Grandma. I died. They keep me locked in my room. Billy lets me out at night. Thank God for Billy and for July-May." She put her finger to her lips and whispered, "Shhh. No one knows. It's a secret. Don't tell anyone. Anyone."

Clearly, she was not dead. Twilight saw Billy look at them from the hall; nervously, he kept turning in all directions, scouting. Clutching her hands together, Grandma continued, "When I lived at Woodland Manor, after my husband died, I let people who ran from plantations hide with me. Many children from Magnolia Bay stayed with me for a night. Tricked James and his hounds. For some time, James never thought to look at Woodland Manor. I helped many children and adults run from bondage to freedom. Then, he discovered what I was doing, and he made me die. You must leave. Leave, or he'll make you die, too." Billy fidgeted. With her forefinger, Grandma touched Twilight's forehead quickly, then disappeared into her room; Billy locked it from the outside. He smiled weakly at Twilight. As Grandma Ghost had done, he put a finger to his lips as if to say, Shhhh, then hurried away.

Grandma must "feel" dead because she's locked away. Have the Canons convinced themselves that she is dead?

An hour had passed since Jackson had put the head cage on her—an hour of pure anguish, focused breathing, Taboo petting, brotherly love, and Grandma Ghost visiting. Surely Jack was in the back perimeter with smelly Bratton. *Now is the time. I must escape.*

In Jack's room, she found some dixies, then stuffed them in her trouser pockets. Back in her room, Taboo was curled on her bed. Tenderly, she hugged him to her chest, then kissed him. "I can't leave you, little mister. Who knows what might happen to you by the mean people here? They already tried to kill you. So, you're coming with me. Besides, I'd miss you too much," she whispered. He innocently blinked. She slid the carpet bag handles over her shoulder. "Let's go, wild boy."

Taking care so no one would see her, she tiptoed out of the big house and went to the paddock. Spirit ran to her. She placed Taboo in the carpet bag and looped the handles on her forearm. She easily leaped onto Spirit. She propped the squiggly bag—secure on her arm—in front of her on Spirit. She didn't risk the time for a bridle, so she locked her fingers into Spirit's mane and grasped tightly onto Spirit's neck with her free arm. She could hear Taboo hiss and growl through the bag. Whispering "this is wild," she nonchalantly rode to the road, and then they ran, nearly flying, high speed—and, she prayed, with Godspeed.

But no such grace fell upon her. Out from the roadside forest just past the entry lane to Magnolia Bay stepped John Bratton. Spirit knew what to do and charged Bratton, knocking him to the ground. Shakily, he stood.

This won't do. He'll get Jack now, and we'll be caught. Spirit, I might never be allowed to ride you or even see you again. Jack might sell you! By the brilliant moon, I will not let that happen!

Horse and rider approached the man. Gliding off Spirit's back, Twilight placed the carpet bag on the ground, then walked to Bratton, pulling her secret weapon from her trouser pocket.

Bratton looked at her with angry, glazed-over crazed eyes. He pulled a pistol from his pocket and aimed at the one who rammed him—Spirit.

"No," Twilight said calmly and confidently. Wondrous Ring glistened in the sun. Suddenly, as if the Earth opened between them also saying "No," bees surged upward from their underground nest. Bratton and

Twilight bent over to hide their faces from the bees; Spirit leaped into the air, hovering above the swarm.

Miraculously, the bees disappeared without stinging Twilight. She straightened, and from the corner of her eye, she saw in the trees a deer jump and run. Bratton was touching his face and with relief and disbelief said, "They didn't sting me." But during the bee scare, he'd dropped his gun. Twilight still held hers. Now, seeing her chance, she kicked his gun into the woods, then jumped onto the still-bent-over Bratton and smashed his head with the side of her Deringer. Though small, it was sturdy, and it made its impact on contact, even with someone so thick-skulled.

Bratton crumpled, face down. Angry, relieved, and scared all at the same time, Twilight bent to feel his neck pulse. He had one. Until Bratton, she'd never hit any person or creature, and it hadn't felt great doing so. This made it twice that she'd hit Bratton in the head. Both times he'd asked for it—he'd threatened the lives of Taboo and Spirit. And her life was threatened if he ran to tell Jack she was gone. Simultaneously, she regretted and was glad that she had hit him. She bent closer, hating his smell but glad she could detect breathing. Spirit glided from the sky, softly landing next to her.

"Thank the good Lord I didn't kill him, Spirit," Twilight said, patting her companion. "Thank the good Lord he didn't kill you." Picking up the carpet bag, she looked inside at the frightened, crouching Taboo. "It's ok, Taboo," she said in the most soothing voice she could muster in her rising panic.

Looping the carpet bag handles over her arm, she leaped onto Spirit without even needing to take a step. She secured one hand into Spirit's mane. Bending forward, she grasped Spirit's neck with her free hand. Looking at the prostrate out-cold man, she said, "It's a good look for you, Bratton."

But her persistent wit and Spirit's speed as they ran toward Memphis didn't lessen the gravity of her situation. She tried not to think, but her chaotic mind nagged her with reminders of her rash decision to be

Jackson's betrothed, her forced marriage, his torture of her, the abusive suppers with his family, the imprisonment of Grandma Ghost, the pain endured by the brave enslaved, and the constant violence against humans that defines slavery.

I am escaping Magnolia Bay, but can I find a way out of this hateful maze of a marriage? Will Jackson arrive in Memphis and drag me back to his deranged life? Or can I pull myself from this wreck and be free?

She felt the amulet Precious Friend, Ember's gift, against her throat. Then, she heard the elusive Voice: *Yes, you can and you will.* She echoed the Voice: "I can and I will."

But then, a different voice chimed in her mind: *You have failed. Failed as a wife, failed as a friend, failed as a daughter, failed all of Magnolia Bay's enslaved, and failed yourself. For no matter how righteous your beliefs and your attempted actions to do what you could to help others, you are a fraud. You accomplished nothing. Nothing. All you have carrying you is your privilege.*

She knew: it was the voice of a Beleaguer.

Leaning even more into the neck of her dear companion, she felt the strength of Spirit's muscles working to take her to safety. "No," she spoke aloud to the Beleaguer that had infiltrated her mind. "My beloved Spirit carries me."

Having a horse is a privilege, the Beleaguer said.

"Yes," she said, "but *I* choose *how* I guide my privilege."

After a few beats, the nagging Beleaguer answered: *You are trying to ride with a cat in a bag; that will never work. You're a loser.*

The direness of her dilemma and the comedy of Taboo in the bag hit her crazed state. She laughed. *By the full brilliant moon, I can't let this cat out of the bag. Not now, anyway.* At her own fun pun, she laughed harder, which abated the Beleaguer. With Taboo in the bag, her situation was so ridiculous that she couldn't stop laughing. With her continued laughter, the Beleaguer fell silent.

She began to think of the good that awaited her. She wanted to see Ember and hear her words. She wanted to see Gallatin and feel his arms.

But more than anything, she wanted to regain herself. Again. *Why am I always losing myself?*

Then, the magnitude of escaping Magnolia Bay and what might happen if Jackson found her before she reached home shook her resolve. She started to see Jackson emerge from that tree over there, from that rock over there, from up the road; she could hear his horse racing to her; she could feel him at her back, clawing at her will.

She held tightly to Taboo's bag and Spirit's neck. *Concentrate on Spirit's hoofbeats*, she heard from the Voice. Her mind fell into the steady rhythm. Four hoofbeats, four hoofbeats, four hoofbeats, swoosh; four hoofbeats, four hoofbeats, swoosh; four hoofbeats, swooooshhh.

With each of Spirit's resounding hoofbeats and of Twilight's pounding heartbeats, the Voice chanted: *Do not break, do not break, do not break.* Swoosh. *Do not break, do not break.* Swoosh. *Do not break.* Swooooshhh. As if sunlight had cracked a dark-cast sky, Twilight felt blessed by the Voice that comforted her and by her mystical pegasus gliding forward, carrying her away with Taboo.

In the rush of the speed of Spirit's pace and the wild conviction of her soul, Twilight joined in the chant with each forward stride and flight: "I won't break. I won't break."

>Four hoofbeats.
>Swooooooooooooooooooooooooooosh.
>Four hoofbeats.
>Swooooooooooooooooooooooooooosh.

This was new! After each fourth hoofbeat—for seven seconds, about seventy feet—they flew. She stated loudly and decisively in liberty's wind:

"I won't even bend."

Chapter 42
Escape

Saturday, July 9, 1859
Evening
The Forest Near Ivy Falls

"Damn the bad luck," whispered Ava, rubbing her swollen, bruised, throbbing ankle.

"No time to be correcting my cursing, Mama. Any minute now, I'm going to be eaten alive by that catch hound, so I'll curse all I want, and I think God won't mind my cursing that hound and those human murderers as I fly into His arms."

Mama wasn't here. Mama was never here. Not since Ava was ten, when the Maryland Pale sold Mama and Ava apart even though they were free. But never mind; Ava always talked to Mama anyway. And she knew Mama heard her and loved her. Ava also knew death was stalking her. Bloodhounds loudly bayed in their deep voices with obvious ominous movement toward her. Within moments, she'd be in death's maws from being mercilessly mauled by the Magnolia Bay catch hound.

She pushed her body into the clump of trees she was leaning against. She was far from the road, but close enough to it so she wouldn't lose her way to Memphis, where the free Rich-tone family would give her food and rest before she continued to the North. They had helped Jafaan and her on earlier journeys. She'd heard that a Pale man also might be aiding freedom champions. Freedom champions—those, like her, facing great challenges to make their way to the North, to freedom—their successes inspiring others to flee captivity. Regardless, she wouldn't make it to either place of refuge in Memphis now.

"Mama, I can't make it to freedom. If only I could fly to Maryland. My magical Moses is there; she'd get me North like she did before. There I was free. If I'd stayed there, I could've lived past fifteen. But when I heard stories told among our people of the evil child-enslaving Magnolia Bay, I knew my calling."

Ava took her hands from her ankle and folded them, speaking now as if in prayer:

"Mama, remember how scared I was when, at thirteen, I walked into Magnolia Bay? There I could use Moses' training and all the survival skills you'd taught me. I helped six escape. I taught reading, writing, and numbers. But then that jackass James. What he tried. He tried it once. He didn't even get close to getting what he was after—because I kneed him where he noticed. I kneed him where he needed pain." Ava chuckled. "Then I ran out of that cabin. I decided I'd never let him near me again. I hid from him. But I knew it was a matter of time before he'd find me and again drag me to that evil place. So, before jackass James could do that, I ran. I bleed woman's blood now, Mama, and I don't want a child yet—and never a child of jackass James's. And, I never want any of jackass James's body parts near me! Fetid thought! So I ran for my freedom. I made my vow and I stuck with it: be free or die trying."

Her lips trembled. "But now, with this hurt ankle, I can't save myself or anyone else. I won't be able to find Jafaan. I can't help little Glory. I told her I'd come back for her one night soon."

Ava didn't want to die. Her ankle throbbed. So did her heart. She said, "I won't cry. They'll see me die, but they won't see me cry." Then, as her Moses had taught her, she prayed with passion. She decided she would die praying.

A twig broke. She tensed. She opened her eyes.

A rare antlered doe walked to her. Just inches away, the doe with gorgeous, intense brown eyes looked directly into Ava's eyes. Immersed in the moment, Ava barely breathed. Ava reached out her hand and lightly touched the doe's neck; her fingertips glowed. The doe circled the girl, reached down, her antlers touching the other female's face, gently pressing the middle of her forehead. With a firm but tender bite onto Ava's worn shift collar, the doe pulled a piece of fabric, turned, and leaped away as if she were flying, her white tail flicking as she disappeared.

The sounds of the hounds faded into silence.

They've gone a different direction! They must be following the deer and my scent on that cloth.

That was all Ava needed. She stood and limped, one step at a time, first to find Jafaan, then toward freedom.

Later, her steps would be for freedom for Glory, Ifeoma, Jimmie, Sally, Ben, Zvi, and as many who would follow her lead.

Chapter 43
Home

*Saturday, July 9, 1859, Night
to Monday, July 11, 1859, Evening
Memphis*

The house sat deathly quiet.

Cara was drinking tea in the kitchen. "Oh, Twilight! You arrived like a ghost, scaring the blood right out of me!" she said. "Why are you back home? What's happened? Is Jed with you?"

"I'm back for good. Just me, Spirit, and—" Twilight let her cat out of the bag. "—Taboo." Taboo shook his head, hissed, blinked his large eyes, and wobbled across the kitchen floor. Twilight bent and caressed his back, calming him from his ride in a bag. "Hey, little mister," she cooed.

"A cat! You brought a cat in a bag on Spirit?" Cara said.

"Yes," Twilight laughed. "I did. I'll get him some cream to lap."

"Milk will be better. First, let's take care of your face," Cara said, placing a wet cloth to Twilight's injuries and asking no questions. Then, she gave Taboo a small saucer of milk and made Twilight a cup of the tea she was drinking, an herbal mixture to encourage sleep.

Soon, Twilight was back in *her* room. She hid her Deringer at the top of her wardrobe. Then, she snuggled in *her* bed, with Taboo curled at her side. Stroking his soft fur with one hand, she held GrandMama's letter, now with one missing page. She read the pages she had again, as she had done every day in the last year. A year gone. What a weird year. She had accomplished nothing in stopping the atrocity of slavery and little in bettering the lives of the enslaved. Further, Jackson had the page of the letter with the dangerous, possibly deadly, secret. Things were worse now than when she had set out to try to do some good.

She'd put first her self-preservation, leaving her friends at Magnolia Bay to suffer. *You are a loser.*

"No! I will not let a Beleaguer fill my mind! I pray, GrandMama, for another way that I can help stop slavery." But keeping the letter had been, and was, a bad idea—and defiant against GrandMama's final words to her. Now, Jackson had proof to enslave her, and maybe even her brothers and sisters—*and my mother! No! I can't let that happen.* Fear soaked her; she breathed deeply several times and petted Taboo, trying to relax. But she couldn't relax. And she couldn't sleep. Because of her resistance to reason about burning the letter, she might have to pay with her freedom and her life. And so might her family.

The next evening in the library and with Taboo on her lap, Twilight felt moved to try her hand at poetry. Writing poetry might help her express her soul thoughts, which she hoped might ease her distress and help her out of the crazy maze of her life. She'd written some verse years before, but when she began working at her father's business, she'd stopped. Now she wrote in the rebellious way of Whitman, without a set metrical pattern or end rhyme:

> My cat sleeps on my lap,
> Unconcerned.
> What does he know
> That I don't?
> Maybe tonight, as I lie awake,
> He'll dream on my chest
> Sending his measured breath messages
> To my heart.

She heard the knocker on the front door, then Ember saying, "Mr. Canon," and then the sound of the door being slammed shut.

Shaking with fear, Twilight placed Taboo on the ottoman, stood, and smoothed her dress and hair. Ember rushed into the library. "Twilight," she said with urgency.

"I heard," Twilight whispered. Even though she had expected him to come for her, she was unprepared to face him.

"I shut the door on him!" Ember said.

Twilight laughed and said, "Good for you! But we must let him in. His anger is dangerous."

Hiding her trepidation, Twilight walked confidently to the door, opened it, and said, "Good evening, Jack."

He entered and took both her hands in his. She flinched as if she'd been hit. "Hello, darling," he said, seemingly oblivious to her severe reaction to his touch and that Ember had slammed the door on him.

Twilight stiffened, said nothing, and pulled her hands away.

"I thought we were reaching an understanding in our marriage," he said. "I want you to return home."

"I am home."

"Twilight, darling, don't be coy with me. We've been married a mere half-year, and look at what's happening to us. I should not have spoken to you in such a manner. Nor should I have sent you away."

"Sent me away? You didn't send me away. I left of my own volition. And not because of how you spoke to me. You tortured me," Twilight said. "Grant me a divorce, and leave, now."

"I won't leave," Jackson said with a strange combination of rage and desperation twisting his handsome face. "I spoke to you harshly. And I broke my word. A Southern gentleman never breaks his word. I'm the one who's wrong."

She continued, "I won't let you order me any longer. You don't know how to treat a woman, or any human, Jack. You're a liar, and you are cruel."

He placed his hand on her shoulder. Through the light silk, she felt it, leaded and hot, almost as if it might leave its impression like the signet of the sealing wax of worn and yellowing letters.

No, not like that. His hand on me is searing, as if he is branding me.

He ran his hand down her arm. She tried to stop shaking, but she couldn't. He said softly, "I knew once how to treat you, didn't I?"

Twilight didn't answer and held in the sickness rising from her stomach.

Pulling his hand away to clutch his hat with both hands, he said, "Give me another chance. I know our marriage can be a fine one."

Twilight was silent.

"You love me. I know you do," Jackson said. Pacing the parlor, he added, "You know that my father is an intimate friend of many influential men. It would be no problem for me to obtain our divorce. If we'd had a child, as you well know, he would rightfully be mine." He stopped pacing and stared intently at her. "I wish to God we had a child on the way. If so, you would stay with me."

"What good would that do, Jack, if the feeling between us is gone?"

Staring hard at her, he said, "Mrs. Canon, enough of this discussion. As your husband, I have the right and the power to order you to come home with me, and I intend to use that right. So I am ordering you now to come home. I will stay here with you tonight; then, we will leave for Magnolia Bay in the morning."

"No."

"Twilight, no more dissension. I'm ordering you."

"So you are. But as I said, I'll no longer follow your orders. I won't go. And, Jack, how can you allow your grandmother to be locked away?"

Jackson inhaled deeply; a fury in him visibly rose. Evenly and with effort, he said, "You've lost your mind, Twilight. What in Liberty's name are you talking about? I told you to stop reading. Fantasy stories are ruining your mind. I have every right to carry you out of here. I have every right to have you arrested for your insolence and disobedience. Then the law would force you to leave with me."

I pray the law will not doom me back to Hell Bay.

Jackson looked long and deeply at Twilight. Tears edged his eyes. "You're a thief," he said. "You stole some of my money. But that's of no consequence. What you did that makes you a thief of the highest order is that," Jackson drew a breath deep into his chest, "you stole my heart. And, my dear, I have two reasons the law will ensure you stay mine. First—you are my wife. Second—" He pulled a folded paper from his inside jacket pocket. "—this." He waved it in front of her face.

The page from GrandMama's letter! Fear gripped her chest; she was silent. "Give me that, Jackson." She placed her right hand lightly on his cheek. Wondrous Ring twinkled. A spark of sunlight glinted through the parlor window. As she'd hoped, her touch distracted him: she reached for the page, but Jackson jerked it away from her fingertips. Dangling it before her, he said, "If you want this, you know where to find me."

"Jack."

"Change of heart, my dear?"

"No. I want to know about Ava."

"Odd. The hounds tracked a deer, not her. Even the deer got away. The poor peasant neighbor is a poor trainer. Bratton, also, is a poor trainer. Maybe a couple more cracks on his skull will help him," he said, smiling at her.

A deer saved Ava!

"We are continuing the hunt. No one escapes Magnolia Bay."

"Leave Ava alone, Jack."

"You abandoned your friends, didn't you, little captive? If you want to know more about what happens at Magnolia Bay, you must return."

Jesse, Harley, and Ember entered the parlor. All three stood with feet apart, arms crossed at their chests, and stern expressions.

Placing his hat on his head and tucking the page back into his inside coat pocket, he nodded to Harley and Jesse, ignored Ember, then said, "I'll have the proceedings started. Good night."

Twilight was leaving for the office the next morning when someone knocked on the door. "Lands a mercy," Cara said, rushing to answer. "Who could it be at this hour?"

There stood Jackson. In the dining room, Twilight clutched the tablecloth. Fear shot through her. *Will he drag me back to Hell Bay?* Then she heard him say, "I've come to call on Miss Rachel. Is she in?"

Cara answered that Rachel was still asleep. Would he mind returning after noon? Twilight tried to clear her head. *Jack is calling on Rachel?*

That evening at supper, she asked Rachel if Jackson had called that afternoon. Blushing like a sunset, Rachel hid her face with her ever-fluttering fan. Shocked, Jesse stared at Rachel. Rachel stammered, "I-I told him it was not-not proper for him to call—until he was no longer married. To-to my—sister."

"He'll be back anyway," Twilight said. "Probably this very evening."

"Why, he wouldn't dare refuse my wishes," Rachel said, dropping her fan and pouting.

"Rachel, do be careful," Twilight said.

"Are you threatening me, Twilight?"

"No," Twilight said. "It's a warning—you don't know Jack."

"Poor, poor Jackson," Rachel said. "Why he ever proposed to you, I could never imagine. Anything, I repeat, *anything* Prince Jackson does will be marvelous in my eyes." She fluttered her eyelashes.

As Twilight had predicted, Jackson did call on Rachel that very evening. And Rachel didn't refuse his visit. Twilight worried endlessly since Jackson knew—and had proof—of Rachel and Jed's heritage. At Magnolia Bay, he could enslave them. Maybe he already had enslaved Jed and was planning for Rachel to be next.

She feared for both siblings, who—charmed by Jackson's capitalistic charisma—might be developing a tolerance for just how nefarious he could be.

Chapter 44
Poetry and Surprise

Monday, July 11, 1859, Evening
Wednesday, August 24, 1859
and Thursday, August 25, 1859
Memphis

Seated on Twilight's bed in dressing gowns and with Taboo snoring softly between them, Twilight and Ember shared their newfound interest—one that seemed to seek them: creating poetry.

"I was working in the garden, and the words came up from the earth into me," Ember said. "It's verse. Not quite poetry. At least not how Phillis writes poetry."

"The same for me," Twilight said. "Verse just came to me in the parlor. I'm writing very freely, like in the way Walt writes. Would you read yours to me, please?"

Ember smiled, nodded, then read:

> "A beetle strolls my garden rows,
> An expert in traversing the earth.
> Suddenly, her back opens, wings appear
> Lifting her as if on an invisible hand,
> And she flies,
> An expert in traversing the realm of air.

Yes, she walks along the ruggedness of ground
As the smallest—she could be so easily crushed.

Then, as if on cue from some unknown source,
She's above us all, smoothly rising
On the heights of flight.

Dear Tiny Beetle,
You are evolved
Much more than I."

Twilight clapped lightly to not disturb the sleeping Taboo. "That's wonderful, Ember!" Leaning over Taboo's snores, close to Ember, Twilight whispered, "You have those wings that magically appear; I know it."

"So do you."

"You whispered to me your heritage, your ancestor Makeda, the Queen of Sheba."

Ember nodded.

"I have a secret," Twilight whispered. After wanting to share this information with someone, but knowing she shouldn't, it seemed as if Ember knew something anyway about a mystical sisterhood. So, she decided to hint a bit: "All I can say is that my GrandMama told me to look for the Wise Ones, and that," she lowered her voice even more, "as a young woman, I am part of a mysterious group of other women. A Sisterhood. I think you are part of that Sisterhood."

"Mama said strange things sometimes, too," Ember said, which was neither a denial nor confirmation of Twilight's statement.

"Did she mention a Sisterhood?" Twilight asked.

"Not exactly," Ember said. "And I'll not say more on it."

Twilight nodded. Maybe saying something to Ember had been the wrong move, but she hadn't said much—.

After Twilight read her Taboo poem to Ember, they agreed to continue writing and reading their poems to each other, with a candle lit, every Sunday evening.

~~~>>>>> <<<<<~~

Six weeks later, news arrived that changed everything.

Telegram in hand, Harley paced and ruffled his hair, thinking. Finally, he stopped and said, "I'll serve as captain for this trip, trustworthy Gaines as engineer. I'll hire roustabouts as deckhands; they won't talk. And there is only one answer as to who should pilot—the only man we can trust fully with these precious passengers—Gallatin. He'll be here tomorrow. We'll speak with him then."

Twilight's grandfather in Evansville had died. He'd left his home and businesses to Twilight, with the businesses under Harley's supervision until Twilight turned twenty-five. Twilight would need to move to Willow Land and run the businesses. Evansville was a Northern city; thus, Ember wanted to go, and so did Jesse. Ember, of course, refused to leave without Menelik. She'd discovered where he was, though she wouldn't confide her source of information to even Jesse. Once they had Menelik, the plan was to smuggle Ember and her children on one of Harley's freight steamers into Indiana. Traveling by passenger steamer or train was out of the question, as Indiana's constitution didn't allow Rich-tone people, even those who were free, to enter the state.

The next day, Twilight peered anxiously out the office window at the wharf, searching downriver for Gallatin. Soon she saw gray puffs in the clear sky, then the tips of the smoke stacks peeked over the horizon. She left the office and went to the wharf, taking in the soft, slow engine "chuu chuu" with the puffs of smoke keeping time to the sound. Before long, she could hear the "tuu tuu" of the paddlewheel hitting the water behind the ship.

Then she saw through the tall wide widows of the pilot house atop the two-story ship, Gallatin standing at the giant wheel. Expertly steering while using hand signals and speaking through the voice pipe to the engine room, he commanded the docking to the deep sounds of whistles, rings of bells, and leadsmen calling the river depth. After the ship was tied at the wharf and the passengers disembarked, Gallatin walked down the plank. He barely hid his delighted shock at seeing Twilight, holding onto the reins of both Spirit and Charger, waiting for him.

"Good day," he said, tipping his hat, concerned, then whispered, "You're here? Is this a dream? I want to take you in my arms and kiss you. But, a death, dearest? You're wearing black. Has Jackson died?"

Twilight shook her head and said, "No, not Jackson. Grandfather. I'll miss his letters. And I miss him." Then she whispered, "To me, Jackson is dead. I'll never return to Jackson."

"Let's fly."

She smiled. "Yes, let's fly."

On horseback, they raced outside of town to a broad brook. Panting, laughing, and hot, they dismounted and walked Spirit and Charger to cool them, then tied them to a low limb of a tree by the brook.

"It's beautiful here; a lovely place for a late lunch," Twilight said as she took a saddlebag filled with food off Charger.

"Perfect," Gallatin said, then untied the quilt from the back of Charger's saddle and shook it out, spreading it by the brook. "Darling, I'm concerned," he said. "You're looking too thin. I'm worried you are ill. Would you like to sit?"

"No," Twilight said. "I'd like to wade."

Impulsively, she slipped off her riding boots, then stepped behind the tree and reached under each trouser leg to pull off her stockings. Gallatin stood by the water. Touching his shoulder lightly, Twilight laughed, bent, rolled up the legs of her trousers, then lifted her skirt and stepped onto a large stone in the water. She looked back at Gallatin and called, "Follow the leader!"

Gallatin laughed, pulled off his boots and socks, then followed her into the brook. Twilight ambled upstream. "You have to step carefully. Some rocks are slick!" she called without looking back. To avoid some rough rocks, she stepped back up to the bank, walked on the grass, then went back into the brook. Stopping, she turned, watching Gallatin follow her every step. When he approached her, she held her skirt with one hand, bent and splashed him with the other.

"Ha! Now you're playing a different game!" Gallatin said, laughing as he guarded his face with his arm. Twilight let her skirt drop into the water and furiously splashed him with both hands. In two giant strides, he was upon her, grabbing her hands and gently pulling her body toward his. Leaning, he kissed her. This was a sensation Twilight had desperately missed, as she had with everything about Gallatin.

"Now *you* are playing a different game," Twilight said.

"I'm not playing," Gallatin said, kissing her again. "And this isn't a game." Intently, he looked at her, then lifted her from the brook into his arms. He carried her out of the stream and to the quilt, laying her gently upon it. They kissed. Then he said, "Your skirt is wet. Let's hang it on a limb to dry." Gallatin knelt beside her and placed his arms around her waist to unbutton the skirt. They kissed, and they kissed, and soon the skirt was off her. "I wear trousers, too," she said.

"Of course you do," he said, smiling. He stood, the skirt dangling from his hand, and gazed at her. He turned to a tree to hang the wet garment on a limb and kept his back to her. She unbuttoned her jacket-style bodice and placed it to the side, then wiggled out of her trousers and threw them, hitting him in the back. He laughed.

After hanging her trousers on the limb, Gallatin shed his jacket and trousers and, in only his shirt and drawers, returned to Twilight, who was leaning back on her arms, legs crossed, watching him. She was only in her drawers and shortened chemise, but she didn't blush. Everything she did with Gallatin, even this, felt right. He stood over her, his feet on each side of her stretched legs. "I love you," he said. He knelt. She uncrossed her legs so they lay straight between his thighs, and he was close, very close to her. Gently, he brushed her hair from her face. "I love you."

"I love you."

He bent forward to kiss her; his thighs touched the inside of hers, uncovered by her open drawers. He caressed and kissed her neck, then tenderly trailed his fingers on her shoulder, which he kissed through the linen of the chemise.

"May I?" he asked.

"Yes." He pulled the chemise up and off her, then caressed her bare skin. Softly, he kissed both her shoulders, kissed up her neck to her chin, kissed her lips, then kissed back down again onto her neck. He stopped. Taking her face in his hands, he said, "I love you. But I can't promise I'll leave the river yet. So tell me to stop. If you are not ready for this, my darling Twilight, tell me."

Smiling, Twilight traced his face and lips with her fingertips. "I want to remember every crease of your face, every muscle of your body, every angle and curve of you," she said. "I want you burned into me, so on those long days and nights when you're gone, I can feel the impression of your body with mine."

Gallatin groaned, kissed her lips again, then said, "I want you to be sure. Should we consider your marriage? The law?"

"The only law I know is written with my heart," Twilight said.

Gallatin unbuttoned his shirt and pulled it off, saying, "Just let me feel your skin next to mine. I won't do more than that."

Twilight whispered, "I want you to do more than that."

Touching bare feet to bare feet, bare thighs to bare thighs, bare abdomen to bare abdomen, bare chest to bare chest, they kissed. Neither had ever felt such warm beauty and loving care as that of their skin touching in pure nakedness and their bodies molding into one.

Chapter 45
Northbound

Thursday, August 25, 1859
to Friday, September 2, 1859
Mississippi River

G allatin agreed to the plan.

After his return from St. Louis, he would pilot Twilight, Jesse, Ember, Makeda-Angel, and Menelik to Evansville on the freighter *Whistling Wind*. It would be Gallatin's last trip for Harley, for, after this trip, he was purchasing a steamship to go into business for himself. He assured Twilight that this was a step in leaving the river because, if working for himself proved profitable, he would stop piloting and work ashore as a steamship packet owner.

As for Twilight, she was moving to a port on a river that Gallatin didn't navigate. But, she'd be in the North, so hopefully beyond Jackson's grasp and the power he held to keep her his captive. Thus, while they were moving farther from each other, they believed these moves would ultimately bring them closer.

"I wish we could stay together all night. I don't want to leave you, Twilight," Gallatin said when they were alone in the library.

"We could stay *here* all night," Twilight said, snuggling her face firmly against his broad chest.

"Here, in the library?"

"Yes, just as we are. I like snuggling with you."

Stroking her hair, Gallatin said, "I'll stay with you until you fall asleep. Someday, I swear on my ship's wheel, you'll never have to sleep without me by your side."

Resting securely in Gallatin's arms, feeling safe for the first time in months, Twilight did fall asleep. He held her there for hours, not wanting to let her go, and watched her serene face. Too soon, he heard the first chirp of the dawn bird, and he knew he must put her in her bed before any family member found that they'd spent the entire night together. He carried her upstairs to her room, gently laying her on her bed.

He gazed lovingly at her. Then he covered her with a quilt, gazed at her again, and whispered, "I do love you, more than the river. Just give me some time, my darling." He left her room, softly closing the door behind him. For a moment, he stared at the door; then, he walked a few steps down the hall to where her bed would be on the opposite side of the wall. Firmly against the wall through which his love slept, he pressed his hands and his face.

The grandfather clock at the end of the hall ticked loudly. As birds joined in a crescendoing morning chorus, the sound of the clock faded. Sunlight slipped through the cracks in the shutters and filled the hall. Pulling away from the barrier between them, Gallatin went to his room.

⤞⤞⤞ ⤝⤝⤝

The next day, Jesse and Ember drove a carriage to a nearby plantation that, Ember said, held Menelik. During the hour-long trip, several deer flitted across the road as performers in an enchanted nature play.

As they traveled, they agreed on an alias for Ember. When they arrived, out walked a Rich-tone man with a Rich-tone boy of about age twelve.

The Pale planter greeted them, and as they walked to the quarters of the enslaved, he said, "I must be getting a reputation for having Riches as fine as Forrest has. A free Rich-tone who owns a small farm a few miles away was just here and made a similar purchase. You probably saw him leaving with his merchandise. In his case—and he's well known in these parts—he's establishing himself as a bona fide planter. But, having little cash, he purchases his laborers when they are young. In just a few years, they are sturdy field hands. With this purchase today, he has maybe five young captives now. I must say, for a Rich-tone, he has some smarts and wherewithal. Most of the peasant Pale planters who do all their own work can't seem to come up with the cash for more than one purchase."

Ember kept her expression blank. She'd heard of rare cases of free Rich-tone people buying enslaved Rich-tone people. However, the purchases of Rich-tones by Rich-tones were usually to free their family members or friends—not to enslave them—and not to be enslavers. So, most likely, he'd been there for the same reason they were—to free someone's child, perhaps his own. Still, her heart wrenched at the thought that, possibly, his intent was not admirable at all.

"Boys! Boys! Come!" the man shouted.

Four boys scurried from the shacks and stood in a line, their faces directed downward. Acting his part, Jesse said to the man, "My house servant Helen is a good judge of her kind." Addressing Ember, Jesse said, "Helen, do you see a suitable boy?"

She walked close to the boys. Even though she was looking for her son, she'd seen him with only spiritual eyes for three years. How would Menelik look at six years old? She walked closer to one boy. *Is this my Menelik?* She stood in front of him and looked into his eyes with her eyes of a mother. There was no doubt; he *was* her son.

Though she desperately wanted to wrap him in her arms, she remained calm. He stared at her. She looked away. He was a smart boy, a brilliant boy. If he recognized her, he'd know better than to say anything. Trying to appear composed, she quickly nodded to Menelik. "He should do nicely." Then she stepped away so as not to reveal her joy.

Jesse paid and signed the papers. In the carriage, Ember said to Menelik, who was staring at her, "Honey, my name isn't Helen. I used that name because we didn't want to take a chance that you'd recognize me in front of that man. We feared he'd keep you just out of meanness if he knew I already know you and love you."

"You're my mama," Menelik said.

"Yes," Ember said, opening her arms.

The boy nestled against his mother, crying. "I knew you'd find me," he said. "Every night, I saw you. I saw you flying above me across the moon."

On the appointed day, September 1, Gallatin disembarked from the *North Star* for the last time. The day was busy with preparations.

Now that the time had arrived, Elizabeth cried to Ember, "Stay, Cherish, I beg you, stay with me!" Then to Twilight she shouted, "This is your doing! You get out of my sight forever! I hate you!"

Ember placed her arms around Elizabeth. Twilight held her breath. Ember whispered in Elizabeth's ear. Elizabeth crumpled onto a chair and said, "Yes. Yes, you are right."

Late that night, Twilight quietly stole into her mother's room and whispered to the sleeping woman, "I love you. I wish you loved me."

To avoid being seen, the adventurers boarded the *Whistling Wind* around midnight. While settling in for their journey, Twilight asked, "Ember, what did you say to Mother that stopped her fit?"

"I said, 'Cherish forgives you. Now, Elizabeth, forgive yourself.'"

The trip north to Evansville, Indiana, typically took at most five days. But this excursion of the *Wind* would be a ten-day trip: instead of having two pilots for continuous travel, Gallatin was the sole pilot. When night fell, he'd tie the riverboat to shore so they could collect wood for fuel when needed, and he could sleep.

Just after dawn, the *Whistling Wind* left Memphis. After helping prepare breakfast for everyone, Twilight joined Gallatin in the pilot house. He said, "Can you guess what I named my ship?"

"Hmmm," Twilight said, hugging his arm. "River Tamer?"

"I like that. But no. Painted on the side, in big blue letters: *Star of Twilight*."

She threw her arms around his waist and said, "You named your ship for me? Thank you."

Gallatin smiled. "It has two meanings, actually. As you said, the first and most important reason is that it is named for you. And the second, well, you'll see this evening at twilight."

As the day unfolded, Ember invented myriad travel games for the children. She, Twilight, and a deckhand experienced with food preparation made the meals, which was a time-consuming task.

Time passed quickly as Gallatin kept the *Whistling Wind* at a good upstream clip of ten miles per hour.

At her hour, Twilight took a meal to Gallatin in the pilot house. He pointed into the western sky and said, "There, do you see it? The first star of the evening, the star of twilight."

"Yes. I see. It is the only star you can see, for it isn't quite dark yet," Twilight said.

"It's the only star you'll see at dusk. And it isn't really a star, but you know that. It, the planet Venus, is a sign to us, as is all of nature, here on the river. When we pilots see Venus, we know the mysterious night will be over us in minutes. Venus is sometimes called the evening star or the morning star, depending on its orbit when it appears to us on Earth. But I like to call it the star of twilight." He winked and lightly touched the tip of Twilight's nose. "Named in honor of the Goddess of Love—you, Twilight."

~>>>> <<<<~

That night when everyone was asleep, Gallatin patrolled the ship. During his rounds, he checked on Spirit and his other precious passengers. Ember, Menelik, and Mekeda-Angel slept on cots near Twilight, who was closest to the walkway. Taboo, lying next to Twilight's face, snored. For just a moment, Gallatin watched Twilight sleep; he burned to lie near her. He wondered how she could sleep so peacefully and not be restless to be near him.

As he turned to go, he nearly bumped into Jesse, who was checking on Ember from the other side of the hay bales. Quietly the two men chuckled. Lightly smacking Jesse on the back, Gallatin whispered, "Why don't you join me in the wheelhouse?"

There, as they watched the night river, they talked of the South's threats to secede from the nation, the upcoming presidential election, their jobs, and any other acceptable man's topic that kept them from discussing what they had in common, what they were really thinking of, what each man was feeling most deeply—the ache to be next to the woman he loved.

Chapter 46
Bad Catch

Early September 1859
Mississippi River

One afternoon, Gallatin squinted and leaned to the side of the wheel, peering ahead at a particular place in the river.

Seated near Gallatin and the wheel, Twilight could discern only what seemed to resemble logs bobbing in the river.

Gallatin said, "Do you have your Deringer?"

"Always," Twilight said.

"Keep it ready. There are a couple of men ahead; see them? They're hanging onto logs. We'll pick them up." Through the voice pipe, Gallatin ordered the engine room to stop the engines.

"Have they wrecked?"

"If so, only off a small raft, most likely," Gallatin said.

"Oh no. I know I sound horrible when I say this, for I'm not at all thinking of their lives, but I wish we wouldn't," Twilight said. "How will we hide Ember and the children from them? What if they tell?"

"I don't see that we have another choice. We can't just pass by and leave them in the river. They could float to land, but there's not a town for miles around. And they could be injured. To make sure they don't tell anyone about us, we'll tell them Ember is your servant and that we are headed back to Memphis after you tend to your ailing mother in Cairo. We'll leave them in Cairo; they'll have no idea we are going to Evansville."

"I'll tell Ember and Jesse."

"Tell the children to get below deck. And get your father. He needs to take the wheel," Gallatin said. "Keep your Deringer ready."

"But why? Do you think a couple of raft-wrecked men will try to attack us?"

"If they didn't wreck, then, yes."

Gallatin went to the deck as Harley took the wheel. Some deckhands reached down to pull the two men out of the water. Lying on the deck, they appeared exhausted.

"I think they've been stranded awhile, from the looks of them," Twilight said.

Gallatin searched the river, upstream and downstream. "Maybe," he said between clenched teeth. "Or maybe they're just good actors."

"What makes you say that?"

"They wouldn't be out here hanging on logs with no wreckage around. I haven't seen any debris along the shore or in the river. Since we're traveling upriver, it would've floated towards us." Gallatin nodded. "Adds up to only one thing. I'll check their story. Take my Deringer," he said sternly. "This way, you'll have two shots if needed."

With a pistol in each hand, she watched as Gallatin walked to the two men.

"I'm the pilot. I suppose you fellows would like some water?" He said to a deckhand, "After we hear how long they've been stranded, get them a drink." To the two rescued men, Gallatin said, "What are your names? And what's your story?"

One man staggered to a stand. "I'm Joe," he said. "He's Kit." Kit crouched and said, "Here's my story." With sudden strength, Kit jumped behind Gallatin, grabbing him and pinning his arms to his sides. Joe drew a knife from a hidden sheath on the inside of his waistband and lunged at Gallatin.

Using Kit as a brace, Gallatin leaned back, raised one leg high, and kicked Joe in the face, knocking him back to the deck. Gallatin rocked forward, loosening Kit's grip. With an elbow, he jabbed Kit in the gut, knocking Kit to the ship's edge.

The deckhand jumped at Joe, who'd staggered up. Joe's arm shot out, slicing the deckhand's arm with his knife. With a scream, the deckhand fell backward, clutching his bleeding arm. Knife in hand and arm extended, Joe jumped at Gallatin. Gallatin grabbed Joe's arm and twisted it; Joe's knife clunked to the deck. Joe bent, reaching for his knife. Gallatin lifted his leg and, with a hard kick, knocked Joe into the river.

Kit pulled a knife and staggered from the ship's edge. Twilight aimed a pistol at Kit and, with practiced accuracy, shot him in the leg. He screamed and fell backward into the river.

During the commotion, a rowboat with three men appeared from a place hidden on the shore and approached the ship. The three men aimed rifles at Twilight, Gallatin, Jesse, and the deckhands who'd appeared after hearing the gunshot. Twilight ran to the ship's edge and shielded herself behind hay bales. With her second gun, she shot the hand of one of the men; his rifle dropped into the river. Jesse shot the other two men. Even though he aimed for their arms, he hit one in the chest.

Harley apparently had ordered full steam, for the *Whistling Wind* was moving fast, and soon the rowboat was far behind.

Twilight ran to Gallatin and hugged him. "By the full moon! You are a fighter beyond fighters!" she said. "Without using a gun, you held off both of them."

"You're quite a fighter yourself," Gallatin said proudly.

"I shot one in the leg; I shot the rifle from the hands of another," she said.

"That's good shooting, I'd say," Gallatin said.

"Have you ever shot a man?" she asked.

"Yes," he said.

"It was easy," she said. "Almost too easy."

"Your survival instincts kicked in. Next time is easier, and harder," Gallatin replied.

Twilight wondered how Gallatin knew this, but she didn't ask. Who knew what a riverboat pilot might encounter on his travels? Gallatin had always spoken sparingly about his travels, but she suspected he'd had many dangerous adventures. Ember was cleaning the bleeding wound of the deckhand. Pensively, Jesse sat next to her. "Poor Jesse," Twilight whispered to Gallatin. "He shot a man in the chest. Probably killed him. Of course, when using guns to defend ourselves, it's always possible, or probable, that we will kill someone. It's difficult shooting with precision with such a small gun, but you made me practice. I'm glad about that. I didn't aim to kill. I never will."

She went to Jesse, put her hand on his sagging shoulder, and said, "I'm glad you were here, Jesse. They would've killed us."

"They're river scum. They make the river a dangerous place for the innocent," he said, looking at her with defiance. "And yet," he added, his expression softening, "it feels strange to shoot someone, to possibly kill. I don't like it."

She took his hand and held it.

Ember looked away from her patient to Jesse and smiled. Jesse kissed Twilight's hand holding his, then said to Ember, "What can I do to help?"

"Fortunately, the wound isn't deep, and it's clean now," Ember said. "Let's bandage him."

Twilight went to the pilot house, where Gallatin sat on the lazy bench while Harley steered. Her father was whistling, and to Twilight, he acted more enthusiastically than she could remember. "Daughter, where did you learn to shoot?" Twilight didn't answer. He glanced at Gallatin, then back at the river, smiling. "A young woman of secrets. Doesn't matter how you learned; I'm just glad you did. I'm proud of you and Jesse. I'm proud of Gallatin, too. Because of his anticipation and keen sense of the ways on the river, we're alive instead of robbed and dead. Those two rotten thieves we fished from the river? We threw them right back in. They were a bad catch," Harley said, chuckling. "You and Gallatin go on and relax now. I'm enjoying myself. I remember enough to pilot for a stretch. I'll ring the bell when I need you, Gallatin. Oh, and ask Jesse to come in here, would you? I want to tell my boy how proud I am of him."

Twilight laughed as she and Gallatin descended the steps to the deck. "I've never seen my father so animated."

Gallatin nodded and smiled. Twilight knew what he was thinking—running the river had a way of putting life into a man.

Chapter 47
Willow Land

*Friday, September 16, 1859
and Saturday, September 17, 1859
Ohio River and Evansville, Indiana*

On the river journey, Twilight comforted Taboo and Spirit.

Throughout the day, she walked with Spirit on the deck and, when they stopped to collect wood, on the shore. Most of the time, she perched on a stool pushed close to Gallatin at the wheel. From that vantage point, she could enjoy observing the river through the pilot house windows while feeling the electricity of her pilot. When not chasing mice, Taboo slept on Twilight's lap.

As they approached Cairo, Illinois, where the Ohio River feeds into the Mississippi, Gallatin pointed north and said, "I'm accustomed to running that way; it's been some time since I've navigated the Ohio. I'll slow a bit since it's a river to relearn." Into the voice pipe leading to the engine room, he said, "Slow will do nicely, Mr. Gaines."

As she contemplated the bending waterway and passing shoreline, Twilight said, "Gallatin, would you tell me about your mother? You never have."

Taking a deep breath, Gallatin said, "That's because I know nothing about her."

"Nothing?"

"Nothing about her as a person—her personality, her spirit, her appearance. I don't know if she was clever or stoic or funny or stern or nice or if she had dark hair or light hair, happy eyes or sad eyes."

"She was beautiful, inside and out," Twilight said.

"Yes?" Gallatin said.

"She had such a handsome son. And she had blonde hair, like yours. Her eyes were green, like yours. She had a caring, gentle soul, like yours. And I bet she was happy, especially when she carried you inside her."

Gallatin smiled. "Many times I've imagined, just as you say, that she looked like me, that she was happy about me, that she was proud of me. But she never knew me. She took her last breath the same moment I took my first."

"She knew you, though, while you kicked and squirmed under her heart," Twilight said. "Did she live long enough to see you?"

"I don't know."

"Doesn't your father ever speak of her?"

"No. Never has," Gallatin said, shaking his head. "I figure he hated her, and that is why he's never said a word about her. I've always felt he was ashamed of me, as I was what remained of her. He didn't give me a name. He calls me Son."

Aghast at the thought, Twilight thought about her father, who'd never been ashamed of her, though she'd given him plenty of reason to be. And her GrandMama adored her and gave her a name. Her mother? *True, Mother didn't name me, sent me away as a newborn, and hates me to this day, but Mother is distressed and not well.*

"Did you ever ask him about her?"

"When I was a child, I did. Repeatedly. But he wouldn't answer me. All he said was, 'Your mother died. She didn't have time to name you.' Finally, I stopped asking."

"Do you know what her name was?"

"I looked in the town records when I got older. Her name was Martha Kent before she married my father."

"Martha Kent Gallatin," Twilight said. "I'm sorry you know nothing about her."

Gallatin shrugged his shoulders. "You get used to it."

"Do you?" Twilight asked.

Gallatin didn't reply.

The next day, after rounding a curve, they could see some buildings. "We're about a quarter mile away from town," Gallatin said. "We'll stop here. Nobody will notice us."

Ember, Jesse, Menelik, and Mekeda-Angel walked down the plank and onto the free soil of Indiana. Twilight followed them, giving each a hug. Jesse didn't let go of Ember until Gallatin gently patted his back. "I hate to leave them here alone," Jesse said. "I should stay with them; I want to stay with them."

Jesse and Twilight looked up at Harley standing near the boat's edge. "I'm sorry, Son," Harley answered. "It wouldn't be best. I think people should see you disembark with your sister in Evansville. We need to avoid any suspicion. What we are doing, though right, is illegal." Harley noted the sun's position in the west. "You'll be returning in your wagon to get them in no time."

Jesse gave Ember a final hug, then handed her his gun. "Stay near the shore, but in those trees, so other boats won't see you. I'll be back just before dark."

Twilight hugged Ember and her children. From her pocket, she took the organza bag of stones, the Power Gems. These three gems were precious to her, as were Ember, Menelik, and Makeda-Angel. "Ember," Twilight said, "the black obsidian protects."

"Yes," Ember said.

"Take these. And you can return them to me very soon."

Ember pushed the bag into her dress neckline, feeling it near her heart. She gave Twilight a quick hug and Jesse a longer hug. Jesse intently watched the family head into the trees.

Twilight shivered. "I'm scared, too, Jesse. But it's a chance we must take."

"There could be wildcats here. Or worse," Jesse said.

"There are many deer here, I'm sure."

Jesse looked at her strangely. "You think *deer* will protect them?"

Twilight didn't answer.

As the *Whistling Wind* chugged away from the shoreline, Jesse hung over the rail. Harley patted his son's shoulder. "It's just a few hours, Son," he said. "They'll be fine. Ember's smart. And the good Lord is watching over those three."

Jesse shrugged. "Yes. The invisible Lord. Three tiny stones. And some deer."

Within minutes, they docked in Evansville. Twilight immediately noticed how different the Evansville wharf was from the one in Memphis. Though busy, it seemed dull without the familiar chanting and singing of the Rich-tone stevedores of Memphis. In Evansville, most stevedores unloading the riverboats were Pale. Almost all the passersby on the cobblestone wharf were Pale. Twilight, holding Taboo and leading Spirit, walked down the plank, then stood, observing the standardized community.

Gallatin joined her on the plank. "What's the matter, Twilight?"

She continued to stare at the wharf, the many businesses and stores facing it, and its bordering street, Water Street. "I was noticing how different the North looks. I'd forgotten. It's been five years since I left; I was only twelve." Twilight looked at him. "Everyone here is free. That's the best part. As usual, I did some reading before coming here. But the facts didn't help me imagine what I'm now seeing. Evansville is about half the population of Memphis. About one hundred Rich-tone people live in Evansville as compared to about three thousand Rich-tone people in Memphis. Of course, again, the most important difference is that the Rich-tone people here, though few, are not enslaved. And here, it's not wrong to be against slavery."

Gallatin took her hand and patted it, then released it, for they were in public. "Actually," he said, "I think you'll find a common attitude in the North to be simultaneously anti-slavery and anti-Rich-tone."

Staring hard at the scene, she said, "And what does that mean?"

"Don't expect the Pale people of Indiana, simply because they don't agree with slavery, to agree that Rich-tone people should live among them. The entire nation, for the most part, thinks America is the Land of the Pale."

"Gallatin, tell me, am I being naive about the North?"

"As harsh as this sounds, here's how many Northern Pale people think: slavery means Rich-tone people and Pale people live in the same towns, cities, and, of course, in the same houses—those of the enslavers—or on the land of the enslavers. So, if there is no slavery, then Rich-tone people can live in communities and areas separate from Pale people. Similar thinking as to why many don't want slavery to be legal in the West."

"Why can't Americans want slavery illegal simply because it is wrong?" Twilight said.

"Honey, you and I know that many Americans want slavery to be illegal because it is wrong. Like us, many want equal rights for anyone who lives in this country."

"Yes," Twilight said. "But more need to feel that way."

"That is absolutely true." Gallatin added, "While many do have a preference for communities being inclusive, another prevalent attitude among Northern Pales is to be in favor of the programs that send Rich-tone people to Africa, particularly to Liberia, which, as you know, was a former colony of the American Colonization Society. Or, people with that attitude say, if not Liberia, Rich-tone people can move to

Canada. Or anywhere, as long as it is outside the United States of America. Remember, the Indiana state constitution prohibits anyone having Rich-tone blood from entering the state. That means free Rich-tone people can't move here, or even enter the state." He leaned and whispered in her ear. "That's the very reason we're going to great lengths to smuggle in Ember and her children. That's why they are waiting alone in the woods rather than walking down this plank with us."

According to Indiana law, I shouldn't be returning. Some secrets are meant to stay secret.

Gallatin took a deep breath. "Our nation is the home of millions of people, hard-working people, who don't have equal rights nor any rights at all. Most aren't allowed to vote."

"Women are half of the population. We cannot vote," Twilight said. "And where are the rights for children?"

Gallatin nodded. "Unbalanced as to who decides how most people will live."

"I tried to explain this to Jack's father," Twilight said.

"And?"

"He with his cruel beliefs exploded all over the dining room. I have so many bad Hades Bay memories."

Taboo wriggled, trying to jump from Twilight's arms. "Be calm, kitty. Do you want me to put you in a carpet bag?" Twilight said, laughing.

Jesse had hired a horse and wagon to take them and their belongings to their new home just two blocks south on Water Street. He'd been hustling about, which seemed to Twilight as if he thought that, by rushing, he could hurry nightfall. After the men loaded the wagon, tying Spirit to the back of it, and with Twilight holding tightly to Taboo, they headed down Water Street. "Look, there's my grandparents' home, Willow Land," Twilight said, pointing to a charming house with willow trees just one hundred feet from the river. "My precious willow friends!"

When the wagon stopped in front of Willow Land, she was unprepared for the depth of emotion she felt at being home again. "Oh, it is beautiful," she said. "My willow friends are everywhere! Look how they guard the home and land. There's the wonderful cast iron veranda on the second story. Grandfather and I watched his riverboats come in from there. By the full moon, it is the loveliest home I ever did see! What an enchanted place."

The housekeeper and friend Twilight loved, Margaret, had passed away shortly after GrandMama died. Opening the door was a housekeeper who introduced herself as Trisha. Inside, Taboo explored his new home. Twilight saw that even the same plants were there, still living and growing, the ones she'd seen her GrandMama whisper to, water, and carry to the side porch on sunny days. "She's still here," Twilight said.

When she entered her magical grove behind the home, she suddenly had more flashbacks of long-forgotten memories—with GrandMama also in trousers! Together they were cracking whips to clip small stones off the fence. Together they climbed trees like cats. Together they sprung onto the back of their beloved horses, Mystica and Spirit.

Apparently, I pushed these incredible memories away. It had hurt too much to remember them, to miss GrandMama. The trainings, and their conclusion when GrandMama had become ill, came back to her, filling her with emotion, strength of self, and confidence in her abilities she hadn't acknowledged in years.

Twilight went to the kitchen to tell Trisha the story she'd devised so they could get Ember without suspicion—that she needed a Rich-tone attendant.

"Not many Rich-tones here," Trisha said. "Those who are here you'll find on the east edge of the city a few blocks from here, near the Canal."

"Edge of the city," Twilight repeated, taking three apples from a fruit bowl on the table. "I'm going there now."

"Oh, Mrs. Canon. Do you think you should? It's nearly dark, and it's not fitting for a woman of your class to travel that area at night."

"It is a neighborhood, and I'm sure it is lovely," Twilight said.

Trisha pursed her lips and put her hands on her hips.

"My brother and Mr. Gallatin will be with me," Twilight added.

Trisha said, "Now that you are here, I'll be leaving. I have a new position in a home that's not as strange as this one. I don't know what went on here before I took Margaret's place, and I don't want to know. All I know is your grandfather contacted me many evenings to tell me not to come to his home the next day. He never gave me a reason. I'll be gone when you get back."

"Well, hello and goodbye, then," Twilight said.

She found Jesse and Gallatin and said, "Let's go."

Gallatin grabbed Twilight's arm and whispered, "You aren't supposed to come with us."

"Well, I am," she said, patting her pocket.

Chapter 48
Rescue

Saturday, September 17, 1859
Early Evening
Woods Near Evansville

"In case we are seen, we need to go through the southeast edge of the city," Twilight told Gallatin and Jesse.

"I told Trisha we were going there to find an attendant," she added. "On the way back, that's the area where we can uncover Ember and the children from the blankets they'll be hiding under. That way, if anyone notices us, it will appear we went there because that's where Ember was supposedly living with her children when we hired her. Since they are hiding a quarter mile east of here, this direction takes us out of our way, but it's our only option. So, Jesse, let's head east until we see the Wabash-Erie Canal."

"I didn't know there was a canal here," Gallatin said.

"There is and there isn't. They began building it before I was born," Twilight said. "They finally finished it about six years ago. It goes to Toledo, Ohio, but I think only one boat made that trip. It's simply not profitable. Determined to have a canal, city and state planners seemed to turn their faces from what was happening before their eyes—the railroads."

"I'd like to turn my face from the railroads, too," Gallatin said.

"It could still prove to be an important waterway, as it seems freedom champions could follow it almost all the way to Canada," Twilight said.

"Interesting," Gallatin said.

Intent on getting to Ember, as if silence would speed the trip, Jesse said nothing until they reached the canal. "There it is," he said through gritted teeth. "Now, back to the river."

Soon the coach pulled by Spirit bumped over the riverbank's unimproved terrain. Abruptly, Jesse stopped the coach and jumped from it, running through the trees, calling Ember.

"Stay in the coach," Gallatin said to Twilight, handing her his Deringer. "Two shots are better than one, as you now know." He leaped to the ground to follow Jesse, then turned to her. "Keep that gun. From now on, keep two with you."

"What about you? Do you have your other gun?"

He pulled out two larger pistols from his pockets, his Colt and his Smith and Wesson. "Now, I carry two," he said.

In her years of knowing Gallatin, she didn't know that, except for planned target practice, he carried more than one. He'd not pulled even one gun when they'd been attacked on the boat. He must've had them in his pockets and just not used them.

※

Gallatin and Jesse had been gone several minutes. Twilight tapped her foot nervously. "By the full moon," Twilight said aloud.

When they returned, Jesse, visibly distressed, was panting heavily. "They're gone," he said. "They're gone. Oh, God, she's gone!"

"Try to stay calm, Jesse," Gallatin said. "Let's drive a bit farther; then we'll look again. Maybe she had to leave this spot for some reason."

Twilight's heart pounded; she drove slowly as Gallatin and Jesse searched. "Stop!" Jesse said, jumping out. Something beyond vision led him to the brush where Menelik was cradling the whimpering Makeda-Angel. Softly, Jesse spoke their names. Menelik pulled his sister closer as Jesse leaned to them and hugged them tightly. He lifted them into his arms and returned to the carriage.

Twilight and Gallatin tucked blankets around the children. "Poor babies," Twilight said. "They are shivering."

"It's not that cold," Gallatin said. "They must be frightened out of their wits."

"Where's your mother?" Jesse asked.

"Two men with a dog came," Menelik said. "Mama hid us under brush. She was hidden but not as good as we were. She shot the gun, but I don't think she got either of them. They took her; they didn't see Makeda-Angel and me, didn't even look to see if there was anyone with Mama. They just grabbed her and left."

"Did the men have anyone else with them?" Gallatin asked.

Menelik nodded. "Five or six other men and women. All chained at the ankles."

"Abductors," Gallatin said.

"In the North?" Twilight said. "Jackson told me abductors scour Kentucky for anyone Rich-tone, including the free, to sell into slavery. Bedford Forrest himself used to search throughout Kentucky for people to abduct and sell. But this is Indiana! It's a free state."

Gallatin said, "Abductors search the free states and abduct free Rich-tone people. Who's to stop them?"

"God be merciful!" Jesse said. "My Ember is in the hands of abductors, and all you two can do is discuss it. Let's *do* something."

"Mama couldn't be far," Menelik said. "They found her just before dark. I heard them say they were going to make camp."

"They'll be on the riverbank," Jesse said. "There is lots of good driftwood to burn there."

Gallatin pulled the blankets over the children. "Twilight, we'll drive until we see their fire. Then Jesse and I'll get out and circle through the trees and come up behind them while you act as a decoy. Drive the coach as close to their camp as the wheels can take on this terrain. Talk to them. Keep their attention as we sneak up on them. What do you think, Jesse?"

Jesse nodded. "We'll make it work."

Twilight said, "It's difficult driving anywhere near the river bank. And where there's not mud, there are trees and brush."

"You can do it," Gallatin said.

Fortunately, the ground on which she could maneuver was vegetation-sparse and firm enough to hold the weight of the coach. Soon they saw firelight by the river ahead of them.

Gallatin and Jesse jumped out and ran into the woods, moving silently. Twilight handed the apples she'd brought to the children.

"I'm not hungry," Menelik said.

"Then just squeeze that ole apple, honey," Twilight whispered. "If you get a little bit scared, see if you can squeeze it hard enough to make apple cider."

"I'm not hungry either," Makeda-Angel said. "I'm making cider, too."

Twilight caressed the heads of both children and said, "Good for you, honey. You're both strong cider makers."

After waiting several minutes to give Jesse and Gallatin time to circle quietly through the woods, Twilight drove the coach slowly, approaching the campfire heedfully. "Keep under the cover," she said to the children. "Don't let them see you."

As sound carried in the night, the abductors could hear the coach approaching before they could see it. A dog growled. A man called, "Stop right there. Tell us who you are!"

"I'm lost," Twilight called weakly with her finest Southern drawl.

"A woman!" a gruff voice yelled. Then she heard snickering. Her skin crawled. "From the sound of your accent, honey, I'd say you're truly lost. That's not a Hoosier accent or a Corn-cracker accent, is it Cyrus? It's a fine, down-home Southern accent."

"The kind my heart's been bleeding for. It's been so long, Rufus. Too long," the voice of the second man, who Twilight now knew was named Cyrus, shouted.

"Will you help me?" Twilight drawled.

"Sure we will, honey."

"We're always ready to help. We know exactly what to do to help you. Drive closer."

Twilight heard disgusting guffaws from both men. When she stopped near their camp, the two abductors were poised to shoot. One was standing, the other sitting. The dog stared at her, growling with teeth bared. "What's a sweet thing like you doing out here alone?" said the one standing.

"I ran away from my husband. He was mean and beat me," Twilight said.

"Rufus, go check inside her coach. See if anybody's hiding there," the standing one, obviously Cyrus, said. To Twilight, he said, "If you're trying to bushwhack us, we'll shoot you."

"There's no one here but little ole me," Twilight said, her pulse jumping.

"We'll see for ourselves, sugar," Cyrus said.

Behind the campfire were seven people chained together at the ankles, hands tied with ropes, and lying on their sides behind the fire. At the end of the group was Ember, eyeing Twilight hopefully. Nervously Twilight fingered the Deringers on her lap, covered by a fold in her skirt. Rufus approached the coach. He stunk. He smirked, revealing missing front teeth.

By the full moon, I remember this putrid pair. It's the breathing manure heap and his buddy from the day of my sixteenth birthday, at Atrocity Square.

"Fine, fine horse," Rufus said. He put his hand out to Spirit. "I'd like this glittery beauty to be mine." Spirit nipped his hand. "Owww! Dammit to hell! Whoa, beast!" He aimed his gun at Spirit. Constrained by being hitched, Spirit shook her head, pawed the ground, snorted, and blew. Fear grabbed Twilight's breath.

"Rufus!" Cyrus called. "Forget the horse. For now."

Rufus backed away from Spirit. He reached into the coach and poked the blanket with his gun. It moved. "I'll shoot you!" he called.

"Don't!" Twilight said firmly. "Those are my children. Please, good sir, don't shoot them."

Rufus threw back the blanket. "Well, well, well. What do we have here? About nine hundred dollars, I reckon. Stand up, little captives."

Twilight's fright became rage. Menelik, sounding like his always-brave mother, said, "No."

"Well, now. Your children?" Cyrus said. "More like your little captives. But they are our little captives now. Stand up, little captives, or you're dead meat."

The children stayed put.

Twilight kept from looking at Ember. *She must be terror-stricken.*

"Get more chains, Cyrus," Rufus called. "Out of the coach, little captives." Cyrus placed his gun in his pocket and fished in a bag.

"Stay where you are," Twilight whispered firmly to the children.

"What did you say, woman?" Rufus said.

"I said, Rufus, you stink worse than outhouse waste," Twilight said, whipping one Deringer up slightly from her lap, aiming for the shoulder of his arm holding his gun. He stared at her in surprise. Cyrus dropped the bag and pulled his gun. The dog poised to attack on command. "Throw your gun down, Cyrus, and keep that dog at bay, or I'll blast what little brains your buddy has right out of his skull," she said, moving up her arm, now aiming for Rufus's head. Cyrus was quiet. Rufus looked scared witless. "Don't move, Rufus," Twilight said. *Where are they? By the full moon, where are Jesse and Gallatin?*

Finally, Cyrus spoke. "Go ahead. Shoot him. Right between the eyes. I never liked him much anyway. Leaves more money for me."

"By the waning moon," Twilight whispered.

"But Cyrus! We're kin! Don't let her kill me! I'm lucky that Riches' bullet didn't hit me earlier; now this? Don't let her do it. I think she's got good aim," Rufus pleaded.

"Shut up, joker. If she shoots you, I'll shoot her. It's as simple as that."

"But then I'd be dead," Rufus called.

"And so would she. She's not thick-skulled like you, Rufus. She won't do it."

Just then, Gallatin jumped from a tall rock, landing on Cyrus and flattening him to the ground. Gallatin stood, pulling Cyrus up with him by the shirt, and punched him in fast succession three times in the face. The dog snarled and jumped at Gallatin. In anticipation, Gallatin raised his leg and kicked the cur in the chest. There was an audible crack; it whimpered and ran.

Rufus bent to pick up his gun. "Don't," Twilight said, firing near Rufus's hand, then quickly aiming her second Deringer at Rufus's face. Rufus didn't.

While Gallatin and Cyrus fought, Gallatin doing almost all the hitting and deflecting, Jesse searched for the key to the chains. Unable to find them, he asked Rufus, "Where are the keys?"

"In my pocket."

With his gun aimed at Rufus, Jesse cautiously approached, then reached into Rufus's pocket for the keys or a concealed weapon. Rufus jerked up his leg and kicked Jesse in the groin. Jesse yelled and doubled up. With strength, Menelik threw his apple at Rufus, hitting him squarely in the nose. Makeda-Angel threw hers, hitting him on the arm. Rufus yelped, pulled a knife from his pocket, and jumped at the children. Twilight shot Rufus's arm. Rufus yowled. His knife dropped to the ground; Rufus followed.

Jesse rifled through Rufus's pockets, grabbed the keys, picked up the knife, then rushed to Ember. Twilight said, "I shot your arm without a thought, Rufus. I've wanted to do that for over a year." Rufus looked at her strangely. She continued, "I have two more guns, and I can shoot both your legs just as easily. Or I can shoot out your brains." Rufus fainted.

Twilight ran to where Gallatin was giving Cyrus calculated blows. With one final punch to the teetering Cyrus, Gallatin said, "That's got it." Cyrus fell.

Jesse had unlocked the iron cuffs that cut into the ankles of the chained. He cut and untied the ropes binding and strangling their wrists. "Hurry away," Jesse said, "before those scum gain consciousness." Four people thanked Jesse, and all six disappeared into the woods. Ember hugged Jesse, then scrambled into the coach, pulling her son and daughter to her.

Gallatin hovered over Cyrus, who was wobbling, trying to stand. Finally, Cyrus stood, swaying worse than any drunkard. "Get yourself and your buddy to a doctor," Gallatin said. "And give up human trafficking."

Cyrus spat at Gallatin. "I'll do what I like. I like abducting Riches, especially free ones. And I don't need a doctor."

"Now you do," Gallatin said, hitting Cyrus firmly in the face, sending him sprawling to the ground and panting. "Get yourself and your buddy to a doctor," Gallatin repeated. Cyrus passed out cold.

Gallatin took their guns and Jesse's gun that they'd taken from Ember. Twilight ripped her chemise skirt and wrapped pieces around Rufus's wound. Thankfully, the bullet hadn't entered his body. He wouldn't bleed to death.

Gallatin, Jesse, and Twilight got into the coach. Gallatin took the reins. Spirit nickered and hurried off to town.

"We had to protect ourselves," Twilight said aloud to no one in particular. Then, thinking of GrandMama, the elusive Sisterhood of Gifts, the men she'd shot on the river, and the man she'd just shot, she whispered, "It's horrible. Forgive me."

She was sure the Sisterhood of Gifts was not about shooting people.

Chapter 49
Friendship

September to November 1859
Evansville

"When you get your divorce documents, I will leave the river. We'll marry," Gallatin said.

Twilight nodded. He kissed her. "Until then, I may not see you, but I will write. And, remember—I am *always* thinking of you."

She nodded again. "Why does love have to be so difficult?"

"If it were easy, it wouldn't be love," Gallatin said.

She pressed her face against his neck and whispered, "I suppose."

"Darling, stop wasting away; please, gain some weight. You're safe now." He kissed her, then said, "No matter what happens, never forget I love you. With each heartbeat and beyond, I love you."

Then, he was gone.

Harley and his admirable, trustworthy makeshift crew left with Gallatin on the *Whistling Wind*, and Twilight settled into a routine in her new town. Each morning she and Jesse went to the office, a room on the side of the general store on Water Street that her grandfather had opened when he, with his wife and daughter, arrived to Evansville in 1834. Its windows faced the wharf, giving them a fine view of the riverboats docking and leaving.

Within days after the abduction—after the safety of Ember and her children had been threatened in the supposedly free state—Jesse brought home two puppies of mixed lineage. "It was a litter of just these two twin boys. I got them both so they'd not be separated," he said. "They'll be large. They'll protect Ember, her children, and you, Twilight."

The puppies jumped and snarled and wrestled with each other, immediately becoming the adorable humorists in the family. When Twilight saw them together, her heart lifted and pierced with the memory of Jesse and Jed, long ago it seemed, being so like the frisky, loving pups. Jesse named them Achilles and Hegemon.

"Been reading your Greek, Jesse?" Twilight asked, amused.

Jesse laughed, then answered, "I like knowing I can give orders to the Hegemon. He'll be a protector hegemon, not the typical one who controls people for his own power. Of course, Achilles is a strong protector name." Responsibly and conscientiously, Jesse trained them, which was also a comic sight, especially when Jesse called their names with the commands, enjoying wordplay. Even though Jesse said the training was serious business, it was difficult not to laugh when he ordered, "Hegemon, come. Hegemon, stay." Or "Achilles, heel."

Menelik and Makeda-Angel fell in love with the pups. Their version of Hegemon's name was Heggie Man or just Heggie, with Menelik sometimes saying Edgy Man; all three pet names for Hegemon caught on with the rest of the family. Even at their young age, Hegemon and Achilles growled their puppy growl whenever anyone not of the family approached either child.

The pups slept in a small room near the back door where boots, shoes, and wraps were kept. Twilight and Ember kept the floor of that room immaculate, as each morning they found Menelik and Makeda-Angel, who had sneaked from their beds in the middle of the night, curled in quilts next to the pups. As for Taboo, sometimes he played with the pups, but mostly he kept his distance, blinking slowly and deliberately at them.

The magical grove behind the home of Willow Land, which Twilight knew was a community of Wise Ones, became a haven for Sisterhood of Gifts exercises. Twilight, Ember, Menelik, and Makeda-Angel named it Wise Willow Grove, but they called it simply Willow Grove. The young women and children trained there—cracking whips, leaping onto horses, jump kicking, and climbing trees. When Heggie and Achilles kept a watchful distance, deer appeared, sometimes nibbling on leaves, sometimes just watching them. Rabbits hopped in the grass, and squirrels ran up the trees. Even when the dogs were nearby, birds filled the place with song.

Twilight enjoyed sitting among the Wise Ones, listening. With her eyes closed, she saw beautiful images and heard gorgeous sounds and lovely words. She didn't understand most of what she saw and heard. It seemed there was a symbolic code she must decipher. Often, she imagined she was vanishing into the willow trunks. Then one day, as she imagined, she did fall right into the willow trunk. Taboo was there! She felt a light: it wasn't seeing light with her eyes, and it wasn't the same as feeling sunshine on her skin. But it most certainly was a light. Almost as quickly as she had entered the tree, she was out again, leaning on its trunk. Taboo walked slowly and deliberately from the trunk, then blinked at her and said, "Mhrrr." She laughed at him, then stood, pondering this unique experience.

As if the encounter had given her a new gift, she knew she could jump high into tree branches. The branches of the Wise Ones of Willow Land were thin; they would never hold her weight. But there were a few oak trees on the property. She walked to one, took two steps, then jumped, landing agilely on one of its branches! She had leaped over the rock walls at the end of that horrid race at Magnolia Bay. But jumping several feet higher was new and very exciting. When she showed her new talent to Ember and her children, they clapped enthusiastically. She hoped, as did they, that they would acquire this ability, too.

Twilight called on the girlhood friends of whom she had fond memories. But she found that after they reminisced about the pasts they'd shared, they had little else to discuss. These former friends never returned her visits, for their husbands or fathers wouldn't allow them to spend time with an "unfeminine" young woman who'd moved to Evansville without her husband, who owned and managed businesses as if she were a man, and who dressed typically in trousers and sometimes in Bloomer costume.

The kind next-door neighbors—the two teachers of the Female Seminary School—were thrilled she had returned. They visited now and then, mostly talking about books and lovely memories of their friend, Twilight's GrandMama.

Still, even with Ember's constant, thoughtful friendship, Twilight felt perpetually lonely. *Where are the women who know they are of the Sisterhood of Gifts? Maybe some don't understand their gifts. Maybe the information isn't passed down in all families.*

After a month, Twilight became annoyed with Gallatin, for she'd been sure she would have received a letter from him by then. But no letter arrived. When two months had passed and still no word from him, she was angry and worried. To further worry her, she had no word yet from Jackson concerning the divorce.

And, she suspected she was carrying Gallatin's child.

Her suspicions were confirmed after she spoke with Ember. "I've had to move the buttons on my jacket bodices; I've been trying to regain some weight that I'd lost, but this seems different," she said. "I'm larger in my middle, and I feel terribly queasy; I have frequent headaches, and I haven't had a monthly. I thought I couldn't conceive. But I must be carrying a child."

Ember nodded, smiling. "A baby! They are so precious."

Holding back tears, Twilight frowned.

"Oh, Twilight, of course you can't be thrilled. If Jackson finds out, he won't divorce you. This will change your life in beautiful ways, but if he finds out, could also change it in ugly ways."

Twilight said, "I had a monthly early in August. But none since then."

Ember said, "The baby must be almost two months along."

"Yes. Eight weeks. This baby was conceived August 24," Twilight said. "The one time I wanted, desperately, to be loved by the baby's father, whom I've not heard a word from in five weeks."

"This doesn't sound like Gallatin. I hope all is well with him," Ember said.

"I don't know what to think," Twilight said. "It seems Father would've heard and would let me know if anything has happened to Gallatin. By the full moon, I'm still married, so this child is legally a Canon. But I'll do everything in my power to keep Jackson from knowing. If he finds out, as you say, he won't divorce me. And then I'd be back at Magnolia Bay. I can't even let Father and Mother know. This baby will be a secret to anyone south of Evansville until I receive my divorce documents."

Twilight said nothing about her baby to anyone else but Jesse. She was known as Mrs. Canon throughout the community, so as her abdomen grew, everyone assumed the child was that of her absent husband, the Southern gentleman whom no one had met or even seen. Though gossipers enjoyed trying to surmise why Twilight was in Evansville while her husband lived in the South, she was treated with distant respect, for she was the granddaughter of businessman Johannes Wild, a man the community held in high esteem.

The days flowed as a full, rich river. Twilight and Ember shared their poems. Through their poetic themes, they realized that they had in common a seemingly otherworldly ability to see and hear "things." Twilight felt safe mentioning again a supposed mystical sisterhood. Ember stated again that her Mama had alluded to a similar sisterhood through stories that could be true, or legend or myth. Finally, Twilight had someone with whom she could share at least some of GrandMama's heavy message. "Can you describe your gift?" Twilight asked.

Ember said, "At night, I fly. Some might call it a dream. But I know I am flying. Through my nighttime flights, I see. The fuller the moon, the better I see. This is how I found Menelik. I also fly when I sing."

"Ember! You sing? Why have I not heard you?"

"I only sing in private or with my sisters. And when I sing, the tips of my fingers tingle. Sometimes, it seems they emit sparkles."

While Twilight had been unsuccessful in rekindling girlhood friendships or making new friends, Ember had made friends with some Rich-tone women she called her sisters. She found reaching out to meet Rich-tone friends easier in Evansville than it had been in Memphis, where the laws constraining Rich-tone people had been numerous and strict. Sometimes, Ember wished she lived among her sisters. While a few families had offered a room for her and her children to live in until she found a suitable place of her own, she decided to stay, at least for the time being, at Willow Land. Mostly because of her feelings for Jesse. But also because of her friendship with Twilight.

That Sunday evening, with candlelight dancing, Ember read aloud her new poem:

> "My sisters shake
> Gourd shells;
> My sisters shake
> Their bodies;
> My sisters shake
> Their entire selves.
> I sing.
> My sisters and I shake
> The world,
> Opening a secret place."

Twilight said, "I like that poem. Makes me sad, though, too. I miss my friends at Magnolia Bay."

"I know that feeling well," Ember said.

Twilight nodded. "So, here's my poem." Twilight read:

> "Secrets, secrets permeate the air;
> Secrets hide everywhere.

Remember: secrets live
If not revealed or told.
Embrace them, if you care,
With your heart and with your senses:
Through Ritual, Love and Faith
Feel the Ancient Divine Order
~ And the ecstatic risks, if you dare ~
Sent from this very moment
And from the days of old."

Reading their poems in front of candlelight became a sacred ritual for the two women, the ritual they believed strengthened protective mysteries and their ties to the Sisterhood of Gifts.

"I wish I could write more like Phillis Wheatley," Ember said. "She had created a collection of skillful poetry by the time she was merely eighteen."

"I wish I could, too. She is an inspiration," Twilight agreed.

They were quiet for a moment, pondering Phillis's skill, which they lacked. Then Ember said, "Oh well."

Both young women laughed.

"Yes! Oh well," Twilight said. "We'll become better poets with time and practice."

"Yes, we will," Ember said.

Each night, Twilight lit a lamp, placing it in the window as had her GrandMama and her Great-GrandMama.

※※※ ※※※

One November night, Hegemon and Achilles barked. Ember found Twilight scrubbing some clothes on a washboard and said, "I heard a tapping against one of the windows in the parlor."

"Where's Jesse?" Twilight dried her hands on her apron.

"Out, caring for the horses. He heard Spirit neigh, so he went to check on them."

"Maybe it was just a tree branch," she said.

"There's not a tree close to the window where I heard the noise," Ember said.

Suddenly, a tap-tap-tap sounded on the kitchen window.

"There it is again," Ember said with a gasp.

Achilles and Hegemon continued their puppy-yap barking.

Ember and Twilight heard a tap-tap-tap on the back room door. "He's moving from one room to the next," Ember said. She and Twilight crept to the back door.

Leaning near the door, Twilight said, "Who is it? Tell me, or I'll open this door and shoot." She had completely stopped carrying her Deringers. With children in the home, her pockets were no place for weapons. And she would be a mother soon, with her baby in her arms or balanced on her hip. So the guns were unloaded and hidden high at the top of a wardrobe in her room. But, whoever was at the door wouldn't know this. She said again, "Tell me who you are or I'll shoot."

A low, soft male voice said, "I'm looking for Twilight Canon. Is this her home?"

"Who are you? Why don't you come to the front door?" Twilight said.

"I'm a friend of Twilight Canon's from Magnolia Bay."

Puzzled, Twilight didn't answer.

"Please tell Mrs. Canon to come to the door."

"I'm here."

He softly sang: "Keep your light bright, so I can find my way home."

"Jafaan?" Twilight whispered. Then through the door, she said, "Jafaan?"

"It's me."

"Jafaan," Twilight whispered in wonder.

Cautiously, she opened the door. Stooping behind the bushes, Jafaan looked up at her. Behind him was Ava. Twilight grabbed their arms, pulling them into the house. "Jafaan! Ava! I'm so happy to see you! Spirit will be glad to see you, Jafaan. That's why she neighed!" Seeing that these were welcome visitors, the pups stopped barking and started wiggling then jumping on the two guests. Twilight hugged her friends and said, "Oh, you are soaked clear through and freezing! Ember, this is Ava and Jafaan."

"I'll get you blankets and dry clothes, and I'll tell Jesse," Ember said.

After Ava and Jafaan were dry and had eaten, everyone settled around the parlor fire. Twilight asked, "How did you get here? How did you find me?"

Jafaan said, "One night, Ava appeared in my shack at Ivy Falls."

"You were at McCay's?"

Jafaan nodded. "He's a mean man but easy to escape. We snuck out. We kept walking north, following the rivers, first the Mississippi then the Ohio. You gave us directions to Evansville, remember? How to get to Evansville by crossing the river from Kentucky. You described your grandparents' house. There had been rumors that you'd left Memphis. We took a chance, and you are here. We are here."

Ava said, "Jafaan and I have traveled similar routes. I was born free in Maryland. When I was ten, I was taken by Pale men and sold away from Mama to a small farm near Bucktown. I met Jafaan there. The expert freedom champion named Moses found us and led us with Jafaan's mama and daddy to Canada. Even there, among our people, Magnolia Bay is known because it is the largest enslaver of our people's children. When we were close to grown-up age, Jafaan and I went to Magnolia Bay to help the children. We purposely let ourselves get caught by that Bratton. Our plan was to do some teaching and to find some children we'd be able to lead away. We were trained by the best, our Moses. Destroyer Jackson always states that no one escapes Magnolia Bay. Well, he is wrong. While we were there, we led six children away at night. Four trips. Four youths and two younger children. We'd get them away into the woods and give them directions. We would get back before morning, so no one knew we were gone. You didn't even know about those who had escaped."

"Your covert missions are amazing!" Twilight said. "No one even mentioned an escape until the day I left—when *you*, Ava, escaped Magnolia Bay."

Ava nodded and said, "It's a miracle I'm not torn to shreds. Mama, prayer, and an antlered doe saved me."

At the mention of the savior doe, Jesse glanced at Twilight and lifted his eyebrows.

"But that is a story for another time," Ava continued. "Twilight, during the time you were at the plantation, Jafaan and I helped two children escape. Months would pass between escapes. Part of our plan was for it to seem random, unexpected. We watched closely. Studied the ways of the destroyers. The Canons wanted to keep the escapes quiet. They always act as if they are in complete control; they don't see what they don't want to see. If they *say* there are no escapes, then, to them, there are no escapes. If they *say* Jackson's grandma died, well, to them, she is dead. All acts. Even to themselves. They didn't even set the catch hound on any of the six freedom champions. Until me. I don't have to say why it was different when I ran. James never got what he was after. He's a strong old jackass. But my knee is stronger."

"James is sick and sickening. Thank goodness for your strength and your bravery. And your knee," Twilight said. She smiled. "So you knew about Grandma. I began to understand how well you and all of the youths at Magnolia Bay could take care of yourselves—that all you needed from me were some things from the big house—when you asked for books but didn't want my help teaching. I understood that you must have had your own, very secret, school there."

"Yes, we taught many children reading, writing, and numbers. The Canons have no idea," Jafaan said. "I'm returning to Ivy Falls to free Sally. She, too, was sold to McCay. I hated winning the freedom race; I wanted to let her win. But Canons make it clear that if the races aren't real, the suspected winner will be hanged. 'Hanged like a dog,' James would say. 'If any of you let another win, I'll see your hanged-dog expression.' After finding Sally, I'll go to Magnolia Bay for our family. I'm worried, though.

So many gone at once, rather than one by one or, at most, two at a time. Enslavers are crazier than ever now that John Brown was found guilty earlier this month. Surely James will set the catch hound on us. Traveling with a young child and a baby will make it more than a trick not getting caught. There are wooded places to hide all along the river, but we'd never get far with the hound on our trail. So, I need a plan."

"I'm going, of course," Ava said.

Jafaan took Ava's hand and pressed it to his lips. "Stay here, please. Your ankle still needs healing. After I return with our family, it's time we go back to Canada. Canada is the safest place to be. The North is not truly safe from men who trade us."

"It's not safe at all," Ember said.

"And there is hostility toward Rich-tone people throughout the North," Twilight said. "You may be free here, but not welcome. There's still that damn Fugitive Slave Act prohibiting a life of freedom in the North. If anyone suspects, you'll be sent back to Magnolia Bay. I've heard Canada is more fair than the United States, though not without prejudice."

"I'm going," Ava said. "On my own, all alone, and with a horribly twisted ankle, I hid in the woods until my ankle was strong enough. Then I found you, Jafaan. Then I hobbled here. I did all that, so I can do this."

Jafaan smiled. "Yes, you're right. Ava, you're a godsend."

"I want to go with you and Ava," Jesse said. "We can take a wagon led by Donner; he's a calm but energetic gelding. If we get your family out at night, we can get away before the hound can find us."

Ember lightly and quickly touched Jesse's hand.

Jesse added, planning aloud, "I'll take the wagon and cross the Ohio on the ferry, but to avoid suspicion, Jafaan and Ava will have to cross at night in a boat. Grandfather had one he used for fishing in the river. We'll take it in the wagon down from the town a ways; then you two can take that across the river, hide it well, and hopefully, it will still be there when we return with your family. The trip should take two or three weeks each way. We'll need enough food for that time, food that won't spoil."

"We'll get you sacks of dried food. You'll have food, just not much variety," Twilight said.

Jafaan said, "On our journey, we'd find apples here, an old ear of corn there. Freedom champions often get caught because they can't find enough food. And the woods are filled with predatory creatures that live there. But even the worst of those aren't nearly as vicious as the catch hound."

"Hopefully, we can avoid all that," Jesse said, "by traveling in a wagon."

Jafaan, his eyes tender, said to Jesse. "It's settled, then. Thank you for the miracle of your help, a horse, and a wagon."

Jesse and Jafaan spent the following day preparing for the rescue; the next night, the three left. Jafaan hid under the boat in the wagon bed; Ava hid under a blanket. Ember squeezed Twilight's arm as she watched Jesse drive away. "I want him to help, even if it's dangerous, though it worries me," Ember said.

Jesse left Jafaan, Ava, and the boat at the river's edge, about a mile outside town. Then he doubled back toward town and took the ferry across. He drove the wagon as near as he could along the Kentucky banks of the Ohio River to the point they'd decided to meet. Jafaan and Ava crossed the river uneventfully.

"Try to find the boat," Jafaan challenged when they met Jesse.

Jesse searched for a half hour, never finding it. Jafaan led him to where it was, hidden in bushes and covered with brush and leaves. Jesse patted Jafaan's arm. "That ought to do it," Jesse said. "Let's go."

Traveling through Kentucky and Tennessee with a Rich-tone young man and a Rich-tone young woman in the wagon was easy, as those who saw them assumed Jesse owned them. In no time, Jesse was fond of the strong-willed, strong-bodied freedom champions. He enjoyed having Jafaan as a male comrade, an aspect of his life he'd missed since he and Jed began disagreeing. Ava was a brilliant conversationalist. They traveled during the day and camped at night. Within two weeks, they were near Magnolia Bay. Thus far, all had gone well.

Late the following night, their rescue mission began. First, they stopped near Ivy Falls. It took an hour for Jafaan to return to the wagon with Sally. A half-hour later, they were near Magnolia Bay. Sally stayed with the wagon and Donner as Jafaan, Ava, and Jesse departed on their mission. Making sure they went nowhere near the catch hound kennel, Jafaan and Ava crept to the quarters of the enslaved. Luckily, the old, beloved watchdog Jasper didn't appear, as his bark would, of course, destroy the rescue, thus re-enslaving Jafaan, Ava, and Sally, and setting into motion god-knows-what to Jesse, possibly enslaving him, maybe hanging him. Soundlessly, Jafaan sprinted to the shack where Ifeoma, Jimmie, Glory, Zvi, and Ben lived. Jafaan started to open the door, then looked toward a huge tree several yards away where Jesse hid, armed and scouting. Ava, limping, arrived and stood by the door, patrolling the area. "It's me, honey," Jafaan whispered as he started inside. Instantly Ifeoma pulled Jafaan inside, hugging him desperately. Zvi also hugged Jafaan. With soft and quiet squeals, Fearless jumped on Jafaan. Kneeling, he hugged Fearless, then said, "We're leaving. Where's Ben?"

"They moved him out of our place," Ifeoma said.

Jafaan cursed, then said, "We'll find him next time."

Jafaan lifted the sleeping Jimmie, carrying him away in his dreams. Zvi lifted sleeping Glory, who started to rouse. "Stay quiet, honey," Zvi said. Fearless stayed at Ifeoma's side.

Silent and stirring as breezes through cotton white, they entered the American night.

Something woke Jed. For a moment, he thought he was in Memphis sharing a room with his twin. Then he remembered: those days were long past. But he had a feeling. Something. He wasn't sure what. He pulled on his trousers, grabbed his rifle, glanced at the drunk, out-cold John Bratton, then sneaked out the door. Someone was running through the forest not far from his cabin. Like a five-point buck, Jed sprinted noiselessly, following the someone into the deep woods.

Suddenly, that someone stepped into Jed's path. Expecting a captive on the run, Jed halted and looked into the face of his mirror image. "Jesse!" Jed whispered in surprise.

Jesse stared at his brother, at whom his gun was poised. He was facing who and what he'd refused to consider when he decided to help Jafaan and Ava—that he might have to confront his twin at Magnolia Bay. He'd hoped that they'd not rouse anyone from sleep. They'd been so quiet. But Jed was there. And Jesse was there. The twins continued to stare at each other without sound or movement. After a moment passed, Jesse said, "Throw it down," nodding at the rifle faltering by Jed's side.

"Throw down yours," Jed said. "You won't use it. Not on me."

Jesse cocked his gun.

"I don't know you anymore," Jed said, dropping his rifle. "If you're crazy enough to become a Rich-tone lover, then you're crazy enough to shoot your brother."

"You're the one who's crazy," Jesse said. "You're a disgrace to the Adams name."

"You're a disgrace to your homeland," Jed said. "You're the one who's changed. You're a born and bred Southerner. But after one look at that Riches beauty, you threw away your land, your people, your heritage—and your own brother."

"You foul-mouthed, prejudiced scum. I didn't change my life for Ember. I hated slavery even before I met her. The summer we spent at Clover Hill was hell for me. I hated watching people being enslaved, whipped, and forced to work for nothing from before dawn until night. I hated watching you practice with a whip, longing for the day you could lash someone. I hated being there, but I stayed because I loved you and that's where you wanted to be. You were once kind. You're the one who's changed. You, Jed."

"So now you steal my laborers. Is this your revenge against me for that summer? I remember it wasn't so bad for you, Jesse. I remember you enjoyed being served mint juleps on the veranda by enslaved servants as much as I did. No, you don't hate me now because of that summer. You hate me because you've become a Rich-tone-loving leech, sucking off the prosperity of King Cotton and mooning over the South's beautiful enslaved."

Jesse uncocked then tossed his gun and jumped at Jed, landing on him, throwing them both to the ground. All the anger over their opposing beliefs, all the sorrow for their lost closeness, and all the passion they still felt for one another rushed out in a barrage of fists smashing into cheeks, fists into sides, fists into stomachs. Over and over they rolled on the ground, pounding each other, looking like one man mauling himself.

After several minutes of vengeful blows, they spent their anger. Jed had been on top of Jesse, smacking him across the face, when suddenly he couldn't hit his brother again. He fell and rolled over onto his back, lying beside Jesse. The bloodied brothers heaved for air.

Jesse turned his head to face Jed; Jed turned his head to face Jesse. The fight had set free all their long-trapped emotions about losing each other. Now as they lay next to one another, they were reminded of themselves as lads who had slept each night in beds placed side-by-side so they could whisper and laugh into the night without waking the rest of the household. Through the pain and blood from the repeated blows of his brother's fist, Jesse smiled; his eyes crinkled. Jed, also bloodied, grinned. Simultaneously they burst into the laughter of brotherhood and with the connection of love they both missed.

As the moon crept across the night sky, they lingered in their laughter, not wanting the moment to stop, for when it did, they knew it would be over forever. But finally, they looked at each other, and their smiles faded into frowns. Jed stood. He gave Jesse his hand, pulling him to his feet. For a moment longer, each man stared at his brother who'd been closer than a brother, closer than they could even comprehend, for they'd been conceived as one. Then, Jesse picked up his gun. Jed picked up his rifle. He said, "I'll give you until the morning. After that, we're after you."

Jesse extended his hand; Jed took it in his. They shook as agreement, as a forever farewell—and as their last grasp of something unnamable and beautiful. For a moment longer, they held each other's faces with their eyes. Then, they released one another.

Jesse turned from his brother and disappeared into the trees to find and help his friends; Jed walked slowly toward his cabin, where he would lie awake until dawn and then would report the freedom runners.

Chapter 50
Freedom Champions

December 1859 to mid-June 1860
Evansville

A warm spell blessed the winter and, thus, the freedom champions.

They'd made it safely back to Evansville. After only one week of reprieve at Willow Land, they said they couldn't take any chances with their freedom. During that week, Ifeoma said little, ignored Twilight and Ember, and directed her love to caring tenderly for Jimmie. Everyone else visited as if they were dear friends.

Their freedom journey plan was to follow the canal from Evansville to Toledo, Ohio. Hopefully, they could cross from there into Canada via a boat or ferry on Lake Erie. Or they might find it better to travel on land further east to Cleveland, Ohio or to Erie, Pennsylvania, then across Lake Erie to Canada. If they decided to stay on land the entire journey, they could travel to Buffalo, New York, then cross into Canada. Ava and Jafaan knew of communities of Rich-tone people living in these areas; they were the most effective in helping their brothers and sisters to freedom. Also residing on their planned route were Quakers, the community of Pale people most committed to assisting the enslaved to freedom.

As they prepared to leave, Ava said, "Jafaan and I will be back. Even though Jafaan wanted this to be our last rescue, we both know we have to lead more of our friends from Magnolia Bay. We are not done yet with our freedom train. One more trip. Maybe two."

One night, under a silver moon, they left with Sam, a gelding that Jesse had recently bought. On Sam's back sat Glory, then Ava, then Ifeoma holding onto Jimmie. Jafaan, Sally, Zvi, Glory, and Ifeoma planned to take turns walking, with Jafaan, Zvi, and Sally being the first to walk. Glory would walk less than the older children. Ava, with her ankle healing, and Jimmie would continuously ride. Fearless followed his family.

As Sam walked away, Jimmie waved, and Ifeoma smiled at Twilight. Twilight smiled and waved.

Menelik frowned, and Makeda-Angel cried at losing their new friends. Jesse and Ember, while sad, were also happy for the chance for guaranteed freedom for the family. Heggie and Achilles whined as the children and Fearless disappeared into the folds of the night.

⇢⇉⇶ ⇇⇇⇠

On the frigid first day of February, Twilight came home in the afternoon to find Ember shoveling the cold garden ground as an outlet for her anger. Ember said, "Did you hear that one year ago this month, a mob of Pale Males burned down a sister's home while her husband was away working on a steamer? On Leet Street near the canal and close to where we gather to worship. I just heard about this today, as folks were recalling that it was a year ago. She and her husband had rented it from Mr. Carpenter, an honorable Pale man. The men who burned it down claimed it was the home of dishonorable women, both Rich-tone and Pale. As if that's a reason to burn down a home? No, sir, it is not! Besides, what they said was a lie. They were looking for a reason to burn down a house of a Rich-tone woman while her husband was away—a woman with probably one drop of African blood."

Twilight's breath stuck in her chest.

Ember said. "I'm baking her some cornbread; it's in the oven now."

"Such cruelty makes me want to scream!" Twilight said.

"Instead of screaming, I've been shoveling," Ember said. Together, they exorcised their fury by shoveling the frozen ground as if hoping to rush the Earth into the newness of Spring. When the cornbread was ready, together, they took it to the couple.

⋙ ⋘

Each night, Twilight continued to light a lamp and place it in the window. To avoid the chance of fire, she put just a small amount of oil in the lamp. Around midnight, the light would go out. Twilight rose before dawn each day to relight the lamp as a beacon to any freedom champions who might have arrived after midnight and were looking for her home—so they could enter her home of safety before the sun shone on their secret arrival.

Ava and Jafaan returned in early February for their last rescue mission. Then, with Jesse—who would stay in the forest to not see Jed—they headed to Magnolia Bay. In late February, they arrived at Willow Land with five children, Ben being one.

Bolstered by the escapes for liberation, enslaved children in small groups began disappearing from Magnolia Bay, as did people of all ages from its neighboring plantations, arriving in the night at Willow Land.

This felt very familiar to Twilight. Fragmented memories of late-night visitors flooded her mind, merging into a complete memory. And then she realized:

My grandparents' home has always been part of the Underground Railroad. The lighted lamp in the window was a sign.

⋙ ⋘

During a misty Spring day, a rather odd yet lovely out-of-towner named Miss Summer visited Twilight. Miss Summer claimed she'd been a friend of Twilight's GrandMama. After spending some time with the woman,

Twilight vaguely remembered her. Over tea, Miss Summer said, "You have a blessed child."

Twilight nodded. "Babies are blessings," she said, believing her words but still feeling in some ways like a child herself and hoping that, when bearing her baby, she wouldn't die.

Miss Summer mentioned twice the importance of listening to "messages from elsewhere." At first, Twilight thought the strange woman was referring to hearing God in Heaven or maybe even the lovingly departed. But then Twilight wondered, could Miss Summer be a Champion of the Sisterhood of Gifts? GrandMama had used the term "Elsewhere" in her letter—.

At that moment, Miss Summer leaned over her teacup, looking into Twilight's eyes, and said, "You remember your training, do you not?"

Twilight didn't answer. *So, you are a Champion.*

Miss Summer continued, "Your grandfather sent you away for your care and safety. Your training ended when you were merely eleven, so you hadn't received the full benefit." She lowered her voice, "And you would not start receiving the sparks of your strongest powers until age sixteen. So, at twelve, and without your GrandMama to care for you in the manner of the Sisterhood of Gifts, you were vulnerable to unseen forces and possibly to certain townspeople. When Margaret, an ally in your grandparents' work, passed away, Johannes feared a new housekeeper would not keep quiet about the freedom champions who came and went. So, he planned that she wouldn't be here the days that they were and, thus, wouldn't be able to care for you throughout each day as your GrandMama and Margaret had done. So, if you recall, it was really when Margaret died, which was soon after your GrandMama passed, that he sent you away. He missed you terribly."

"That's why Grandfather sent me away from my home? How do you know so much? I have so many questions. Tell me what you know about the Sisterhood of Gifts. It is all so mysterious and secret."

Miss Summer smiled. Patting Twilight's hand, she offered an exasperating explanation: "You must find your answers." After promising to visit again, she left.

⇶ ⇷

Jesse learned prized secrets, such as Rich-tone people in Evansville offering overnight hiding places to freedom champions within their homes and even places of work. While Rich-tone communities throughout the area provided the safest shelter to their kindred freedom champions, Jesse also learned that a covert group of some Pale people in southwestern Indiana, called both the Anti-Slavery League and Anti-Slavery Society, had been formed in response to the Fugitive Slave Act of 1850. Jesse discovered that a member of this league, Mr. Willard Carpenter, who provided shelter to those crossing the river for freedom, was their grandfather's friend. Also that the fishermen Twilight had heard about as a child, upon being signaled by a Rich-tone Kentuckian man, shuttled some freedom champions from Kentucky to Evansville in their boats.

But Evansville was just a stop along the way for the freedom champions, and helping them enter the state was still illegal. Further, the crazed nation had intensified with mania, set off by heightening tensions from John Brown's raid on the Harper's Ferry arsenal in mid-October the year before. So Jesse, Twilight, and Ember swore themselves to secrecy about what others in the area were doing—and, of course, about what they themselves were doing. Twilight believed that the fewer people who knew, the better, as lives were at stake: the lives of the freedom champions, and of Ember, Menelik, Makeda-Angel, Jesse, and—of utmost importance to Twilight—the life of Kent.

Kent Adams Canon, born June 1, 1860, was the unexpected miracle of Twilight's life.

Bearing Kent had been excruciating. If it had not been for Ember, who knew just what to say and just what to do, Twilight would have screamed relentlessly to high heaven. For hours, all Twilight knew was

Pain. She forgot she was bearing a child: she felt she was being tortured, and for what, she didn't know, as it seemed oddly unrelated to the act that created life. During those hours, she cursed Gallatin for never being with her when she needed him. Until she'd experienced labor before childbirth, "by the full moon" or some tame variation had typically been her strongest words. Those hours before pure, innocent newborn ears emerged from her body, she used words no lady, and very few gentlemen, would say.

But after Twilight saw the tiny new life emerge from her, all cursing left her. When her unseen baby had been growing cradled within her, she had felt a unique connection. Then, when she first saw her child—now an individual and not part of her, his own little person—love for him was total. This love became enveloped in his cries for life. This was the most overpowering feeling Twilight had ever known. The miracle and mystery of it, the beauty of it—she knew then that creation was magnificent and secret.

The word "precious" planted firmly in her mind and heart, especially concerning life itself. *Life is precious*, the Voice began repeating. From that moment of his arrival into humanity, she and Kent lived in a dream world of Love, a beautiful place Twilight never imagined could exist. What's more, her baby needed her. She was his mother. He was her child. He loved her just because she was. Never before had her existence mattered so much to anyone.

Her baby was born alive and healthy. And she hadn't died. With those facts alone, she knew she had so much more than many women. And now, though she wasn't quite eighteen, she considered herself a woman, not a child, as she had a child.

Achilles assigned himself as guardian of the small human. Heggie became the guardian of Menelik and Makeda-Angel.

Twilight wished Gallatin could share with her the joy of watching their child, of playing with him, of loving him. But he'd never written. He'd never contacted her father concerning her. The Voice had gone oddly silent except for repeating *Life is precious*. Regardless, the Voice had always been silent about Gallatin. She was convinced that for the rest of her life, all she would ever have of Gallatin were some fine memories and his perfect child.

Gallatin had lived so long with constant torment that he was adapting to it. It had been eight months since he had seen Twilight. He missed her feverishly. When he'd left her, he thought it would be easier to leave his beloved Mississippi River to work from an office on the Ohio River shore. But it wasn't.

When he'd returned to *Star of Twilight*—his riverboat—and his hands and mind again guided the vessel with or against the current, he felt that giving up piloting would be giving up himself. Moreover, believing himself to be a man of honor, he upheld his pledge to the Large Mystical and its messengers Miss Summer and Mr. Fall: to allow Twilight to discover her identity before he joined her as a companion.

Of course, he often thought about writing Twilight to try to explain, which is what a gentleman would do. He'd promised her he'd write. But whenever he took up the pen, his hand froze—he did not know what to say to her. He hoped that somehow, through their closeness, she understood.

And would wait.

Chapter 51
Nation Ablaze

June 1860 to Tuesday, November 6, 1860
Evansville

The United States of America, North and South, was ablaze.

In May, Abraham Lincoln had been nominated for President on the Republican Party ticket, the new moderate, liberal-leaning party that opposed slavery and challenged the far-reaching, deep conservatism of the Democratic Party administration.

To hear the talk about town and to join in on discussions of the state of the Union, Jesse began spending frequent evenings at the Courthouse, at Mozart Hall, and at the taverns along Water Street. With his excitement over Lincoln's nomination, one would have thought that Jesse knew the man himself. The news had the same effect on many town citizens, for Lincoln had spent his formative years on his father's farm a mere fifty miles from Evansville.

However, Evansville's close social and commercial ties to the South contributed to other citizens supporting the Southern cause. Southern unrest had gained momentum, with Southern conservative leaders declaring that if Lincoln were elected President, their threats of secession would come true.

"One older fellow by the name of Jerold Grissom," Jesse said one evening, "is taking quite a stand against the purpose of the Union. He's outspoken and causes heated debates at all the taverns by saying that the only way to preserve the Union is to let the Southerners live the way they wish, to let them keep their enslaved people, to keep slavery in America legal. He was with that mob who burned Ember's friend's home in February of 1859. Grissom is trouble. He loudly claims to whoever will listen that we're a strong nation today because of our national and foreign trade due to the South, so why would we interfere with a method that works? I've argued with him on occasion, and so has his own son, Frank, whose beliefs oppose his father's. Frank, several other young gentlemen, and I are helping to form our city's Lincoln Wide Awake Club. Many young men are wide awake and are calling ourselves Wide Awakes. There's more support for Lincoln than not. After all, it was in these parts that Lincoln developed his honorable beliefs."

Twilight never heard from Jackson, thankfully, except that also meant no divorce papers. However, Twilight and Harley wrote frequently, exchanging concerns, such as how the impending secession would hurt their river trade businesses and their family. She told Harley that Jesse, she felt, would join the war on the side of the Union, if it came to that. Harley replied that his heart couldn't be more burdened, for though Tennessee didn't favor secession, Jed had stated that he'd gladly join the Southern army and die for his land.

One Sunday night, Ember read her new poem to Twilight:

> "Geese fly South,
> Then fly North,
> Loudly sounding their path:
> In the winter, to the warmth

Of the South!
But when it gets too hot,
The North is the place to fly."

Abraham Lincoln was elected President of the United States of America on November 6, 1860. His inauguration would happen on March 4, 1861.

Chapter 52
Division

Tuesday, November 6, 1860
to Friday, March 1, 1861
Evansville

Southern aristocracy, no more than a castle of sand at the ocean's edge, melted in the rising tide of democratic consciousness that President-elect Lincoln represented.

During the three months between Lincoln's election and inauguration, Jesse's time in town increased. When he was home, all he could speak about were the rumors of secession and war, his loyalty to the Union, his admiration for President-elect Lincoln, and that American slavery must end. Saddened by his absence, Ember and her children spent more time with their friends near the edge of town. Twilight fretted over business matters. But her one true joy was Kent.

He was quickly becoming a big boy. By nine months old, he was already demonstrating speech and wit, and he was pulling up to walk. "I love you," Twilight would say to Kent, pointing to him. Balancing at the wall and copying her, he would point to himself and say, "uv oo." Then he would point at his mother and say, "uv oo." Copying Kent, Twilight pointed to herself and said, "I love you." It wasn't easy for Twilight to say she loved herself. However, saying those words was an essential part of the frequent game with child and mother, and with time, became easier.

March 1, 1861. Jackson walked into Twilight's office. Though shocked, for the flash of a moment, Twilight was reminded of the first time she'd seen him looking so distinguished at Atrocity Square in Memphis. The memory immediately turned to disgust, igniting her lingering fear.

"Jack. Jackson. I didn't expect you."

"I don't need to notify you of my arrival, my wife," Jackson said, grinning.

"Why have you come?"

Jackson reached into his jacket pocket and pulled out some folded papers. "I could've sent these to you, the papers ending our marriage, but I wanted to bring them, to watch you rip them up, and then we can return together to Magnolia Bay." He leaned toward her lips and whispered, "I've missed you."

Twilight stepped back. "It's over, Jack. Thank you for bringing the documents. I'll sign them now."

He closed the office door, then turned to her, smiling. *Blast of the moon*, she thought, wishing Achilles or Spirit were there. But just a few minutes earlier she'd let Achilles out for a run. She had walked the short distance to work that day, carrying Kent. So Spirit, who would knock down the door to protect her, was in the Willow Land yard. Then, Jackson saw Kent cruising along the wall toward Twilight. "Sitting for someone's child, Twilight?" Jackson laughed.

Twilight said nothing. Kent left the wall, bent down, crawled to her, grabbed her leg, and pulled himself up. "Ma," he said, gazing adoringly at her.

"Ma?" Jackson said, startled. "A son? My son! Why didn't you tell me I had a son?" Tucking the papers back into his jacket pocket and reaching down to Kent, he said, "This makes all the difference in the world."

Twilight hurriedly picked up her son. "Let me have him," Jackson said.

Clutching Kent tightly to her, Twilight shook her head. "This doesn't change anything, Jack. We're through. I don't want to be married to you any longer. Why do you think I didn't let you know about Kent? I didn't even tell my family about him because I didn't want you to find out."

"I had a right to know. He's my son."

"What about Rachel? I thought you two wanted to be a couple."

"We've spent many memorable moments together. She's a fine Southern lady." Jackson bent close to Twilight's lips again and breathed heavily. "But no one has the passion you have, my wife." Then he stood straight. "And, now I see you can bear children, and a son at that. So pack and return with me. As your husband, I order you. Remember, by law, you are my property."

"Property? When will men learn that people cannot truly be owned? Maybe in our 'great' America, you can own someone's body and actions with documents, violence, and torture, but you can never own someone's spirit. And you will *never* own me."

"I do own you. You are my wife. It is the law."

Twilight frowned. *He is right that, legally, women and their actions are owned.*

"I can force you to come home with me," Jackson said. "I can easily enslave you. But, I won't. Rachel will have me. Or Victoria, of course. Regardless, I'm taking my son. In a divorce, as you know, the husband is entitled to the children and all property. A woman gets nothing, not even her children."

"Will!" Twilight screamed, calling the clerk in the attached general store. A young, robust man ran into the office, pushing past Jackson to Twilight. Twilight shoved Kent into Will's arms. "Will, take Kent! Get away!" Wildly barking, Achilles scratched at the door. Will ran carrying the crying Kent, who was reaching for his mommy and screaming, into the general store.

"Jackson, please, you'd be happier without me. And I want my son. Just let me sign the papers, then forget about us. You and Rachel or you and Victoria will have children of your own. Please."

Jackson grabbed the back of her head and pulled her to him, smashing his mouth on hers. Releasing her forcefully, he threw her backward, nearly throwing her to the floor.

Catching herself against the wall, she stood, walked forward, then said, "Jackson, give me those papers, then get out of here."

"Stop telling me what to do, woman. I'm the man."

Twilight steadied herself, poised and waiting.

He looked at her long and hard, then squinting his eyes and cocking his head, he said, "Have some of your friends—the ones from Magnolia Bay—visited you recently?"

"I didn't and don't have any friends at Magnolia Bay, you know that."

"My captives," he said, drawing back his hand and smacking her across the face.

Her stance perfected, she barely flinched. Not touching her stinging cheek, she said, "Did that make you feel good, Jack? You're *such* a man. Go ahead, hit me again. Do it, Jack. Show me what a man you are." She squinted her eyes. "Just try it."

At her fearsome attitude and fearless words, Jackson chuckled awkwardly. "You *are* bold. And consistent." Then, frowning, he said, "So, you've helped my captives escape, have you? That's theft."

"I don't know what you are talking about," she said evenly.

"You have. I know it. And that only gives me more determination to take you back to Magnolia Bay and turn you into a proper lady. And I'll do it, too, if I have to bind and gag you every day and night and leave you with the captives to rot. I *will* break you, Twilight."

Staring straight into Jackson's eyes, fists clutched at her sides, Twilight said, "I won't even bend."

Jackson drew back his hand again. Twilight felt a scream and tears readying at the thought of being hit a second time—and on her swelling face—but she held them back and stood staring straight at Jack, defiant. He stopped. He let his arm drop. "Fine." He threw the divorce documents at her. She picked the papers off the floor. Leaning on her desk, she signed, dated, and wrote the time on both documents, then handed

Jackson one copy. "I'll leave then," he said. "But I'm taking my son." He started for the doorway where Will had vanished with Kent.

Twilight had one last chance, and she took it, risking it all. Mentally beseeching God and Goddess and GrandMama and the Voice and the elusive Sisterhood of Gifts and the Moon, she implored this would make him leave Kent and her alone once and for all.

"You don't have a son to take," she said.

Jackson stopped. Turning slowly to her, he said, "What are you saying now, woman?" Pointing to the general store doorway, he said, "That boy in there is my son. And I'm taking him to his home. My mother will raise him better than you ever could."

"Come on, Jack. Really? You only see what you want to see. Notice his age. Kent is not your son."

Jackson's face contorted in rage.

She continued, "The last time we were together was early February 1859. Kent was born more than a full year later. He is only nine months old. Our child, if we had one, would be fifteen months old."

Eyes blazing, Jackson yelled, "You sneaky, witchy enchantress! You gave your body to someone while being married to me?"

Twilight screamed, "Leave me alone!"

"Who was it? Who'd you lay with, you sneaky sorceress? It was McCay, wasn't it? I'll kill him!" Jackson yelled. He clenched and thrust his fist to smash it into her abdomen, where she'd carried a child he hadn't sired. But that was *her* sacred space—no way would she let him hit her, or even touch her, there. Her training made her quicker than his fist. She pivoted to miss his hit, then shoved her body into his side. Caught off guard, Jackson took a second before he could right himself. She leaped backward, landing across the room twelve feet away from him, far from his grasp.

"I could have you arrested! I could have you hanged! For harlotry *and* for theft!" Suddenly calming and lowering his voice, he said, "But you're not worth any more of my time." He spat on the floor. "I curse the day I met you. But I'm still taking the boy. He has Rich-tone blood."

Grasping the Power Gems in her pocket with her left hand, she said, "No." She touched her amulet necklace with the fingertips of her right hand. Wondrous Ring and Precious Friend at her throat warmed. "You will not take Kent from me. You will not enslave him," she said, her body ready to attack. She knew aiming her Deringer would be an effective threat. She would not pull the trigger, but even aiming a gun at a man might end her in jail. So might one of her jump kicks right into Jackson's gut or groin. Kent needed her. Jail was not a good place for a mother.

Jackson turned his back on her and started to walk into the general store to find Kent. Twilight took one step, then leaped across the room and twisted in the air so that her right foot soundly bumped Jack's back, smacking him into the wall. Deftly, her feet touched the floor, then she jumped backward and landed without a sound, again twelve feet from him. Just as Jackson, confused, turned from the wall to see her standing across the room, Will, still clutching Kent, burst through the door. Achilles, growling and ready to attack at Twilight's command, followed, with Marshal Marks entering last.

"There he is, Marshal," Will said. "He's been yelling at Mrs. Canon, and I know I heard him hit her."

"Who are you, sir?" Marshal Marks asked.

"Jackson Canon, Marshal," he said, eyeing Achilles' teeth. "Get that rabid dog out of here. I wish no row with the law of this fine town. I merely came to coax my wife to return with me to my plantation outside Memphis, but she refused. So, as of moments ago, we are now divorced. I have the signed documents with me. But I am taking my boy."

"Did you hit her?" the marshal asked.

Twilight was hanging onto Will, gently pressing her swelling and bleeding face next to Kent's tiny body. "Ma," Kent cried, wrapping his arms around her head and burying his face into her hair. Achilles, eyes fixed on Jackson and growling low, teeth still bared, stood beside her.

"I see you have hit her," the marshal said, walking over to Twilight. "I don't take kindly to a man hitting a woman. But since you were her husband when you hit her, it's legal, so there's nothing I can do or say about it. By your admission of signed papers, you're divorced now, so leave her alone."

Twilight held desperately to Kent and Will.

The marshal looked at Kent holding onto his mother, sobbing into her hair. Then to Jackson, he said, "And I suggest you go back to your place—your Southern plantation—on the next steamer or train out of here. I know what the law says, but this boy belongs with his mother."

Lifting his chin, Jackson said, "I'll gladly return to my home in the South. This land of Lincoln smells of conceit. And deceit." He walked toward the front door, then turned. "But let me remind you, Marshal, that it is still against the law—even in the North—to assist the enslaved in escaping for freedom. And it is a crime for any Rich-tone—free or enslaved—to enter Indiana." Pointing at Twilight, Jackson said, "That woman has aided my enslaved laborers in running for their freedom by harboring them in her very own Evansville home."

"No," Twilight said. "Have you spun off your axis, Jackson?"

Jerold Grissom had entered the store in time to hear Jackson's accusations. He looked at Twilight, then at Jackson, then at the marshal. "What are you going to do about that, Marks?" Grissom said. "The woman should be locked up and her house closed. Or burned."

Almost imperceptibly, the marshal's eyes widened. He said, "That's no concern of the law, Jerold, unless I see her do it with my own eyes."

"Then what are laws for?" Grissom said. Shaking his head, he added, "Sometimes a man's got to take the law into his own hands."

"Not while I'm marshal."

Grissom protested, "You can't see anything happening at that home, Marshal! All those trees around it hide any goings-on."

"Don't question my vision, Grissom. Now, why don't you two gentlemen cool off at a tavern until Mr. Canon's riverboat or train leaves?"

With a pat on Jackson's back, Grissom said, "Fine idea. I'll buy you a drink, sir."

Jackson said, "I accept." Then, slowly, he pulled a piece of paper from his inside jacket pocket. Twilight held her breath. He stepped next to her and waved it in front of her face. "The incriminating page of your dear letter. If you want this, my darling, you know where to find me," he said, tucking it back into his pocket, smiling smugly. Then he left with Grissom.

Terrified, she prayed for a miracle to get her out of this dilemma. She'd been naive to not burn that letter as GrandMama directed. The "one-drop rule" meant Kent also was at risk of being enslaved. And that's surely what Jack had meant to do once he learned Kent was not his son.

Still, at that moment, she closed her eyes and smiled, for in her hand she clutched her divorce documents, and in her arms she held Kent.

Now, if only she'd hear from Gallatin.

CHAPTER 53

LEARNING

Friday, March 1, 1861, Evening
Saturday, March 2, 1861, Twilight
New Orleans, Louisiana

"I want to remember every crease of your face, every muscle of your body, every angle and curve of you. I want you burned into me, so on those long days and nights when you're gone, I can feel the impression of your body with mine."

In a New Orleans tavern, Gallatin poured himself another whiskey and savored the words Twilight spoke to bless their lovemaking so long ago. With the next drink, he recalled each moment of their bodies' passionate expression. Lost in his memories, he paid no attention to the uproar of drinking men concerning the news:

Lincoln's inauguration hadn't yet happened, that being on March 4, three days away. But even though Lincoln had not yet served an official day of his presidency, the Southern states, one by one, were falling further south, crumbling from the nation that had boasted being the united land of the free.

South Carolina had seceded from the United States of America—the Union—in December 1860. In January 1861, Mississippi, Florida, Alabama, Georgia, and Louisiana had followed South Carolina's lead. In February, Texas seceded. Just days later, Jefferson Davis was inaugurated as provisional president of the provisional government of the Confederate States of America—the Confederacy—which had created a provisional constitution.

Men were arguing as to why Virginia, what they called the grand Southern slavery state, had not yet seceded. Or why Tennessee, with Memphis being the largest inland cotton-and-captives-trading port, did not seem interested in seceding. And what of Kentucky, Delaware, Maryland, Missouri, Arkansas, and North Carolina, all states with legalized slavery? Would they secede?

Gallatin poured yet another whiskey. The hair ribbon Twilight had given him was entwined with the fingers of his left hand; he lifted the glass with his right and downed the pour. He'd be in New Orleans just one more night. Tomorrow he'd visit his father, as he always did when docked in Orleans. But this time, he wanted to know something specific.

"Hello, Son." Gallatin's father, Zeke, moved just slightly, forward then back, in a rocker on the front porch of his clapboard home.

Gallatin sat in the twin rocker next to his father's. "Hello, Father."

Slapping his own knee, Zeke said, "Well, it looks like our land is finally rising against the tyranny of the Union. Thank God. We Confederates—we're Confederates now—need to stand up and fight for what we believe. Let's see how long the North can thrive, or even survive, without our cotton." Slapping Gallatin's knee, Zeke stated, "When an army's formed, you'll be joining. And I'll be proud of my boy."

Gallatin shook his head. "No, Father. I won't join the Confederate Army."

Rising half out of his rocker, Zeke said, "What? My son won't defend his land?"

"This isn't my land, Father."

"It is your land, just as sure as I'm sixty-five, poor, and rocking on this porch. You were born and raised here, Son. The South's been good to you."

"Father, the river's been good to me."

"The South is your land," Zeke said with a look of reprimand.

"The river is my land, so to speak," Gallatin said. "But, Father, I didn't come here to discuss politics."

"What else is there to discuss? That's all there is these days."

Gallatin studied his hands to avoid meeting his father's eyes, saying, "I want to know about Mother. You've never spoken of her."

Zeke rocked rapidly. After a moment, he stopped. "You never asked before."

"Yes, I asked. When I was young, several times, I asked. But you never answered me, so I finally stopped asking. If you loved her, you would have spoken of her, isn't that true? But since you've never said a word, you must hate her."

Closing his eyes and slowly shaking his head, Zeke said, "Oh, no, Son. I loved your mama more than anyone has ever known love before. Still do. Not a moment goes by that I don't ache to see her again, hear her laughter, or touch her cheek."

Stunned, Gallatin said nothing for a moment. Then he said, "So, why have you never talked about her?"

Concentrating on his clasped-together gnarled hands, Zeke said, "It hurt bad enough just thinking about her and knowing I'd never see her again. Talking would only make it hurt worse."

"Father, have you no idea what that did to me? I was a child who never heard a word about his mother. I am a *person* who has never heard a word about his mother."

Zeke said nothing.

"Can you talk about her now? Can you tell me about her?"

Unresponsive, Zeke sat, not even rocking. For several minutes, father and son sat silent and still on the Southern porch. Then Zeke's eyes brightened, and he spoke for nearly an hour of all he could remember about the only woman he'd ever loved. When he was finished, he said, "Funny. It didn't hurt to talk about my Martha."

"Did she see me before she died, Father?"

He nodded and said, "Yes, Son. She was weak, but she wanted to hold her boy. With you in her arms, your mother smiled as I had never seen her smile before; she looked like an angel shining on you. Then she kissed the top of your head and was gone." Gallatin's father bowed his head and wiped his eyes with his hand. He looked at his son and said, "Nothing, Son, is more precious than the love of a fine woman. Nothing. Not the South, not your work, not even your life."

Zeke sighed. "I didn't learn that until I lost her."

Chapter 54
Decision

Saturday, April 13, 1861
Late Afternoon
St. Louis, Missouri

Six weeks later, in a St. Louis tavern, Gallatin poured another whiskey.

After seeing his father, he'd made a risky run, as it was still winter, to St. Louis. Then Nature, with a March hard freeze, gave him the time to drink and think. Now mid-April, the river ice was melting. It was time. No longer could he stall; he had to make a decision. "It comes to this," Gallatin mumbled to himself. "Which do I want more? The feel of piloting the Mississippi or the feel of Twilight's body against mine? My own single identity? Or knowing Twilight is with me as my true friend and my true love? The river as my companion? Or Twilight as my companion?"

Interlocked with the fingers of his right hand was her hair ribbon. When he put it to his lips and nose, he believed he could still smell the lavender scent of her hair. Tipping his head back, he finished one last whiskey, and all he could see was Twilight's eyes, her face, her smile, her hair, her form. Banging the glass on the table, he stood. He fished around in his pockets for coins, which he threw on the table.

He knew. The decision was made.

He was going straight to the telegraph office to apologize to Twilight, to tell her he'd left piloting the river, and by morning, he'd be on his way to her. In his head, he started composing what the telegraph, which would be read by the operators, would say. Maybe: *Deepest apology. Left river. Arriving soon.* Surely Jackson had finalized the divorce by now. And if he hadn't, Gallatin decided he'd wait in Evansville with Twilight until the divorce papers arrived. Never had he felt so sure of anything as he did, finally, about spending the rest of his life with his love, Twilight.

And as for his vow to the Large Mystical? Well, he had made a vow to Twilight with his body and his love, and he felt like a rotten man for not honoring that vow to her, his most important vow.

As he turned to leave, two Army officers, one on each side of him, grabbed his arms. "What is this?" Gallatin demanded.

The ranking officer, a captain, said, "I'd lower my voice if I were you, Mr. Gallatin. We don't want any trouble. We just want to talk."

"Then let go of my arms. You're treating me as if I were a criminal," Gallatin said as the officers ushered him out to the street. As they walked, Gallatin said, "This won't take long, will it? I have business at the telegraph office before it closes, and it's getting late."

The captain opened the door to a building facing the wharf and waved his arm, signaling Gallatin to step inside. The other officer, a lieutenant, followed. "Take a seat," ordered the captain.

"I don't think so," Gallatin said. "I have to send a telegraph, and I have no business with the military."

The captain sat behind a big desk. The lieutenant stood at attention at the door.

"Suit yourself. At least for now," the captain said.

Gallatin stood.

"We've been monitoring your abilities as a riverboat pilot, Mr. Gallatin," the captain said.

"I want to know what is going on. Who are you?" Gallatin said.

"It is not important that you know who I am. What you need to know are my mission and my authority: I am assigned by the War Department to, in this area, scout for and recruit the best pilots on the Mississippi River."

"For what reason?" Gallatin asked.

"For the purpose of reconnaissance. And for a show of strength. Some of our states along the Mississippi are unsure of their loyalties. We need a few Union steamships patrolling the shores of Missouri, Arkansas, Kentucky, and Tennessee. All those states are still within the Union, and the Army plans to keep it that way. You'd be doing your country a great service if you sign this paper saying you will work for us as a pilot."

"I don't want to join any military," Gallatin said.

"You wouldn't be joining the military."

"I don't want to work for any military," Gallatin said.

"We know you are from New Orleans. We could lock you up as a Confederate spy if you don't cooperate."

"Are you trying to blackmail me?"

"We don't have to try," the captain said. "We have our orders, which come from the White House. Do you have authority higher than that?"

"I am sure Mr. Lincoln would not condone your recruiting method. False accusations. Blackmail. And why would the Federal Army want a pilot from a seceded state?" Gallatin said.

"It doesn't matter where you are from, only that you are a top-notch pilot. We'll pay you as a civilian pilot, not as an enlisted soldier. You'll be an employee of the Union. But because you are from Louisiana, you'll not have contact with anyone. You'll not be allowed to send letters or telegraph messages. When you're not piloting, a guard will keep you honest."

"Why me?"

"As I said, we've been watching you. You, Mr. Gallatin, have a stellar reputation and the most impeccable record of any pilot on the Mississippi. Among pilots, your record is remarkable—exceptional for one so young. We could not pass by the opportunity to recruit you into our service."

"I see: being the best isn't always best," Gallatin said.

"You may not know it yet, but the papers will be filled with the news. The first battle of the war was yesterday and today. The seven states of the Confederacy attacked—and took—Fort Sumter."

Surprised, but refusing to show it, Gallatin nodded.

"Oh, don't be thinking that the Confederates have a fighting chance, Mr. Gallatin," the captain said. "That bunch of farm boys can't outfight an established national military. We'll squelch this secession, this ridiculous war effort, in nothing flat. Three months at most. Naval plans are to construct more gunboats, but we'll never even need to use them. Still, our orders are to be prepared, and currently, that includes the western rivers. Rivers, being inland waterways and within our nation's interior, are under the jurisdiction of the Army, not the Navy. Besides, our Navy is equipped with sea vessels, not river vessels. If the war lasts longer than we think, which it won't, we might need to develop a river fleet, in which case we would need the aid of the Navy. Who knows? The Army and the Navy might work together to fortify our rivers. We could even have our own brown-water navy if ordered to take the Mississippi River as part of a blockade. But, for now, the Army merely needs a few good pilots for a few reconnaissance steamers that will display strength and our American flag. We'll add some light artillery to the steamers. We'll hire the ablest men to run them. You, Mr. Gallatin, will join us. We need you. You should be eager to serve your country."

The captain pushed the paper to Gallatin. "Sign here. It states that you will work for hire, not as a soldier but as a civilian, for the United States of America, as a reconnaissance gunboat pilot."

Ignoring the paper, Gallatin looked at the captain.

The captain returned the look straight into Gallatin's eyes. "Mr. Gallatin. Sign, or go to jail."

Loyalty overtook Gallatin. Certainly not a loyalty to the Confederacy or the Southern cause, but a loyalty to, most certainly, a Southern trait—his own determination to not be forced to do anything. Further, if he signed, he'd not have contact with Twilight until after the war, however long that would be.

He disagreed that it would be over in no time. Maybe the Confederates appeared to be just a bunch of farm boys. And maybe, logically, they couldn't stand up to organized armed forces. But several Southern men had fought in the war with Mexico. They had skills. Once they got organized, they'd be formidable. Besides, he'd never known a group of people with as much raw energy, determination, and fanaticism about their beliefs as the Pale Southerners had. True, their zeal was misguided and wrong; he always held in check a continuous anger at the South, his Southern brothers, for enslaving people. Slavery must stop. He wanted to aid the abolitionist cause. But he would not tolerate being forced by the Army, the Navy, or whoever, to pilot a gunboat.

"I'll go to jail," Gallatin said.

"I think not," the captain said with a crooked smile.

The lieutenant stepped up to Gallatin and pressed his gun against the trapped pilot's skull. "Sign," the lieutenant said, cocking the gun.

The captain handed Gallatin a pen and said, "You see, Mr. Gallatin, this is war."

Chapter 55
Call to Arms

Saturday through Tuesday
April 13-16, 1861
Evansville, Indiana

Jesse was insufferable upon hearing the news.

The Confederates started the Civil War on April 12 by attacking the Federal garrison at Fort Sumter, located on an island in Charleston Harbor. On April 13, the United States Army commander of the Fort surrendered, meaning the Confederates won the first battle of the war.

Fortunately, no one was killed. Yet, the Confederates were victorious. And the Confederates had been prepared, even having constructed in the months prior an ironclad vessel as a floating battery that controlled the harbor.

Jesse paced the hallway and the parlor, back and forth, back and forth, ranting that Lincoln had better get busy and keep the promises he'd made. Lincoln did, appeasing Jesse and many other angry Union men—and some women who were determined to find a way to fight—when, on April 15, just two days after the surrender at Fort Sumter, he called for volunteer troops from state militias to fortify the Federal Army in stopping the rebellion.

Squaring his shoulders, Jesse said, "I'm signing up. We must stop American slavery."

Ember grabbed his hand. "Oh, Jesse. This will be over soon. They don't need you."

Smoothing her hair, Jesse said, "President Lincoln has called. Governor Morton has called. It's only for a three-month term. Everyone knows we will squash the rebellion in less than three months. And, darling, what if everyone felt as you do? No one would volunteer."

"I don't think that's going to happen," Twilight said. "All I hear is too much eagerness to fight." As she spoke, she, Makeda-Angel, and Menelik were chasing Kent, for he'd mastered walking and was fast, grabbing everything in sight. "I'll have to store away each and every item in the house," Twilight said, laughing. She caught her young son. He giggled. She hugged him tight to her and said, "I thank God every night that Kent is only ten months old. I'd dread having a son fighting in a war. And I hope there's no war when Kent is old enough to enlist."

Menelik and Makeda-Angel ran through the house. Kent wiggled from his mama's arms and ran with them. The children were the light of the home. Kent found delight in everything, laughing at the silly antics of Menelik, Makeda-Angel, the dogs, and Taboo. Though tiny, he showed a mature finesse for a toddler and tried playing the games Menelik and Makeda-Angel created.

Ember began to softly cry. "I love you, Jesse."

Gently placing his hands on the sides of her face, Jesse said tenderly, "Don't you see, darling? This is for us. When we win this war, slavery will be abolished. And when that happens, all people will be equal, as our nation intends."

Looking at him through tear-filled eyes, she said, "The greedy power-hungry are spread too wide and too far, and prejudice runs too deep, which makes me doubt Rich-tone people and Pale people will ever be allowed to marry."

"Of course we will marry, honey. That's what this war is about, equality and freedom. And when slavery no longer exists, all Rich-tone folk will be free, as free as faded folk. If we're all free, why couldn't we marry?"

Ember shook her head. "I'm free. Evansville is a free town. And yet, you and I can't be married here."

Taking her hands, Jesse said, "It'll be different, Ember, after the war is won. I know it will. Mark my word, the war will be over in no time. Three months. And if it is like Sumter, with no casualties, no death."

"Why can't there be freedom without war?" Ember said.

Twilight said, "That should be the case. But, since it seems there's too much meanness for that, it also seems fighting is going to happen. And if they are going to fight to keep slavery, we must fight back to end it. To finally end it." Watching Kent, Menelik, and Makeda-Angel play, she said, "Some things are worth fighting for. But that can mean killing and dying, and, of course, I wish that were not true."

As her son scampered with his friends, Twilight added, "And even though we know that this war is about the fates of all enslaved people and ensuring they all are free, I want to remind you of President Lincoln's inaugural address. He basically stated that he would not free those enslaved but would uphold the laws already in effect, including the Fugitive Slave Clause of our Constitution, and that he would continue to support states making their own decisions about slavery."

She took a deep breath. "Of course, by his inauguration in March, seven states had already seceded, so his main concern in his address was probably to keep the nation together above all else, and claiming other than what he did might have toppled the other enslaver states to secede. Still, it doesn't seem the Southern states believe him. After all, while politically moderate himself, he did run on the liberal-leaning platform of the party created to end slavery. The real issue is that our nation, while allowing prejudices, inequalities, and Pale Male supremacy, does not endorse slavery. If it did, there would be no Southern dissension."

"He'll free the enslaved," Jesse said. "That's understood."

Twilight nodded. "Or he will take great steps to that conclusion."

"He knows what he is doing," Jesse said. "In his inaugural address, he was supporting the rights of the states to govern themselves. What better stance to keep the United States intact as a nation? Consider this: if the

Confederates succeed in their secession, win the war, and remain their own country, they will have established an entire country of legalized slavery. And our United States will be a separate country with no say over what the Confederate States as a nation decide to do. If the country stays intact with both North and South, as President Lincoln is determined to do, then with time, slavery will be abolished in the South because the United States as a country will demand it. So, first things first. President Lincoln is smart. First, keep the nation together, which is what his speech was about. Then, abolish slavery nationally. Again, if the South is a separate nation, slavery will continue. If it stays part of the Union, in time, slavery will end. But now there needs to be a brief war first, to reclaim the seceding states."

"Strategic," Twilight said, nodding.

Ember said, "Just days ago, Virginia voted against secession. Then Fort Sumter happened. Now I wonder if this attack and victory by the Confederates will energize Virginia into joining the Confederacy after all."

"It might," Twilight said. "And we don't know yet about Arkansas, North Carolina, Missouri, Delaware, Kentucky, or our family's state of Tennessee. As of now, they are still states of the United States. But remember, Jesse, that even though Tennessee has not seceded, our brother most likely could enlist directly with the Confederate army rather than by a state militia. Soon, he might be out there fighting, as you will be, as enemies."

Jesse's jaw became rigid; he said nothing.

Indiana men responded zealously to the call to uphold the Union. That very day, Governor Morton informed the President that his state could ensure ten thousand volunteers, which was double what the President had asked for from Indiana. Eager to be in the midst of the organization of the troops and the "real action," as Jesse called it, he and his friend

Frank Grissom decided to join by directly going to Indianapolis, where the Indiana Infantry Regiments were being organized, rather than joining through a community-organized militia.

The next day, Jesse and Frank boarded the train for Indianapolis. As she watched him go, Ember said, "That man holds my soul, Twilight. Honor be blasted; I wish he'd made love to me."

"I know what you mean," Twilight said, hugging Kent. "By the full moon, Ember, I know exactly what you mean." Placing her arm around Ember's back and shoulders, Twilight said, "Your day will come, Ember. The day for you and Jesse will come."

That night, Ember wrote this poem:

> Pink embraces the sky as love,
> Spreading its blushing warmth
> Into each morning.
>
> I no longer wonder if there is a reason
> For hatred and pain,
> Because I can see each day
> That pink surrenders to the sky
> Of blue and gray.
>
> Then blue and gray
> Blaze each evening
> Into red,
> Into morning
> Bruises, wounds,
> And mourning
> Blood.

Tucked away in her home in Massachusetts, a woman named Emily was writing poetry.

Years later, women of the Sisterhood of Gifts would read Emily's poems and recognize this poet as a sister with the talent of reaching into the heavens and pulling to Earth complex and perfect images and soul songs.

Chapter 56
The Divided States

April 17, 1861, through July 1861
Evansville, Indiana
Mississippi River
Virginia

Five days after the Civil War began, Virginia voted to secede from the Union. On the issue, the state was fractured: a majority of delegates from the northwestern section of the state had voted to stay with the Union.

Twilight's daily routine included visiting the post office for any correspondence that might arrive concerning her businesses. Also, in case her father wrote. Which he did. And also in case Gallatin wrote. Which he didn't. But now, she and Ember had an even greater reason for those daily visits—to see if they had a letter from Jesse.

They received his first letter in the second week after he had left. Dated April 22, he told them the details of what had happened since his arrival in Indianapolis. He and Frank had been sent with thousands of other men to camp in the barns at the state fairground, renamed Camp Morton. Governor Morton had chosen Lew Wallace to be Adjutant General of Indiana. General Wallace organized the volunteers into six regiments, Regiments 6 through 11, as Regiments 1 through 5 had been Mexican War Regiments. Jesse and Frank were assigned to Regiment 9, which was officially the 9th Indiana Infantry Regiment—Company C, under Colonel Milroy. The talk was that, within days, General Wallace would become Colonel Wallace, commanding Regiment 11, with plans to secure the Evansville port and surrounding area in May. Jesse expressed regret at not being in the 11th so he could be near Ember and Twilight; but, he explained, the 11th, under Colonel Wallace's command, was only for those seasoned men who had already served in militia companies. He added that his regiment would see action soon.

The next day, she got the letter of all letters—no, not from Gallatin. From Jed. Folded were two sheets of paper: on one, he had written ten words: *On my way to war. I love you, Little Sister.*

The other was the page from GrandMama's letter.

Arkansas seceded from the Union on May 6, 1861.

Kentucky, Tennessee, Missouri, Delaware, Maryland, and North Carolina had not seceded.

Because Kentucky was an enslaver state located between the North and the South and was staying with the Union, it was contested between the established Union states and the newly-seceded Confederate states. Almost daily, troubling events surrounded northern Kentucky and southern Indiana river border towns, including Evansville. As Jesse had relayed, the 11th Indiana Infantry under Colonel Wallace arrived in Evansville in May for blockade duty.

North Carolina seceded from the Union on May 20, 1861.

Virginia ratified its Ordinance of Secession, thus formally seceding on May 23, 1861.

Jesse's last letter from Indianapolis informed Twilight and Ember that his infantry, nearly eight hundred men strong, would be leaving May 25 for Virginia's western region.

⋆⋆⋆

At the end of June, Twilight and Ember received a letter from Jesse written and sent from the battlefield of Philippi, in western Virginia, the first land battle of the war. Dated June 4, the day after the Battle of Philippi, Jesse relayed that the battle lasted only minutes. He wrote:

> *Our Union forces had the rebel troops on the run. Thankfully, neither side suffered a fatality. My buddies and I are heartened that the war will be quick with a Union victory in no time. Most likely, the 9th will see more action in this area, sending the Confederates running. With no fatalities at either Sumter or Philippi, it seems these battles are skirmishes, soon to end in our favor.*
>
> *I have great admiration for the color guard, the men who carry and guard our colors—our noble flag bearers who also bear exceptional bravery. They keep us organized. They risk their lives, unarmed, to do so. Enemy fire targets them to disorganize and demoralize us.*

He wrote of his friend Frank and of new friends. He was especially fond of one young soldier named Private Ambrose Bierce. Jesse wrote:

Private Bierce, soon to be twenty years old, is kind and intelligent, with a sharp wit. His stories and his love for words and puns keep many a soldier entertained. Private Bierce likes to invent word definitions, and he talks about someday compiling them into a droll dictionary.

Twilight and Ember sent letters to Jesse twice a week and, because his infantry regiment was on the move, they hoped he would receive at least one of them. Ember held her letters from Jesse to her heart each night as she watched the moon, knowing Jesse was watching the moon at the same time as she. At night, she found it difficult to find him when she flew. So, with all her heart, she sang at church in hopes she would fly and see Jesse.

One Sunday morning, Ember invited Twilight and Kent to accompany Menelik, Makeda-Angel, and her to church. "That is," Ember said with a chuckle, "if you didn't drink too much last night to attend church today."

Laughing, Twilight said, "Drinking—oooo, that brandy. Long gone days, Ember. Long gone days."

Inside the Leet Street house where the African Methodist Episcopal Church congregation met, people chatted and laughed; babies were passed between relatives and friends to cuddle. Ember, with a voice that ascended to miraculous places, sang with the congregation. She also sang a solo. Hearing her made Twilight happy and Kent smile.

June 8, 1861: Tennessee was the last state to secede.

The four remaining states with legalized slavery—Kentucky, Missouri, Delaware, and Maryland—did not join the Confederacy, choosing instead to continue as states of the United States of America.

The Union continued to deliver mail to the South through June. However, it was unclear if the Confederacy, which had established its own postal service, had delivered the mail dispatched from the North. Twilight sent letters to her father but received none from him, so she lost all knowledge of her family in Memphis, now part of the Confederacy, and of Jed, a soldier of the Confederacy. She shook with anxiety when she realized that her twin brothers, bright spots of her life in Memphis, could very well be trying to kill each other.

Though she'd given up on ever hearing from Kent's father, still she thought of him, wondering where on the river he was—and what was he thinking?

Gallatin was thinking of Twilight.

As the water moved perfectly against and onto the shore, he was thinking of his body caressing Twilight's curves, they moving perfectly together. He was thinking of his bad luck in being forcibly "recruited" by the War Department. He was thinking of his lousy timing in being on his way to the telegraph office to contact Twilight when he was circumvented. And now, there was no way to contact her. He pressed her hair ribbon to his lips.

Gallatin was thinking of the war and his place in it. He was piloting a reconnaissance light-artillery gunboat on the Mississippi, patrolling the contested state of Missouri, split with its own state-wide civil war between those who supported the Confederacy—the secessionists—and those who supported the United States—the loyalists. His assigned mission was to show Union strength and gather information to keep St. Louis, the Missouri shoreline, and that section of the Mississippi River under United States control.

Inadvertently, Gallatin had become a Union spy.

Some young men who were murky on politics joined the Missouri secessionist militias only to reassess their loyalties, realize they didn't want to be traitors or fight against the United States, then desert within weeks. Many others, dedicated to the Confederate cause, joined the state secessionist militias with fervor. No doubt about it, Missouri—an enslaver state that voted to not join the Confederacy but be neutral within the Union—was a hotbed of division, a state version of the national turmoil, meaning Gallatin piloted waters heating to the full boil of war.

The Camp Jackson massacre of May 10 was one such scalding occurrence. After Brigadier General Lyon had safeguarded the federal arsenal at St. Louis from attack by traitors at nearby Camp Jackson, secessionist unrest triggered gunfire, possibly from a civilian. Union soldiers returned fire, killing nearly thirty civilians. Riots ignited. The area was part of Gallatin's patrol, but his ship was to display—not use—force.

Gallatin was thinking: *My missions, so far, have been only reconnaissance—and evacuation, if necessary. Though this steamer is clad in timber and equipped with guns, it could not withstand prolonged attacking firepower. Soon, however, there will be more steamers as gunboats, clad in tin and in iron. In time, I might be transferred to one of those. I pray never to be a pilot of death.*

※※※ ※※※

As the landowners of the South eagerly joined the Confederate army, plantations were often left to the management of planter wives, the older overseers who stayed behind, or the enslaved overseers and drivers. With this power shift, changes in routine, and fewer men with whips, the enslaved found more opportunities to escape captivity. Many more freedom champions came to Twilight's home from Magnolia Bay and other plantations. Children and adults were in one night and out the next. Twilight worried ceaselessly after Jackson had told Marshal Marks that she hid freedom champions who'd run from Magnolia Bay. But the marshal patrolled Water Street no more frequently than usual, and he never called on her.

Still, Twilight organized each day with extreme caution. The Indiana residents who sided with the South blamed the abolitionists for the war. Pejoratively called Copperheads, these Confederate supporters were banding together with outrage for those who did not agree with the main reason the Southern states wanted their autonomy in making laws—keeping slavery legal.

Grissom was one such angry Confederate supporter. What might happen if Grissom continued his accusations of her? Could he gather a mob to try to get her arrested? And what might happen to Ember and her children, whose arrival in Indiana was undocumented and illegal?

~~>>>> <<<<~~

The lamp burned in the window.

By the burning lamp each night, rocking Kent to sleep, wrapping him in her arms as he slept, Twilight often gazed into his serene face and pondered. On June 16, she'd turned nineteen. From sixteen—the birthday she learned she had power—to her present life at nineteen, she'd moved to a plantation, married, befriended the captives, left Jackson, given her heart to Gallatin, made love with Gallatin, moved to Evansville, took over businesses, started hiding freedom champions in her home, carried and bore an enchanting son, gotten a divorce from Jackson, and tried to forget about Gallatin.

As for Twilight's power? She was starting to understand that while sixteen most definitely was the age of power, her skills were ever-emerging. And that if she wanted to continue to experience the mystical dimension, she needed to focus on those magical events. Since running businesses on her own, aiding freedom champions in her Underground Railroad station, worrying about the war and her brothers' places in that, and becoming a mother, her attention hadn't been on the mystical. She was sure that it was because of her focus on worldly matters that her otherworldly experiences hadn't increased exponentially with her age.

Ember, her dear friend, had been with her through all the changes. So had Taboo, her shadow. And Spirit, her always-steady companion whom she cared for, brushed, and walked, but since becoming a mother, seldom rode. However, now that Kent was old enough, she reveled in holding him against her heart as they nearly flew for short stretches on Spirit.

A poem emerged as Twilight found herself missing the flying strides of the longer rides on her beloved Spirit:

> My horse, numinous beauty,
> Commands each space
> Of standing, walking,
> Running, nearly
> Flying.
> Spirit is my lesson.

The thought of Grissom and other Confederate supporters in the town directing their hatred at her stuck in her mind like a needle. *After GrandMama and Margaret died, Grandfather sent me away to keep me safe. Are the children and Ember safe at Willow Land? What would happen to Kent if I were arrested for welcoming freedom champions into our home? What would happen to Ember, Menelik, and Makeda-Angel?*

She didn't want to stop welcoming freedom champions. But she had to protect Kent, Ember, Menelik, and Makeda-Angel. The thought repeated: *What would happen to them if I were arrested?* With the war, all was uncertain. From Jesse's letter and from newspaper reports, she tried to believe she wouldn't have to worry much longer, as the war would soon end with a Union victory.

Divided ideologies. Enduring dogmas.

The first major battle occurred on July 21, 1861, near Manassas, Virginia—about twenty miles from Washington, D.C.—and was called the Battle of Bull Run by Northerners.

The troops under Confederate General Thomas J. Jackson, known after the fight as "Stonewall" Jackson, stood firmly as a stone wall. Confederate General Beauregard's forces, yelling the rebel yell, broke through the Union line. Some Union troops fled toward D.C., as did civilians on nearby bluffs who'd been watching as they enjoyed food and drink refreshments, viewing the battle as entertainment. The Confederacy claimed victory.

Unlike Fort Sumter and Philippi, Bull Run amassed deaths of a devastating number of both Union and Confederate soldiers—estimated at one thousand killed and three times that number wounded.

Surprised, the Union finally had to accept that the Confederacy was a formidable enemy, violently dedicated to its cause, and that the war would not end in three months.

Or maybe ever.

Chapter 57
War

August 1861
In particular 4:40 p.m. to 5:00 p.m.
On Tuesday, August 27, 1861
Evansville

One gusty afternoon at the general store, customer Jacob Messick told Twilight that he and his nine-year-old son Johnny were enlisting.

Beaming proudly, Jacob placed his hand on Johnny's shoulder, stating that his boy would be "joining up" as a drummer.

This news deeply saddened Twilight. She liked Johnny. He played with Kent whenever he visited the store. Though a young child, Johnny soon might be in the war since the morale-boosting musicians played during drill and also typically during the actual battles. She prayed he'd live to see the war end.

By August, Evansville had organized its first regiments: 1st Battery, Indiana Light Artillery and 1st Regiment, Indiana Cavalry.

Even though river trade was nearly defunct, Twilight continued to work at her office attached to the general store almost daily. Usually, she took Kent, who, seated in front of her on Spirit, gleefully giggled as they nearly flew. But sometimes he wanted to play with Menelik,

Makeda-Angel, Achilles, Heggie-man, and Taboo. On those days, Ember watched him tenderly and carefully as if he were her own.

The night of August 26, Ember enjoyed a great surprise when her sister Dove and two young men, Noah and Samuel, arrived from Magnolia Bay. Chattering constantly, the sisters were thrilled to be together. Seeing family members reunited, Twilight witnessed a celebrated miracle. Though eager to leave for Canada, the trio decided to stay until the following night, August 27, so that Dove and Ember could visit for a full day. Twilight stayed home that day.

Late that afternoon, Twilight needed to collect the mail at the post office. When she started to dress Kent for the outing, he pouted. "Play," he said.

"You want to stay and play with our visitors?" Twilight asked. Kent nodded his head.

Ember smiled. "I'll watch Kent. It's best if we stay in the attic while you're gone; I want to get as much visiting in with my sister as I can before they leave tonight, and I don't want to whisper," she said.

Giving Kent a big kiss and hug, Twilight said, "You know that Mommy loves you bigger than the whole world." Hugging him again, she said, "You're my life, little Kent. You're my life. I'll be home soon."

"Bye-bye, Mommy," Kent said, then gave her a smeary kiss.

She handed the pouch with the Power Gems to Ember. Ember slipped them into one of her apron pockets. Then, she lifted Kent and started up the stairs. "We'll be fine," she said. "Heggie and Achilles are outside, guarding. See you soon." Then she added, "Maybe take your guns since Kent won't be with you. Confederates could arrive anytime. If they want Kentucky to turn, they might attack here and claim all areas south of us." Twilight nodded, then closed the door to the attic stairway.

She took her Deringers from their hiding place high on a wardrobe shelf. Outside the house, she loaded them both and slipped each into a pocket.

Into the typical overcast pre-autumn Indiana day, Twilight and Spirit nearly flew. With no saddle, she felt that her body and her horse's body were one—she was a centaur. And all the dead men from ancient Greece watched her, envious.

At the post office, a soldier's letter—as marked on the front—was waiting for her. It was addressed in an unfamiliar script—so not from Jesse.

Worried, she hastily opened it. It was dated July 18, 1861. She scanned to the bottom, to the signature. It was from Jesse's friend Ambrose Bierce, now with the title of Sergeant. Twilight crumpled onto a bench as she read the carefully written words of Sergeant Bierce, describing Jesse's friendship, his dedication to the cause, his humor and intelligence, and mostly his bravery in serving his country. The letter stated:

> *Private Adams died at Laurel Hill in western Virginia, the second battle for the 9th Regiment, saving another soldier, Private Frank Grissom, who, unfortunately, was mortally shot two days later at the battle at Carrick's Ford.*

After many words of condolences, Sergeant Bierce added that he, too, had saved a soldier at Laurel Hill, a soldier who later died. For his bravery, Bierce was promoted to Sergeant. He wrote:

> *The same promotion would have happened for your brother had he not died in the act of such bravery. He died with honor, serving his country to keep our nation indissoluble. Your brother is now promoted to a better land, one with kindness, one without prejudice and killing.*

She clutched the letter to her constricted chest, trying to breathe.

Four other small letters were folded inside the envelope. These, Sergeant Bierce explained, were found in Jesse's pocket. Jesse had written on the back of each letter. One said, "For my beloved Ember, in the event of my demise. Your Loving Jesse." The other said, "For my dear sister Twilight, in the event of my demise. Your Loving Brother." The third: "For Mother and Father, in the event of my demise. Your Loving Son." And the fourth: "For Jed, in the event of my demise. Your Loving Twin."

As if the postal clerk had been the one to give her the news, she clasped his hand, bent her head, and cried into their intertwined knuckles. He shook his head woefully, knowing, because of the times, what the letter was about.

She and Spirit left for home, stopping near the river. She thought about Jesse, remembering his ways. She read the letter he'd written for her. Beautifully and succinctly crafted, he told her how important she was to him, all the things he wanted her to know if he never saw her again. At the river, she whispered, "Jesse is dead. Do you hear? Do you care?" But it was just a river. She cried, "Gallatin, where are you when I need you?" She sobbed as if her body was being ripped open from the inside.

Fifteen minutes passed. Spirit, who always stood patiently for Twilight, had become agitated. She pawed the ground and neighed. "Yes, Spirit. Let's go home. I must tell Ember and give her Jesse's letter."

As they galloped, she noticed a great curve of smoke coming from somewhere close to the wharf. Without a command, Spirit leaped, and then they were actually flying—only inches off the ground, but definitely flying.

Panic rushed inside Twilight. That smoke was too close to her home. At Water Street, she saw the nightmare was true—her house was on fire! Everyone inside could be trapped in the third-floor attic! A crowd was watching it burn. A bucket brigade had assembled, but the people with buckets of water could do little to deter the monstrous flames greedily consuming the inside of her home. Their greatest concern was keeping the fire from spreading to the neighboring homes. Spirit landed, and with a haunting echo, Twilight screamed, "Noooooo!!"

Leaping from Spirit, she ran close to the house, yelling, "Kent! My baby! Where are you, my baby? Ember! Makeda-Angel! Menelik! Dove!

Noah! Samuel! Get out of the house! Can you hear me? Kent! Oh, my baby Kent!" She slammed the side of her body against a blistering door, but the ignited behemoth pushed back with searing intensity from the inside. She ran around the house, looking for a way to open any door or window. But all were bursting from the erupting heat exhaled by the fire-breathing, fire-breeding monstrosity.

She could hear barking from inside the house. She scanned the two attic windows that were ominously small and vacant, like the eyes of a cacodemon dragon. Then, at one window, she saw the frantic faces of Samuel and Dove. Through the second window, Noah, holding Kent, was trying to squeeze through.

"Kent! My baby!" Twilight leaped high into the air.

She could see her frightened boy. He could see her. He called, "Mommy! Mommy!" She reached toward the window. Noah thrust his body through the window, holding her terrified tiny child with one arm and steadying himself with the other. Twilight could leap high, but she couldn't hover. She had nothing to land on except the gabled second-story roof, but it was an inferno. She was floating to the ground—clawing the air and calling to her son—when Spirit appeared. Spirit, too, could jump high but hover only momentarily. Twilight pulled herself onto Spirit's back.

She reached for Kent's tiny hands as Noah held him toward her. Mommy and Baby saw each other's faces. They touched fingertips. But the demonic blaze reached to grab Spirit, scorching her and Twilight. Spirit couldn't sustain the hover. As they started to drop, it looked as if Spirit's mane rose in full flame. Twilight screamed for Kent. Then she witnessed the ultimate horror that would never stop terrorizing her. With a bloodthirsty determination, the sizzling flames thrust upward from the second-story roof to swallow the third-story attic and its windows, hiding Noah and Kent from view. She heard Kent calling her. Then, the second-story roof caved, bringing down the entire house. The second-story veranda crashed onto the front porch. The house disappeared in a collapsing explosion. Spirit landed—thankfully and strangely her mane was barely scorched—and Twilight jumped to the ground. With an animal shriek, Twilight ran as close to the flaring pyre as the reaper heat would allow, then watched and waited, wanting to believe she'd see Noah emerge from the remaining flames, carrying Kent.

Seconds passed, and she saw nothing but flames. No Noah. No Kent. No Noah. No Kent. No Kent. No Kent. "Kent!" Twilight screamed. "Kent! Kent! Keeeeent! Oh nooooo, Kent!" She charged toward the ravages left by tireless blazes.

A man ran after her then pulled her away. "He's gone, fine mother," he said, holding Twilight tightly so she couldn't break free. Tears streaked the man's face. "Your boy's gone. Leave it be. You'll only harm yourself if you go in there." Kicking and scratching, Twilight, a roped panther, fought. But the kind man was stronger. He held her tightly. Blisters welted her face framed by scorched hair.

Finally, with its fury spent, the destructive force retreated. Still no Kent.

The walls had fallen in. Exhausted, the hellfire lay dying. The bucket brigade disbanded.

Waking from her hope that Kent was alive, Twilight slipped from the man's arms to the ground, crying in horrible tones, echoing the chorus of lost souls. Several people from the crowd ran to her, bent down to her, but no one knew what to do with the wailing mother.

Breaking into her grief was the sound of gruff laughter. Pulling up her heavy head, Twilight saw Jerold Grissom about fifteen feet from her. Laughing violently, he stared at her. "How do you feel, Mrs. Canon, seeing your home destroyed?" he snarled, laughing again. "You're the one I was after. I thought you'd be inside. But, no matter. I've done away with your house of evil, where you kept Rich-tones against the law. Such evildoings as yours caused this war—and killed my boy!"

Fury gave Twilight the strength to stand and face Grissom. She shrieked, "Killed *your* boy?"

Everyone backed away.

"It's my son who's dead, you pigeon-livered ratbag! You killed my baby!" she screamed.

She heard Kent's little voice saying, "Bye-bye, Mommy." Spinning around to look behind her, she saw nothing but ruins in dying flames. Her mind continued haunting her with his voice. "Bye-bye, Mommy." Tears came as her chest heaved with sobs and with hate-conceived everything.

"Was that your boy?" Grissom laughed. "I saw him in the window. I thought he was a little enslaved boy hiding out. Your boy. All the better. An eye for an eye. I was after revenge because you killed my boy. He died at Carrick's Ford. Found out today from a letter sent by Sergeant Ambrose Bierce of Frank's regiment, the 9th. A Union regiment." Grissom spat. "My boy died fighting for the wrong side. Isn't that a spillin' guzunder!" He spat again. "My boy wouldn't have been in that war—because there wouldn't *be* a war—if people like you had obeyed the law and let the Confederates have their Riches."

"I didn't kill your son!" Twilight screamed. "*You* killed your son with your ugly, diseased prejudice. The Confederacy will kill all its sons with that same prejudice." Breathing hard and fast, Twilight said, "My brother died *saving your son* at Laurel Hill. That's what I found out today!"

Walking closer to her and shaking his fist, Grissom said, "Well, because of you, Frank died anyway."

Spirit ran toward Grissom. Twilight stretched her arm with her palm facing Spirit and shook her head. Spirit backed away.

A protective rage possessed Twilight. She stood face-to-face with the man who'd killed her child. Her greatest instinct as a mother had been to keep her child safe. She failed, and she hated the murderer from whom she'd been unable to protect Kent. "You set fire to my little boy, my baby, burning him to death!"

Grissom mocked, "'My baby. My baby.' Oh boo hoo." He stepped closer, laughing in her face.

From each pocket, Twilight pulled her Deringers. She cocked both and aimed the right one. She felt herself firing into the heart of the jeering Jerold Grissom.

He stopped harassing. He fell backward.

She could've wounded the hell-damned heckler, but she didn't. She killed him, the murderer of her child.

An eternity passed. Sunlight parted the clouds.

And then she saw Grissom standing before her. He wasn't dead. She didn't take even a moment to puzzle at his appearance. She aimed the second Deringer straight for his heart. Before she pulled the trigger—

"Mommy." Baby Kent. He was standing between Grissom and her. "Mommy." He looked into her eyes. She fell to her knees, dropping her Deringers, reaching for her child, crying in relief and gratitude, and whispering, "Kent. Kent. My angel Kent." He took a step toward her. She reached to embrace her truest love. He stepped into her arms. She hugged him, pulling him forever into her heart. She knew. He was there, but he wasn't. She fainted.

⇝⇝⇝ ⇜⇜⇜

A kaleidoscope of faces, the faces of her loved ones, broke into her mind. She woke. People familiar and unfamiliar were standing or kneeling around her. One person was carefully dabbing a wet cloth on her forehead. Spirit reached her nose to Twilight, touching her face.

Struggling with the weight of life and death, Twilight stood, but only because she had the help of hands about her. Long minutes passed. She crumpled, then crawled toward the fallen house. She had to enter that house; she had to stop the destruction; she had to stop the murder of Kent and the murders of her other loved ones waiting inside for her. She was nearly there.

Again, she fainted.

Chapter 58
Wise Willow Grove and Ember's Moment

Tuesday, August 27, 1861
4:30 to 4:40 p.m.
Evansville

Hidden in Willow Grove, a mother with her two children watched the fire rise and the commotion of people running around the burning home.

She, her boy, and her girl couldn't see what was happening in the front yard. They didn't know if Twilight had returned. Twilight hadn't, and she wouldn't for another five minutes. The mother held onto her boy and her girl, an arm around each; she pulled them close to her as they sobbed.

Just minutes earlier, the entire group within the house had been playing a game, hiding an object then giving clues as to what it could be, each in turn guessing. They all decided they needed things from nature. Ember reached to pull Kent into her arms to take him with her, Menelik, and Makeda-Angel to Willow Grove. To not be seen, the three visitors couldn't leave the house.

Usually, Kent would be eager to join this type of activity. He loved wandering among the sturdy trunks and swaying branches. But this day, strangely, he'd adamantly shook his head no, and, as toddlers are inclined to do, stood his ground as if staying was his mission. Ember knew he'd be safe with Dove and the young men. She, Menelik, and Makeda-Angel would be away for a short time.

The three went into the grove with their protector. With Hegemon following, Ember felt safe from the ever-present possibility of abduction by human traffickers, a fear from memories she always carried. Because Kent was inside, his defender Achilles should have stayed by the house. Instead, Achilles had looked at his brother, then at the back door, then at his brother, then at the back door, then at his brother, whined, stood and ran with his brother.

Deep within the dense grove, they concentrated on finding pebbles, leaves, grass blades, feathers, dandelions, and other wonders of nature. Makeda-Angel giggled, holding up a treasure. "An acorn, Mama."

"Among all these willows? A squirrel must have dropped it from his chubby cheeks." The family laughed. "Let's find him," Ember whispered, looking around. That was when she noticed Achilles and Hegemon intently digging, fixated on their pursuit of something in the ground. "Achilles! What are you doing? Get back to the house, now!"

Achilles pulled his nose from the dirt and faced the house with his ears erect, alert. He barked, then raced from the grove to the house as if on harm's trail. Heggie barked, too. "Something's wrong," Ember said, "Come on, children." When they neared the grove's edge, they saw fire blasting from the inside through the windows of the home. Achilles must have found a way inside, as he was nowhere to be seen.

In shock, she stared, holding onto her babies tightly. Heggie stayed at their sides, whining. Her mind screamed: *Baby Kent! Dove! Samuel! Noah! Oh dear God, no!*

She'd left the house only minutes before, and now her loved ones must be trapped in the attic, suffocating, dying, or, by the looks of the flames reaching out the windows, already dead. Neighbors were surrounding the house, throwing buckets of water on it. As the flames raged, Ember told the children to stay put while she went to join the people lining at the pump, filling and passing buckets.

But then, something stopped her—she feared for her babies' safety and did not want to leave them alone. She remained among the willows, trying to comfort Menelik and Makeda-Angel.

She heard shouts of commands, cries. People were screaming, "They're trapped! Everyone inside is dead! Or will be soon! They'll all die!"

Twilight's sweet baby! She'd promised to keep him safe. She'd failed. How much longer until Twilight arrived at this devastation? Could she already be there, in the front yard? She must try to comfort her. But—after letting her baby die, how could she ever face Twilight? Dove, oh, her little sister Dove! Gone! Noah. Gone! Samuel. Gone! Though she knew this horror wasn't her fault, Ember felt responsible. The facts didn't matter; for the rest of her days, she would suffer at the death of baby Kent, her sister, the two young men, and Achilles, forever wishing they'd been outside the home with her and her babies—safe.

It was strange that a fire had started. Fires happened. But it was daylight, and no cooking fire was burning. It was August, so no fire for heat. No lamps had been lit. But sometimes, mean people burned homes, as the mob had done in February 1859, destroying her friend's home. And then she thought it had to be the Confederacy raiding the free city of Evansville!

This was the war. It was everywhere.

This fire, which Ember might never know, was ignited at nearly the moment she, her children, and the guard dogs left for the woods. Jerold Grissom had poured oil inside through the windows, then tossed oil-soaked, lighted torches inside. It had taken him less than three minutes. If Achilles had stayed, he would have stopped Grissom.

Achilles' one weakness was his brother, whom—only on this one occasion—he followed rather than staying true to his purpose: serving and protecting his humans. Wickedly twisting the will of Fate, in the short time Achilles trotted away to play, Grissom arrived to kill.

Fate and Destiny say, "We never decide if someone acts humanely, or not. We merely provide the setting for a person to make the choice. To be humane, or not."

Grissom had the choice. To be humane. Or not.

⋙ ⋘

Soon, as if its motive was to be tragically violent but brief, the fire started to die. New thoughts sparked Ember's mind; a plan ignited.

Suddenly, she knew what to do.

She had to escape the invading Confederacy. Surely they were arriving on boats. Being right on the river, Willow Land was probably the first place the troops had torched. They might be marching the streets at this moment. If she and her babies didn't get away from Evansville immediately, the Confederates would drag them back into slavery.

Staying in Evansville had always been a huge risk: even though free, she and her children had been smuggled in. It was illegal for them to be there. Her plan was clear—she and her children had died in the fire. That's what everyone would think. No one would look for them. They'd go to Canada. Presumed dead, no matter what outcome of the war, she would never have to worry that they'd end up enslaved. Never again would she let that happen to her babies or to herself. Never. Never. Never.

To be believed dead, they couldn't be seen by anyone. They had to leave when no one would notice, so it had to be immediately, during the commotion. She had to take this chance. She'd thought many times about taking her babies to Canada, escaping with some of the freedom champions who'd sheltered overnight in their home. Just today, she'd considered it again—leaving this very night with her sister, Samuel, and

Noah. But, the thought of Jesse always stopped her. Now, because of the fire, if Jesse did survive the war, he would think she was dead.

What if she left something that Twilight—and only Twilight—would know was a message that she and her babies were alive? Twilight was smart: with a clue, she'd figure out that they had disappeared because they'd run to freedom in Canada when it was clear the devastation was relentless—and that somehow they had slipped from its blazing jaws. She would realize that their escape would have to remain a secret to all but Jesse. But what clue could she leave that only Twilight would understand?

Then she knew what her message could be. In her two large apron pockets, she always carried essential items. One was Twilight's gift, the poetry book by Phillis Wheatley. The book opened in her hand to the poem "A Funeral Poem on the Death of C. E. an Infant of Twelve Months."

Quickly, she tore a small piece off the top of the page with the first six lines of the poem. She took a pencil from her pocket. In the margin of the page, she wrote:

> By the full moon
> I will see you.
> Always.

She whispered, "Stay safe, Twilight. You're a sister." She stuck the paper with Phillis's poem fragment and her own words to Twilight onto a broken branch. This was the best she could do.

Jesse. She almost stopped, thinking of him. She loved him. Desperately. But more desperately she loved freedom, freedom for her babies and for herself. She couldn't have Jesse. And she couldn't have freedom. Not here. Not now. She knew the truth. She wasn't abandoning Twilight or Jesse. She was saving her babies. And herself.

Somehow, after the war—if slavery were abolished—she would find Jesse and Twilight. Her nighttime flights or song flights would aid her in her search. But figuring all that out was too much to think about now. Now, her priority was freedom.

Her boy and girl were sobbing uncontrollably, saying over and over the names of Kent, Achilles, Taboo, Noah, Samuel, and Auntie Dove.

She took a deep breath. The narrow opening of precious time for freedom was closing like a soon-to-be-locked door. *We have to leave now.* She knew of several freedom routes to Canada that their visitors had taken. She could do this. She could affect their futures.

Strong, however, was her feeling that it would be easier to crumple to the ground and cry like her babies, cry until life sprang from her tears soaking the always-regenerating earth. Stronger was her determination and focus, which dammed the mounting tears.

Then, watching the dying fire, she thought of her name. Ember. She could have died in the fire. Was that what her name was supposed to mean? *By an ember I came into the world, and by an ember I will leave.* Had she escaped her fate?

As if her mother was whispering the knowledge in her ear, she understood: *An ember is created by a nearly gone fire still smoldering. Within an ember is the spark that can start a new fire, a new passion.* She heard a clear, distinct Voice inside her: *You are Ember. Ember Free.*

Her stomach tightened. She put the book back into her right pocket, where she always kept their freedom papers and some dollars. Without fail, in case her babies got hungry, she kept bread in her left pocket. She'd forgotten that, just an hour or so before, the left pocket was also where she'd slipped the tiny stones in the organza pouch—Twilight's Power Gems.

Waiting for their mama to take charge, Menelik and Makeda-Angel watched her through their tears. She grasped her son's left hand in her right hand and clasped her daughter's right hand with her left. She said,

"I am Ember. I am Ember Free. I am free to create my fate. True to my name, I burst into flames of a new fire, the fire of freedom."

Overhead, a dove flew.

As the family, with their guardian beside them, set off through the willows to a new destiny, a doe jumped across their path.

With wild conviction, Ember said, "This is our chance. Our chance to be truly free."

Chapter 59
Twilight's Time

*Wednesday, August 28, 1861
to Monday, September 16, 1861
Evansville, Then Along the Ohio and Mississippi Rivers*

The doctor said her burns, cuts, and bruises would heal fairly quickly, but Twilight knew the real wounds were forever.

Marshal Marks entered the side room of the doctor's office, where Twilight was sitting on a cot. "Grissom will stand trial next week," he said. "There are more than enough witnesses since those gathered around heard him confess to you that he'd started the fire and intended to kill by doing so. I've no doubt he'll be found guilty. Maybe he'll receive a sentence."

"I didn't kill him?" Twilight asked, her mind numb as if in a death fog. "I have a memory of shooting him and a memory of not shooting him, wanting to, but Kent was there, as if he were protecting Grissom—and protecting me." She clutched the marshal's sleeve. "Where is my baby?" The marshal didn't reply.

"Grissom killed him, didn't he?" The marshal patted her hand. Her hand dropped from his sleeve. She said, "What did I do to Grissom?"

"You pulled your pistols. You aimed—straight for Grissom's heart. You cocked them, but you didn't fire either one. You don't remember?"

Twilight felt odd. "I remember two different things—I remember shooting Grissom. It was easy killing him, the murderer of my baby. But then, Grissom was there again, alive, and Kent was there, too. Kent didn't want me to kill Grissom." She wiped her tears and flinched at touching her tender skin. The doctor scurried in and lightly blotted her tears then her brow and cheeks with a damp cloth. "Kent's right. I don't want to kill." Putting the cool cloth in Twilight's hands, the doctor scurried back to his office.

Marshal Marks said, "From what witnesses say, it looked certain you were going to kill him, shoot him straight through the heart. You were so crazed no one knew what to do. No one interfered. But, you stopped. After aiming first with one pistol, then with the second, and looking ready to pull the trigger on each one, you stopped, fell to your knees, and dropped the guns."

"It was Kent. He was there. Between Grissom and me. He walked to me. I hugged him to me. I held him to my heart."

Marks shook his head. "Whatever happened saved your life. If you'd shot and killed Grissom, you'd be noosed for killing an unarmed man. The law—not you—decides who receives justice."

The law, meaning a judge and a jury of only men. Well, maybe my life isn't worth saving, but my soul is. Somehow, Kent had been there. His love for his mother saved her soul.

"I don't want to be at the trial," Twilight said. "With all those witnesses, I'm sure you don't need me there." Wiping her hand lightly across her brow and pushing back her hair, she added, "Marshal, I'm leaving. I have nothing here."

⊱✦⊰

"Doesn't add up, does it, men?" Marshal Marks said to Doc and to Enoch, the town-health-official-and-undertaker, the three meeting in Enoch's office. "Doesn't seem to, anyway. We have pieces of the puzzle, so to speak, and I don't mean that with any disrespect. Facts left by such great destruction are unclear at best. Fragments of the skulls add up somewhat, but not size-wise, as Doc here says."

"Freedom runners?" asked Enoch.

"She is suspected," Marks said. "Grissom claims that's the reason he set fire to her place, after he found out his son had died at Corrick's Ford. Some said they saw an older boy crawling through the attic window with her little boy, trying to get on the second-story roof. But the Rich-tone attendant living there, Ember, had a son. Probably was him. Others said they heard Mrs. Canon calling several names. But then, it was complete confusion for everyone. And I think Mrs. Canon's mind was off its spindle." He looked out the window, checking to see that all was normal on the streets, then added, "A few said they saw her jump up to the window and that her horse jumped, too. But I give that no credence."

Doc said, "Stories and mystery follow that young woman. Have you seen how it looks like she flies on her horse? Just slightly above the ground. So maybe they are making a very long leap. Or are running very fast. It is hard to know for sure."

Marshal Marks said, "We've all seen that. Yes, she's a mystery. But she's not magical. No one is."

"No one that we can attest to," Enoch said. "Anyway, there was no need to spend too much time and effort in that mess trying to put together parts. Volunteers, Doc, and I did what we could. We don't have the manpower to figure this out. I say, Marks, let's go with her story. Also, we can't discern accurately her two dogs, so let's bury all remains together in a family grave. I'm not troubled about figuring out who's who. Because her boy was so small, so different than the others, we could identify what's left of him, we think." Enoch shifted his weight from one foot to the other, then added, "What's troubling me is preparing what little is left of him so that he can be an apt traveling companion; you understand my meaning." He dabbed at his eyes with his handkerchief, then said, "I do have a small airtight metallic case from a company claiming that stored bodies in such a case have lasted months to years. And I'm having a well-sealed box made to put the case in. This war will make embalming a practice soon, like the embalming Thomas Holmes did with President Lincoln's friend, Colonel Elmer E. Ellsworth. But the rest of us don't have that ability yet. So I think the case I have is the best bet for the young mother."

"She's still insisting she take with her what remains of her boy's body?" Marshal Marks asked.

The other two men nodded somberly. Doc said, "She didn't want to know what's left of her son. She said that she wanted him with her. That she would not bury her baby so far away from his mother. That she'd find somewhere to settle, and his remains would be there with her. She is adamant about not leaving him behind."

"You can't blame her," Enoch said.

"Still, not entirely rational," Doc said. "But then, who in this country is?"

⇝⇝⇝ ⇜⇜⇜

The doctor insisted Twilight stay in his care for two full days. During that time, she barely left the cot. After exactly forty-eight hours—on the evening of August 29—she went to her office to make arrangements with her loyal friend and employee Will, who was caring for Spirit. Twilight and Will agreed that when she left town, Will would run the businesses, which she would still own. To him, she deeded what was left of Willow Land, mostly land with willows, some chickens, and Donner. Through the diligence of the bucket brigade, the stables and shed had not caught fire.

Then, she and Spirit returned to the charred debris and dirt, the ruins of a once-lovely life. Taboo, eyes wide, crouched high in an oak not far from the pump. "Taboo! You're alive and here. Oh, thanks to Eternal God and the full Goddess Moon," she whispered. Without any other thought but her love for Taboo, Twilight glided up, landed, balanced on the branch, and lifted him to her, cradling him, then glided back to the earth. "You poor boy. Have you been in this tree for two days?"

Cuddling her frightened friend, she swayed her body in a steady slow rhythm, as she'd often done to soothe her baby Kent. She wanted to whisper words of comfort to little Taboo, but she couldn't. She walked to the edge of Willow Grove, stopping before entering the Wise One community. She found her voice and said, "Wise Ones? No. It's not true. You willows are good for easing a headache, but you're not good for anything really serious. You can't do anything about freedom. You can't protect us. You can't save a life. All I have to say to you is goodbye."

The teachers next door brought her hugs, blankets, and cream for Taboo. Because, miraculously, Spirit had not sustained any burns and only very light scorching from the fire, Twilight was able to hitch her to an express wagon. She loaded the wagon with Spirit food, Taboo food, the blankets, and other essentials. Stara, a woman from Ember's church, came with a loaf of bread and a pan of cornbread. "We miss Ember and her babies," she said. Patting Twilight's hand, Stara added, "It's time." It didn't matter to Twilight what Stara might mean. Twilight took the food gifts and hugged her.

Then, Miss Summer appeared. Though surprised to see her, Twilight's mind was in shock, so nothing made sense. Miss Summer hugged her, then said, "I'd hoped to get to know you better, but you're doing the right thing to leave. It's time." Drowning in her deepest grief, Twilight was trying to merely breathe, so everything seemed painful, distorted, and odd. But Miss Summer said something that sounded really weird: "Your destiny should never have included such tragedy. Destiny should have cooled Fate. I *am* sorry. You have one more trial, and then you will know."

"No," Twilight said, "no trials. I'm not going to Grissom's trial. They don't need me to prove his guilt. Everyone there heard his confession. But even after being found guilty of murder, the man will get nothing but a slap on the hand anyway. The law doesn't care about the victims of Grissom's crime—children, women, mostly Rich-tone. The law cares only that Grissom is a Pale man."

Miss Summer said, "Grissom will pay his dues. Someday. Somewhere. Somehow. My dear, you have other concerns."

Then Twilight, Taboo, and Spirit pulled away from Willow Land. In town, she collected the box holding Kent's coffin—with what was left of her baby securely sealed inside. She stopped just northeast of town at the large family plot in the cemetery, a final resting place without skin-tone division. She knelt at the simple collective grave that, just hours before, had been dug and covered, holding, to her understanding, what remained of Ember, Makeda-Angel, Menelik, Dove, Noah, Samuel, Achilles, and Hegemon. However, she was aware that town officials, not knowing of the three freedom champions who'd arrived, believed the grave held Ember, her boy and girl, and the two dogs.

Twilight touched the black walnut root guarding her throat, which she always wore. She thought of adorable Makeda-Angel. She remembered her crying for her mama on that cursed block. She thought of clever, strong Menelik, who had faith that his mother would find him someday. She thought of dear Dove, who, miraculously had reunited with her sister, only to share Ember's fate of dying by the ember. Valiant Noah had overcome horrors at Magnolia Bay and nobly tried to save her baby's life. Kind Samuel, as did the others, had dreams of freedom. He, Noah, and Dove had just made it to free soil.

"You're all free now," she whispered, touching the site that also held the sweet and loyal canine twins.

She thought of Ember and Jesse, both now gone from her but together somehow, somewhere. "My dear friend," she said, "the time for you and Jesse has come. You can love each other without fear now. You'll find no prejudice in God's land."

She also spoke love to the resting places of GrandMama and of Grandfather, their gravestones side by side—Felicia Wilde Wild and Johannes Neumann Wild.

Then she left.

Behind the ruins of her home, the tree at the edge of Wise Willow Grove let free the piece of paper, allowing poetry to float with the wind.

Twilight, Spirit, and Taboo trekked west. Sleeping under the stars most nights, they stayed some nights at farmhouses that took in travelers. After two weeks, they had journeyed through southwestern Indiana, then into and through Illinois, reaching the Mississippi River.

The Mississippi River—whole unto itself, yet part of the North and of the South. After looking downriver, Twilight headed upriver. North. The road followed close by the river.

This was the Graveyard section of the Mississippi. Here and there, drowned ships poked their bows like dead faces through the water. By early evening, she saw a clearing at the river's edge and drove there to camp for the night. Pulling the wagon to a stop, she got out and sat on the bank. It was then she realized how fatigued she felt. And how lonely. So lonely. To journey further seemed hopeless. Life seemed hopeless.

She reached into her pocket and touched GrandMama's letter, complete with all pages now, thanks to Jed. GrandMama's gift, Wondrous Ring, felt so heavy, as if it were a weight tied to her hand. GrandMama's gems were buried with Ember. The black obsidian hadn't protected her child, Ember, Ember's children, her other friends, or her guardian pups. They were all bones and ash now.

The entire idea of the Sisterhood of Gifts was a sham, and so were GrandMama's too-precious words. GrandMama wasn't whacky, but the ideas she shared with Twilight were. GrandMama had been duped by her mother, who'd been duped by her mother, and so on. Twilight didn't feel part of a caring Sisterhood. Everything she'd done since opening

GrandMama's letter had resulted in one thing and one thing only—her baby was dead.

"Sixteen is not power, GrandMama," she said. "I had no power at sixteen. I have no power now. I've always been powerless. There is no power for women to claim. I did very little to help the enslaved. I couldn't even keep my baby safe." For Kent, again she sobbed as if her body would split apart.

The glinting of the setting sun on the river caught her attention. She watched the water moving, moving, moving somewhere, so peacefully. Hypnotic serenity. Hypnotic, hypnotic, hypnotic. Serenity.

She wanted to feel as peaceful, no, to *be* as peaceful as that water flowing, flowing, flowing somewhere. She'd go with the water, flowing. It would lull her along, gently carrying her body somewhere. Somewhere where Kent was, the only place she belonged.

She stood, went to Spirit and unhitched her, removing her rig. Hugging her strong neck and kissing her nose, she said, "You've been with me through it all, Spirit. I love you. I will always love you. No matter where I am. Go on now. Find a meadow filled with grass." Spirit didn't budge. Taboo blinked deeply at Twilight and lifted his chin to her. Twilight kissed her beloved buddy who'd escaped Magnolia Bay with her and had been her shadow ever since. "I love you, Taboo. Forever and always."

Twilight pulled the tiny box off the wagon and pushed it partially into the river, knowing that the current would take it with time. To the box, she said, "My little angel boy, I love you in a way I never knew was possible. You are my life. Without you, baby, I have no life." Vivid memories of his smile, of him running about, calling her, kissing her, laughing with her, and of the sweet, warm way his flesh smelled as he pressed his face to hers appeased her for a breath. Then she said, "Yes, I will see you again. This very day." The thought cheered her. "I can't wait to see you," she said. "I'll be there, my angel, in just a few moments."

She took GrandMama's letter from her pocket, kissed it, and placed it inside her bodice, near her heart. She whispered, "Finally, GrandMama,

I will destroy this letter so no one finds it. Not by burning it—though, I should have burned with this letter and with Kent."

Slowly she waded into the river. The water welcomed her feet, her ankles. She heard it whisper, *Come to me. Come to me.*

The water caressed her calves, her knees, her thighs, her hips, her waist. *Come to me. Come to me.* The empathetic water bobbed, edging upward to take her.

Come to me. Come to me. Come to me. Come to me.
Come to me. Come to me. Come to me. Come to me.
Come to me. Come to me. Come to me. Come to me.

Faithful Spirit wanted to intervene, to go into the water to pull Twilight out. But, she sensed this was Twilight's time. So she stood at the river's edge in trust that her human would do the right thing.

A bald eagle swooped onto the water, splashing a bit onto Twilight's neck encircled with Ember's amulet gift, Precious Friend.

Come to me. Come to me. Come to me. Come to me.

Breaking the serenity of the water's caresses, another voice echoed in whispers. She tried to ignore it, but though soft, it was relentless. *Life is precious.* It was the Voice.

She only wanted to think of the river and how it would take her gently, peacefully to be with Kent that very hour. She envisioned him waiting for her with his arms open, walking to her, as he had done when saving her from being a killer. All she wanted was to see her little boy again. All she wanted was to feel his presence near her. There was nothing else.

Fracturing her reverie of seeing Kent very soon, she heard, *Never give up.* GrandMama's voice. Memories of her, the woman who never gave up, crowded in on Twilight's weary mind.

"Nothing is more important than being with Kent," she replied with agitation. Then she heard her father's voice saying, *Buck up, and take care of you.* Then Gallatin's voice saying, *Never lose your fight, Twilight.* Then another voice, her own, saying, *Some things are worth fighting for.*

"Leave me alone!" Twilight screamed. "Go away! I don't want to think of GrandMama. I don't want to think of my father or Gallatin or my idealistic philosophies. I want to see Kent again. I ache too horribly for him. I can't stand it any longer. I must see him! And I am tired of the fight! I want it over!"

But pain's hypnotic spell was broken, allowing Twilight to see what she was doing. Though she wanted the hurting to stop, the fighting to stop, though she desired peace, and as desperately as she wanted to see Kent, she didn't want to kill.

Nearly chest-deep in the river, Twilight lifted her head. Searching the red-streaked sky, she raised her arms and screamed, "Hey, you! What do you want, anyway? What do *you* want? Do you want me to live in misery? Pain! Misery! Death! You love it all, don't you? Almost all of the millions of enslaved people lose their children! Ember was an exception in keeping Makeda-Angel and finding Menelik! But for years, she thought she'd lost her son! The enslaved lose their children because of greed and cruelty! How do they bear it? You could stop our suffering! But you never do! You could stop slavery! But you just sit on your throne of clouds and watch us all flounder about down here, crying, hurting and suffering! Well, the pain of losing Kent is too much for me to bear! What is it you want from me? Tell me!"

Dropping her arms, she continued to search the darkening sky. "Oh, I know. I understand now. If I died, you'd lose the sport of watching me, Twilight Wild Adams, fight. And suffer. And fight and suffer. Haven't you gotten enough lately? Kent suffered and died. So did Ember and Makeda-Angel and Menelik and Dove and Noah and Samuel. And thousands of the enslaved. And hundreds of our boys—Jesse, Frank Grissom, and maybe even Jed. More will die. You know this! You see all, and yet, what are you doing about it?"

Breathing rapidly, Twilight raised her voice again. "It's blood you want! You like blood, don't you—blood from sacrificial lambs. Is that all my little lamb Kent was to you? You even watched your own son, who only wanted love and honor for you, bleed from nails driven in his hands and feet. By the full moon, it's blood you want! Fine! Watch this!"

She stomped out of the river up to the wagon, shuffled through a bag, and found a knife.

She marched to the river's edge, then made a small cut on her left palm. Though a slight slice, it was painful, sending her screaming in agony. She pressed her lips to her wound, kissing it.

Dear God. How could I have deliberately hurt myself? By the full moon. Kent would never want his mommy to hurt herself.

Kent. Oh, Kent, my love.

She thrust her bleeding palm into the gloaming. She yelled, "Here! Blood! Is that what you wanted from me? Are you happy now? Well, then, maybe one of us is happy. Because I'm not. I feel worse than miserable. And now my hand hurts like the fires of Hell. But that's nothing in comparison to how horribly I hurt from losing my son!"

As blood ran off her palm, down her arm, dripping onto her face, and dropping onto the river bank, she searched the deep red, cerulean, and violet darkening sky, but she heard no booming voice. She heard no small voice. She heard no whispers. She heard nothing. Nothing.

The first star of the night winked.

Thrusting her bleeding palm higher, she said, "I know what you want. You want people like me to live on and on, continuing to suffer, as you watch to see if our spirits will break."

Looking into the heavens, clenching her wounded, bleeding fist above her, enunciating each syllable, she said, "Fine, Mister High and Almighty. Try to break me. Go ahead. Try. But I will tell *you* something."

She drew a breath.

"I won't even bend."

Chapter 60
Finally

Monday, September 16, 1861
Twilight, Evening, Night
Mississippi River and Bank

Halfway through the Graveyard with its hidden dangers, Gallatin's twelve-hour shift at the wheel of the Union gunboat had just ended.

Peering out over the river near the steamer's edge, Gallatin thought he heard screams echoing on the water. He went back to the wheel house. To the co-pilot who'd taken his place at the wheel, Gallatin said, "Did you hear screams?"

The co-pilot nodded his head. "Could be the screaming of a lost soul from one of these dead ships. Navigating the Graveyard is always weird."

Something on the edge of the east bank caught Gallatin's eye. It was a woman, maybe still a youth, slumped near the shore.

The co-pilot saw her, too. "Hey, look sharp, Gallatin. Not a lost soul. Unless she's dead. She's wearing black; must be in mourning. Wish we could stop to check on her, but gunboats can't be stopping for every person we see along the river. Especially not in this stretch of shrouded hazards. Though, she has a fine horse. Could be used in the cavalry."

Too familiar to Gallatin was her long black hair that fell about her body and over the box she was slumped over. And the horse nuzzling her certainly resembled Spirit. She moved. So she was alive. It couldn't be Twilight and Spirit—too much of a coincidence, Gallatin thought. But something buried under reason started to take over.

Slapping his co-pilot on the back, he said, "A Union gunboat would be the disgrace of the war if we stopped to check on a female." The co-pilot laughed. Gallatin added, "I saw her move. She's probably just sleeping. And I don't think the Union is in dire enough straights to warrant taking her horse for the cavalry."

They were passing her then, and Gallatin took a good look back at what he could see of her face resting on that box. The gorgeous golden horse continued to nuzzle the woman. Spirit would do that. And did he catch a glimpse of a cat? Taboo? It could be Twilight. Gallatin shook his head, deciding he must need rest and that the sore way he missed her made this woman appear to him as Twilight.

And then, the golden horse raised her head in Gallatin's direction and, as horses do, neighed a loud call to a friend.

"Fantastic horse," said the co-pilot.

"See you in twelve," Gallatin said, hurrying down the steps and walking swiftly to the back of the ship. He couldn't imagine why Twilight would be on the Illinois riverbank. But if there was the slightest chance it could be her, he would not risk losing her again. Diving into the river from near the stern of the riverboat was life-threatening. Even though the steamer was a side-wheeler, getting pulled back into the paddles was possible. Or he could get caught in the undertow. Either way, he'd die. But he had to risk it. And he had to dive off near the rear, for anywhere else he'd definitely be pulled into the side-wheel paddles—and he'd be seen diving. If he didn't hurry, he'd be seen anyway, for he could hear the infernal whistle of the guard who always watched him, the guard now looking for him, coming his way.

Quickly he pulled off his boots, pushed them inside his trouser belted waistband, took off his jacket and threw it down. He dove into the river, swimming vigorously away from the boat. Then he felt it, the undertow. It was strong, very strong. It grabbed his legs, and he was almost out of breath. He sliced and pulled through the water with his arms, but the river grabbed him and pulled back with a mightier force.

The Mississippi River did not want to let Gallatin go.

Caught in its grasping whirlpool, Gallatin swirled around and down: he saw his mother, he saw the *North Star*, he saw the *Star of Twilight*. Then, all images coalesced into one—that of Twilight. Her face was before him. With powerful arms, he reached for her. She smiled, then burst like a shattered mirror, taking with her Gallatin, who burst through the water and into the air, gasping and flinging his arms. He gulped air. Then, he swam to the shore.

Shaky but alive, he stood on the riverbank and breathed deeply. Then he did something he'd never done before—he knelt on one knee and bent his head, resting it on the other knee. "Thank you," he said. "And, please, let it be her." His boots were still pressed between his body and trouser waistband. He tugged the soaked leather boots back onto his feet, then sprinted toward her, feeling more alive than he'd ever felt.

When he got close, he stopped sprinting and walked up to her. She was seated on the ground with her body bent over the wooden box. Her horse nickered. "Spirit, it *is* you," Gallatin said, hugging the horse's neck. "You called to me, didn't you, Spirit?"

Taboo sat atop Twilight's back. "Taboo," Gallatin said. Taboo lifted his chin to Gallatin. Kneeling next to his love, he said in a whispered awe, "Twilight."

⋙ ⋘

Twilight was dreaming. In the dream, someone kept saying her name. Then, slowly, her mind registered that it was a person speaking to her, not a dream. She started.

Gallatin touched her face. "Twilight," he said.

"Gallatin?" she said, bewildered and certain it couldn't be him kneeling there on the desolate bank of the Mississippi River.

"I'm here, honey. I was piloting that gunboat that just passed. I saw you here. Then Spirit called to me. Thank God I saw you. I jumped off, and it's a miracle I'm alive, for a strong undertow had me. But I'm here, honey, with you, like I should have been years ago."

He sat beside her, put his arms around her, and pulled her onto his lap. "The river is a waterway. But you, Twilight, are a person, and the person I love more than anyone or anything in the world. I'll never leave you again. From now on, I am here for you, no matter what happens. Finally, it is all so clear to me. I don't care what you know or don't know about your destiny. I don't care about any promise except the promises I make to you. I am here with you. Forever. That, I promise."

Twilight said nothing.

"Darling, what has happened? You're wearing mourning clothes. And you're traveling alone in this desolate area. What is it?"

"Oh, Gallatin, there was a fire. A Confederate supporter set fire to our home. I'd been hiding freedom champions who had escaped the South. My home burned, killing Ember, her children, and everyone inside."

"Twilight, my God." He shook his head as tears welled in his eyes. "My God."

Looking down at the box lying at their feet, she said, "The remains of the most precious boy you could ever imagine lie in a casket in this box. Kent. Killed in the fire. And I almost shot the man who killed my son. I almost shot him, right through the heart, with the Deringers you gave me, Gallatin. But then Kent, my child, was in front of me, between his murderer and me, holding his arms to me, saying 'Mommy.' He stopped me. Our son saved me."

"Our son?"

"Yes, our son, Gallatin. *Our* son," Twilight said, smiling wryly. "You are Kent's father. I wanted to tell you, but I never heard from you."

"My son?" Gallatin said, staring at Twilight, then down at the box. He gently moved Twilight off his lap. He stood, walked to the box, then dropped on his knees next to it and placed his hands on the top, then on the sides, then on the top. He looked at Twilight. "My son?" She nodded.

He looked again at the box and said, "Oh, Son. Oh, Son. My boy." He folded his arms around the box, hugging it, rested his chest and face on the top, and wept.

Three deer walked from the trees to the river. After drinking, they sauntered in a wide circle around the couple, then flitted back into the woods. Two hummingbirds appeared, hovered near, then flew away.

They drove the wagon a few yards to a concealed spot in case the gunboat was looking for Gallatin. Hopefully, he'd be forgotten and listed as drowned in the Graveyard.

As the sun settled, the moon appeared: it was her turn. She added light to the night. Gallatin gathered driftwood and built a small fire. The fire crackled. With Twilight safe, Spirit and Taboo rested.

Tenderly, Gallatin held Twilight. He said, "You've been through so much. Too much. Tonight, I want you to rest in my arms." Gently, he took her left hand, bandaged in black, and cradled it in his. "Tomorrow, we'll head north to Canada, or would you like to go West? California? Or Santa Fe?"

"I don't care, Gallatin. You decide," Twilight said wearily as he stroked her hair.

"I'll never leave you again," he said.

Twilight was silent.

"Believe it. We'll be married in the first town we come to. We'll settle somewhere, get some land. We'll bury our son on our land." Holding her hands within his, he kissed Twilight's forehead.

Her eyes were closed. He kissed each eyelid lightly.

Finally, her body was next to his. He whispered, "Now that we are together, what more could life give?"

"Yes," Twilight said, the secret letter pressing against her heart.

"What more?"

Dear Wild Conviction Champion ~

Thank you for being a Champion by joining Twilight on her quest.

While you've been reading, Twilight has learned much more about her mystical abilities and enhancing her powers. If you'd like to know what this means or would like to contact me, please check out my website: marydezember.com.

I'd love to hear from you!

On my website, you can find:

- My contact page;
- Where to sign up for my newsletter with bonus materials;
- A reader's guide and other supplementary material about the story;
- News and information about *Wild Conviction*, my other publications, and my events.

Let's continue questing! *Mary*

Acknowledgments with Notes About Story and Research

Thanks to the Wild Conviction Village Members ~
It takes a village to raise a novel such as this one. Deepest thanks and love to Elaine Ritchel, Sean Ritchel, Tom Ritchel, T. A. Niles, Dr. Galaxy Dancer, Teresa E. Gallion, Cyndi Sanchez Bleicher, Shiela McDermott-Sipe, Dr. Deborah Turner, Dr. Scott Zeman for attentively reading—and for your valuable insights, caring support, lively encouragement, thoughtful discussions, and lovingkindness. Thanks and love to those who read selections at various stages of writing and revision, providing supportive and helpful comments: Maria Ritchel Wahl, Tony Ritchel, Carol Gentry Nurrenbern, Dr. James Capshew, Jules Nyquist, Kate Padilla, Dr. Sylvia Ramos Cruz. Thanks to so many others who've cheered me on.

In Loving Memory ~
Love to those who believed in me and this novel over the many years I've worked on it but are not here for its publication—Elaine Schaffer Dezember, Garnett Dezember, Charlotte Sauter Dezember, Tobias Pino, Mary Dudley, Richard King Johnson, Pastor Roberta Meyer, Dr. Scott Zeman. You are always with me, never gone from my heart. My love to my beloved buddy Sammy Dezember—my own darling little Taboo—for knowing how to make me laugh and for being by my side during my writing and crafting of several drafts. And for lifting your chin to me in love and acknowledgment and saying, "Mhrrr." Sam, you are always with me, never gone from my heart.

***Author's Notes* ~**

Wild Conviction has been challenging to write and is the result of many years of work. To create of sense of authenticity for the historical setting, I have done extensive historical research, consulting numerous sources over several years. Some information from before 1861 can be difficult to verify, with source material sometimes differing. In addition, historians continually uncover new information, and ideologies of the period are subjects of ever-evolving scholarly work.

This is a socially conscious novel, a fictional coming-of-age adventure in which the protagonist confronts social issues and contends with white privilege, male privilege, economic privilege, and the marginalization of women and children.

Historical and contemporary derogatory words are avoided. However, difficult situations do occur. Comments, conversations, and actions by certain characters that show prejudice, abuse, racism, and misogyny are part of those characters' personalities and are not my beliefs.

Beta readers and sensitivity readers reviewed my writing for possible—while unintentional—instances of being unaware, insensitive, or culturally appropriative.

For this novel, I created a scenario within a historical setting in which the terms Rich-tone and Pale are used for skin tone. My intent is to create and tell a story using skin tone terms that might provide insight differing from the historical and contemporary words and connotations and to tell a story without historical and contemporary derogatory terms. Language, even individual words, can be effective in creating awareness.

***Author's Note On Historical Figures and Research* ~**

Wild Conviction is a work of fiction. Characters, names, titles, places, organizations, and events are fictitious or are used fictitiously. References to historical figures, persons, names, titles, places, organizations, or events are used fictitiously and are intended only to provide a sense of authenticity. All other characters, names, titles, places, organizations, and events are products of my imagination, and any resemblance to actual persons, living or dead, names, titles, places, organizations, or events is entirely coincidental and is not to be construed as real.

The following minor or mentioned characters were real people, and these historical figures were in the locations specified by the novel. Of course, their participation in the imaginary lives of the major characters, who are fictional, is fictionalized: Samuel Clemens (who took the pen name Mark Twain years after his time in Memphis in 1858, reportedly in 1863) and his brother, Henry Clemens, both of Hannibal, Missouri; Nathan Bedford Forrest of Memphis, Tennessee (who, in 1867, would become the first Grand Wizard of the Ku Klux Klan); Emily Dickinson (referred to as Emily) of Amherst, Massachusetts; Jacob Messick and his son Johnny Messick of Evansville, Indiana; Ambrose Bierce of Warsaw, Indiana and Elkhart, Indiana.

There are many other historical figures and persons who are mentioned but do not appear in the story, such as Phillis Wheatley, Lucretia Mott, Frederick Douglass, Harriet Tubman (who is referred to, as she was historically, as Moses), Queen Makeda (Queen of Sheba), Empress Mentewab, Walt Whitman, (William) Shakespeare, Francis (Fanny) Wright, Sojourner Truth, Solomon Northrop, "The Fugitive Slave" (who was Harriet A. Jacobs, pseudonym Linda Brent), Charles Dickens, Stephen Foster, Sir Walter Scott, George Washington and his wife and relative, Thomas Jefferson, Henry Deringer, Marcus Winchester, Marie Winchester, Andrew Jackson, Rachel Jackson, Thomas Affleck, James Henry Hammond, David Christy, the daughters of the (Eugene) Magevney family, Horace Bixby, William Brown, (John) Klinefelter, John Able, John Everson, Abraham Lincoln, Willard Carpenter, Lew Wallace, Thomas Holmes, Elmer E. Ellsworth, Nat Turner, John Brown, (Oliver P.) Morton, (Robert H.) Milroy, Jefferson Davis, Thomas J. "Stonewall" Jackson, (Pierre Gustave Toutant) Beauregard, (Nathaniel) Lyon, Jesus, Moses and his wife and father-in-law, Adam, Eve, Cain, Abel, the unnamed author of *Wuthering Heights* (who was Emily Brontë, pseudonym Ellis Bell), the anonymous author ("A Lady") of *Every Lady Her Own Shoemaker*, the unnamed owners of the home burned on

Leet Street and the unnamed men who burned it, the unnamed Quakers who bought Woodlawn. The unnamed fishermen and the unnamed African American man from Kentucky who signaled them probably were actual people. Other unnamed possible contributors to the Underground Railroad.

Research Sources ~

While I consulted numerous research sources, I wish to acknowledge the source from which I use quotations and a few additional sources that provided valuable information and a sense of the historical time period, as follows:

Source With Quotations Used With Permission

Quotes from Lucretia Mott—originally from a speech delivered at the Fourteenth Annual Meeting of the American Anti-Slavery Society in New York, May 9, 1848, also printed in the *National Anti-Slavery Standard*, May 18, 1848, and from *The Liberator*, pg. 168, October 15, 1841, Vol. XI No. 42—are from *Lucretia Mott: Complete Speeches and Sermons*, edited by Dana Greene, Edwin Mellen Press, New York, 1980 (on pages 31, 32, 78), and are used with permission from The Edwin Mellen Press. Thanks to The Edwin Mellen Press and to Professor Herbert Richardson, Editor-in-Chief, The Edwin Mellen Press.

A Few Sources From Which No Quotations Are Used But Provided A Sense Of The Historical Time Period

Thanks to Willard Public Library, Evansville, Indiana. Special thanks to Lyn Martin, Special Collections Librarian at Willard Public Library, for help in locating *Evansville Journal* newspaper articles of 1860. Special thanks also to Vanderburgh County Historian Stan Schmitt, Special Collections Assistant at Willard Public Library, for information on burials in Oak Hill Cemetery around the time of 1861, and specifically, that there were no specified segregated burial areas. Additional thanks to Stan Schmitt for verifying that one of the first African American congregations in Evansville, Indiana—African Methodist Episcopal

Church—met on Leet Street, possibly in a house church, during the time of the Evansville, Indiana setting of the novel.

Special thanks to Gary Johnson, Reference Librarian, Newspaper & Current Periodical Room, Library of Congress, for locating the article about Sam and Henry Clemens in the *Memphis Daily Eagle and Enquirer*, June 16, 1858, page 3, column 1.

Special thanks to Glenda Chavez for help in finding period information about caskets, preservation of the dead, burials, and in particular, this helpful source: *The History of American Funeral Directing* by Robert W. Habenstein, William M. Lamers, 4th Revised Edition Revised & Edited by Howard C. Raether, 5th Revised Edition Revised & Edited by Kathleen A. Walczak, National Funeral Directors Association, 1955, 1962, 1981, 1995, 1996, 2001.

Enslaved Women and the Art of Resistance in Antebellum America by Renee K. Harrison, Palgrave Macmillan, a division of St. Martin's Press LLC, New York, 2009, provided valuable historical instances of subtle methods and covert acts of resistance by enslaved women on plantations—crucial ways of maintaining identity and agency.

On Jordan's Banks: Emancipation and Its Aftermath in the Ohio River Valley by Darrel E. Bigham, The University Press of Kentucky, Lexington, Kentucky, 2006, provided valuable information, including: the first African American churches in Evansville; the burning of the house on Leet Street; the African American man in Kentucky who aided the enslaved in crossing to Indiana; people helping covert travelers into and through Evansville as they moved along Underground Railroad shelters for freedom.

The Book of Negro Folklore, edited by Langston Hughes and Arna Bontemps, Dodd, Mead, and Company, New York, 1958, is a source for information about the heritage of Dove and Ember that includes hoodoo beliefs (in particular pages 183-185: "Origin of the Voodoo Cult" and "Hoodoo"). [Note: The family custom of naming a baby told by Dove is my creation.] *The Book of Negro Folklore* is also the source for the story Twilight tells Jackson about Cain and Abel—"Origin of

Races," page 155. This book is one of numerous sources about the diaspora stories of the flying Africans.

I have read varying references about how people were bought and sold in antebellum Memphis. There were markets with yards, similar and in addition to the one run by Nathan Bedford Forrest. They were called slave markets, slave marts, negro markets, negro marts, Negro markets, and Negro marts. Additionally, auctions of people might have happened on a block or not on a block, either at Market Square or at Auction Square, or at both, or possibly at neither. It seems unlikely that antebellum Memphis, known then as the largest inland slave market, would never have had public auctions of people. In this novel, there are two scenes in which auctions of people are conducted in a town square on an auction block. I decided to include the auctions with a block in a town square—the unspecified "Atrocity Square"—based on the first-hand account by Allan Pinkerton about his 1861 visit to Memphis, in which he describes a public auction in a square that used a block. Source: *The Spy in the Rebellion; being a true history of the spy system of the United States Army during the late rebellion, revealing many secrets of the war hitherto not made public, compiled from official reports prepared for President Lincoln, General McClellan and the Provost-Marshal-General*, by Allan Pinkerton, Chapter 12, pg. 191-192, published 1883.

Memphis in Black and White by Beverly G. Bond and Janann Sherman, The Making of America Series, Arcadia Publishing, Charleston SC, Chicago IL, Portsmouth NH, San Francisco CA, 2003.

A Brief History of Memphis by G. Wayne Dowdy, The History Press, Charleston, SC, 2011.

Blacks in Tennessee 1791 – 1970 by Lester C. Lamon, published in cooperation with The Tennessee Historical Commission, The University of Tennessee Press, Knoxville, 1981.

The concepts from Senator James Henry Hammond are taken from his speech before the United States Senate, March 4, 1858, "On the Admission of Kansas, Under the Lecompton Constitution," also referred to as the "Cotton is King" speech, which includes his "mud-sill" theory.

Source: *Speech of Hon. James H. Hammond, of South Carolina, on the admission of Kansas, Under The Lecompton Constitution. Delivered in the Senate of the United States, March 4, 1858*, Washington: Printed by Lemuel Towers. 1858. Found on and with thanks to the Internet Archive, Oberlin College Library Anti-Slavery Collection, Oberlin College and Conservatory, Oberlin College Library.

In Chapter 6, Tarnished Mirror, the character Harley says: "Sam told me, 'To correct Brown's behavior and his speech, I pummeled him and his parlance.'" This is fictional dialogue I created to summarize in one sentence and with my words what Sam Clemens/Mark Twain describes in a longer passage about his confrontation with William Brown in Chapter 19 of *Life on the Mississippi* by Mark Twain, Boston: James R. Osgood and Company, 1883.

Additional Notes ~
The name Precious Friend for Ember's amulet necklace gift to Twilight was inspired by a sculpture my friend Mariam Ehteshami made for me, which she entitled "Precious Friend."

It is interesting to read about the Lincoln Wide Awake Clubs and to research the American political parties, platforms, names, and how they have changed. In the years just before the Civil War, the platform of the newly formed Republican Party leaned liberal, and the established Democratic Party was considered conservative. Today, the Republican Party is considered to have a conservative platform, and the Democratic Party is considered to have a liberal platform.

The names Carrick's Ford and Corrick's Ford are both found for the same battle in historical documents. Ambrose Bierce uses Carrick's Ford in his story "On a Mountain" and in his book *Iconoclastic Memories of the Civil War: Bits of Autobiography*. Thus, that is the spelling I use for the fictional letters of Bierce in the novel.

Adams Avenue in Memphis is also referred to in historical documents as Adams Street. I have chosen to use Adams Avenue in the novel.

As noted earlier, the family custom of naming a baby told by Dove is my creation.

The lyrics to songs sung in this novel are my creation, most of which I created in the spirit of African American Spirituals of the antebellum period sung by the enslaved.

Poems that are written by the characters Twilight and Ember are my creation. The epigraph poem is my creation.

The tilde or swing dash sign (~) found in the letter by the fictional character GrandMama and other places in this novel has a space before and after it and is not used in any conventional or defined sense. For example, it does not mean "approximately." It is GrandMama's artistic way of writing a sign to replace a dash or a colon—basically, her way of showing a pause in writing. Sparingly, I have used "GrandMama's swing dash style" similarly in other places of this novel.

About the Author ~ Meet Mary Dezember

Mary Dezember, Ph.D., earned her doctorate in Comparative Literature with an emphasis in Comparative Arts from Indiana University. She is a poet, author, Professor Emeritus of English at New Mexico Tech (New Mexico Institute of Mining and Technology), and a scholar of the arts, literature, and writing.

Her writing examines the historical basis for contemporary social issues and the rite of passage to identity, including the hero's emotional and intellectual quest. A lover of the beauty and power of language, she states: "We spell words and, arranged well, words can put a spell on us."

Mary believes that it helps to make life magical, even if that means simply donning a tiara, cuddling a cat, channeling the muse, talking with a unicorn, or reading a good book. She is seen on the right—photo by Sandy Dierks—visiting a sweet kitty in March 2022 at Catopia Cat Cafe, Albuquerque, New Mexico.

Mary lives in the Land of Enchantment.

Author photo, left, by Jason Collin Photography.

You can find out more about Mary, her books, poetry, short fiction, blogs, workshops, and events at marydezember.com.

Made in the USA
Coppell, TX
30 September 2023

22234381R00268